Lindsey Mackie left her native Yorkshire to study English at the University of East Anglia where she met her husband David. Their family now live in Buckinghamshire. It was on a nostalgia trip back to Norfolk that the short story 'Olim' surfaced and eventually grew into this novel.

Lindsey is an award-winning singer and writer of many songs and acclaimed short stories, one of which won the Adfam writing competition. The CD that accompanies this novel introduces you to her music.

To Toby

with warm wishes

Lindsey xo

ASO

A Novel

Lindsey Mackie

Copyright © 2008 Lindsey Mackie

The moral right of the author has been asserted.

Apart from any fair dealing for the purposes of research or private study, or criticism or review, as permitted under the Copyright, Designs and Patents Act 1988, this publication may only be reproduced, stored or transmitted, in any form or by any means, with the prior permission in writing of the publishers, or in the case of reprographic reproduction in accordance with the terms of licences issued by the Copyright Licensing Agency. Enquiries concerning reproduction outside those terms should be sent to the publishers.

Matador
9 De Montfort Mews
Leicester LE1 7FW, UK
Tel: (+44) 116 255 9311 / 9312
Email: books@troubador.co.uk
Web: www.troubador.co.uk/matador

ISBN 978 1906510 459

Typeset in 11.5pt Stempel Garamond by Troubador Publishing Ltd, Leicester, UK
Printed in the UK by The Cromwell Press Ltd, Trowbridge, Wilts, UK

Matador is an imprint of Troubador Publishing Ltd

For my family

Acknowledgements

David, my deepest love and thanks for your constant loving dedication, creativity and critical discernment over every word in every draft.

Loving thanks to my dearest Mum and Dad, darling Frances for your encouragement and Cornwall memories, to good friends for all their support, to Jo Swinney my friend and gifted fellow writer for her help and Faith Davies for her Norfolk journey guide.

Finally, thank you to Evie and Abbie for all the shared joyful moments and the lessons you continue to teach me.

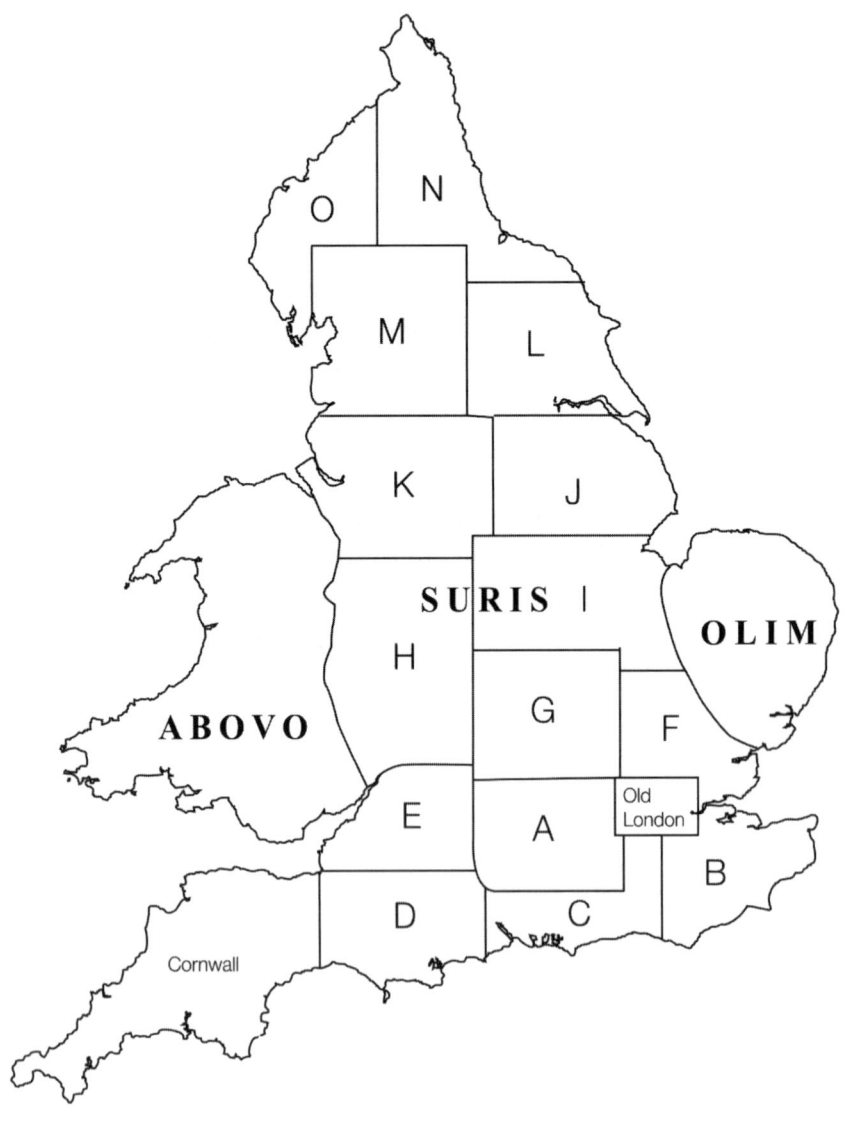

CHAPTER ONE

Abovo

There was never silence, even here in Abovo.

Taking her daughter's hand, Rachel Develin stepped off the trolley, walked over the flats and onto the speckled dunes. They stared out to the horizon, to the hundreds of white turbines whose towers sentried the coastline. After last night's storms, their whirring blades roared in protest as the winds blasted across the wet sands.

"Can I use your scope?" Bera asked. She pointed the optic, searching until the yellow base of the towers became visible.

"All the boats are out. Fish yields are excellent from the nurseries at the moment."

Rachel glanced sideways. Should an eleven year old be so… earnest?

"Are you still enjoying your lessons?"

"Oh yes. Mater says I'm progressing well and should achieve Juvenilia early. I'd like to specialise in Food Engineering. People always need to eat."

Rachel bit her lip. Where had this gravity come from? Not from Ben with his wicked sense of anarchy, constantly bubbling under the surface… but from her.

She stretched out her hand and stroked the sleek black cap of hair.

"Come on. I'll race you."

Bera tore away, her legs splaying clumsily and her arms flapping, unused to so much liberty. Rachel followed with her steady trained pace until the sharp wind peeled back her cheeks, her breath burst urgently out of her.

Keep on going. Don't stop.

She overtook the child, leaving her panting and laughing simultaneously.

"Unfair... crabs... look... on a field trip... hah, hah!"

Running. Always running.

"Mummee... wait for me!"

The wailing jerked her to a halt. Umbilical cords never shrivel. How long since she had heard those words?

She swung round, arms outstretched, beckoning. And soon they sprawled, entwined and sandy, one hand cradling Bera's head, echoing those first few precious months of weaning – before Abovo swallowed her up.

Bera suddenly separated, locking her elbows, her face clouding.

"Can we stay here all day? Joy-time finishes at four."

"I said we would be back for lunch. We'll catch the trolley up to the headland first."

It was the one place high enough to see a clear horizon uncluttered by turbines, storage facilities and boulders brought in to reinforce the coastline. Although, if one looked hard enough, the tip of the wave power plant was just visible with its circus of floaters, rafts and tubes driving the pumps underneath. Dimly, Rachel remembered the old religions. Since the Age of Division, energy and water had commanded a zealous awe the priests could only have prayed for.

"What's out there?" Bera smiled. It was a regular question.

"The rest of the world."

Returning to Ark 60, Bera asked tenuously.

"Would you... I mean... well, I know there's only one child allowed per couple but... would you have liked more?"

"Oh yes." The feeling that curled around those two words surprised them both. "If it had been possible. But... it takes a lot of resources to make a baby"

Bera patted her mother's hand maternally.

"At least you had me. The Maters can't have any!" She lowered her voice conspiratorially. "Remember Mater Dawn? She was supposed to have 'fallen', that's why she was expelled to Cornwall... with all the others who won't..."

"What?"

"You know... contribute!" she hissed.

"Aah."

Must the indoctrination be so absolute?

The early spring sky was shot with apricot and in the distance Snowdonia's white-capped range came into view. A final corner and the trolley followed the long avenue leading up to the Ark. By the way her feet unconsciously came together, the straightening of her cape's grey folds and the compliant readjustment of feature, Rachel felt her daughter's recent expansiveness constrict, and she buried a sigh.

She was committed to this way of life. It was right for children to be reared in Abovo. In this structured, secure environment with its prevailing harmony and purpose.

But it lacks... and this prickling doubt will not stop creeping along my spine... it lacks.

"Are you Grade three Fidelis or four?" Bera interrupted her thoughts.

"Four."

"Jona Mailer says her mother's Fuel Engineer four and Jona says my name would have been better if you'd called me 'Rabe'."

"What d'you think?"

"I like 'Bera' better."

"Good."

They reached the high gates. The large metal plaque announced Ark 60, with the distinctive scroll insignia used throughout ASO.

"Fidelis Develin returning with Bera." She spoke briskly into the vopass and the gates slowly opened.

A protective ship? Possibly. In appearance more like a fortress of metal and stone topped with its glass conning towers. Here the Abamater and her Maters lived and shared.

In the entrance hall Bera's own Mater Ruth met them.

"Oh Fidelis, I'm glad you're early. Abamater has just told us that Magnamater's transmission has been brought forward today. It will be held in the library in fifteen minutes. If you would like to accompany Bera, you are most welcome."

Rachel nodded appropriately.

"Find a good seat for your Mother, Bera."

So, smoothly and without question, authority was passed like a baton. Mater moved forward imperceptibly, bringing her pale eyes, with their suggestion of sea, level to Rachel's own.

"I am pleased to permit the book of poetry – despite the twentieth century references. Nourishment comes in many forms."

"Thank you. I have another request. I wonder if I might take Bera out to Broad Sound. There is a seal colony and bird observatory there. The new hydrogen plants at Milford Haven are supposed to be an extraordinary engineering feat. It might involve an overnight stay at a nearer Ark. 39 is close, I believe." She added innocently. "Wherever you think is best."

"There's much to consider. I would have to gain approval and it may take a little longer than your next scheduled visit – perhaps a written proposal."

They parted graciously, yet as she watched a flushed Bera chattering with Faith Orph, her dormate, she felt resentful.

Let them try and deny me, a Fidelis officer. At least I can bring joy. Orphans like Faith have no one. At fourteen she's the youngest ever to be nominated to train for Matership. How would I feel if Bera declared an interest?

As she joined them, she noticed Faith hurriedly turning off her visometer screen.

"Hello Faith. Anything interesting?"

The girl reddened. "So much information."

"Mummy, why are all the history files empty before the Age of Division?"

"It doesn't relate to modern ASO." Faith interrupted quickly.

"How are your Materdom studies going?"

"Well, thank you Fidelis Develin. It's a privilege to nurture the future." Faith said modestly.

"It's a 'vocation'." Bera emphasised.

The familiar distant hum grew from the bowels of the Ark, vibrating through every floor until it surrounded them. Thus summoned, the bobbed and smocked children filed in silently, accompanied by their Maters whose dark inky suits and pale snood-framed faces made them appear like a row of highly polished marble pillars. All bowed as Abamater stepped up slowly to her raised chair.

Rachel cast Faith a sideways glance and wondered. The girl stared ahead at the screen where Magnamater Beatrice looked out benignly.

I empathise with this one. A kindred inscrutability. She appears to be listening intently but those clenched knuckles suggested an inner struggle.

Rachel had followed Faith's progress with a mixture of compassion and admiration. Always carrying her Orph branding with dignity, she seemed to have used her loneliness as a weapon to sharpen her intellect and cut through the Juvenilia's grades like a razor. Obviously Rachel had conducted background checks since Bera spent so much time in her company, but had found nothing ominous. In fact Rachel was one of a handful of people who knew that her parentage was quite distinguished.

"Children. I humbly greet you today…"

She watched all the necks slightly stiffen in automatic response to the voice they heard every day. To them, Magnamater was a commanding constant – like the sun or food or sky.

Once the broadcast was over they processed out and Bera whispered conspiratorially.

"I don't really listen. It's nice to watch her face but the words are like a background… sort of bubbling frothy water in a fountain. Why does she say the same thing all the time?"

"Mater Ruth says that it is important for us to connect with the greater whole in Suris where we will eventually live.

Although recently, I have wondered if anyone so powerful could ever be… humble." Faith answered gravely.

The acute observation was too sophisticated for Bera.

"Maters stay here!" Bera argued.

"We will remain relevant. There is no better, more vital cause."

"So you won't mind about never having a baby then?" Bera persisted, returning to an old topic.

Faith shook her head.

"Mater Dawn was a sobering reminder. I could not imagine the disgrace of expulsion to Cornwall or standing on that last dangerous coastline with a strange untouchable world before me. I would have no point." She shivered.

Together they slipped down to the Refresher hoping to beat the queues. No. A long line of infants bobbed before them like fawn coloured ducklings and they stood behind Mater Richard, one of the few men.

"I enjoyed your mechanical sciences project, Faith. A lot of work has been done on radiation seeking robots but incorporating pulmonary and bi-sensular response is an interesting idea."

"Thank you Mater. I'm sure someone's already working on it somewhere."

"Nevertheless, what an inspiration you will be one day."

They sought a corner away from the throng and Rachel watched as Faith mechanically divided her plate of soy, kelp and salad into starches, primary proteins and vitamin groups as she ate. The girl finally flushed under her scrutiny.

"I like to imagine the fields and waters they came from, their passage through the provinces and their final delivery. Motion – it's a game I play." She finished eating in silence and Rachel understood that she would have infinitely preferred solitude.

She rose and tilted her head respectfully.

"Enjoy the rest of your time here Fidelis and your trip to Snowdonia." Already a Mater's sheath enveloped her.

At the ASO circle, Faith rinsed her hands in water falling from its two wavy lines. Forty-five steps to the entrance hall, sixty-seven to the main door, seventy-five to the field and then she strode out to the perimeter fencing, her brown frock coat flapping, unaware that they had followed behind her at a distance and now watched her tall thin figure grow smaller.

"She always goes there during Joy-time. She likes to crouch down in the long overgrown grasses."

"What does she do?" Rachel asked, vaguely disquieted.

Bera shrugged. "Nothing. Just stares out into the dark forests beyond the borders... you can't be seen from the conning towers... I think," she added quickly.

"How do you know?"

"I went a couple of times... it's a bit boring really."

They roamed as far as they could over the waterlogged fields, down to the energy and water stations and onto the patch of scrub which allowed the only view of the lush valley with its swollen streams and oxbows.

She felt Bera nestling into her side.

"Is Daddy's hair brown or black?"

"Brown." Rachel was amused.

"I was drawing a picture – for genetics... I couldn't remember... Will he come soon? I... I love seeing you and I know I'm luckier than most because you can come every fortnight instead of monthly but..."

Rachel was stung by her daughter's emotional maturity.

"Of course darling. He misses you so much. It's just the nature of Transmissions but I will insist he takes time off for a visit next month. Now we should go. The trolley will collect us in half an hour."

She had been gratified that Abamater had invited her to escort Mater Lee and four girls on their field trip to Snowdonia. Later, as they reached the Precipitation park tucked into the beginnings of the first range, she insisted that they stop and appreciate the five white peaks, that they breathe in the fine air and notice their freedom. It was so easy to follow without looking up.

"We should make the most of this view. One day it could all be completely covered in snow and glaciers again."

She taught them how to light a fire, cook a basic meal, cross the stream while protecting their packs and manage their supplies. As the night temperature fell she herded them into the cabins and allowed them some squealing leeway before silencing them into sleep. No one argued and Bera knew better than to take advantage. Her mother was Fidelis and the Mater was grateful for her authority in this unfamiliar territory.

At dawn Rachel emerged to see Mater Lee dressed but snood-less, her bald pate gleaming white against the green hillside behind as she softly mouthed a rhythmic incantation. She watched curiously. The Fidelis included certain meditative procedures as part of their training but this seemed to be more like contemplation. If there was any subtle tension between the Materhood and the Magnamatership it was in their refusal to relinquish or explain this unobtrusive but undeniable dimension to their vocation. Why not? As long as they did not seek to inculcate the children and it improved the quality of their care.

After five long minutes Mater Lee turned.

"Thank you for waiting."

"After breakfast we will do a thorough muscle group warm up before abseiling."

She was indomitable. Flexing and revelling in old unused parts of herself. Pure physicality. In the moment. No thoughts, strategies or investigations.

She struggled to conceal her pride as Bera's natural strength and balance outshone the others on the cliffs and in the canoes. In contrast, another child barely seemed to occupy her own skin, walking on every surface as if it were lunar and staring helplessly about her when presented with equipment. It was a direct result of their prescriptive sheltered lives where resourcefulness or initiative were not needed and more often discouraged. Yet by the end of the session they had cajoled each other into success and the beginnings of team awareness.

There was a new energy as they returned home to Ark 60 and Rachel nodded to Mater contentedly smelling the ozone in their hair and clothing

"Home feels smaller" observed Bera.

"For a while" said Mater, her arm guiding Bera forward.

Another goodbye. Momentary panic of separation. The child's left hand floated freely into the dusk and waved, before the gates swallowed them up. The trolley moved on immediately. She had learned not to crane her neck around.

Inside the grounds, a flurry of brown-suited boys hurtled like rats across the field and at their heels a clutch of Maters swooped like inky ravens. Their intended destination was obviously the spot where Faith often visited. Lights bounced erratically across the skyline.

"What's going on?" one of the girls asked.

"Quickly! Inside!"

In the dorm Bera watched as a canopy was erected and the area was floodlit throughout the night. Faith's bed remained empty.

Rachel boarded the locomoter, suppressing her usual urge to run back to the Ark and demand her daughter.

Eleven years and I still feel the wrench!

"A fortnight's not so long... not long." She muttered bleakly.

Still, her job with the Fidelis allowed little else. Looking upward, she noticed a small, protesting chink of blue in the sky's depressive grey blanket. These days a storm did not clear the atmosphere but left a dirty hangover through which the sun rarely broke. Its reluctance was their punishment, judging them undeserving.

Oh for that vivid brightness that heated my face and left me drenched and languorous. Those idle days that elongated and stretched into evening. Lying on my stomach, watching dragonflies hovering over the pond, only occasionally seeking a refreshing sip.

In her driven occupied days, responsibility coursed through her veins so hard that sometimes she thought it would burst through her skin. There was no time for whim. But then, few in ASO had. Oh, there were prescribed, carefully selected choices. But after a while, who wanted a vending machine life?

Select 'A' or 'B', go to 5, add mixer and pick up your small, approved packet at the bottom. One could show initiative and flair as long as it enhanced your function. It was too tight and she was haunted by the suspicion that if they were deprived for much longer of that freedom to make glorious, colourful mistakes, they would shrivel back to sophisticated insects.

As the locomoter sped into province E, she considered how an earlier traveller might have felt.

The Ancients could have taught us so much. A slight shift, a notch in time's belt and we could erase the last one hundred and fifty years. Use them only as a warning – a sealed canister to be breathed into once. Essential training so that you could recognise the poison, the narcosis.

Her thoughts were interrupted by the bleeping transor. Josie Kitchener calling. Her supervisor. Although more recently tested, their friendship had lasted for years.

"Hello Josie."

"Rachel, I know you're routing back to 'B' at the moment. I'm afraid I have to ask you to return to Ark 60."

"Why... is Bera?"

"Bera's fine. Are you secure?"

"Yes."

"An elderly man was found unconscious on the borders of Suris and Abovo last night. Abamater believes he was trying to corrupt a group of young boys by offering them drugs on which he may have subsequently overdosed. He was Peter Marchant, eighty years of age, Olim resident of course. Known political activist, ex-shadow Home secretary who strongly opposed Division. His cell had been dormant for some time but if the rumours of current dissident activities in Olim are accurate, it is likely that he will have influenced them. He... was supposed to quite a character. His grandson, Pajo Marchant lives in Ark 60 – there's obviously a connection. Can you investigate, report back to B and then continue on to Olim. See what you can dig up. Sorry, I know how much you have on but this raises so many sensitive issues with Magnamater's office."

We're all feeling the strain, like ships timbers, creaking with the expectation placed on us. There's a malady – duty is calcifying our very bones. Even Josie with all her energy and resilience has aged. Troubling to see her face twitching with nerves, sallow with fatigue.

Stepping onto the returning locomoter, she caught sight of her own grey reflection. Slate uniform, silver close-cropped hair – it was always a shock. Like her grandmother after the chemotherapy, or her mother in the grip of anthrax poisoning. How the gene pool hovers above us, eludes the mysteries of youth and finally settles into our cracks, like beautiful rooting powder to tell us where we have come from. But like the rest of her generation, with their shrivelled ovaries and growths and early lines, she resented it.

Not yet! Not yet. I'm only 37!

An unexpected sob caught in her throat, which she cleared like old leaves, and thrusting her chin upwards, dismissed her momentary vanity.

As if it mattered!

Whatever Bera believed, Fidelis could access anything. She paged up Marchant's history. The file triggering her own memories of that key time. His famous, passionate 'Division is Disintegration' speech uttered to a stunned nation now made him seem like a harpooned pre-historic in its final thrashings. Mum insisted that she listen to it. She remembered her father saying gloomily that he could feel trouble brewing like a tornado as early as 2025. The world had had too many faiths and too little trust – despite all the memorandums of understanding, alliances and unifications. Everyone was so busy agreeing what they were not going to do and watching each other like hawks, that their peripheral vision did not pick up on the trans-national free –wheelers and swarms of fanatics spreading their ivy roots over porous branches. Whether it was ideology, trafficking, information or just desperate thirst, they underestimated how unstoppably clever, committed and callous the enemy was. So the calamity of the Turkish World Peace summit in 2028 sent them reeling, as with a single dismissive swipe so many heads of state and their supporting bodies were killed outright. Immediately, there followed a series of international concurrent assaults on airports, key government establishments, hospitals and strategic satellite stations. Weapons of Mass Destruction were used on the United States, United Kingdom, Pakistan, Israel and China. And whilst all the Intelligence and Military forces united to identify the insurgent groups they could not have predicted how contemptuously their own information sources and technologies would be harnessed to destabilise, misinform and ultimately damage them.

So in an atmosphere of suspicion, borders were re-established, treaties so long in the making resealed their lips, turned up their collars and retreated into dark corners. The cosmopolitan complexion of society decreased as different ethnicities returned to their country of origin and found themselves unwelcome strangers. Suicides rose to new levels. Scapegoats were legion.

Everything that Marchant's generation had worked for crumbled, and all they had fought against re-established itself.

But all this had merely been the third round – a few body blows to send old Britain reeling. It was the next final phase she remembered most clearly. Her sixteenth birthday. Thursday. She was on a school trip to the coast. Her father was attending an air display on the Downs. There was a party arranged for the evening and theatre at the weekend. Mum called before she got on the tube to come home.

The detonations were simultaneous. Porton Down. All the major London stations. South Bank. Birmingham. Manchester.

And all that brilliant summer day, planes dusted crops, fields and people with deadly toxins. Anthrax seeped into the ventilations shafts of stations and airports to cocktail with the chemical agents Sarin and VX. Smallpox whistled through the largest cities while dirty bombs housing untried, synthetic and ultimately unpredictable viruses swirled before a dazed medical community, mutating and unresponsive to treatment.

At first, everyone had flu. The illusion did not last.

The stench of rotting flesh. Shivering in queues for uncontaminated water, clinging to her younger sister who wailed for her lost parents.

So it was out of this cloud of screaming panic that Magnamater Olivia stepped. With her specific expertise on post-viral attacks and her experience as part of the Directorate for Chemical and Biological weapons, she was able to mobilise a wide-ranging body of military, medical and fuel technology experts and initiate a rescue period. It had become impossible for anyone to trust politicians – few were clean and uncluttered by commercial concerns. It was one of the reasons why, in the aftermath, she and her board were able to cohere ASO so persuasively and it was decided that society would be best served by dividing into age-related regions. Trained professionals in Abovo situated in the West cared for the young. The majority lived in Suris, from where the country was administered under the guidance of an elected board and led by the Magnamater. Even the name inspired confidence. Then in the east, there was Olim, where the elderly were resorted. The fourth region, Cornwall, hosted the high security prison. It was also home to those who were unwilling to conform to the new procedures. They were allowed to live as they chose with no interference and no assistance.

And here, twenty years on, everything ran as smoothly as the loco' pulling out of the station, leaving Rachel to re-board the trolley. Magnamater Beatrice had acceded eight years ago, after Olivia's tragic death. All was just about as it should be.

I don't want to have to interrogate an old man. I want to take Bera back to the beach and truffle for shells, collect pointless pretties and purr over them. I can't think of one single frivolous possession.

She had seen the site where he had been found and now, listening to the Abamater conclude her report, she briefly glanced around the conning tower's interview room. Apart from one solid wall and the solar-panelled roof, it was as if they sat in an acoustically sealed glass bubble while overhead the world stretched limitlessly and offered no distraction.

"… We must be grateful he was allowed such a short time with Pajo and the older boys were mercifully too sensible to accept anything he offered them. But the fact that he came so close fills me with horror and of course, has prompted a complete review of security. Indeed I will be raising permeability issues at the next Abamater's conference."

Rachel nodded and looked down at the scanimages. It was a while since she had seen an Olim resident. She had little frame of reference for this wrinkled, hairless man with his collapsed mouth and emptied face. His body sprawled awkwardly, covered in a muddied coat with a torn hem.

This pathetic heap, dissident? Reviled corrupter? Surely a last mission would have a more dignified cause? She read the pathology. Heart condition, one previous attack and the usual slow growth cancers. A variety of regular medications.

"And the boys have said he offered them drugs?" She asked doubtfully.

"It would seem so."

"Which they refused?"

"Yes."

"Did he offer Pajo anything?"

"Yes, but he also refused."

"Would it be possible to interview them, individually?"

"Is that necessary?"

Was that a flicker of concern behind the lenselets?

"I shall not keep them long."

"There was another involved."

"Oh?"

"Faith Orph. It seems that she… facilitated their meeting. It is of some concern. We have conducted our own interview but…"

"I understand." Rachel grasped the implication immediately. Their own creature, in whom so much was invested, had flouted every convention and expectation. They needed to know why.

"I will see her after the boys."

The boys repeated their consistent accounts perfectly. The pills had been green and he had been disappointed at their refusal. When they had returned they had found him slumped forward in the grass.

She sat informally on a sofa so that he would not be intimidated and once he shuffled in, she shepherded him to the seat next to her. She leaned her head to one side so that when he did finally look up, it would be into a softened neckline.

"Tell me everything you can remember Pajo but take your time. There's no hurry."

She heard his epiglottis click, the breath whistle through his parted lips before his surprisingly low murmur began.

"Last night she tripped me up in the Refresher and whispered that she had something to tell me and to meet her at seven in the quadrangle once the Maters had gathered for Sharing in the main tower. We met in the cloisters. Boy's quarter. She told me that Grandfather Peter was there and wanted to see me. I asked why Mater had said nothing but she just said it was unofficial and that he was ill and it would be my only chance and that he had presents."

"So you were tempted to go?"

"Yes… but I didn't want to…"

"Carry on." She used the most persuasive tone.

"We waited 'til the early morning food trolleys had come through the gates and then we slipped out and crawled round the outer wall. Then Faith squawked like a seagull and he sort of fell out of the dark woods with his hands stretched out."

"How did you feel when you saw him?"

"I was very shocked. I told Faith to stay. She was going to leave and then I asked him what he wanted."

"And?"

"He said he wanted to introduce himself. See me. Tell me… how much he… loved me." The boy continued to stare at his knees.

"I said he didn't even know me. Daddy had told me he killed people."

"And how did he respond?"

"Said he could never deliberately hurt another person but he used to work for something called a gov'… gov'…"

"Government?"

"That's it and they had meant well but had made some mistakes. Then he asked me about my hobbies and I said practical sciences, fishing and eating and he told me that he and Daddy used to go fly-fishing and camping and cook sausages made from real meat under the stars and Daddy once caught a massive Pike, which is a fish, in the estuary."

"And the gifts?" She asked gently, reeling him in.

"He had a package but I said I didn't want anything from him and I ran away. He was very old but he seemed all right. He said he loved me." He looked up, visibly upset, struggling. "Dad always told me he wasn't to be trusted. He'll be furious when he reads the report that I even talked to him."

"No listen Pajo, this was not your fault. You learned that your grandfather wanted to see you. You listened and left. That was respectful although, as you rightly suspected, it would have been more appropriate to consult Mater. However you did report everything and if you remember anything you are expected to inform us. You may go now."

His face cleared of responsibility and reassured, he left.

So where were these gifts to which Pajo referred? Lost? Had he lied and accepted them? Did someone else have them? Or maybe she was being too literal. Perhaps the package was a ruse and the gifts were merely Marchant's own words or thoughts. That would be a manipulation typical of his sort. The boys' dorms had been searched and nothing discovered but she could not afford to let it rest there. She read the list of Marchant's belongings. A few Asons. Idientiband. Out of date locopasses. Maps. A variety of different permitted drugs and some items of clothing. Unremarkable swag.

She moved back to the desk for her next interview and lowered the blinds. She wanted full attention. The knock was firm. Rachel deliberately waited before responding.

"Yes. Come in please."

Faith Orph's skin stretched taut over her skull. Yet in a few short hours there had been a transformation in her expression. A layer peeled away. There was none of Pajo's fear but a new steely clarity in her eyes. Had Rachel just failed to notice it before? Faith also gazed slightly beyond her right shoulder, as if the view behind was more worthy of her attention. An interesting and mature technique.

"Are you well?" She purred gently tilting the last word upwards.

"Perfectly. Thank you."

"I'm relieved. This must have been an ordeal for you."

The girl did not reply. *Such composure.*

"In your own words and omitting no detail, describe all the events over the last day and a half."

"In Joy-time I often go down to sit by the perimeter fencing."

"Why?"

"I like to think, be alone, listen to the birds, that sort of thing. He came from nowhere. Shocked me. He squatted down and spoke in short gasps as if he had been running. He introduced himself. Asked for my name, checked it was Ark 60. He seemed unwell. Took out a small bottle. Called himself a silly old fool for getting so excited. Put a small green pill under his tongue. I asked him what he wanted and he said to see his grandson Pajo Marchant. He obviously wasn't expected. He wanted me to pass on a note. I said he could have arranged a proper visit. He said Olimians weren't allowed to see their grandchildren, that families shouldn't be separated, that there was so little time and that he was in my hands."

"Why do you think he trusted you?"

"I don't know. Afterwards, I thought so hard about it. I knew I should report it immediately… but…" For the first time she looked directly into Rachel's face. "He had risked everything to come here. Forced by… something. Blood pressure. No one would ever make such a journey for me. Shouldn't I make it possible for them? So frail and harmless. He was my first old man…" Her voice finally cracked and she continued, her story echoing Pajo's.

"And when they talked I saw for a few minutes there was understanding between them. Then Pajo ran off and all the light and hope left his old face like loose, falling scaffolding. I felt so sorry, I offered to go after him. But he seemed happy just to have seen him. He thought he might have sewn a little seed and said I'd helped... ." She trailed off.

"Did he give you anything to pass on?"

"Yes."

"And?"

"I put them in my locker. Pajo would not accept them."

"Have you examined them?"

"No."

Only a vocalise expert would have noticed the hesitation.

Rachel calculated quickly. *She may have had time to duplicate. A second more thorough search would have to be conducted. Intellectual contamination can not be contemplated. I have to prod closely to the soft heart of the problem. The girl is discovered but utterly calm.*

"You have risked everything for one short meeting. Everyone believes Materdom is your right and only choice, Have you considered your position?"

The girl stared steadily. "I have always believed it to be the highest calling, yet when he crouched in front of me, all I could hear was the need in his voice."

The Abamater would be appalled.

Marchant was being held in the isolation chamber within Restoration. Whilst it would be unseemly to bring him up to the conning tower, Rachel had requested that he be moved from a bed into a hard seat and brought into the darkened antechambers that ran parallel with the wards.

The Doctor met her and silently handed over a medical report. She was clearly profoundly uncomfortable in the murky waters of geriatric care, her daily remit being the rafts of responsive and treatable paediatric viruses.

"I followed your orders to use adrenalin. He is just revived – I cannot guarantee for how long. The recovery will, I suspect, be temporary. As you… instructed, he is alone facing the wall in the middle of room ten. He will not see your entrance and low level white noise is being piped in."

"Can I administer further shots via Epipen?"

"Well… yes but I would urge extreme caution… I mean… it could be too much for his system."

"Nevertheless if I could take one now."

In her laboratory, the medic prepared the extra dose with misgivings. It was easy to forget that one did not achieve Fidelis status without complete ruthlessness. She felt compromised and powerless faced by this stiff automaton.

"Once you have switched off the soundtrack you may leave the unit. We are not to be disturbed under any circumstances."

She pictured him on the other side of the wall. Disorientated, weak, fearful. Muscles tensed and cramped. Every sense alert. She had lost count of how many of these she had done, although this was her first Olimian. It would require a delicate and imaginative balance of intimidation and restraint.

She slipped inside, acclimatised to the dark and listened to his laboured wheezing. Then she skirted around the perimeter to avoid shifting the air current. As she drew level with him she switched the lights on full with her remote.

He sat calmly, unperturbed, legs crossed and eyes shut. His voice rumbled like old machinery.

"Not quite the shock you hoped for, eh? Poor eyesight has made my hearing exceptional." A grimace turned north on his face and he grinned up at Rachel. She noticed how his smile parted the hanging folds of his face, like a stone rippling on water. Large, knotted, mottled hands sat loosely folded on his lap.

Although his gaze was cloudy, it was direct.

She sealed her countenance and set her pitch low, allowing her mouth to open only enough to deliver.

"Doubtless, you will want to keep this brief. It is required that you wear a veriband to authenticate your statement." She leaned forward and attached the thin strap to his wrist.

"I take it my consent is not needed." He said dryly.

"You are Peter Marchant, eighty years of age, resident of Olim?"

"As you see. My mug-shots probably don't do me justice."

"Are you aware that your unapproved presence here breaks all resorting rules and usually incurs a custodial sentence?"

"Yes but then I think that my life is already a kind of sentence."

"That is but the first of several charges I will be bringing against you."

"Goodness... and barely a question asked! How incisive!"

"It will save time and your... limited resources if you confine your responses, Mr Marchant. Why are you here?"

"I wanted to see my grandson, Pajo."

"Without authorisation."

"I knew permission would not have been given. My son Josh has broken off all contact. I... I have made a recovery of sorts from my first heart attack but I do not have long... They tell me that I am riddled... and I wanted... needed to see the boy."

"Why?"

He raised his head slowly and straightened his upper body to its full length. For one moment Rachel thought he might even try to stand.

"So that I might become something to him. Instead of a dangerous black hole to be avoided at all costs."

"You have not succeeded. His friends accuse you of offering them drugs. He is terrified of you... he instinctively senses corruption."

He stared into her. She knew how she appeared... she had studied reptiles closely.

"No..." he said finally, "I do not think so. Whisper into a lobe just once and it will echo and there are many ways to leave an impression."

"We will find and eliminate what you have left."

"And reveal your absolute insecurity... that is how dictatorships flounder. You have made monsters of us all but I do believe in Karma and your actions will revisit you... in the cold dispassionate gaze of your own child's eyes as she hurries away from you, without a backward glance, embarrassed by your outstretched hands. By the love that helplessly drips from you, from us all, our life- blood. We would spend the last drop for a moment of recognition. The generations feed on each other like benevolent parasites. You have condemned us to rattle around our country compound... old beasts staring out onto the savannah... knowing the cubs wander without guidance, in the unseen distance."

"They are protected from you."

"They are suffocating. You have stolen them from us. You come riding in like blinkered lancers, each prodding the ass of the next, never getting close enough to the ground to smell the discontent or question those who have given you authority. There will be changes... vengeance, Fidelis Rachel Develin... you are known but you will not be remembered."

I'm used to antagonism but his passion is surprising. It's so... personal.

"I would have thought that you and your friends would have had more than enough to occupy you without taking on such an arduous journey. Are you at the vanguard? Am I to order extra security at Olim's borders?" Deliberately, she adopted a more wheedling lighter tone. If there was any cell activity she had to unearth it.

His breathing had become more stertorous, yet he clicked his tongue and waved his hand dismissively.

"Your mother would have been disappointed. Give Jennifer and Charlie my love. Josh, Pajo and my other grandchild will know in due course that they meant everything to me. This was not a trip... it was a suicide mission and it is... complete."

His heat disappeared suddenly like sun swallowed by thick cloud. His head slipped sideways as if he dozed.

No! I had not finished! She felt for a pulse reaching for the epipen at the same time.

"I... con... clude..." she hissed as she injected the point into his thigh.

She held his slumped form upright by the shoulder and peered into his grizzled face.

Gone! And he had controlled his own departure. Could one decide to die?

I have seen so many deaths but my hands have never shaken so and I know I'm not imagining that high-pitched insistent whirring. The sound of departure. I'm freezing and my spine feels as if it'll break through the skin.

She fled.

It took her several minutes to collect herself before she could summon the medic.

"I want a post mortem performed immediately. Please call me when your report is complete."

The doctor nodded, avoiding her eyes.

Although, protocol required she be escorted, she made her way outside alone and gulped in the fresh air.

Your mother would have been disappointed...

How dare he!

Later she was able to steal a few moments with Bera.

"Everyone's in a funny mood. The Maters are whispering constantly and Faith's insisting on early lights out and hardly says a thing. Can you stay a little longer?"

"Not this time, sweet one."

... Embarrassed by your outstretched hands...

Mater's appearance at the doorway prompted Rachel to drop her arms more quickly than she wanted to. There was a new guardedness in her manner. Rachel was used to the shift. Fidelis first. Mother afterwards.

Abamater studied her cuticles.

"An inevitable death. The post mortem states that death was due to massive cardiac arrest and that he had already had a heart attack. He would have known how dangerous the trip from Olim would be to him. My immediate concerns are with Pajo."

"I felt it important for him to feel free of any sense of responsibility. You are of course expert in counselling so he will be supported. I am certain that he will not suffer any lasting upset but I am less confident about Faith Orph. From a security point of view, vigilance is necessary. Especially if she attempts any further communication with him."

Abamater tried hard to veil her anxiety.

"Indeed?"

"She experienced a definite conflict of interest at the critical point when discernment was necessary. I am unsure whether the crisis is permanent. Obviously you will need to reflect on her tutelage. Perhaps a consolidation course? Or an organised retreat?"

"Indeed!"

Abamater rose, indicating that their business was concluded.

Yet I suspect that Marchant's death will not be so easily folded. My report will state that this had merely been a frail man's last attempt to reconnect with his grandson. There's no real evidence of drugs or other harmful exchange, although his final defiance was unexpected. I won't include his promise of revolt; it would only cause more paranoia in the Administration.

CHAPTER TWO

Suris

It was only by travelling that one really noticed the changes in ASO. People rarely commuted to the next burgh, let alone out of province. It was not encouraged and travel passes were hard to obtain. So, as they passed from Abovo into province E, Rachel reminded herself that it was her privilege to see sights like the vast Hydroelectric power stations straddling the magnificent dams on the river Severn and the acres lush with spinning turbines, growing like monstrous, three-petalled flowers the height of old style high-rise buildings. All along Suris' rivers sat the commanding precipitation ports where engineers quietly manipulated water's natural weather cycle.

Yes, everyone should occasionally be reminded of the true priority. Inevitably people defined their status by grade and therefore how many Asons they earned, but there was so little to spend it on. Apart from the weekly thrill of gambling at Asonetta when, for a couple of hours every Saturday, squares throughout Suris became impossibly congested with people staring slack-jawed at the screens. And, while they could keep upgrading their domestic technologies, persuading themselves they had control, the real currency – to the last drop – was here. The preservation of water had seeped into every single consciousness.

Stoically, they all bore the wet winters with the constant flooding, storms, tidal surges, landslides and hurricanes, especially in the coastal areas, and tolerated the parched summers. The challenge was to keep the water available and desalinated, so the water engineers had become heroes, latter-day gladiators.

As the locomoter's path intersected with an old motorway, she marvelled at its emptiness save an occasional food distribution trolley or fuel transporter. She could just remember a rush hour, the locked grid. Now the only small road vehicle was the 'Har' used by Magnamater and selected officials. Ben had once flown in an 'Air-Har'. The Magnamater had wanted to transmit some birds-eye footage of ASO's geo-structure. He said that for all the apparent sophistication, from the sky it looked like a simplistically cut child's jigsaw. Provinces clearly demarked into fifteen portions, which in turn each housed their ten small, highly organised Burghs. The countryside rolled around them filled with its stations, plants and turbines and endless networks of intersecting pipes, throbbing with fuel, water and energy. So much effort for such a small concentrate.

She contacted Ben's desk at Transmissions. His face came into view topped by the dark hair standing in familiar peaks where he had run his fingers as work's pressures mounted.

"Oh… hello Rachel. Bad time, I'm afraid. Magnamater's broadcasting from here tomorrow as part of her 'get in touch with the provinces' tour – so everyone's jumping and since the system's gone down so much recently, I've got to make sure we get capacity at the right time. How was Bera?"

"Fine. Well. She really enjoyed the trip. I think she misses you. Sends you lots of love. I said that you would try to make the next visit."

He raised his eyebrows, clearly vexed.

"I wish you had talked to me first before promising. If I have to disappoint her it makes me look like the bad guy. Obviously, I want to see her too."

He glanced sideways quickly and nodded to someone off screen.

"I have to go. Sorry Rachel." Leaning forward, he looked at her for the first time. "There's too much going on! I'm dying to have you back. I'll see you later."

It was in the rising flush that climbed into the nape of his neck and the two crimson pools on each cheek that she read his heightened state. He loved the adrenalin rush. His shoulders were like gangplanks from which stress nose-dived. She remembered him at seventeen. Already six feet four, a set of perfectly proportioned muscle groups, the waist a little ill-defined but he exercised, striding the stage and dwarfing its student dimensions. His voice boomeranged from the floor-boards and up into the rafters. It hit her in the forehead, in the third eye that should have seen further and known better and she was smitten.

Dazzled.

And after they finally met, for the first few months she found herself screwing up her slightly down-turned eyes, trying not to stare at the expanse of teeth, the wide high bones scaffolding those extraordinary lapis blue windows. How not to show it, the depth of the fissure. She kept the surface calm and unruffled, her gaze steady while underneath there were rocks falling. He searched for signs of hysteria, possession or jealousy and finding them absent, cradled her chin. She would never be threateningly beautiful. So he swooped and soared, dropping little gifts like quarry into her lap. And in the mirrored half-light she saw her irises dance unrecognisably as he loosened all her tightly wrapped secrets and gave her back permission to laugh.

When Josie eventually met him she said he was dangerous, a smiling virus. Maybe she had been right. Rachel never asked what she really meant because, for the first time, Rachel had caught something without Josie clearing the path.

Ben's big break came just before Division became a certainty. Everyone had to re-define themselves but it was harder for him. ASO did not need actors. Transmission was the obvious choice although ultimately technology bothered him. He liked things in front of him. You couldn't grandstand on a two-inch screen but to his credit he had managed to carve a reasonable career and subsume most of his ego. It emerged in an occasional flamboyance. An unnecessary scarf worn all day, its ends deliberately frayed. Why not?

Recently, she had shaved her demands on him and his time to the minimum, sensing that in some way she could not divine, more was expected of him. After years of holding the superior role, enjoying his support, this new distracting careerism was unwelcome. If she were honest, she resented it. Especially in light of her recent failure to achieve grade 5 when Josie had recommended a 'more imaginative and less dogmatic approach'. She accepted the conclusions but privately railed and began to investigate transfer possibilities, but he had refused to consider it.

As Josie had with Andrew, she had taken Ben for granted.

Her transor sounded. Josie, with that uncanny knack for reading her over the miles.

"Rachel. Business finished at sixty?"

"Yes. I'll have the report for you tomorrow."

"Oh of course. No I'm just making sure that you're still okay for tonight."

"Tonight?" Rachel stared weakly.

"He forgot to mention it then. Ben asked us for drinks at about nine. Andrew said he'd make some eats."

"Fine. Good. See you later then."

It was pointless to debate. She had spent a lifetime doing that. Yet somehow there was still glue between them. Just.

A flashback to their two families at that Regimental gala evening in 2028. Josie's father Kenneth, resplendent in uniform and medals and that strawberry blonde hair which even a regulation haircut barely contained. Josie on his arm, her inherited curls cascading down her back. He used to call her his open sunflower. The conquering Viking and his consort, descending. The mothers waited at the bottom. Suitable audience for Josie's diaphanous blue dress that shimmered and floated on its own breeze while Rachel followed behind. Even then conservative, contained and hot in her green velvet. How she hoped that they would be unable to read her inner turmoil as she grappled with what she had just seen. They hadn't known she was there watching from the bathroom. A witness to the final rule broken. The unmentionable forbidden country that Josie and Kenneth had walked into. She was repelled but never spoke of it.

Josie went on to do her cadetship and they didn't see each other again for two years. The space was needed.

My childhood's been sucked into the past, sealed over like an ice age. All the things I used to worry about. She pulled at the edges of her jacket regretfully. *Yes, hemp is marvellously durable and light. I should be grateful to the inspired Material scientists who spend every waking hour devising broader applications and improving resistance and durability. Yes, the re-cycler is a wonderful innovation but sometimes when I post in a damaged article for regeneration and press the requirements button, I want something pale and flimsy to come back. Bera will never have a pastel party frock.*

The locomoter sped through Province A passing Magnamater's official residence in Burgh 2. It was one of the few to be centred in an old city, accessible with its wide orbiting road but outside contamination range of London and as the low-rise, multifunctional buildings had already been built, it was a flexible base from which to originate ASO.

She felt the familiar judder of hermetic seals tightening over the carriages and tried to remember how the capital had once looked. Anyone you spoke to would have her own snapshot. The streets littered with non-specific dirt that seemed to seep through the pavements at will. The trains filled with scraps of human debris. Abandoned coats, plastic cups, newspapers and half–used packets. The concrete blocks and rusting metal that speckled the embankments. The colours, the clash and the chaos. Fossils had amber but people had the walls to impregnate with their own layers of gaudy slap-on. Poster after poster after poster. Spectacular evidence that such creatures as us had once existed.

Now a strictly forbidden 'No-Zone', the locomoter kept outside a five-mile exclusion area around the river. Apparently there was little to see but crumbling, empty decay and a stagnant river occupied by disintegrating burnt out hulls. No one wanted reminding of the fetid past, so the threat of permanent expulsion to Cornwall's high security prison seemed unnecessary. Besides, regular water and air tests taken ten miles away proved there was still enormous biological volatility.

"Province B, Burgh 1," came the announcement, and the door slipped back.

She breathed in deeply and looked down across the Burgh. Home was too warm a word for it. Base was more apt. Work was here and her sister Georgia. *I haven't spoken to her for over a week. Should feel more guilty. Then the onus is always on me. Leave it until tomorrow.*

But no, her aching feet thought differently and she found herself walking into the centre and towards Weaning, glancing up at the civic block where Ben worked in Transmissions and where Fidelis and Engineering were located. The food trolleys had finished their deliveries and the refreshers had emptied after lunchtime recess. Mid-afternoon and the streets were quiet except for the odd straggle of loitering youths whose barking silenced as she passed. It was ridiculous to allow them a break while they were still training. It sent the wrong message. At the ASO fountain the screen above waited opaquely for the next Magnamater broadcast.

She reached the Restoration building and slipped through the side door into the pale blue crystal-clean interior. A place where every lit corner was known. A place that aroused the most complex set of feelings. One came here to be healed or to receive maintenance shots or to enter the nocturnal world of Cloning, Natal and Weaning through the laborious Viral detection and Sanitisation suite.

So visiting was a lengthy commitment.

She inhaled and exhaled deeply before stepping into the enclosed scanner walkway manned by a clone who diligently examined every cell.

"Thank you Fidelis. Please proceed to the changing area for sanitisation. Enjoy your visit."

As the temperature rose at the mouth of the cubicle, she began to feel uncomfortably hot in her uniform and nodded in anticipation of the next clone's instructions.

"Greetings Fidelis. Please undress and hang your clothing in the locker provided. Then step onto the walkway wearing the protective goggles in this sealed packet. My colleague will supply you with your disposable suit at the other side. Enjoy your visit."

Carefully she hung every item of clothing onto a full-length slim rail and pressed an entry button. The rail slid smoothly into a space that sealed immediately. Then a few steps, during which she had learned to keep her eyes front, and onto the first section of narrow moving walkway. The goggles intensified the blue. She could be surrounded by a summer sky. The opaque screens adjusted to her size. A faint hum as she passed through the microwaves and stifled that moment of concern about their safety before the next door slid open and she entered the cleansing suite. She steeled herself for the high-density antibacterial sprays whose smell would cling stubbornly to her skin and hair until her next shower. Then she was dried by a brief warm jet of air before stepping off the walkway. A clone with shorn eyebrows solemnly handed her a white disposable suit, mouth mask and gloves similar to his own. Gently, he took the used goggles from her hand. His watery down-turned eyes remained firmly on hers. He was unaware of her nakedness.

"Thank you for your cooperation Fidelis and enjoy your visit."

She joined the queue of other visitors, all encased like lozenges, and waited for the shuttle.

This was not an age when anything could be left to chance. Every step in life was tightly monitored and controlled. Was there really a time when the meeting of sperm and egg was dark and hushed? A haphazard mystery? A blessed kiss blown down from above? Now, one's arrival day was a meticulously planned conception. It had to be. The legacy of contamination seeped into every water and air cell, leaving an almost infertile population. So each couple tried endlessly, with quiet persistence, and gritted teeth, willing one precious embryo to hold on. Hold on! Ben had not recognised that there was a hole to fill. Why must they change from a united, water-tight, hard-skinned mammal cutting through life's waves at high speed to smaller, spinier beings, dragging in and out on their own separate tides?

"Can't we just see what happens?" came the regular hiss in between assessments, injections and timed interference.

Everyone was doing it but it was not discussed and once successful, you did nothing else.

I can remember Mum working until her seventh month when she carried Georgia! Astonishingly casual! It wouldn't be allowed now. Pregnancy. Oh the bittersweet responsibility. The resentment towards he who was not. His freedom. The terrible blankness. Words, for so long my precious arsenal, had hung limp and flapping in the breeze. The disconnecting fog from where I could see everyone speaking and moving without being able to touch them. Even my own skin, anaesthetised. The lurching, swinging gauges. Hot to cold. Cavernous hunger to bloat. Mouth splitting rage to bleating, regretful whimper.

I was occupied with ungrateful gratitude and the unfamiliar, for which there was no training programme.

The air is so pure in here, stifling. From Cloning, to Natal to Weaning – a few long sliding corridors. It's amazing that the babies' lungs don't collapse under the weight of real life when they're finally transferred after the nine-month weaning programme, to Abovo.

I remember those three unforgettable months of real family life, of bonding, routine and scanimages. Ben wrestling with his demons. Afterwards, the long journey back. Stricken. The greatest agony of my life. Even now, I can't not think of it. No wonder few women can conceive more than once, their ancient biology so denied.

And as the shuttle hurtled through to Weaning, she realised that she could not have endured it again.

Like a slow suffocation. Like being given a fifth heart

chamber. Fill this. Breathe into it. Encase it with love. Relinquish it. No, I couldn't have done it again.

Still, Georgia could. After Luge had died so unexpectedly, I swear I heard her very veins coursing and howling with grief. Thank goodness for the safe delivery of Gelu. Of course they had had Luge duplicated and Cluge was actually quite effective with basic chores. They hoped that he might have a future in the Distribution unit as other clones had before him. Loading food trolleys requires scrupulous cleanliness and attention to detail but you can already see signs of aging. All this technology and they still hadn't eliminated rapid cell deterioration once clones reach thirteen.

I can't remember a time in my whole adult life when I haven't fretted about Georgia. The lot of the elder sibling. Enforced maturity. Always trying to fill the vacuum that Mum and Dad had left.

At seventeen she had struggled to deal with a thirteen year old who bleated and whimpered inconsolably. As a toddler, Georgia had freely laughed, cried and charmed and so it followed that in adolescence she would hang out her pain and joy in equal measure. Rachel had never dared, there wasn't the space. Her plumbing was subterranean and the tremors so deep, they only occasionally rippled the surface, astonishing herself and everyone else with their ferocity. She spent the years after Division watching her youth trickle away, embracing a new world with one arm around her sister and grieving, exhausted at the end of each day. So much discipline.

Too soon!

As she approached Weaning 10, she could see her brother-in-law's vivid red curls over the top of the screen. He was deep in conversation with his sister Kate whose authority here had been a constant comfort as she had insisted on overseeing the birth and weaning.

"How is everything?" Rachel asked lightly.

"Fine. Both doing well. A little colic but nothing abnormal."

Kate's measured, dove-grey tones immediately soothed and as always, Rachel felt a strong kinship with her.

Georgia stirred sleepily and Rachel was relieved that the urgent anxiety that had creased her face for months had disappeared. The only vestige of despair was in the eyes. Two days after Luge's death, they had turned from a striking green to the darkest of browns – as if everything that defined her had been sucked into those orbs like voracious black holes intent on collapse. Her face had undergone a unique and permanent transformation and no one had mentioned it.

She stood at the foot of the bed watching her sister.

"Hello Georgie. This is the life, eh?"

"Hello back. Long time no see. Work keeping you busy?"

Rachel kept her smile firm. Georgia had learned to distil this air of martyrdom to a refined jus. *When is she going to stop making me feel guilty for having my own life. She's surrounded by friends. Always has been and clings to them like a bur to fur. Perhaps I should be less independent. Ben and Josie were all I ever needed. Familiar watering holes to which I'd faithfully plod back. What happens if they dry out?*

"It has been demanding. I've been in Abovo this week. Travelling to Olim tomorrow."

"Oh, poor you." Georgia was not listening but her pout softened, "Would you like to see her?"

The room stilled further as Luke laid his daughter, like the most fragile of offerings, into Rachel's folded arms. Could anyone ever explain how the ground falls away and the outside world splinters into irrelevant fragments in the face of such beauty? A baby is a revelation. It clarifies purpose.

Rachel nodded softly her breath shallow in her chest.

"She has your hair, Luke."

"We programmed it... and her eyes," replied Georgia. "She's having the operation to see to the palate and the extra earflaps next week but Kate says it's very minor surgery. It's best to do it now... before..." She tailed off. "Rachel, we're thinking of applying for relocation to E so we can be nearer to Abovo. Course we don't know which Ark allocation we'll get but we think it will be 56 – close to the border. We were wondering if you could… speak to Allocations… given the circumstances…"

"It's early days yet." Luke interrupted.

"But we are thinking and I just wanted you to know because as it gets closer…" Her voice rose.

"Of course. I understand. It isn't really appropriate for me to intervene. Take time to consider all the options. Ultimately, you wouldn't actually see her more often…"

"I know that." Georgia snapped. "But you can't blame me for grabbing every opportunity. Although I would hate for you to have to compromise your position. I know it's your primary concern. Perhaps if you looked sideways occasionally you would have noticed how 'busy' Ben is these days and… how is dear Josie?

Rachel quickly exchanged glances with Luke whose face rippled with discomfort.

It was ever thus. She was a tornado, pulling everything up into the vortex and spewing it out. *It's why I keep my distance… I can't stand the storm damage.*

She passed Gelu back to him.

"I… will make enquiries. Enjoy every second," she urged them gently, realising suddenly how drained she felt.

"I've always thought the East rather lovely," Kate offered, as Rachel took her leave.

Back into the arctic light, she leaned her head against the shuttle's cold walls.

I've never understood the female capacity for spite. It's such a small weapon.

Outside, she began to walk towards Residential, but had to stop to remove her boot and adjust the loose lining. Through her stockinged feet, she could feel the constant throb of generators and pulsing pipes.

To the south the valley dipped away. On the horizon, she could just see the tips of the turbines serving Burgh 2.

"If I ever make it to Grade 5, I'm going to ask to move to

the last row... see something more then the next row's back wall." She told no one.

It was felt desirable that there was some Fidelis presence in the centre. As she traipsed past each three storey, pre-fabricated row, all on raised platforms and meticulously designed with large south-facing windows to catch every available sunray and tiny slits north side, she sighed. There was something fundamentally heartless about concrete whatever the engineers said about organic communities.

All these solar roof panels and tight design and the flat still depends on my own body heat to warm it up.

Later, while the shower jets spat out hot water and pummelled her aching muscles, she remembered her father flapping newspaper in an open grate, waiting for the spark to catch and the blast of heat as it roared. He had seemed heroic. *I'd love to light a fire somewhere.*

She leaned back against the granite and did not notice the slight dip in temperature, the subtle shift of air as he stepped in front of her, deflecting the water. Opening her eyes, she smiled slowly and stretched.

"Hello."

They stared into each other as he washed, then stepped forward, skin to skin.

He cupped her cheek.

"Are you hungry?"

Even after all these years they had not exhausted each other – they had not had the time. Similarly riddled with duty, with every minute accounted for, it was remarkable that they still managed to uncover layers of unabated passion. Shared time was often lost so they secreted visinotes for each other. She carried a slim wallet of his best in her breast pocket. Slivers of love.

Dried, splayed, he pressed her insteps tightly and pulled her by her feet, down the bed towards him. ASO bought her uniform but here with her soles thus held, she was truly owned. His fingers tightened around her throat with just enough pressure to claim control. She had never worried – the danger was only ever a frisson, an implication. Yet tonight she found herself struggling for breath. His mouth formed a gag over hers. A flash of red hot panic before he released her and they rolled and pawed feverishly, battling to keep the moment.

Afterwards, she tipped any food she could find onto a tray from which they ate noisily, draped around each other.

"So how was she?" he asked finally.

"Growing fast. Too serious. I rattled a bit of it out of her. The field trip did them all the power of good. She was… the best. So strong. You should have seen her abseiling down this cliff. I thought the Mater Lee was going to weep. I… resent the control they have."

He was taken aback. "Why? Nothing's changed has it?"

"No… I… no. She does miss you more than she says. If you can come next time then I…"

"You're right and I will," he interrupted quickly.

"It all got rather eclipsed by an incident though."

"What d' you mean?"

"Well," she breathed out heavily. "It's work, so I won't bore you with all the details but I was actually on my way here when Josie ordered me back to Abovo. An old man was detained at the Ark, trying to see his grandson… d'you remember Peter Marchant, Shadow Home secretary before Division?"

Ben nodded, "But he must be ancient!"

"Eighty. Got himself all the way to Abovo. Faith Orph of all people helped him to talk to his grandson."

"What? Bera's dormate?"

"Yes. Marchant said he knew my mother… well at least he said she 'would have been disappointed'."

"How strange." Ben glanced at his wife's face.

"What happened?"

"He died." She replied flatly as she lifted the tray from the bed.

CHAPTER THREE

The evening

It had become something of a performance like those annual pantomimes where everyone did exactly as they were supposed to, with few surprises. In Ben's carefully lit room, she watched the three of them move across the tiles in slow motion, like a three-tiered human horse. Josie the head, Ben the body and Andrew, of course being the smallest, the rear.

There were always bear hugs even when they hated each other. Andrew and her exchanged their usual light but sympathetic kiss whilst Josie and Ben shouted for the first half hour.

"Hey Wolfy, are your teeth getting whiter or is it your hair growing darker?" Josie teased.

"Leave him alone. He keeps a lot of chemists in Province C going," Andrew returned, arranging small rolls of pastry onto the platter that Rachel had silently handed him.

"Perfect works of art as always, Andrew. I wouldn't have the patience."

"You need to like food to make it, Rachel sweetie," Josie purred.

There it is. The first little nip at my ankles.

"And you certainly do Josephine!" Ben let his gaze slide down to Josie's well-rounded hips.

"We all have appetites, Ben. Well... most of us."

A new level of tension lingered. All that history locked inside its brown sacking like a snatch of doomed, scratching cats. Rachel's scalp stung.

"Now children." Andrew posted a canape into each of their mouths.

"Well come on. She was the one who stuck lumps of cheese to her arse and painted 'Cut out the Middle man' on her chest at the Fidelis Convention."

They all laughed gratefully.

"You know perfectly well that was to piss Butcher off, young man." Josie drew a melodramatic hand through her bleached out roots.

"Not merely you trying to draw attention to yourself, darling? Anyway, are we drinking?" Andrew looked at Rachel who raised her eyebrows to Ben.

"The syndicate pays off again." He punched the air while Josie echoed the gesture with an appreciative "That man! You see if it wasn't for the likes of us, you two would be absolute teetotallers by now."

"Well I know I've had my issues with it.... being illegal and all that but I have to admit, a bit of local oblivion doesn't hurt." Rachel had to make the concession. *Sometimes it's the only thing that gets me through these evenings. What I can't say is that I'd willingly forgo both.*

Silently Ben poured the pale lime coloured wine into tall beakers calculating how long it would take each of them to grow belligerent. He had done it so often that he knew all of their levels. She noted grimly that Andrew and she had considerably less.

"How are your folks, Andrew?"

Andrew's pointed chin puckered.

"All right. Stoical, I suppose. Dad doesn't say much but Mum's scared. She's taken up knitting."

"It's better than wringing her hands constantly," Josie interrupted from the kitchen table where she sat, swinging her legs backwards and forwards dangerously.

Like a cat flicking its tail and looking for trouble.

"Well they've never been apart. Twenty-five years is a long time. Yet when I was last there they bickered, oh you wouldn't believe how much. I kept wanting to shout 'you haven't got long, enjoy each other.' But I just kept finding ways to take Dad to the allotment. I know he's happiest there."

"He's a saint. He'll have a new lease of life when he resorts. That's why it's such a good system. A breathing space. He deserves a bit of fun." Josie returned.

"I'm not so sure. All of those simple rituals and rhythms we create around each other. Organic. It can't be explained because others wouldn't be able to understand it, not fully anyway. She knows how much to fry the soya, so it's burnt at the edges. He knows her feet get cold at night so he fills a water bottle even in summer. That sort of thing."

"Oh please. I've always thought routine was over-valued. Anyway Andrew you never heat a bottle for me."

"You've always been very hot-blooded dear. And your parents spent more time apart than together."

"That was his job as you know. The Admiralty's a career where you can't cherry-pick your assignments."

"Oh of course," he added soothingly. "All those waves."

A small innocent phrase. Rachel took a larger gulp than she had intended and watched Andrew do the same and wince.

"It's too acidic for me. I'm getting old. Any new ones for the gallery, Ben?"

He nodded over to the alcove whose wall was covered in beautifully framed three dimensional and holographic pictures. There were two of their parents in much younger times but the images were mostly of Bera, Ben and herself. Above, in an arc of gold letters he had written.

"When We became Us."

She had taken most of the images on visits from which he was almost always absent. They had just been snapshots for him to glimpse the changes but he had insisted on blowing them up like wall-paper. In the corner sat a model of a wind turbine that Bera had made and asked Rachel to give him. He wrote back full of praise and indeed visitors never left without a guided tour. In the square afterwards they might ask themselves why Rachel always fell silent and hung back from all his detailed anecdotes. The moving images unnerved her.

It should be titled. "Moments I have Missed."

She never entered the space. Everything was covered in dust. It felt like a shrine.

Ben looked at Rachel.

"I did take a couple from the camping trip. She enjoyed it so much you know."

"Best co-ordination!" Ben boasted.

"Well, yes she was good," Rachel owned "But she also showed a lot of maturity, good leadership and took the initiative unprompted."

"We'll make Fidelis of her yet," Josie said.

"What about Transmissions? She'd be at the heart – the veins and arteries of the Asoan body," Ben said pompously.

Andrew sniggered.

"And Fidelis are the white blood cells," Josie retorted.

"Oh please." Rachel glanced at their glasses. Discord was coming early.

"Well you're her mother. What d'you want for her?"

Rachel considered her hands for the longest possible time before replying.

"Happiness. To be the best she can be."

"Yes. I might have expected that. Sounds like my mother."

"You never gave your mother credit. She was wise and noble and truly compassionate."

"Yes well she was very 'good' wasn't she? Her response to any of my problems was 'shall we pray about it together?'" Josie retorted.

"Oh, but she gave you so much practical support too!" Andrew argued.

"It wasn't enough."

"My mother used to say something similar," agreed Ben. "Don't get me wrong, she was a great listener, just not to me. I think she wore herself out, nodding and filling in the silences between all the different communities. She forgot to watch herself. I still choke when I think about the guy who murdered her. A white suburbanite whose only defence was 'everyone hates a tourist.'"

"What about your Dad?" Andrew asked gently.

"Mac? Oh well Mac was... remote. A great engineer, apparently. Unique bridges. There was a family joke that Mum made links with communities and Mac linked countries without ever really understanding them. My over-riding memory is of slithering into corners at night without being noticed, trying to unscramble the whispered phone calls."

"At least children are spared all that misunderstanding these days. All that maternal claustrophobia," Josie added.

"Every marriage has its tension spots. And not all mothers are 'claustrophobic', as you put it!" Rachel felt her inner heat rising, defensively.

"It's a mother's duty to raise independent women."

"I think I do."

"Only because of the way we live. Without Abovo you'd be just like every other generation."

"How do you know? How can you possibly know what I would be like? You, who have no frame of reference whatsoever, you're not qualified to comment!"

"Yes I realise my infertile status does prevent me from joining your exclusive club, Rachel, but that doesn't prevent me from having an opinion based on all of the testimony I have heard. There are very few women who got it right then or have the chance to get it wrong anymore. It's just the reason we have to support the infrastructure that's been so painstakingly put in place and not let woolly indeterminate thinking persuade us otherwise. And actually we should be recognising the qualities needed for Fidelis early just as the Maters do. And like the Maters maybe one of the essential criteria should be childlessness so that there are no distractions. You'd be the first to admit that you were not the same after having Bera."

"And didn't you let me know it... Boss. I think that's a ridiculous idea. So many talented, suitable women rendered ineligible. It's prehistoric thinking. Even before Division women had fought for centuries, earning the right to choose. I take it this is all your own work and doesn't represent current thinking from 'above'?"

"It's a complicated area," Andrew pleaded, hating the open hostility and the fact that his childless heart still ached.

"Yes… yes it is," Josie glanced at Rachel who sat tight-jawed, rotating her fore-fingers around each other. "Oh, I'm sorry Rachel, you're right. Who am I to make judgements? I just think historically too many women became unsuitable mothers because society expected it. If I'm really, really honest, I think that one of the advantages of contemporary life is that only the women who are really committed do have children and…" She paused and swallowed. "It must be both incredibly hard and much easier these days. You don't have all the responsibility."

Rachel smiled thinly. "That's true. Sometimes I wish we did. But I would hate to leave the legacy of disappointment in her that both your imperfect but fine women seemed to have left in you."

"Cards anyone?" Ben refilled everyone's glass. "I think we've still got one pack intact after the last time."

"Oh that was so funny. I haven't laughed so much in ages." Josie slapped her knee. "Just the sight of Rachel tearing up all the picture cards into tiny pieces, shouting, "I AM NOT COMPETITIVE! Brilliant!"

And there it was. Solid ground once more.

The red drained away from behind her eyes and their faces came back into focus.

Yet there's something not quite right. I'm used to the combat. No, it was more subtle. I've heard parts of the speech before. I know Josie's voice patterns like my own. It was too forced. Who had she been trying to convince?

A couple of hours curled behind them peacefully until she felt her eyes closing.

"No stamina!" Josie's gentle sneer came from far away but was enough to rouse her.

She watched the horse sashay with slightly less coordination towards the door. Josie, somehow smaller, had nestled into Andrew's shoulder.

"Tomorrow then!" someone's mouth slurred.

She stood and lurched towards the bedroom door seeing them all still hovering at the threshold.

Just go. Go!

She swatted irritably at the air and in response their hands fluttered loosely in half waves.

Don't come back!

CHAPTER FOUR

Working

In her dreams, they were dashing across a path of burning embers, giggling for there was no pain. But as she woke, her laughter became whimpers. She reached out behind her, felt the hollow where a child might foetally curl after a nightmare. She had sensed him leave. Draining the last of her water she padded through to the kitchen and re-filled her glass. Her epiglottis clicked in the darkness.

"Ben," she murmured. All the rooms were still but it was only when she saw his empty transor-cradle that she realised he had gone.

Why? Work? Had he said he was going back and I've just forgotten? Or in the basement? Of course! He would be recharging the fuel cell. An odd time! It was two in the morning, well into curfew.

Fumbling she found her transor – no message. There was no reply from the basement pager.

She would not rest. Hurriedly, she dressed, pulled on her overcoat and slipped her stunner into the pocket. Outside, the biting wind almost blew her over and bullied clouds across an obscured moon. The basement was locked. Her transor beam provided the only faint light as she skirted close to the residential blocks and hurried up to Transmissions.

This is too familiar. Those endless nights when insomnia haunted my pregnancy. The heightened hearing. My restless twitching limbs. The wandering from room to room. His nocturnal absence. The more weight I gained, the more gaunt and hollow-eyed he became.

Then the night came when she followed him to that discreet corner of the burgh, watched him slip inside, welcomed. A state run service like food or energy. So that the pregnant Asoan would not be 'bothered'. She made it back to the square before a yowl broke through.

There was a register that she regularly scrolled, endlessly imagining whom he might have picked. At night their faces hung over her like dispossessed spectres. Her jealousy spilled out in a vulnerable moment with Josie and she regretted the confidence immediately when Josie had said she was 'too much of a purist'. Since Andrew wasn't that interested she had been using the service herself for years. Still she looked into it and managed to establish that there was someone specific. An exotic Oriental in a time when such features were rarely seen.

His moods ran the gamut. Bright and breezy to sullen and withdrawn. Bitter pride kept her silent. Empowerment came from an unexpected source. One afternoon she opened the door to a swirling snowstorm and Josie's mother from whom she had kept her distance over the years, barely able to look her in the eye.

"I heard you were struggling," Marianne said simply, handing over a potted blue hyacinth.

Over tea, she first held Rachel's hands and then cradled her as hot tears soaked her shoulder. Afterwards Rachel sat open-eyed and humble as Marianne prayed for her marriage and the unborn baby.

"I used to put a photo of Kenneth's latest conquest on his pillow. It didn't change anything but at least he was aware that I knew. There were no scenes."

Rachel took her advice. It was never discussed but Bera's arrival changed everything.

Didn't it?

Why am I doing this? Stop now.

The clone patrol allowed her admittance into the building but insisted that no one was working.

"Thank you but I must insist on checking my husband's offices. He has left some important work behind."

"Of course Senior Fidelis. You must check. Thank you for visiting."

It was only when one stood in Transmissions that it was possible to appreciate how extraordinary the technology was. Much was so instinctive and sophisticated that engineering was more orchestration of many finely-tuned parts. She found his station, sat at his seat and stared at the central platform where images and information hung, suspended on their own small screens, waiting to be assembled, given meaning and then broadcast. It demanded a creative spirit. She had forgotten this in Ben.

His desk was covered with a series of schedules. In the corner stood a frame holding a composite of scanimages. Bera at about seven; Josie and her at the last promotion ceremony and an old copy of a snapshot of his parents. It was an eclectic collection. She did not recognise the wooden frame. She examined it more closely, admiring the old fashioned inlays of marquetry. She had not seen anything like this in years. As she was replacing it she felt a flap in the inner side of its stand. A thin empty pocket, enough to hold a small cardette or visinote.

Unexpected.

Outside she re-traced her steps but stopped under a stairwell as she noticed an intermittent beam approaching from the energy stations in the bottom west corner of the Burgh. He ran past. Hooded. She followed at a distance and watched him let himself into their flat.

"Where were you?" He whispered huskily as she slipped into the bed some five minutes later,

"Basement. I... needed an extra cell for my trip to Olim."

"Mhm... night."

Her beating heart refused to stop skipping.

In the morning she found him, carefully removing his gumshield to reveal that unnatural polar smile.

"Morning, how's Harry?" she asked. An old joke. He was

the only person she had ever known who had a favourite tooth and named it!

"Still the boss! Have you seen my tweezers, Rachel?"

"There on the top shelf." She pointed while studying herself in the mirror and fingering her grey spikes distastefully.

"There's no need for it you know, Love. So many different colouring agents out there. Easy, quick. I could do it for you. You've so little hair it would take five minutes."

"Could you? I mean would you... prefer me dark again?" She asked casually.

"No, no that's not the issue. It's entirely up to you."

"It's the keeping it up, with my schedule... maybe I'm just not vain enough."

"Well you've got a good face and a great body – you should feel more proud."

Side by side they dressed. So similar they could have been related with their well-shaped limbs and compact bodies. He looked younger. His olive-toned skin was still remarkably unlined while she had a witch's pallor.

"I'm running late. Short of trousers. Could you take these to the recycler for me?"

"And what colour would we prefer, Sir?"

He smirked "Oh I... let's go brown,"

She heated bread and protein slices and arranged them in the shape of a smiling face on his plate. Any opportunity to make a connection, but he ate mechanically, preoccupied and she sensed again that new unspoken restlessness snaking its way in their grass. Now was the time to ask him.

Why does he still disarm me so? Even after all these years. I can be brutal with the rest of the world. For once just be bold with him. Don't let it fester.

"You know last night when I..."

"You and Josie got a little edgy, I thought."

"Well, she's impossible sometimes but what I..."

"She does go on but she's solid. Full of integrity."

"In many ways yes but what I wanted to..."

"I've got to go." He stood abruptly. "I'll see you later."

"Well maybe, it depends on what..."

"Oh, the fuel cell needs recharging." He shouted from the open door before disappearing.

Typical. Was it always going to be like this? I try to fix a beam of coherent light on him, on the two of us, while he scampers away. Maybe it's unrealistic. We've had to be independent for too long.

As she walked through the centre, Transmissions was already cordoned off and projection engineers were adding another multi-screen in readiness for Magnamater's arrival. She bought a news-file and tried to read the moving text. It was becoming smaller, harder to read. She would have to get her lenses examined.

... Lupin and Soya production up... Long-awaited breakthrough in high-powered fuel cell capacity... Airhar flies further... Efficiency in CHP plants pays off... Increased unrest in Northern provinces where clashes with Fidelis and expulsions are on the increase... "Don't ignore us" says ringleader... Beat the Beetle... Crop managers celebrate total eradication of pests... Marriage made in Hempen... wonder crop's applications just keep on growing...

Once inside the Fidelis building it was hard to be anything other than sober. Its interior had all the moods of a winter sky. From the slate grey desks to the insinuation of blue on the walls – everyone took everything seriously. The salutes were crisp, the greetings brisk. At the verification grid, she stared ahead allowing for eye assessment, placed her ten fingertips on the print panel and announced herself for vocal recognition. The receptionist watched her screen silently.

"Good morning Fidelis Develin. Senior Fidelis Butcher asks that you report to her immediately."

"Right. Is Fidelis Kitchener in yet?"

The receptionist checked. "Not as yet, Fidelis."

If one looked, one could find a redeeming quality in most faces. Sadly, not in S.F. Butcher. Economic features peered from a flat, ill-defined expanse, save two deep vertical grooves running in-between her eyebrows to meet with a larger horizontal on her forehead. She was Pi – cross, rational and fundamental. A bristling stick, whose presence her subordinates avoided unless necessary.

She finished reading.

"So, you will be travelling onto Olim today?"

"Yes, Ma'am. If that is what is required."

"I am sure it is. I am still unconvinced about Marchant. There's a general sense of unrest in Olim. Your line of questioning should extend to anyone associated with him. I would also like you to spend some time at the Learning Centre in Norwich. There's a lot going on there that we would like to know more about without raising alarm. Circumspection, you understand."

"I believe that Fidelis Kitchener has been our Olim expert."

"Indeed. She left all the relevant files for you. You will find them at your station."

"Is she expected in today?"

"Later. Ah, Magnamater is about to broadcast. Shall we go?"

She rose and Rachel dutifully followed her down to the concourse where the large Asograph turned gyroscopically, awaiting transmission.

On the other side of the civic building, Magnamater Beatrice settled back into the transparent seat from which she always broadcast. She was known for her composure and seemed impervious to the local technical difficulties that Ben and his team were encountering.

Those used to seeing her via transmission would have been surprised at her smallness, the delicacy of her jaw. Her square, tiny hands rested like sleeping doves in her lap. No one would suspect how tightly they gripped each other. As if they relaxed their mutual clasp, they would freely float away. It was only her hair that suggested an inner uprising. Hemp-oil did contain it but off-air there was little time for grooming so she allowed its grey spokes to fizz and spur at gloriously unpredictable angles. Occasionally it was trimmed and, in truth, she would have preferred to shave but she needed to make a distinction between herself and the towering, shorn severity of Olivia's administration. She believed that an implied wildness might endear her to the increasingly indifferent Asoans. She had the retinal scan figures and knew that while receivers were on, people were not watching and polls suggested that they were only half listening. That's why this provincial tour was so important to bring the Magnamatership and her new proposals to the public.

From the gallery, Ben timed commencement.

"Friends, good morning. I speak to you today from the beautiful primary Burgh of Province 'B'. At the start of my tour…"

Unremarkable, thought Ben. Without her specially dyed robe, the blue of unknown oceans with its grey piped edges, she could pass unnoticed in the streets until she spoke and then her mellifluous, surprisingly low tones would soothe and persuade us. Probably.

"… And I am excited to announce that by next year we will have new leisure facilities to host, amongst others, an inter-Burghian low-ball sports league. We hope to extend this to an inter-Provincial competition and to facilitate this, there will be a relaxation in travelling restrictions and an increase in locopass availability…"

Rachel stood slightly behind her supervisor noting her stiff carriage, her shaved hairline and her head that moved slightly to scan any reaction in her team as they listened. She turned sharply to Rachel who nodded enthusiastically in return.

Actually, it was a good initiative.

"… So, I send you our eternal promise to keep ASO united in truthful transparency…"

As soon as the address had finished Rachel slipped away and at her desk began to leaf through the files on Marchant and his family members, recent activities and a general history. Her heart sank. They were a mess. New levels of disarray. Even for Josie.

Ben watched the Magnamater's advisers spirit her down to the waiting Har and on to a whistle-stop round the new Hydrogen plant. His assistant grimaced.

"I'm sure she means well. But it's just tinkering. Fundamentally she's disconnected and the distance just keeps on growing."

"Well, who knows. Thank you people. Take a break."

He watched his team drift, relieved and disengaged, down to the refresher and returned to his desk. Unobserved he gripped the frame and slid out the expected card. He read.

'Activate E links'. So much to be done he could not remember a time when he had felt this excited. Then he remembered the nape of Rachel's neck which was at that moment being encased in a hooded overcoat as she walked up to the locomoter.

She sent a text.

"Well done. Love you always" and an accompanying visimessage of her lips blowing a kiss.

He sighed and leaned back in his chair, cradling his head in his interlocked hands. He stared up into the roof void, imagining the sky beyond.

So much intensity between them and then nothing. It was unnatural. Like a war.

CHAPTER FIVE

Olim

She would have two hours to read and conduct a visilink interview with Peter Marchant's son Josh, who worked as a crop engineer in province F. He responded quickly. Fidelis were not kept waiting.

"I understand that you will not be attending your father's funeral in Olim."

"I can't possibly. We are in the middle of harvesting early soya," he replied impassively.

"Indeed. Yet you are only in the next province."

"My father and I were not close and we have not spoken in five years. I can't shed any light on his life in Olim and have no idea what possessed him to trek across to Abovo – but it was typical of him to act without reflection or regard for others. He liked the big platforms and gestures. My mother had to live with it all her life. I am grateful that she has been spared this."

"Have you spoken to Pajo since the incident?" Rachel asked.

There was a pause.

"I have spoken to the Ababmater and his guardian Mater and am assured that he is unaffected. I'm confident that they would have alerted me if there had been a problem. It's visiting next weekend anyway."

"I tend to agree. He seemed more concerned to have done the right thing and that you would not be angry with him. Perhaps some reassurance would help. Although obviously the Maters know best."

He bridled. "So I understand that you will be conducting a rigorous investigation. Good! I wish you well."

"Please be aware that I may need to contact you in the future. Particularly if further details come to light."

There was little point in pressing him. Like so many Surisians related to dissidents, he sought only to distance himself from his parentage. It was the approved way.

Yet it strikes me that if the situation had been reversed, nothing would have stopped Marchant Senior from making contact to reassure himself that his son was all right. Is Josh now typical of this generation? Did Division encourage such distance and coldness? I know why there's concern in the Magnamater's camp. They take nothing for granted. The stability of a coherent ASO can't be jeopardised by unauthorised migration. Although one can't actually prevent Surisians removing their children from Abovo and relocating to Cornwall where supposedly they can live as they choose. Frankly I have my doubts about that, but the numbers are increasing.

Enlarging the miniaturised files on Marchant's sister Jennifer Lacy and brother-in-law Harry, she noticed a coded security lip, highlighting at the bottom of the second page. It was her code. She scanned the lip with her transor—

"Rachel. Talk to Diana – Olim – J."

The message immediately scrambled and dissolved. She sat upright, quickly glancing round the carriage for witnesses.

Diana who? Why this subterfuge? She watched the flattened acres of Province 'F' flow by, fighting a mounting irritation. The landscape grew denser as they began their passage through thick pine forests. The locomap told her it was Sandringham – an entrance to Olim. It would not be long. Somewhere, outside to the right, the old king lived in isolated retirement. He had not been forced to resort since his children had abdicated from their royal status and contributed as normal citizens. It would have made the Magnamater seem petty.

She disembarked alone onto a platform bathed in brilliant, low afternoon sun and, shielding her eyes, could just see a woman walking towards her.

It would be Jennifer Lacy. Her status required a salute but a palm was already outstretched, so hesitantly Rachel grasped the papery fingers.

"Welcome Fidelis Develin. I hope your journey was good."

Rachel buried her surprise. *At seventy-five, she is still an astonishingly pretty woman.* Blonde curled hair crowned a face skilfully highlighted with cosmetics. She wore a soft flowing outfit made from materials Rachel did not recognise.

"We can walk back to the village. It's not far. I understand you're staying at the Swan? Would you like to interview me there or come to my home?"

"Your home will be fine."

Rachel followed her onto a tree-lined street. A white sign with black lettering announced 'Lime Avenue'. So quaint that the roads were still named. They passed rows of single-floored, pastel-coloured houses, decked with flowers.

"Do you all live in these places?" She asked, disbelief slipping out unintentionally.

"Of course. Why not?"

"They seem so... ornamental."

"They are. But we also grow our own food in the gardens and in communal allotments and participate in the livestock breeding programmes on the farms, obviously."

"Livestock?"

"Well chickens, sheep, a few cows."

"You eat meat?" Rachel was incredulous.

"Yes," the elder woman replied, amused. "Here we are."

They stepped up the path and Jennifer waved briefly to a man who merely nodded and continued digging.

"Edward York. William's younger brother. Perhaps you remember."

"Of course!" How could one of the chief engineers of Division be forgotten?

Once inside, a large beast approached her wagging its tail.

Disgusted, Rachel lifted her hands involuntarily.

"Down, Bingo!" Jennifer clapped.

"You allow guarding animals to live inside?"

"He was Peter's dog. You must be hungry."

Without waiting for a reply, she brought out a prepared tray from the cooling box. Rachel's stomach somersaulted but she made herself eat cautiously. Hunger showed vulnerability. Oh the need! Fresh, moist, white bread encased unidentifiable delights. A depth of taste she had not experienced in adult life. Cake – light and suffused with a delicate sweet fruitiness. There was no stopping her mouth, which, like a child, ran down the hill ahead of her.

"How do you sweeten your food?" She asked noisily, wiping crumbs from her cheek.

"Honey. We have apiaries in each village. I don't expect Surisians have much time for baking."

"It is not a priority, no."

She savoured the fragrant herbal tea and thought regretfully of her usual thick brew. This felt like a seduction.

She shook her shoulders.

Business.

"Thank you. It is required that you wear a veriband to authenticate your statement."

Jennifer nodded her assent and extended her wrist for Rachel to clip on the narrow strap, adding, "Generally though, I find it saves time to tell the truth."

"Tell me about your brother."

"He was an intelligent, compassionate and humorous man."

"How did he spend his time?"

"He played chess, a little light gardening, he swam, cooked, socialised. It's a lively community."

"Did he belong to any organisations?"

"Yes. The Bowling club. The Marine society. The Antiquarians."

"What is the last one?"

"A history group, really. You become very interested in the past as you get older."

"Was he in contact with anyone from abroad?"

"The odd e-mail. The Learning Centre at Norwich has access to trans-national networks. He spent a lot of time there. We all do. Everyone's studying something."

"Did he often flout the resorting rules?"

She returned a level gaze.

"Infrequently."

"Can you explain his presence in Abovo?"

"He wanted to see his grandson."

"Without authorisation?"

"He knew permission would not have been given. Josh had broken off all contact. It's not complicated. He knew he did not have long and it was his last chance. I..." she sighed, "did not try to stop him."

"And the drugs?"

She laughed hollowly.

"After his first heart attack he carried his beta blockers everywhere. The trip was obviously too much and the second attack killed him in Abovo. For the record, he hated all medication."

"Children have reported that he tried to give them drugs."

For the first time Jennifer's face tightened and her lowered reply had gravel in it.

"They... are mistaken."

From nowhere, her husband Harry slipped in.

"Hello my love."

They kissed and as he softly stroked her cheek, Rachel looked away, embarrassed.

"Fidelis Develin, this is Harry."

He appraised her. Good bones. Awful hair.

"Welcome. Why are you here?"

Directness never threw her.

"There is concern that, given his reputation, Mr Marchant's behaviour might indicate a more orchestrated operation."

Harry's lips twitched.

"With respect, that sounds paranoid."

"We can not afford to be complacent where the security and welfare of our children is concerned," she retorted.

"And that is achieved by keeping them away from the

supposedly corrupting influence of their grandparents, is it?"

"No. If the guidelines are followed, there is always the opportunity…"

"You're wrong! Ask yourself Fidelis if your parents had survived how would you explain to them that they were not to be trusted to spend time with your daughter. Never to see her, cuddle her, sit her on their knee? And moving on, how will you feel when your daughter sends you a scanimage of the grandchild you will never kiss?"

His voice whipped over her, as it used to across the school hall.

"I will accept it as the best way," she retorted staunchly.

"How long will Surisians delude themselves that their fragile society is sustainable? It's just a temporary stasis, a holding bay. This resorting to Olim is nothing more than Age-Apartheid – but you're probably too young to know what that means. History, if you but allowed yourselves to read it, would tell you that segregation cannot last. No matter how you seek to justify it."

"I have read and lived enough to know that it was the arrogance, self-interest and materialism of your generation that betrayed us. What could not be controlled was ignored. Collectively, you failed to notice the holes appearing under your feet. The fanatical uprisings, the underground nationalisms, the water shortages!"

He exhaled slowly.

"Yes… there was too much of everything… so many causes… all that information. People clinging to driftwood on a swollen sea. But we all have to be free to make mistakes, to learn, to change. You've become slaves to a fixed, flawed idea and let yourselves be persuaded that we are dangerous because we can't be adjusted to your way of thinking… I…" he grimaced "Get off your box, Harry… sorry, I think I prepared that speech a long time ago. Look, wouldn't you like to… see another country? Taste something new?"

He stuffed an oversized slab of cake into his mouth as he spoke.

Rachel pooled everything within her to resist this onslaught, to keep all her doors open.

"Yes," she said finally. "I would like to try chocolate again."

Jennifer's face broke tenderly. "Oh my dear, I wish I had some to give you. There is so much missing. I'd love to have a chat with my daughter – face to face, without an appointment. We feel we are the victims here, in the clutches of a social experiment in its dying stages."

"It's not…"

"Please. The family is like a ship – if you are cut loose from it then you are anchorless, a castaway. It was my first cause. It defined and dignified me. I still have so much to offer, to pass on. What should I do with my experiences, my memories? The need to be needed does not stop according to your age or where you live. I feel like an amputee… but the pain's here."

She laid a hand across her chest.

They all fell silent.

"You are married, are you not Fidelis?" Harry asked.

"I am… united yes."

"Don't you miss your daughter?"

"I have my work."

Jennifer noticed the tightening in the officer's jaw. She exhaled dreamily.

"From the moment my baby slipped out of me, ambition floated away like a lost balloon."

"I believe that the Maters expertise is superior to any skills I have."

"I always find experts a little unnerving." She leaned forward, "Tell me, Fidelis, did you conduct the final interview with Peter?"

"Yes."

For a few silent seconds, Jennifer's head shook and she seemed to be struggling. Then she looked upwards and Rachel saw how grief greyed her face.

"I… I know what you people are capable of. I hope he did not suffer."

"No. Even at the end he was in full control. He sent you his love."

The older woman nodded. "Was there anything else before I take you over to the Swan?"

"No. Thank you for now."

'You people'... that's it. I'm a 'people'. No. Separate the issues. Never personalise. Keep the armour intact. They mustn't know an arrow had penetrated. Let them believe me obtuse, and indifferent to their sorrow.

"I would like to talk to other members of the Antiquarian society. Can you give me their names?"

The Laceys exchanged glances.

"Locally, Edward York and Susan Pelucci are two that spring to mind. You can contact them via their board at the Centre in Norwich or they often hole up at the Swan for a drink – you might see them there."

Her transor beeped.

"Ah, the Magnamater's transmission." This she watched, noting their indifference as they chattered and cleared the table.

As they walked through the village, she was amazed at the unoccupied open spaces. It seemed so wasteful when in Suris every millimetre was accounted for. There was even a small, unused area of water, just lying there with birds floating on it! The people she did see ambled unhurried, others lounged on benches or participated in an activity on the green, rolling and slowly trotting alongside balls. Occasionally a rider slipped by on an old bicycle, staring at her as if she were an unwelcome low-flying exotic. She recognised a church from its spire and coloured glass windows.

"May I look?"

Inside, she marched without hesitation up the aisle and stared around her.

"So is it used as an Information Centre now?" Her voice rang unexpectedly loud.

"No. The church is still our valued place of worship. We

gather here to pray... praise... ask forgiveness and remember." Harry replied quietly.

"I see. It... I don't want to cause offence, but it seems too easy. After everything that has happened in all of our lifetimes."

"No. Not at all. Belief is harder than disbelief and the world has always been imperfect."

At the altar, she ran her hand unceremoniously along its surface and looked down into the pews where Harry now sat with bowed head. She listened. *Should there be rustling, fingers of faith scurrying out of the wood to encircle me with welcome? Should it come from outside or within me? Would it hurt or be bright when it happened? I can't hear anything.*

He did not stir as she passed him. By the door, she leant her forehead against the ancient stone, wondering if by osmosis, understanding would seep through.

Later she sat alone in the corner of an oak-beamed room, seemingly invisible to the gathered Olimians, and ate a steaming unknown supper before retiring. Her head sank down into the pillows and an old mustiness. Her transor sounded and Ben's face appeared.

"Are you secure?" His face was tense.

"Yes."

"Right. It's bad news Rachel... darling..." His voice caught, his face buckled as tears fell. "I thought you should know as soon as I... I've just... Andrew called... They've found Josie earlier... her body... by the river in Burgh 2. She drowned. Apparently. I mean it's just unbelievable. We only saw her last night Rachel. There's been no official announcement but as if this wasn't enough they've asked Andrew to leave the flat – it's been sealed off. Extreme, don't you think? He's in a bad way. I've said to stay over 'til he goes to his sister's. Hope that's okay? Are you all right?"

"I don't know." Dully, she remembered a swimming lesson at school. "She was a great swimmer. They always put her on the last leg of the relay so she could make up the time. Did Andrew do the I.D?"

"Yes. He said she didn't look like herself. Wished he hadn't seen her. Can you get back?"

"I'll speak to Butcher in the morning. There'll probably be a post mortem. Andrew will need some help with the arrangements."

Ben stared. "Ever the practical one. I just... don't know what we're going to do now. Without her." He rubbed his face roughly. "I'd better go. Are you sure you're all right? I know how much there was between you."

"Yes. Years."

"Well try and get some sleep."

"Yes. You too."

She sat on the edge of the bad, her hands cupped expectantly, waiting for a reaction.

Was this our friendship then? The first love after family. All those minutes and emotions somehow vacuum-packed to make them portable, manageable. All that jostling competition. All that loving enmity. Mutual witness and judgement on each other's unfolding lives. Knowing where I had come from, what I was before we all had to change. Shared, irreplaceable time. And how often have I longed to be free? Numbed myself because you left me no choice. You were so bloody big and loud and bossy... just wouldn't leave me alone, let me grow into my own shoes... I had to get away and yet I never have, have I? And I'm going to spend a sleepless night remembering every expression you ever wore and feeling guilty. And nothing's ever going to be the same because you're just going to leave a big fat hole, aren't you?

"Aren't you?" Her savage hot words sliced the still air and her limbs shook so much she buried herself under the covers waiting for the next phase to wash over her.

As the morning's light drifted in, she washed in cold water, grimly noticing middle age trenching her cheeks and loosening her jaw-line. It became less possible to disguise a sleepless night. Then she sat, trying to order her thoughts and structure the day. She would visit the Learning Centre in Norwich, identify the Antiquarian society members and any other organisations that seemed to suggest 'dissidence'.

"So much dissent here. I'm not sure I'd recognise the threatening type!" she said aloud. She felt discernment flapping its wings, lifting from her shoulders and heading south like a migrating bird.

I must hold tight. She stood erect, recalling the hours of rigorous discipline at the training school. Her arms outstretched, like long piers from whose ends she would roll her energy until it ran like mercury back into her and set. She sent deep breaths that cleansed her veins like easterly winds

A door knock interrupted her.

"Breakfast!"

The hosteller's wife gloomily handed her a heavy tray on which lounged more food than she might normally eat in a day. She was unaccountably cheered by the prospect. Eggs, cooked bread, tomatoes, golden-coloured puffed grains. Then, some unrecognisable thin red tubes of... meat? Three dark black discs, veined with white, edged the plate. She arranged herself at the window to watch the village wake and without looking down, ate her way purposefully across every plate.

Grimly, she contacted Fidelis administration and asked for SF Butcher.

"She is unavailable at the moment. Can I take a message?"

"Would you ask her to contact me as a matter of urgency please."

Then another impulse gripped her. She keyed in the familiar digits. Josie's number was still activated. It switched to message after six transmits. And there she was. Every caustic syllable of her. 'Leave an interesting message or don't bother!'

"Come back!" She choked.

The line died. *The thing was that unless the transor was being worn there should not have been a line. It had certainly not been water damaged so who had it?*

Her feet padded down the carpeted stairs – it seemed unnecessary to cover a floor so. But then heat conservation was hardly a priority here, with warmth leaking from every one of its ill-fitting windows and doors. In the empty lounge there was still a sense of occupation from the night before. A cocktail smell of earth, bodies, food and... connection.

Outside, the pale blue eastern sky announced a tempting coastline that she would visit later but for now she made her way through the village to the station. The small brick and flint cottages clustered randomly together, all facing in different directions. Energy supply must be a challenge – it seemed reckless. She could hear the far off hum of the turbines but the prevailing sound was of crisp quiet flecked with the odd crescendo of a bird's chorus.

"Admiring the picturesque, Fidelis?" A voice sounded too close and startled her. Edward York stood, hands buried deep into his pockets, his cadaverous face tilting to one side.

"I was just wondering about your energy supplies."

"Were you?" He smiled dubiously. "Oh we have plenty of alien technology. It's just that it's an important part of Olimian sensibility to place it more discreetly. There are biomass plants everywhere. Willow, hemp, oilseed and sugarcane are all grown here. So we use it immediately at site – little transportation, very efficient. Don't forget, some of the finest brains in fuel technology now live in Olim – happens to us all! Going anywhere in particular?"

"The station. Norwich."

"Me too. Do you want some company?"

"Thank you."

I'm not sure about this man. There's an underlying superciliousness in his manner that I don't like.

"So, uncovered anything interesting, yet?"

"Everyone has been very helpful," she replied carefully.

"Yes, well there's probably nothing to find. Marchant was a straightforward rebel – always knew where you stood. Easy to get over-anxious about death, seek unnecessary explanation."

"An admirably pragmatic approach."

"I say all that... I'm still struggling with my brother's passing."

She was about to ask more but was distracted by a chestnut brown horse cantering urgently through the meadow. Catching sight of them, it abruptly stopped and slowly walked towards them.

"Jennifer's horse. I believe his name's Poncho."

She held the wooden post to steady herself, felt the breath freeze in her chest. The space shrank small between them as she reached out and tentatively pattered her fingertips over the velvet blaze, watching the steam rise from his gleaming flanks. His tail flicked and his mouth began to rout hopefully.

"I have nothing," she murmured softly.

"Always hungry, that one." Edward turned on his heel and reluctantly she followed.

As the locomoter climbed the elevation out of the town she was able to look back at the cluster of houses and the sea waving a 'come on' in the distance. The next station was upon them before she had time to draw breath. A sign for 'Links Hotel' caught her attention.

"What is Golf?"

"It's a game played on a long series of linking grass courses, where one uses an iron, a kind of long metal bar with a curve at the bottom, to 'putt' a hard ball into a small hole. It takes a long time and they tell me it demands skill and tenacity. My brother was supposed to be quite good."

"How did your brother die?"

"A remarkably virulent blood cancer that turbo-charged its way through him and killed him within a month of resorting here… apparently," he said dryly.

They left the station on the same piece of track before curving inland and cutting through woods. Still so unspoiled.

A square towered church on the right. A round towered church on the left. *Were so many really necessary?*

"So, doubtless, you will be visiting some of the countless remaining churches in Norwich then? There's one for every week of the year you know."

"Probably just the Learning Centre."

"Ah yes, the great emporium – something for everyone. I'm there myself."

"Oh?"

"I'm studying astronomy… after spending a lifetime looking down…" He fell silent.

On either side, she noticed stretches of water, on whose banks sat reed-fringed quays leading to pretty houses with wide projecting eaves. From memory their style begged snow.

The odd traveller cursorily nodded from drifting flat-bottomed boats, some ornately decorated, She turned for explanation.

"Man made lakes, more popularly known here as The Broads. Some link into the canal network. People spend a lot of time on the barges. Why not? There's still a lot of water and a little bit of time left."

It was like looking through a kaleidoscope. Fragments of an earlier age where sheep, cows and pigs grazed peacefully with the acres of vivid rapeseed stretching out behind them. The next station reinforced the image with its wrought iron railings and overhead lantern lighting.

"The station's actually a private home but they've kept the original Victorian signage. Lovely isn't it?"

The turbines on the brow whirred like incongruous intruders and as the landscape opened out she caught glimpses of small stone towers, some with blades, others wasted to stump, flanking the roadside.

"Windmills. Part of our heritage from the Dutch. Big renovation project to fully restore them. See those houses over there? With the beautiful distinctive gables? Dutch."

"Who were the Dutch?" She had lost her reluctance to appear ignorant. She just wanted to know.

"People from Holland. One of the low-lying countries on the North Sea. It may seem impossible to believe now that the British once fought, invaded, traded and were occupied by other countries. Here in Norfolk, we had much more in common with them than with the rest of Britain in many ways. It wasn't a bad thing. A natural enlargement. The prospect probably terrifies you, does it?"

She shook her head, refusing to be baited and besides, they

were drawing closer to Norwich and the broadened river with its riverboat houses and waterside activities demanded her full attention. People roamed freely. Eating, drinking, bare feet dangling towards rippling water. Sunlight glinting over surface. Loose. Living.

On disembarkation, she followed him as he walked over to a porch housing a row of two wheeled cycles.

"There are trolleys but they take ages. Norwich is so hilly, you see. Most people take a bycle, will you?" he asked lightly but she read the challenge. She had never ridden and was not going to lose every shred of dignity by learning in front of him.

"I'll take the trolley," she said stiffly. He unclipped two bycles.

"Come on, I'll give you a quick lesson. I thought you Fidelis could do anything."

He began circling in front of her. "Woo-hoo," he sang "look, no hands!" and lifted his arms into the air.

Despite herself, she grinned. "Show off!" He came to a halt.

"You try. Come on. I won't laugh." He lowered his voice. "Should watch some of the old girls – fleshy buttocks like ballast – can't even see the saddle."

They found a short even path. She clipped her files across her back.

"Look ahead. Straight back. Grip the bars firmly. Turn the pedals with your feet." She steered, wobbling and uncoordinated until a raised bump threw the wheel out and she toppled headfirst over the handlebars and onto the cobbles.

"Damn!" She pulled herself up, furiously.

"On again. Just think you can tell all your friends and you don't need a fuel cell."

It was suddenly important and for the next thirty minutes, he cajoled and helped her back until she could do it.

"I'm late!" he said suddenly. "Follow me if you can."

He tapped lightly on her shoulder. She had a vague memory; of her father's hand in the hollow of her back; of him running behind her; his cheer for her independence.

"Thank you so much Edward – you are very kind."

"My pleasure" he beamed.
I've been wrong about him.

An awkward and physically demanding journey followed as she kept banging the insides of her ankles. Finally she climbed onto the flat and cycled along the wide avenues with the spring blossom raining its petals over her like confetti from an old style wedding. A light breeze at her back, she felt life coursing through her, dampening that space where she knew the grief should be sitting.

The Learning Centre was disappointing. She could find nothing edifying in its grey symmetry. It was ugly like Suris.

"I have to dash to my lecture. I don't know where you want to be but there's the library and the theatre's next door."

He hurried away over the concrete concourse and disappeared up inside the high breeze-blocked buildings where interlinking walkways led to tower blocks, lit with activity. Inside she watched people file into the various halls, theatres and side-rooms in animated exchange. The boards were covered with notification of events, classes and speakers. It was astonishingly vibrant.

To her right, two women paused outside a room.

"Oh. It's been cancelled. What a shame," one said regretfully to her companion. "Diana Fielding was one of the most influential biologists of her day – quite a powerhouse, even now. I hope she re-schedules."

In the library, she was amused by the archaic print and lens registration but the information was surprisingly extensive, and the Antiquarian file was more illuminating than she had hoped. No small local club, but an international organisation that met twice a year. The last meeting was hosted abroad in Paris, France. The list of attendees included Marchant. Its mission statement declared a pursuit of learning and development through the sharing of international historical perspectives. The precise nature of this pursuit was carefully unmentioned but the membership was clearly trans-national and, despite the age profile, committed to travelling.

How were they getting there?
A low groan rippled through the library as line after line of flickering screens indicated a power cut. She had time to miniaturise the file before cessation.

On the return journey she considered the society. Certainly regular communication overseas was discouraged, but not forbidden. Was it not reasonable for like-minded people of an age to contemplate the past and share their thoughts? Ostensibly, these activities seemed harmless. However, overseas travel was a different matter. She accessed the previous year's travel permit requests. Unsurprisingly there were no familiar names. If Olimians were managing to leave ASO, there surely was the possibility that foreigners could be landing without their knowledge. Security in the coastal provinces would have to be re-examined. The Magnamater's office would have to be briefed and possibly undertake some delicate negotiations with the administrations in Europe. It was well known that it was not an area of her role that Magnamater enjoyed. The first few points of her report were thus noted before the memory of Josie bolted though her and forced her to slump back into her seat, overcome.

At the hostelry there was a subdued air. The Laceys were eating their lunch at a crowded table and nodded briefly before continuing. Her temples and scalp were now tight from lack of sleep and her eyes watered constantly. She needed fresh sea air.
"Where will I find the nearest beach?" The hosteller barked out some vague directions that she forgot immediately and so left, bearing right and keeping the sea clouds and circling gulls in view.
The first dunes were more like small sandy hillocks that made her calves ache as she climbed and as they grew and the sand bracken thickened, she struggled to keep afoot. At the final brow she could look out to sea. The whirling wind turbines seemed a galaxy away. Nothing could have prepared her for the vast expanse of sand stretching wider and flatter than any she

had seen before. Its strata of pale brown shingle, topped by pools lying in strips of lilac and grey muddy flats rippling softly until the land joined the sea in a final golden ribbon. A private flirtation between earth and an unseen sun.

Bending, she rolled up her trousers, took off her boots and strode forward. How long since she had felt this cold wet yielding underfoot? She made little progress towards the retreating water's edge and so instead turned and walked in parallel, noticing a promenade of incongruously multi-coloured beach huts nestling into the corner. By the time she had reached the decking, the sky was flooded with a sunburst of apricot and blue. The first miniature house was painted pale green with ornamental shells threaded on fraying twine cascading from its small window boxes and chimes hanging in its doorway.

She sat and stared, determined to watch the colours play out. But instead, faint echoes distracted her. *The noise of children combing beaches. Fathers lifting little bodies above the encroaching surfing waves. Siblings patting endless sandcastles and quarrying new depths that would soon be refilled by an indifferent returning tide. The watching women content to weave their generations together in unforgettable sandy moments. I can feel their soft, sighing breath.*

Then another echo. *Josie's voice. Gritty, collapsing sandwiches on the beach. Sheltering from the rain in the little house which was like a box of sweets or stripy pyjamas.* The east coast must be littered with such estatelets, yet she pulled up onto her feet and walked along, enchanted by the care that had been lavished on each house to give it an identity. Normal rules did not apply, hence the anarchy of colours and daubings and, on each letterbox, a printed name. She passed a couple that might have fitted but there was no specific link. Growing tired, she was about to turn back but the next orange and yellow candy strip made her stop.

It was called 'Picnic'. Her attention was drawn to a painting on the side panelling. A family sitting around a table-cloth covered in sandwiches, cakes and fizzing bottles. Two girls with flaxen hair and bulging cheeks. Two adult females, one dark, one fair and a blonde male. Above each, one could just make out a faded name. Marianne, Kenneth, Kim, Josie and Diana. She stroked Josie's forehead and gave a small mock salute to the dark female. Josie's Aunt Diana. *Found. Now what?*

There must be a registry of ownership.

The Fidelis in her turned heel and made her way back to the village where she found a local office attached to the church. Here she pored over a handwritten ledger until she came to 'Pebblars Course', the street name she was seeking. 'Picnic' was registered to Diana Fielding. It also gave a reference for another property in the village itself.

I'm not sending a message. It's too formal. I'll just go and hope she's there.

But the layout of the village confounded her with its intricate streets and alleyways and she found herself back in the green, her transor bleeping. Senior Fidelis Butcher.

"Are you secure, Fidelis Develin? Reports have been confirmed that Fidelis Kitchener's body has been found in Burgh 2, near to the site where she had been investigating two similar vagrant murders. Tragically, it seems likely that she may have been the third victim. The relatives have already been notified and the funeral has yet to be announced. Have you any updates for me?"

"Uhm, nothing substantial but I would request permission to return to Suris early. I understand that Andrew Kitchener is unable to occupy their flat and will be staying with us. I think he needs the support and to be frank I am not likely to conduct as thorough an investigation as I would like, given the shocking news."

"Then I suggest you rally your considerable resources and endeavour to complete the task so that you can return soon!"

"Thank you Ma'am. Security has just become compromised. I will be in touch."

"Of course. I commend your professionalism at this difficult time."

"You Cryo!" Rachel muttered.

Every Fidelis received vocal training. How to recognise the nuances of fear, uncertainty, inaccuracy, joy and deceit. Sometimes one became so acute to the waves, the veriband was a needless formality. She had detected something, indistinct but definitely hidden, in the layers of her superior's voice and it filled her with an even greater urgency to find Diana Fielding.

When she found the house it was less adorned than some but the small garden boasted a glorious tree covered with pink, outsized, goblet-shaped flowers. Above the doorway hung a familiar double helix, crafted from shells that waved gently as she knocked.

She was met by a woman of average height, with a plain flat face and reddened eyes. She was younger than Rachel had expected.

"Fidelis Develin. I'm Susan Pelucci. We've been expecting you. Come through."

As she passed, two candles flickered in the alcoves, casting elongated shadows on the wall. She had made this journey from door to room many times. A bringer of bad news has a soft noiseless tread. There was a face to wear but she found her features would not settle, playing and twitching uncontrollably like children oblivious to the hush of grief.

Into the living area where no body was laid out but the air was still and remote like an ancient tomb.

"Please sit. Diana will be with you shortly."

There were a few pictures on hangings but each wall was shelved to the ceiling and stacked with books. Moveable steps stood close to the door. She realised that she had not planned this interview. There was no frame of reference. She had never lost a close friend before.

Suddenly Diana stood before her. Age did not necessarily corrupt beauty. While her hair was snow white it still curled abundantly from her high forehead. Her face supported by exquisitely carved wide bones and brow. Her large dark eyes, round and un-hooded stared unblinkingly down at Rachel. She was taller by some six inches. She motioned for them both to sit at the table and as she wrapped both hands in front of her like an owl folding wings, there was no doubt who would control the conversation, yet she remained silent.

Rachel began, "Good afternoon. I am here to pass on my condolences. Josie and I have known each other a long time. I will miss her very much."

"Yes."

So much restraint housed within so small a word.

She did not know how to break out of the role, to lose the uniform and ask the question.

"She was so committed to her work... so highly thought..."

"STOP!"

It flew out like gunshot, its force skimming Rachel's face, so that she jerked back.

"I remember you. We both had the same black hair – so shy – always trailing after Josie with your serious little face. It went deep with you even then."

Rachel could hear the fault-lines, the vulnerability, and struggled to still her lips but despite her efforts, air hissed through to become a whisper.

"She left me a note – 'Talk to Diana'. Nothing else. I have no idea why or what she was up to. Have you?"

For the first time she heard her own bitterness.

Susan joined them and slid a file across to Diana.

"The official explanation is that she was killed by vagrants roaming the streets – a rare occurrence during curfew, I understand."

"There is spasmodic unrest," Rachel acknowledged.

"My sources tell me that she was drowned and found not in the estuaries of B but by the Thames in Old London."

Rachel took a few moments to unravel the implications.

"But that's ridiculous! Josie wouldn't break the no-zone restrictions. She had too much respect for the anti-contamination policy. As we all do! Your information's flawed."

What have I landed myself in? Even Josie would never have put herself at risk like that.

"Why do you think that Josie's message to you was left surreptitiously?"

She struggled to follow the train of thought.

"It was on the files passed to me which she knew I would read… in… particular circumstances."

"Those being?"

The older women waited.

Rachel felt impatience and apprehension in equal measure. *Who do they think they are dealing with here? Come on! Don't drag it out like some laboured lesson for a clone.*

"Presumably," she said slowly, "in the event of something happening to her. So what did she want you to tell me?"

"Firstly I have to say I was… am unsure of your nomination. Your reputation as a committed Fidelis is well known."

"Indeed, commitment has always been a prerequisite. Does such loyalty disqualify me then?" She replied dryly.

"When I expressed my doubts that you were an appropriate choice to replace her, she said that she trusted you above all others because you needed the truth and that given your history and all the… family connections, you would want to become involved."

"In what?"

"How much did you know about her current caseload?"

"Burghian unrest. She was conducting a province by province survey."

"Josie's investigations were of a far more profound nature than Burghian unrest. A team of micro-biologists have fission track dated and analysed water and air samples every year for the last twenty years and have found that for the last ten, there has been no contamination."

Rachel laughed, "But it's been proven."

"By whom?"

"Well the authorities, the entire scientific community. What would be the point?"

"Usually a myth is perpetuated to retain control. The question is why keep an area sealed off needlessly?"

"And how do we know that these microbiologists and their results have any credibility?"

"I handpicked them myself," Diana answered quietly.

"And Josie knew about this?"

She nodded.

Rachel noticed Susan Pelucci was taking notes.

This is madness. These were some of the brightest people we had. What have they become? But... maybe that's the problem. They used to signify and now, in Olim, they feel redundant. Here is a cause, a boat.

She spoke deliberately.

"Josie was passionately committed to ASO, to its coherence, to the creed of Transparency."

"Yes and for a short time, it did hang together. So it should, it was planned meticulously. You will never have knitted Rachel, but let me tell you that once you have dropped a stitch, it leaves a hole, a weakness and if one pulls at the yarn, the whole garment will eventually unravel. Josie had great wisdom and a rare clarity of vision, qualities which she believed you share."

"What do you want from me?" Rachel interrupted.

"Josie's work was incomplete."

"Oh, you mean slithering around in places she should not have been, collecting who knows what and getting herself killed was not enough for you?"

"She was no dupe. Once she knew what we had discovered, she could not ignore it. Her conscience would not let her," Susan snapped, speaking for the first time.

"A few microbes do not make a... conspiracy. I, for one do not want a country and a way of living so fragile it destroys itself on such scant evidence."

"You want a quiet life then, Fidelis?" asked Diana coolly.

Rachel was stung. "No... but you must realise how this seems."

"Like two old women with not enough to do, making trouble?"

Diana stood and leaned forward.

"I know you have a report to compile on Marchant. At the Learning Centre you will find history files, particularly about the Age of Division, which cannot be seen anywhere else. Do some reading. Ask yourself some new questions. If we can clarify anything else let us know. We will talk again."

It was a dismissal and Rachel left with the feeling that she had disappointed them.

In the icy darkness with a glittering sky overhead, Edward York stood in his garden, staring intently into a large telescope.

"Did you find what you were looking for?" He asked briefly without averting his gaze.

"Not really. What about you?"

"Huh... homework!" He tutted. "The course is good except for the female lecturer – bossy with it... Oh... there you go!" he exclaimed softly, whistling.

"Anything interesting?"

I'm getting to like this truculent man. At least you know where you stand.

"Have a look." He made a minute adjustment as she stared into the lens.

"See the bright star. That's Orion strutting his stuff... and if you scan north-west there's Taurus, with all her weeping women... even up there, the women are either moaning or telling us what to do."

"You have such a low opinion of us!"

"Not all. But most. I was so glad to resort. Used to be surrounded by dominatrix – hated it – not like my brother. He couldn't get enough – happiest under a big female thumb!" He glanced across quickly. "There I go, being indiscreet again. Mind you, that's one thing I like about getting older. Can say what you like! You won't go without a 'goodbye' will you?"

Later in her room she noted precisely what had been said onto a secure lip file – it amounted to little. Yet she knew that she would have to return to Norwich as bidden. The curtains did not pull tightly, letting night stream in. She lay gazing out and tried to find form or feature in the scattering of stars while her aching limbs shifted on the soft mattress until they found the impression her body had left yesterday.

CHAPTER SIX

Abovo and Olim

At the same time as Rachel journeyed to the Learning Centre, Bera was watching another black stroke being placed by her name on the register.

"Three days in a row, Bera. It won't do. Your Mother would be disappointed. Do you have an explanation?"

The girl shrugged and Mater had to exercise more restraint than normal. "Bera?"

Bera traced a sun with the tip of her boot. *Tell her anything.*

"I'm tired. Not sleeping well. The dorm's colder since…"

The Mater softened. "I see. You are missing Faith? Well we can do something about the temperature at least. Perhaps a milky drink last thing will help. Are you eating properly? Making sure you take all your supplements?"

"Yes."

"And you're feeling well in yourself? Not struggling with anything?"

"Yes. No."

"Well join the circuit training now and… try and enjoy the day."

And as her feet thumped the ground and all she could hear were the regular pants of the children running in front of her, she stared into the white sky and thought of Rachel.

How often does she wonder about me? After she's walked back into her important life. There's no room, is there? It's very easy for her, really. Let someone else worry if I'm well and taking those stupid pills. She wouldn't even know what I eat. I know Dad can't come but at least he calls. Sometimes I wish... I'd... I'd just like to hear her voice more. I know Mater's right and... I'm getting too big to be... It's almost worse when Mum comes because she's got to go again. She should just stop coming... I'm going to say something.

From the conning tower the Abamater watched.

"I do congratulate you, Ruth. Class ten are such a strong team. Particularly the Develin. She could go far."

Rachel deliberately chose a remote spot in the archive section of the Learning Centre. She wanted no attention and no distraction. The volume of information on events leading up to the Age of Division and before in the late twentieth century was astonishing. Undaunted, she scanned the years, seeing for the first time the accumulation of insurgencies from the turn of the century and the tightening of restrictions, as it became obvious that terrorist cell activity was rife in Europe. She noted Marchant's extraordinary career path. He seemed to have had great international credibility and was a constant guest at conferences, embassies and institutions throughout the world, even during his apparent fall from grace after the 'scandals'. The old newspaper headlines blazed "Marchant's Marriage Farce!" with a picture of Alana Marchant and young Josh leaving the family house with suitcase. A further picture showed the couple reunited on the doorstep.

"Welcome back to the fold Peter!"

She listened again to his "Division is Disintegration" speech from the lower chambers of the old Houses of Parliament, warning against the dangers of social engineering, of trying to control the flow of a dynamic fluid population. He argued passionately for the principles of asylum with such heart and conviction. The lobbies filled with rapturous ovation as he almost fell back onto his seat, spent. It made the Magnamater's addresses seem tame and contrived. Then the attacks of 2028 and 2029 happened. The world peace summit.

The amazing photograph, with every attendee linking arms in a gesture of unified aspiration. She miniaturised the file without knowing why. There had been so few survivors. Then she scrolled on to the isolation units, the overloaded hospitals, the burning shells of previously glorious buildings. The Houses of Parliament. Canary Wharf. Lloyds. Most of Fleet Street. That silly Ferris wheel. St Paul's Cathedral.

Those were days of keynote speeches, of Royal weddings, of street celebrations and one way or another many of the powerful or significant were eliminated. The timing was viciously, uncannily accurate.

She watched the video taken by planes flying over abandoned fields where livestock rotted – she could still smell the stench of decomposing flesh. Despite the highest security, the remaining military establishments, army barracks, naval installations and even armed force units overseas, succumbed to pathogens in the food and water.

Why were international vaccine stocks at a mysterious, all time low?

It's the first time I've really appreciated how exhaustive and extraordinary the orchestration was. Like a firework display, each event unfolded into the next, a total choreography. Easy as spraying insects. Not a random, sporadic set of revenges but a single-minded campaign.

Mum used to say that she could identify the culprit by how clean his hands were – the problem was that conductors usually wear gloves. How could I have not looked at it this way before?

Her transor sounded. A coded message was coming from Ben.

... Rachel. Andrew has just given me a disc he found in their basement on a self-timer. Josie wanted it to be passed to you if anything should happen to her. Can you access a terminal so I can miniaturise and send? Safely, Rachel! Lv B

She keyed in her terminal reference and waited. The image that came through was undecipherable – a haphazard grid of interlocking lines upon which there was an occasional asterisk or circle. The words 'Merope... closing in' and a short series of letters and numbers.

What am I supposed to do with this Josie?

Her transor sounded again. Senior Fidelis Butcher's small muddy irises stared back. She set her face and listened, thankful that the screen by her side could not be seen searching for definitions of 'Merope'.

"Fidelis Develin, Magnamater herself will be visiting Olim tomorrow to announce various unifying initiatives to the full council meeting. Your presence is required and I would like a full brief when I meet you at the conference suites there. Fidelis Kitchener's funeral will take place in province B the next day."

As Rachel nodded her assent, she noticed the terminal screen starting to flicker and managed to press the save button while keeping her gaze firmly on her transor until Senior Fidelis finished.

I have to be so careful. If Josie had involved herself, the Administration could already know. And if she was compromised then in time I could be too. Miniature surveillance is a science in itself. So many sophisticated strategies and techniques. Once they've lost confidence. But maybe I'm being overanxious. I am legitimately following an official course of enquiry here. Don't have to justify myself.

She left the deserted centre and cycled back to the station, wondering if her search had been productive. On the locomoter, the results proved scant.

… Merope… one of the Pleides cluster in Taurus…

She kicked the seat opposite and caused a raised eyebrow from a fellow traveller.

Was that it? Means nothing to me. I won't have time to revisit the files before the meeting. But cluster implies stars. Talk to Edward.

He was pruning some flowers that climbed and fringed his front door.

"Any time for roses in your busy life, Fidelis?" He snipped a deep crimson bud on a long stem and handed it to her. "It's called 'Dark Secret'. Starts black and blooms open up to a vivid carmine. Smells like nothing on earth."

She breathed in deeply and gasped. The scent surged through every cavity – seduction.

"It's unbelievable."

He chortled.

"Ooh, we'll corrupt you if you stay much longer, Fidelis."

She smiled. "I need your advice."

He stood aside. "Come in. How can I help?"

"It's a… It's a private matter." She was running risks but felt instinctively that he could be trusted to be discreet.

"I want to know about Merope, the Pleides and Taurus."

"Oh, how lovely. I thought it was going to be something much more conspiratorial. Well… let's see." He pulled down various astronomy encyclopaedias and laid them out before her.

"This is the constellation of Taurus which houses the cluster of seven stars called the Pleiades named after the seven daughters of Atlas and Pleione. The myth tells that they were nursemaids and teachers to the infant Bacchus and that the great hunter Orion caught sight of them walking through the countryside, fancied and pursued them for seven years. Finally Zeus answered their prayers for delivery and transformed them into doves and, on their deaths, placed them amongst the stars. There's another version that tells of them committing suicide through grief for their father's eternal torment at having to support the world, which in turn was his punishment for rising up against the gods of Mount Olympus." He smiled broadly "Keeping up?"

"Yes, yes. And Merope was one of them?"

"Indeed. Merope, the eloquent. Maia, the eldest, brightest and most beautiful. Asterope the lightening twinkler. Celaeno, the swarthy. Elektra, the amber coloured one who seems to flow. Alcyone the protector and Taygete the long-necked one. Pleione means 'to sail', making her daughters, 'the sailing ones' and also they rise in May which was the start of the new navigation season for the Greeks. Their influence is supposed to be of sweet guidance but depending on the legend you read, they also have a reputation for disorder and blindness. Injury to the eyes is common in all nebulous clusters. I could tell you about their half-sisters, the Hyades who are here if you want?" He pointed.

"Sure."

"There are four but Aldebaran or 'the torch' is the brightest and most obvious. Hyades means 'rain' because of the wet season that accompanies their rising in May and November. As storm-bringers, they have a more violent influence and wept so many tears on the death of their brother that Zeus placed them amongst the stars alongside their half-sisters. So they co-habit but don't talk much! Is that enough?"

"Yes, thank you. For now. If there's anything else perhaps I can follow it up with you?"

"Of course. It would be my pleasure. Gives me a chance to show off. But you're not going to tell me why you want to know?"

"Not yet. I... can rely on your discretion?"

"Of course. Our 'Dark Secret' then."

"You are kind, Edward."

As he showed her to the door she noticed a picture.

"Oh, isn't that... ?"

"The great Olivia and my brother William? Yes... before Division... At an international something or other."

"He was a handsome man."

"I suppose so." He was noncommittal.

"How tall *was* she?"

"About six foot four – making him about armpit height to her."

Acrid. A bitter smoke curls around the words whenever his brother's mentioned.

"It's likely that I'll be returning to Suris soon, Edward. So thank you again."

"It has been my pleasure, Fidelis."

"Rachel."

They shook hands until he quickly swivelled her round and motioned upwards.

"Just about there... Don't forget to look up sometimes."

Magnamater preferred to 'chair in the round' as she called it. Such positioning involved everyone, even if the audience was tiered. It also provided her with another opportunity to differentiate her tenure from her predecessor who had favoured a more regal style that doubtless alienated many.

Today, as Rachel looked down from the gallery, she watched the elders' reactions as they listened to Beatrice's announcements.

"These changes will allow greater mobility between Olim and most provinces in Suris. Licence applications will take less time to secure and stay permits of one week will be available. There will also be opportunities for reciprocal study and stewardship of information. We hope to involve the many experts amongst you in our leisure and extracurricular programmes. The Asoan way of life is now so established that we can all look forward to a new period of enlargement, stimulation and cultural renaissance."

"I note Magnamater, that there is no mention of a relaxation in the non-interaction between Olim and Abovo." Susan Pelucci remained seated to pose her question.

"Small stages. Small steps." Magnamater answered with her customary, sentence-end smile.

"Our grand-children's small steps are the very ones we wish to witness, Ma'am. How can it seem rational to you to prevent what was acceptable when we lived in Suris, being unthinkable when we are forced to 'Resort' a few miles further east? Is not the measure of an advanced society how it treats it's older citizens?"

"Or how it protects its young!" Magnamater answered coolly, clearly disappointed by the lack of enthusiasm. She was sufficiently observant to notice the hostility twitching on every older face? They were not appreciating everything she was saying. She leant forward and with every word stretched out her hands and pulled them into her chest. It was meant to look all-inclusive and appealing but to Rachel she looked like a rather desperate octopus.

"I am genuinely interested in how we can enhance the

quality of life in Olim. I want to be able to assure every member of this society that we are fervently committed to providing the same level of care to Olimian residents as to those in Abovo. People must expect that life will continue to offer physical and intellectual opportunities and be diverse enough to offer emotional connections. So, in what other areas could there be improvement?"

Beatrice drew herself up in her chair. Susan Pelucci stood suddenly and walked into the centre of the forum so that she could face the Magnamater.

"We need to update the grid. Some of the more remote communities are still experiencing intermittent energy supplies. The coastline continues to need reinforcing as the sandbagging is insufficient to protect the low lying communities from flooding. Extra provision for the infirm... Chair transport upgrades and additional and more readily accessible ramps on the locomoter network which in itself is proving inadequate, needing more links to the smaller towns. Practically speaking we need more engineers to build them. But these are the same requests we made a year ago. You must forgive us if we seem less than encouraged by your promises."

"I hear what you are saying and I think," she swung around to her assistants who were recording and notating the interview, "that we are now in a position to actively review our plans and hopefully bring forward some of the practical applications." She smiled and rose. That was it. There could be no specifics here.

Susan remained standing, her arms hanging loosely at her side. What did this woman mean? What did she ever mean?

The tour round the facility was little more than a quick glance, pausing in the library only long enough to read the lists of study courses, before being whisked away to the modern arts displays in the next building.

"I note the terminals are all switched off," commented Senior Fidelis Butcher. "How far back do your records go?"

"We have so many power cuts these days, we tend to

conserve energy unless required. It's hard to be accurate – we have lost so much information over the years especially on the twentieth century – but we get by. If you would like to sit and look through some of the files, please feel welcome!"

It was deliberately evasive but Rachel had the feeling that no one was meant to be convinced.

They waited side by side until the last of the Magnamater's retinue had disappeared into the foyer then turned to face each other, a few suitable inches apart. She could no longer avoid the conversation.

"Your report so far suggests that you have not discovered anything new about Marchant."

There was a certain Fidelis way of communicating in public. The lips barely parted to allow only a whisper while the tongue enunciated with total clarity. It was the result of hours of training in front of a mirror.

"Indeed," Rachel spoke into her superior's left cheek. "While the Antiquarians are undoubtedly international, with a mean age of seventy plus, their pursuits are more intellectual than active. I have a list of members with profiles, details and agendas of meetings over the last five years, but there seems to be nothing ominous in its disposition. However, I do strongly recommend a review of the southern coastlines whose current porosity could very well be compromising Asoan security."

"Thank you. Your recommendation is noted. Have you found the Olimians cooperative? Anything unexpected?"

Momentarily, their eyes locked.

"No Ma'am."

Rachel read something complicated before Senior Fidelis blinked. "I will see the completed lists at Fidelis Kitchener's funeral."

She turned on her heel and left Rachel alone, gloomily anticipating the years of cold consultation with her superior.

Overstrand was deserted on her return, except for a ponderous game of bowls on the green. She closed her eyes and tried to imprint the clear smell of ozone, the brightness and stillness. She visited Diana Fielding. There would not be the opportunity to talk to her at the funeral and there was much she wanted to say. But the house was locked and shuttered.

Returning to the hostel she was stopped at the doorway by Jennifer Lacey. Inwardly she grimaced. She preferred to keep a distance from previous interviewees, especially relatives of those she had interrogated.

"Oh, Fidelis Develin, I was going to leave this for you." She handed her a brown packet. Inside was a thickly wrapped oblong bar of chocolate. Rachel looked at her quizzically.

"It's not contraband, or ancient. A traveller from Europe brought it back recently... I thought you might like to try it... if it's not too corrupt. You are not allergic to milk, are you?"

"No. Thank you. Thank you very much."

"Good luck Fidelis."

Her salute changed its mind and extended into Jennifer's hands. She was struck again by the older woman's poise, her beautiful long neck and finely drawn profile.

"What was your profession before resorting, Mrs Lacy?"

"Many years ago, I taught dance, ballet. Very frivolous."

As she stepped lightly away, raising her arms in a final departing wave, a breeze caught her skirts, wrapping them around her and Rachel glimpsed the younger woman gliding across a floodlit stage.

Later, her packing finished, she sat by her bedroom window, unpeeled the wrapper and nibbled cautiously. It was like sex. It slithered into every pocket of her mouth. She could just remember it being freely available. Restraint and time was lost in a few gorging minutes and soon there were only flakes spotting her uniform, telling tales.

A high wind blew her down the platform, lifting and swirling the autumn leaves as high as her waist. Too many trees, too close to the line. This whole place could do with structuring. Perhaps she should suggest it? Or not. Maybe by the time she reached fifty-five she would want more, need to loosen her hold. The locomoter sped out of Olim and into the darkness. She could not settle. Her spine prickled, her calves bounced with unexpressed tension. Something was crawling over her, coursing through her, like the chill after a long hot summer's day.

CHAPTER SEVEN

Suris

The following morning she had cause to regret her excess, as she hung over the toilet seat.

"So just how big was this chocolate bar that I'll never taste?" asked Ben, rubbing her back. She flapped his hand away ineffectually.

"Well, as long as you enjoyed it, eh! I have to go. Broadcast is in two hours. I'll see you at the funeral. Afterwards I want to hear about Olim."

Would there be an afterwards? A time when all the impossible knots and tangles between Josie and me would be untied?

She slumped backwards against the tiles.

"It's so typical of you! Always have to have the last word! You just had to involve me in your muddy little conspiratorial world didn't you? When are you going to let me off the lead? If I could have just gone to Olim, done the work and come back. But no… and now I've no choice… as you knew I wouldn't. I can't ignore what I've been told and I can't do this job unless I'm absolutely certain… it's the only fuel that works. So I need someone independent, a scientist to refute or corroborate what Diana said. Someone trustworthy and discreet who won't laugh in my face. I don't think they exist. Damm you, Josie!"

Her transor bleeped. Luke.

"Rachel. Is this a convenient time?"

"Of course. How is everyone?"

"Fine. Gelu's put on three pounds. Georgia's well…

today." Rachel nodded sympathetically. They had always understood each other. He had taken the baton of responsibility from her. "Anyway, I'm ringing to say how sorry I am about Josie. What time is the funeral?"

"Three."

"I'd like to come if I can. Kate is on duty should there be any problems."

"I may see you later then. Thank you Luke."

It had made her think.

She contacted Kate. "Can I come and see you briefly?"

"Anytime. Have you spoken to Luke?"

"Yes. I was thinking of coming in shortly. Would that be convenient?"

Later as she waited for Kate who sat in lengthy dialogue behind closed doors, she completed the final paragraph of her report. Eventually, three men emerged, glancing briefly at her before slipping away. Kate's usual pallor was broken by two high spots of colour on each cheek.

"Rachel. How are you? How was Olim?" Rachel read her distraction.

"Good. I met some interesting people. Thank you for seeing me at such short notice."

"I'm always here for you, Rachel."

"Actually, it's not about Georgia. I... some interesting and challenging issues have arisen recently and I... find there are few people whom I can confidentially approach to try and find answers. A high level of discretion is vital."

"You know that I am bound to keep everything that we discuss confidential. Besides which we are family. How can I help?"

"You studied virology, didn't you?"

"Amongst other things."

"Would it be possible to take air and water samples from areas of high contamination, without risk?"

"Possibly – under rigorously applied procedures."

Rachel took a deep breath. *Here we go... just like stepping off a cliff.*

"And is it feasible that, despite the general consensus, the no-zones may no longer be contaminated?"

Kate's face remained impassive as she calmly contemplated the prospect. A true scientist.

"The environment was so toxic it would be hard to imagine that such significant changes had occurred. It was the mutations that were unpredictable rather than the original diseases. That is not to say that there would definitely be permanent instability, but it's likely given what we know, and it would need regular tracking over years, decades even, to be sure. The official virologists in Restoration are scrupulous but could anyone be asked to take such a chance?"

Her tone was slightly compressed, as the muscles around the larynx tightened. Imperceptibly louder, the last sentence had a more public quality.

"But is it possible?"

"Anything is possible."

"Thank you Kate."

"I don't feel that I've helped. We should see each other more often," she squeezed Rachel's arm as she showed her out.

And that's the bottom line. Could anyone be asked to take the chance?

Rachel knew Surisian funerals were brief but had no real comparison as she had never attended one in Olim and the mass burials after Division had been urgent and impersonal.

They filed into the small square building that nestled into the hills on the furthest corner of the burgh. The Administrator gave the one eulogy. He praised her office, commended her contribution and ignored her soul. Rachel hunched over the wooden bench, gripping the rail to prevent the anger and loss from shooting out of her fingertips.

It's just the husk of her. Before Division someone who really knew her would have spoken. Family or a friend. I would have said that she was more alive than anyone I've ever known. That her force moved everything it touched. And that most people loved her. That's not something that this man could ever know unless he'd asked. Whoever stole her must have been really determined.

Then he pressed the multi-switch that concurrently lowered the coffin ready for cremation and initiated the recorded accompaniment for the 'Song of Mourning'. They all knew the words – there were only three songs to learn. The others being the 'Song of Unity' for uniting days and a broadly applicable 'Song of Joy' for any other gathering, written by Olivia herself.

Why should they need more? Who had the time to write songs? And who had the strength to sing them? Yet she found herself joining in despite her strangled throat.

Outside the air was still, the sky white. They processed up to the brow of the hill where the Administrator handed Andrew a small slate-grey cube at which he stared and made to turn over. The Administrator gave a slight delaying gesture and pointed to the ground, where an inset metal plate waited. How could all the infinite complexities housed within one body be reduced to ashes and contained in such a small space? Andrew set down the cube, murmured and the plate slid open, sucking the cube in at high speed. He inhaled sharply as if in echo and continued staring down for a few minutes before rising. She heard an unexpected sob from Ben. Slowly the entourage followed Andrew down to the sealed crematorium doors.

There were more people in attendance than she had realised and many she did not know. Despite the job, Josie had always had a busy life. In the commiseration queue, she noticed Diana Fielding and Susan Pelucci file past and then huddle together further away. Rachel held back with Ben until the remaining few had filed past and Andrew's parents stood alone. She took Ben's arm and sensed his tension. Reluctantly he stepped forward to join the older couple.

"He's devastated." His mother worked her fingers together. "She was his life – well, you know that Rachel."

"We'll be there for him." Ben offered. "Perhaps he can stay for a few days?" he suggested to Rachel. His mother looked hopefully at her. Andrew's wildness that morning had alarmed her. She did not know how to comfort him. Her life was dissolving before her. Soon her husband would go too. She wanted to go home. She wanted to sit in her rug-covered corner seat, stare out over the estuary and watch the birds.

"Yes. That is a good idea." But Rachel's thoughts were on the dark-haired woman whose mannish face she did not recognise and who engaged Diana's full attention while Susan nodded. The wind caught their black scarves as if to wrench them up into the clouds.

"Would you excuse me a moment?"

Diana noticed her approach and the three women immediately separated and began moving up the hill. Anyone else would have missed the short murmured exchange. It took her a few moments to understand it and by that time Ben and Andrew had reappeared in front of her.

"Rachel. I'm escorting my parents back to the Locomoter. Thanks for inviting me to stay."

Andrew looked hollow as if his insides had been sucked from him and his voice slipped small and reedy from dried lips.

"It's my pleasure, Andrew. See you later then. Ben, there's something I forgot to mention to Diana."

If I'm quick, I might catch them before they board.

Although she still felt delicate she sprinted and quickly came abreast with Diana and Susan.

"What does 'sail on' mean?" She panted.

The women continued walking.

"It's just an expression," Diana replied impassively.

"Don't you mean 'invocation'?"

"Interesting choice of word," Susan joined in lightly.

Rachel reigned in her voice.

"I know that 'Pleione' means 'to sail', that the Pleiades were her daughters and ultimately Josie wanted me to know that in this sisterhood, she was Merope. Does that make you Maia, the eldest, the boss?"

They stood. Black expressionless pillars reminding her of old immoveable stones, of Maters. Suddenly she wanted to batter them with her open palms.

Do they not understand how much damage I could inflict?
"Is this why she died? On some blind mission for you? Something you're too old to do for yourselves?"

She felt herself spiralling, tears finally breaking her banks and falling from her thrusting chin.

Diana snapped. "Do you really think I would involve myself or Josie in some erroneous cause if I didn't believe it was essential? Yes, Josie was fearless and I do feel responsible, terribly responsible, but we have to press on, expose the lies. Now, will you help or hinder?"

Rachel swayed.

So, it would always have come to this.

She remembered the trip to a gorge with its spectacular waterfalls. The only bridge was a hollowed-out tree-trunk with thin, fraying rope linking an occasional metal pole on one side. Some twenty feet below, the current flowed hard and the eddies swirled. Josie ran across, as if on solid ground.

"Easy. Come on!" she yelled across the divide. The great gap between her courage and Rachel's own caution.

Her vision blurred, her legs leaden.

"Just keep looking at me. Don't stop!"

She followed the voice and the outstretched hand. There was nothing but the reaching hand.

All right Josie. All right!

"You better have had just cause. You better have been right Diana. Because if you're not, this loose family connection we have won't protect you."

Is that how easy it is? Dip my head, slip under the fence and into collusion.

Andrew finally gave up moving the food around his plate, aware of his friend's scrutiny.

"I'm sorry Rachel, it's good... I just..."

"Of course. Don't worry. Leave it." Ben poured another drink into Andrew's tumbler.

"Sure you don't want one, Rachel?"

She shook her head.

Andrew slid his palms across the table like a newborn foal splaying his hooves.

"Thank you both for being here."

They each took a hand. She loved the ease with which Ben crossed the male barriers.

"You see... I just can't... can't... accept that there is no more... both... just... me. Fudging a life... single. Despite everything, and I do know most of it you know, she... we... understood each other so well. I'd forgotten how... incomplete... how tatty... I felt... before her... I used to have," he laughed bitterly, "awful body odour. She told me as soon as we met. Who's going to notice now? I mean, I knew I wasn't enough for her. Her joB came first."

He pronounced the 'B' hard and loud like a bullet, an enemy. His turbulence was rising up, like a whirlwind, waiting to consume them all and she realised how inadequate she was to the task of comfort.

"And all that loyalty... I didn't get much of it but she was so loyal... all her causes, conspiracies and secrets... like pets... they took her over. In the end, I was just getting the scraps..."

She knew he had to say these things but it was unbearable and then... rescue... a power-cut.

She leaped up.

"I'll go."

As she made her way to the door, his sobs broke into the darkness and hung suspended and unattached. Ashamed and relieved she pulled the handle.

There are probably no spare fuel cells unless Ben's seen to it. I'll have to re-charge.

The temperature had dropped considerably and she took the steps in threes, noting absently that some flats still seemed to have power. She coded and slipped into the basement, feeling her way round to the fuel boards – the light from her transor was slight, but enough to see the cell was empty.

"I don't understand why he let it get so low," she tutted.

"He didn't. I drained it."

Low, a subterranean rumble that whipped the strength

from her knees so that she fell back against the units.

"Maia has sent me. Are you okay?"

"Was it necessary to be so surreptitious?" She hissed, recovering her balance and tensing every muscle.

There was no response. Out of the shadows she was handed a small wallet.

"Inside is a cardette. I need a full set of fingerprints and voice and saliva samples."

"Oh really?" she snorted. "And who are you exactly?"

"Celaeno."

"That's as much as I'm going to get, is it?"

"That's right. Can we continue?"

Having complied, Rachel returned the sample and watched as Celaeno cross-referred her details.

"You will appreciate the need to be certain. This second cardette is saliva responsive. Maia has recorded a visimessage. You might like to make yourself comfortable. I will re-charge the fuel cell while you listen."

She moistened the card, no wider than two thumbs, no thicker than a fingernail and inserted it into her transor. Within seconds Maia's face appeared and she began speaking.

"Much of what I say you will have to accept without proof. It will be difficult so allow yourself to intuit gradually. In history, there are many examples of dictators who have succeeded in galvanising public opinion, destabilising the society and imposing a new, albeit temporary order. Success depends on precise timing, opportune manipulation of circumstance and thorough knowledge of the temperament and fears of the culture. One needs charm, conviction and utter ruthlessness. I have only known one person capable. We went to college together and shared a first work posting. Not that it lasted long, She was a luminary even then and her career trajectory was spectacular but… easy. From a distance I watched her, showered with awards, chairs and postings, growing bored. And boredom breeds corruption. I know you have recently re-read the chronology leading up to Division. You will have seen how incisive the attacks were in this country. Many people knew the desirable targets but few actually knew how to penetrate them so effectively.

It was only the beginning – a means to hatch a sulphurous egg, before the gases settled. ASO – her 'see-through' society. It is extraordinary that her theomania has lasted this long, but the fault-lines are everywhere and we have to help them surface. Our information suggests that despite appearances of enlargement and openness, there is a new phase of social manipulation being planned. We have eliminated many sites and we believe we know where to go. It has taken years of strictly coordinated research and activity to reach this point. Thus, there will be no independent acts of initiative. My darling Josie grew impatient – you will not. You will maintain total secrecy, even from Ben. Celaeno has instructions for your first duty. I welcome you warmly as 'Merope'."

The transmission ended.

Realising that Celaeno would be watching her carefully, she kept her face expressionless.

"So, what now?"

"You tell me, do we proceed?"

Is this how Josie was first persuaded? Could she have ever doubted her own aunt? Sexual duplicity was one thing but I still can't believe she was capable of this. To have become someone so completely different without being noticed. I'm not sure I can but maybe I have to, to keep them close. They're all mad of course. Is it infectious? Will I suddenly lose the power to reason? Unable to distinguish between one set of truths and another? And how do I shadow box my way through a life with Ben or Bera for that matter? I know too much now. I made my choice when I chased them up the hill.

Slowly, so slowly, she returned a nod.

"Tomorrow night, take the sealed locomoter across Old London to Station 53 at the bottom of the M1 road. The station is sealed so you will need to leave via the air exchange shafts. I have provided a schematic of their location – it will be cramped but not too uncomfortable. Once out, use a hover to travel down the A41 road to the Marylebone district. I have marked on the map the area you need to monitor and specifically the building onto which this surveillance disk must be attached. Stay for three hours. This is a Hover with its own fuel cell pack. Have you used one before?"

"A while ago. What are you expecting me to see?"

"Maybe nothing."

"To whom do I report?"

"I will be in touch."

"And all this without protection?"

"That's your leap of faith, isn't it?"

"Why can't you do it? Why do you need me?"

"In certain circles my face would upset people so I keep out of the light. Like a bat or a mole. A Fidelis is expected to be mobile. That's why we like to have one of you on board."

Celaeno pulled her hood tighter, made her way to the door and left.

Moments later the light returned and Rachel found herself staring down at the bag she had been left. Briefly she checked the contents, familiarising herself with the hover's components and then hid the pack at the back of a cupboard.

Her transor blinked.

"Rachel, is everything all right? You've been ages."

"The cell was completely drained… I couldn't find a spare. I'm coming up now."

"Andrew's dozing so be quiet. I think I've heard enough for one night."

Upstairs, she padded past Andrew, curled and sleeping, and into her darkened bedroom. Ben's arms encircled her and pulled her to the floor.

"You're too good at stealth," he murmured, as they rolled and tumbled.

"All the grief. Dying… makes me want to cling on… control… everything."

She was taken aback by his force, his need. Her limbs responded, but in another carriage, she was calculating.

Later, lying in his arms, she said, "I've got another set of interviews to do for this Marchant investigation. Unfortunately, it's got to be tomorrow night."

The words slipped out, nocturnal insects, creeping across the pillows towards him.

"Why don't they just let it drop? Poor old sod," he whispered, already husky with sleep.

Is this how you do it then, Josie? With mislaid pockets of time, unaccounted for, lied about.

CHAPTER EIGHT

Station 53

"Are you still going to Abovo tomorrow?" he asked over breakfast.

"Mhm." She nodded realising that she had forgotten.

"It's just that since I'm not needed at work I'd like to come. Remembering what you said. It's ages since I've held her."

"Yes, she'll love it."

That's so strange. I should feel more pleased that he's listened. But Bera's become my territory. I'm the link and he's not... relevant... Shame on me for even thinking that! So childish.

To still her nerves she spent the day organising paperwork, tidying and completing reports.

At lunchtime she bought extra kale broth from the trolleys, which she cooled and carefully spilled over her uniform so that her later change of outfit would seem plausible.

"It's raining. Take a waterproof," he said distractedly pouring over his schedules.

"I've got to get to zone F and back so I'll be late. Don't wait up."

It's not a direct lie. More of an omission. Here I go, retreating into the arms of a stranger, an illicit tryst. It makes everything else seem mundane.

Crossing the burgh square, the lights were already flickering. There had been so many power cuts recently – drains on the grid were taking their toll.

People could not charge their cells quickly enough, so they stayed at home not noticing the lengthening curfews. What was there to do anyway outside in this all-permeating drizzle?

The locomoter trip due north-west was uneventful. Two passengers disembarked. She recognised the station where she had come as a child to a tennis tournament. Then, it was always heaving with enthusiasts, queuing and camping out on the streets filled with traders. Now it was deserted and she alone boarded the northbound locomoter.

The departures were less frequent so she had time to secrete herself, hood up, into the carriage corner, away from the cameras that she knew were mounted in the centre aisle.

She occupied the time trying to identify any small differences in the interior. The seals around the window frames and doors were thicker. Would they really be enough? For the first time she wavered. She had brought breathing membranes and filters but some of her skin would inevitably be exposed.

Why am I risking myself? Because a clever woman told me to?

The journey started.

A few innocent miles passed before the floor began to vibrate and the carriage itself hissed as metal plating slowly grew like a second skin, over the entire locomoter.

Hermetically sealed.

She felt the temperature rise and the air close in. As they sped she sat in the half-light and imagined the river brooding under its bridges; trawled through fleeting memories of Old London waiting to be kissed awake.

What am I doing? Stop! I want to get off.

What if they were wrong? What if it was still rank out there? What if tiny deadly spores still ricocheted around the atmosphere waiting for some new organic host to pollute?

She breathed slowly to combat her rising nausea and centred on the middle spot. It always had a face. Bera.

As the extra skin began peeling back and the locomoter shuddered to a halt, she prepared to alight.

Face dipped, she slid out of the carriage, noting the layout for her return. As an intersecting terminal for F, G and A provinces, it was busy. You rarely saw such a mixture of grades, uniforms and occupations under one dome.

Working her way through a series of interconnecting doorways and short flights of stairs, she found her way to the airshaft entrance. Luckily she had anticipated that the bolts would be substantial and had brought a laser wrench. They did not loosen easily and on the final turn her wrists were already aching. She had to leave the porthole slightly ajar, desperately hoping it would not be discovered. Before climbing up the shaft, she swung the pack onto her back, set her contamination sensor and fixed a breathing mask to her face. Then, she scrambled upwards. Halfway, she stopped and looked down at the thin sliver of light receding underneath. In the darkness, her body trembled, overwhelmed by the sense of confinement, her breathing hoarse and rasping, another creature.

Nobody made me do this

Instinctively she climbed, and on reaching the rim, her feet found the two straddle points, allowing her a stronghold to start on the upper bolts. They released much more easily and suddenly she emerged, not into another tunnel but into the open, with Station 53 behind her.

Ahead, the empty grey roads loomed into the distance. To her right she noticed a viaduct that would provide cover to set up the hover and orientate herself but her first task was to monitor the air. She held the thin tube up into the night and waited. Long enough. Her arm seemed suspended, unwilling to bring the truth back.

Come on... come on! She clicked through the various categories deliberately mouthing the results so she would consciously understand. Clear. Clear. Clear. She looked about her foolishly seeking a witness.

I want to go home. But I can't go back to when I didn't know. There's a scent to follow.

Under the curve of the viaduct she laid the pieces of the hover side by side. It was years since she had assembled one from scratch but the hours of night-time manoeuvres came back to her and the few parts slid together easily – apart from the fuel cell which would not attach. After repeated attempts, panic set in as without it nothing would function. Then she realised and laughed out loud at her own stupidity – it was upside down. She called up the miniaturised map on her transor and began to transfer to the pulsing navigator screen. She could see now which of the many roads would take her down to Marylebone.

She set the hover level to the minimum one foot and gingerly stepped onto the platform, forcing herself to breathe steadily through the mask membrane. *Trust.*

The controls were basic but efficient and as she pushed the lever forward, she thought how Bera would love this.

The air was crisp with no sign of the earlier dampness and the navigator gave the only light. She felt exposed in the middle so kept to the kerbs passing row upon row of old-style crumbling houses whose glassless windows gaped like toothless mouths, As her confidence grew, she lifted higher and sped faster past the ancient shop fronts, their signs faded and indecipherable.

She could not marry her memories of city bustle, dirt and blowing refuse with this terrible silence, this barren dereliction. Something rustled down an alleyway making her grip the handles tightly and push the hover on.

As the final crossroads came into view, the buildings grew in height and ambition. She had forgotten the architectural vanity, the lack of coherence. How did they ever justify filling the space so? She recognised the busy arterial into Old London and brought the hover to rest on the far side, by an anonymous-looking block.

The front entrance was set back, shrouded by a solid concrete portico. Cautiously, she walked up the five steps. This was apparently where she would keep her vigil. It was only after she had tucked herself into the corner that she understood the intended focus for her attention. There, some five hundred yards ahead of her, she had a perfect and complete view of Marylebone Station. It still retained some of its vintage grandeur, although its iron gates were replaced with large heavy metal doors, closed and airtight as they all had been. It seemed pointless but there were worse things to look at.

Everything changes here. I don't want to take a reading. Don't let there be any contamination. Her hands shook slightly as the sensor showed CLEAR.

The sensor could be faulty but there's nothing to be done about that... not here... not now. Just take out the surveillance disks and focus.

For their size, they had astonishing range and sensors with self-legislating, retractable lenses. They would also record stills of any changes to the normal static environment and each would individually send their data to a mother monitor. She fixed them high into the stone pillar, made some minor adjustments and discreetly peered up and down the road. There had been a waxwork museum down here whose legendary, daily queues snaked and merged into the heavy traffic.

Localised blasts had bleached any natural colour from the stone buildings, leaving them with an unfinished appearance. Equally the posts and signs were buckled, peeling or blank.

After an hour she began to feel some minor cramps in her calves and back, so standing up, she concentrated on a series of pilates flexes to enliven the muscle. Then she checked her fuel cell levels. Although she had taken a slow-release fluid capsule just before she left, her throat was dry and her bladder full. Her urethracat pricked uncomfortably. Despite years of wearing, she would never get used to relieving herself so but when the pressure finally became unbearable, she gave in and relaxed.

Unfinished.

Frozen.

Disbelief paralysing every function.

From nowhere a food trolley crawled up the narrow lane to the station. Several people ambled in its wake, casually throwing the occasional inaudible comment.

Under the arches the two driver clones waited patiently, staring ahead from the cabin of the trolley.

The group settled to one side, stamping their feet to ward

off the chill. Someone must have said something funny as they all burst out laughing, one punching the other's shoulders.

And then they all suddenly moved forward and away to the left hand side of the station's entrance where they disappeared from view.

I can't believe how normal this seems. Here, in the middle of this wasteland, this no-zone.

Like workers changing shifts...

Unprotected.

She blinked as a camera shutter might, having taken the vital shot.

The image imprinted unforgettably onto her.

Her transparency.

There must always be trust.

Nothing else happened in the next two hours. She wrote an account in longhand and stored it inside her boot lining, thinking all the time of Josie, of her beloveds, and as she mounted the hover, flying fast and fearful under the clear glinting night sky, she felt her inherent scepticism liquefying, becoming lava and beginning a slow reformation into igneous angry rock.

So who are you? You, who are stealing my life from me, detonating all those bridges. I will have you!

Her re-entry to 53 was mercifully straightforward although the connections were slow and by the time she reached home she was shivering and dizzy with exhaustion. She had never felt this spent. From the guest suite, Andrew's snores reminded her to keep quiet.

In the dark, she sank onto the bathroom floor and emptied her urethract into the toilet. She managed to wrap it back into its pouch, wash and crawl on all fours into the cold side of the bed where she lay clenched, sleeplessly waiting for dawn. It was to his credit that Ben remained quiet beside her, staring, wide-eyed and wondering.

Over breakfast, they bumped around each other, uncoordinated and numb with tiredness.

"Did you eat late last night then?" he asked, noticing her empty plate.

"No. I... just not hungry."

"I won't be able to go to Abovo after all. Beatrice wants her 'keynote speech' broadcast throughout the day. I hope you didn't say anything to her. Perhaps you should give it a miss too. You look worn out."

"No... Bera... you know."

"I've barely seen you recently."

She slumped over the table, running her hands through her hair.

"I know. I'm sorry. Josie's... going puts a bit more pressure on. Do you think I should tell Bera yet?"

"Does she have to know? It will only upset her."

"Oh I think so. I think it would be wrong not to... she did see her occasionally."

"Well I do believe in being honest with children but perhaps wait 'til she asks."

He curled his palm around her cheek.

"I don't think anyone of us is going to get over losing her. You've still got the most beautiful profile I know."

His tenderness reached in and lifted her lips into a half smile.

Now's my chance. Turn my back on it all. Grab what's left to us. Force him to come

"I think we should both request some absence soon," she said gently.

He sighed. "Oh Rachel. I'd love to but it's not a good time to..."

"Okay." She stiffened abruptly and turned away.

They did not speak until he left.

"So, I'll see you in a couple of days then. Andrew's just surfacing. Kiss Bera for me... Oh, by the way, Senior Fidelis Butcher rang on the land line for you last night. Your transor wasn't receiving apparently. I just said you were out."

The door closed.

The comment had been so light... 'just said you were out'...

but she heard there were steps down the words. The question. Should her superior not have known she was working?

She showered, watching the rivulets of water corrupt her reflection in the mirrored tiles. Her fingers pulled and kneaded her cheeks.
Why couldn't they have just let it lie?
It's too big.
I'm not Josie.
Let them find someone else.
It was bathroom bluster.
She heard her transor bleeping and stumbling out on wet feet, she ran to the bedroom.
"Fidelis Develin. Senior Fidelis Butcher. Will you be in this morning before your trip to Abovo?"
"Yes. I intend to be."
"Will the Marchant report be complete?"
"Yes."
"Good. Please leave it with the Administrator."
"Indeed."
Must the woman always be so dispassionate?

Once at the office she filed her report quickly and walked down to the foyer to collect some soup from the trolley. The clone had just dropped a carton and its contents had splattered the uniform of a clerk from their office.
"Stupid Half-head!" She hurled over her shoulder.
Rachel smiled sympathetically into the clone's dejected face. His huge eyes pooling uncontrollably.
"I'll have soup too. Smells good!"
The clone brightened.
"It is good."
She sat and watched the overhead screen as Beatrice began her address.
"Fellow Asoans. It is my pleasure to greet you this day with more details of my mobility initiative."
Distracted by the Magnamater's hair which continued a

shock-headed passage as if in flight from its origins, Rachel could still hear a certain excitability under the calm vocal icing.

"This new structure applies to all areas but the 'no-zones' where contamination levels remain high. I dream of a day when ASO emerges a healed whole, cleansed and free from its past."

She sipped her soup, tasting an underlying metal and remembering Jennifer Lacey's honey cake.

"I am also pleased to announce that 'comment boxes' have been erected in the foyers of all Fidelis buildings and I invite you to contribute with your own ideas and experiences."

As if anyone would be tempted.

Beatrice appeared to be finishing as the screen folded in on itself and Rachel watched the Fidelis, released from the paralysis of duty, slip back into action.

Yet she stayed.

A vivid memory of the family kitchen. Her mother flushed, rolling and cutting pastry and her father painstakingly filling each case with mincemeat. Her mother patting home the covers, fluting the edges and brushing them with egg. Her father dredging icing sugar like a vigorous snowstorm whose sweet back draft caught in her own throat as she inhaled. The irresistible soft crumbling and scorching heat within. An unexceptional precious moment and her heart stabbed as she searched fruitlessly for something comparable in Bera's life.

"It goes too quickly," she had spoken unintentionally.

"Yes," agreed the clone gently, extracting the crushed carton from her clasped hands. "It does."

CHAPTER NINE

Abovo

It was as the locomoter crossed the hydrodam and she gazed down at the large impossible surge of water beneath the arching bridge that she felt a new vertigo and found she was weeping.

Instinctively she contacted Ben. Behind him, colleagues flitted in and out of view. The scheduler's voice counted down to the next broadcast. It was the worst time. He frowned.

"Yes!"

"Ben, I can't remember what Mum looked like. Her face. How could I have forgotten? I have the photo but it was taken when they were young – not as they were when I last saw them. And I know they both loved music but their voices have gone from my head. What was Dad's favourite colour? I should know. It's my duty to commit them to memory – or else they truly die because I've failed to treasure them enough... and what about Bera? Locked away..."

He shrugged helplessly.

"I think I understand what you're saying but I don't know where it's coming from. I mean obviously losing Josie... you're desperately over-tired. Why not stop for a few days? Give you a bit of space to let out all this raw... distress. Sort out your thoughts, your priorities. You know it occurred to me we could keep a diary for her – record our days... send it to her regularly." He beamed triumphantly. A solution in a moment of inspiration.

"A scrapbook," she returned bitterly. "Rags and bones of a life – it probably wouldn't be allowed."

"Well not necessarily. Look you're too far away for me to help you. But this life is what it is – no one's fault. We do our best, that's all. Bera will understand that. Make the best of your time with her – for both of us. At least we've got her. Poor Andrew has no one now Josie's gone. I've got to go."

Frustrated, he watched her shaking her head and rang off.

She could see the dark shadows flitting through the conning towers before she reached the gate. There, it seemed to be ages before anyone responded to her. Irritably, she walked up the drive noting the new fencing cordoning off the fields.

Even more like a prison.

The great hall door was locked.

"This is Fidelis Develin. I am here to visit my daughter Bera," she enunciated in slow cold tones. Sophia, one of the older Maters answered.

"Sorry to have kept you Fidelis Develin. There are high security procedures at the moment. If you would care to enter I will escort you up to the library where Bera will be brought." She followed the Mater, her heels clicking loudly on the stone floor.

"Regretfully Fidelis, there are no excursion permits being issued."

"What a great shame."

She was angry. All this way to stay inside, surrounded by files and screens.

"I know Bera does benefit from a change of scene. Are you absolutely sure, given my position…"

"We can make no exceptions." Sophie interrupted.

They passed by two Maters who lapsed into silence.

"Please be seated Fidelis. I have to ask if you have brought anything with you today?"

"No and I am aware of your clearance requirements."

The Mater nodded stiffly, "Just so," and then left.

She waited and then sprung to her feet. In the silence the

whirr of a remote camera was audible. This was new level of control. Can it really have been prompted by the Marchant affair alone? Casually, she walked round the edges of the room assessing the camera's range. It was a new Mater who ushered Bera in with one arm around her shoulder. Rachel felt an unfamiliar jealousy.

"Mummy!" Bera smiled and took Rachel's outstretched hands. Slowly she allowed herself to be pulled into her mother's chest while her arms dropped lightly to her side. Rachel kissed the top of her head.

Yes. This small creature. This is what defines me. Yet the last time I was here she broke free of Mater, leaped onto me and almost floored us both.

Mater stood impassively. Noticing, Rachel tilted her head.

"I… I will return in two and a half hours. I… have you been made aware that this is a restricted visit?" She wrung her hands miserably.

"Indeed." Rachel's reply was measured. She did not want any obvious displeasure to be reflected onto Bera.

As if she had been running through an autumn wind, Bera had a new skittishness, circling the tables and switching on the visometer screens.

"We're doing a course on Marine Biology. It's amazing what lives in the sea." She cast a sidelong glance. "I know Daddy's not coming. I got a message through."

"Did you?" Rachel was surprised.

"Oh yes, he's always messaging, Just to 'keep the channels open between us', in case you forget to pass anything important when you come."

"I don't believe I ever have before," Rachel replied slowly. *Where had this… coldness come from?*

"Still, this time I really did think he might make it. I know all these new opportunities are opening up. Has he changed much?"

"I… no. It's been a difficult time since I last saw you."

"When I graduate I want to work in Hydro-engineering. I don't like people much."

A second mutinous glance towards the monitor. So she was aware of it.

"Great idea. You can teach your Daddy how to swim while you're at it!" she replied, stepping towards the window as she spoke and knowing Bera would follow. They both looked down into the fields.

"Favourite food?" Lightly, she began an old game.

Bera's response was automatic and quiet. "Cheese." And then it sunk lower. Rachel was taken aback.

She's learning fast.

"Faith Orph has disappeared. A few days ago. We woke up and she had gone. Didn't even say goodbye."

"Has any explanation been offered?"

"Abamater said that Faith had been very troubled and that we all had to sincerely hope that she could be found and brought back to this or another Ark so that she could be looked after and comforted. Mater Ruth said that we all shared a responsibility to care about each other. They've increased 'Sharing time' but I don't want to talk about stuff and I don't think that Faith was sad... I think she was... bored."

Bera nodded as if to emphasise her point.

I have to concentrate. There's little enough time to percolate my own feelings adequately as a parent – so little time to get the right messages across and leave her with the sense of something solid when all I want to do is stroke her. Examine her minutely and uncover all the subtle changes that this life had pilfered from her. The lengthening jaw, the widening shoulders, the growing breast buds and the gaps in her teeth. Reign it all in. Don't mention Josie... Maybe he was right.

She collected herself and replied.

"It's impossible to know what someone else really thinks. But it is terribly sad if she was so uncertain or unhappy and didn't feel she had anyone to talk to. Running away is never the answer."

"Mater said she had a wonderful future ahead of her. Maybe she just didn't like the look of it." The child speculated adroitly. "Anyway, we're not supposed to discuss it. I don't suppose you count. I mean you're separate aren't you? Your favourite food?"

"Chocolate."

Please let me count. Did Mum go through this with me? Did she feel the same need to weep like a baby, need my comfort, to be understood? Or would I have run away? Tried to follow Dad down the road. Because a mother's tears are too hot and they scald. Reign it in Rachel

"Why did you want to be Fidelis?"

"I… believe in Justice. I always did actually. Even when I was your age. Hated getting the blame for something Georgia had done or said. I never liked amoral behaviour. Do you know what I mean by that?"

Bera wrinkled her nose.

"Yes, I think so. Is killing people amoral?"

Where is this going?

"It is completely undesirable and to be avoided at all costs but very occasionally if the level of danger or wrong-doing is so severe, for instance if someone is threatening the safety of innocent lives, then a casualty may be unavoidable."

"Who decides? People like you?"

"These days… people like me. Why do you ask?"

She flushed and remained silent.

"Bera?"

"There's talk. That you killed the old man. Pajo doesn't say anything. Was the old man really that dangerous?"

"Now listen darling. The old man was in the wrong. He should not have been here. But he died of something called a heart attack. He had been very sick. Believe me, my chat with him had nothing to do with his death. I promise you. It was in his hands."

She looks relieved. I wonder if she's being bullied.

"I wish you'd do something different. I mean I know you love your job and everyone thinks you're really strong and brave. But I wish you could do something different. But…" she looked at her mother doubtfully, "there's not really time now is there?"

"I'll think carefully about it. Have you read any of those poems?"

The air easier between them they quoted the poems, which to Rachel's delight, Bera had memorised with gusto. At the end of the fourth Bera turned quickly

"I'm glad you came, that I've got you to visit."

"And I you." It was all she could allow herself. Soon the sounding buzzer stilled their laughter and heralded in Mater Ruth with the new novice.

"May I speak with you, Fidelis?"

Bera craned her neck as she was being ushered away.

"'Bye Mum. I'll see you soon. Somebody's birthday coming up," she said playfully. But Rachel could see the effort. Her child was not happy and there was nothing she could do.

Mater continued. "I only wanted to assure you that Bera is in the best possible hands and is doing so well."

"Is she? I thought that she seemed preoccupied... well more... remote today. She mentioned my job and for the first time expressed ambivalence towards it. Is she being bullied?"

Mater blanched.

"If you don't mind my commenting, I think that she misses her father. Whilst his regular messaging is, of course, permitted, it reinforces his absence. Not that she has said this. I just sense it."

"In all honesty, I had no idea it was so frequent. I will talk to Ben."

"Don't misunderstand me, Fidelis Develin. I'm not saying he should stop but perhaps the odd visit to reinforce his commitment would be more helpful."

"Yes. But in your opinion is she happy?"

"She is growing up. We see this shift a lot. All the teenage changes come earlier these days and with those come more reflection, less openness. They don't want what they have and yearn for what they don't have. It is not you at fault."

"No. I am so sorry to hear about Faith Orph."

"Yes. We feel her absence keenly. It is a lesson to constantly keep our channels open and remain pragmatic. It will not happen again."

It was the only time that Rachel had seen any Mater

expressing fallibility. As she descended into the entrance hall, Maters murmured softly in clusters.

They're like birds, piteously clucking and brooding over a pillaged nest.

Once aboard the locomoter, it took little for her to drift into sleep.

Bera was lashing the last cords around the raft. It was beautifully constructed. Behind her the ocean pounded onto the shore.

"But what if your Daddy falls off?" she heard herself screaming.

"He's got a suit and I'll just strap him on with the safety harness."

Ben flapped into view wearing an old-fashioned diver's suit, his elongated black flippers slapping the wet sand. He smiled obligingly at Rachel.

"I'll be fine. Could even be fun."

She laughed herself into awakening. Ben had always been such a clown. Not so recently. Ruefully she rubbed at a new stain on her jacket. "I'm such a mess," and reached into her pocket for a cloth.

Nestled in its folds… the unexpected.

A cardette that had not been there that morning. The carriage had been empty when she had boarded and remained so. How then?

She moistened it and then slid it into her transor and waited.

… *Merope. Your installation has been successful and we are witnessing growing activity. We have narrowed down similar no-zone sites in Old Birmingham where assistance will be needed, starting next week. Unusual mobility is increasing from Magnamater's office in province A up to province G. Please wait for Elektra to contact you with dates and instructions…*

She felt more like a fly on treacle unable to extricate itself from the dark stickiness. How had this got here?

Such sleight of hand required great skill, to go undetected.

Then it came to her. The unusual contact; the outreach to her elbows; the warm gesture of trust; eyes locked to engage her; A short subtle journey to her pocket; a little pressure to push the disc home.

Briefly the floor rose to meet her and yawned away.

Mater Ruth.

Slate-grey clouds had smothered the last of the blue as she disembarked and strode down the causeway. Halfway, she knew she had to stop and crouch, overcome by a rising dizziness. She did not remember a time when she felt so weak. He had been right. It was time to stop. She slipped quietly into the flat but the raised voices stayed her by the door.

"Didn't you realise I knew? All the little notes and snatched meetings. You bastard. I just got to mop her brow afterwards."

"You're completely wrong, Andrew. You must believe me."

"Believe you... how can I. Would Rachel believe you?"

"Don't bring Rachel into this!"

"Why not? Hasn't she got a right to know that it's all a sham?"

"You don't know what you are saying. You're upset!"

"Don't patronise me, Ben. I know what I saw."

"It was work, Andrew."

"Some. Kind. Of. Work. Friend."

What were they saying? When was the ground going to stop moving like this? I should not hear any more. Softly, she let herself out and fled to the basement. She set the lights low and sitting cross-legged, slowed her breathing into a meditative state to summon the Fidelis creed.

There is a large cloth and into the middle I will place my fears. No people or faces just ideas. Then gather up the corners and carry it to the window where I will empty the contents outside and the breeze will disperse them.

Couldn't this be explained by Andrew's overwhelming sense of loss, looking for someone to blame? Josie was always complaining about his irrational side. But still, why would Ben and Josie have any sort of 'work' relationship that I knew nothing about? This is hopeless. Everything I touch is loose and unstable. Why do you have to keep doing this Ben? Why can't you just settle for what we have? What had Georgie said? 'Perhaps if you looked sideways you would see how busy Ben was... and how is dear Josie?' It had been such a sly aside. Typical. As usual I chose to ignore it. But I have to know.

"Georgia, it's Rachel. Look I know it's a little late but could I come and see you now?"

It was unique for her to be turning to her sister for clarification. That had always been Josie's role.

"How are you?" she asked her sister an hour later.

"Oh, I'm all right. My blood pressure's too high so I have to take one of these twice a day to lower it." As Georgia spoke she placed a capsule on her tongue and swallowed.

Rachel grimaced, "Does it act quickly?"

"About half an hour. I'm more worried about Cluge. Wish I could give him some of my steam!"

"Oh?"

"Well, you know clones have much lower blood pressure anyway? His has started to drop dramatically over the last week. Kate says we have to prepare ourselves. It's the most obvious sign of shut down."

"Oh I am so sorry."

"Yes... Luke's spending some time with him and tomorrow will bring him here just so he can see Gelu for the last time. Anyway..." she glanced up. "What's going on? You look tired."

"I am. Feel like I am traversing the country at the moment and the funeral was upsetting, you know. I need to ask you something, Georgia."

"Sure."

"Last time you... implied that there was something going on between Ben and Josie. Am I mistaken?"

Georgia reddened. "Yes, that was wrong of me. Luke was very angry."

"Nevertheless," Rachel persisted, "you must be honest. Why did you say it?"

"Oh Rachel. It's not important. Ben's a good man and Josie's gone. Let it go."

"I cannot," Rachel gasped. "When do I ever ask you for anything? I need to know."

"I don't want the responsibility for this."

"You do not have it. I am giving you no choice."

For a few moments she remained silent.

"All right. All right. Over the years we've all got used to Josie… well… being in charge of you all. Yes it did annoy me. Here was my strong elder sister constantly subservient to her. But I started to notice more recently that whenever we all got together, there was more of a… how can I put it? More of a connection between them. Lingering glances. Touching. Then I… we saw them three times. Once down at the reycler. It was brief but intimate. He… sort of stroked her cheek. Their faces were really close. They didn't see me. Then at the energy station, close to curfew. Then when I was in the late stages in here, Luke had to go up to Transmissions to advise on a food science programme and saw Josie was with Ben, at his desk laughing, obviously close. Instinctively he didn't want to stay. And you know how level Luke is." She ran her hands through her thinning fringe and peered up. "But as Luke says there could be a perfectly reasonable explanation. It's important not to jump to conclusions. I mean… I know I have… but that's because I'm so… stupid sometimes. Oh I'm sorry, Rachel. You deserve better from me." She looked miserably at her sister who had sat staring at her interlocked hands.

"What will you do?"

"Nothing for now. Some thinking."

"Look there's the drinks trolley. Can I get you anything?"

"No, I am fine… actually… yes… something hot."

It should hurt more to hear this. You wrecking ball Josie. How could I have been so obtuse? I think I must have a piece missing. Maybe I've become a Fidelis programme rather than a series of synapses leaping to make their emotional connections.

Even in the middle of all this I've just made a decision.

She had just enough time to pocket the capsules before Kate appeared on her evening rounds.

"A pleasant surprise, Rachel."

"Georgia has been telling me about Cluge. It seems so quick."

"It's always harder to tell with clones. Generally they are slower, more economic in movement, rarely make eye contact or engage in conversation. Unlike so many who seem almost oblivious to their environment at least Cluge has a personality and tries hard to reach out. Sadly it's only when they start collapsing that we know anything's amiss."

"How do you manage the... last ?"

"We give them a little kick start with adrenaline but it's a short term solution obviously. There comes a point when they just stop responding."

Kate put her arm round Georgia as she handed Rachel her drink. "Have you taken your medication tonight?"

"Yes, thanks Kate." Her eyes flickered over to the cabinet. "Oh! Did I? I can't remember."

"Yes you did," Rachel confirmed. She drained her cup. The hot liquid scalded the back of her throat.

Shame on me. It's Georgia's health I'm stealing here. And who am I to call Ben a liar?

"I must go. Good to see you, Georgia."

"Oh. Are you Okay? I mean... you can always contact me on the transor if you can't get in."

As Kate slipped out, Rachel kissed her sister tenderly on her forehead and whispered.

"Thank you. Please don't worry."

She spent the next two hours in the basement monitoring all the footage from Marylebone on her own surveillance disk. She knew everything that the Pleiades knew. In another twenty-four hours she would have collated a pattern of shifts and routines for activities there. This is what she was trained for. She stood outside deeply gulping the night air.

With every exhalation I'm blowing away a bit more restraint. What a naïve little foot-soldier I've been.

The flat was cold and empty. Relieved, she took advantage of their absence to gather the necessary equipment. Epipen for stimulation, Sedpen for sedation. Vicorder and a plastic wrist strap recorder which would not trigger any alarm systems. She remembered a previous undercover assignment when she had used glasses with a minute plastic lens attached.

The problem is they're special issue – I'll have to get into stores tomorrow.

Then there was nothing more to distract her and she found herself in his wardrobe, frisking his uniforms and pockets, checking the soles of his boots and minutely examining the contents of his drawers.

How can a life be this impersonal?

"Stop humiliating yourself," she told her reflection.

And even while she was promising herself sleep she began leafing through the years of scanimages, looking for any signs, any recorded gesture that would add weight. Nothing to feed the bloodlust. Unsatisfied and alone she fell into bed.

CHAPTER TEN

Digging

Every morning I'm grateful for sleep's blank interlude. How it scabs over the day's open wounds. Like a small boat listing indecisively on a thrashing high sea, first light brings calmer waters. I know the role I have to play.
He stands dressed, whole and complete.

"Just arriving or just leaving?" she asked lightly.
"Both. I was called in last night… system went down. You were late back."
"Yes. Problems at work."
I can be vague too.
"No Andrew?"
"Apparently. I haven't seen him. He was talking about going back to the flat today."
"Yes. Perhaps he has been here long enough."
"I advised him to get away. Take a little time off if possible. He may find applying for a transfer easier. So many memories here."
"Is that what you would do then? If anything happened to me?"
He seemed startled. "Well… uh… I don't like to think of it. Probably not with the way things are."
"With all these new… openings you mean."
"Well, yes, it's a… vibrant time."
Yes. Something or someone has reinvigorated him. Can it really have been Josie? Damn you both.

"Well with Beatrice's marvellous new mobility who knows where we will all end up?"

He nodded uncertainly.

"Have a good day, Ben."

She turned and left the room.

Later in the Fidelis building she waited for a busy time when many desks were occupied and there was a steady flow of officers before slipping down to the sensitive stores area. Her position allowed her access but she could not avoid signing for the glasses and the obligatory user guide from Jocelyn, the stores manager. Her blinking transor shocked them both. S.F. Butcher.

"Fidelis Develin. I know you are in the building but you don't appear to be in the office. Can you to report to me as soon as possible."

"Oh she's a misery," grumbled Jocelyn. "You know what butchers did before Division, don't you? Carve up meat. She's wasted here."

Rachel smiled despite herself.

She felt her superior's eyes on her as she slid the case into her holdall before stepping over to the private office.

Senior Fidelis Butcher gave a curt nod to enter.

"Sit. Andrew Kitchener's body has been found on the steps leading up to his flat."

The words thumped her back into the chair. Her throat constricted tightly.

"How?"

Not sweet harmless Andrew. Please not.

"This morning. About eight. Although you were not first on the scene, I would like you to take up the enquiry. See the body before post-mortem. The flat has remained sealed since his wife's death."

"I will re-examine it."

"I would like a report as soon as possible."

Senior Fidelis Butcher watched the monitors and waited for Rachel's exit from the building before making a call.

"He was found here. But given the extent of his injuries it's likely that he was pushed with a good deal of force from the next level up probably just outside his own apartment." The forensic officer David Poulter explained to Rachel.

"How long had he been dead before he was found?"

"Between seven and eight hours. I will be more exact after the post-mortem."

"I would like to attend."

"Of course. Shall we proceed inside? It should be straightforward enough. The flat has remained sealed since I was last here."

"Do you have a full contents disc?" Rachel asked as they climbed the final flight and walked towards the door. She needed a distraction. How many times had she followed Josie's long stride taking three steps at a time. She had not dared bring herself here since she died.

"It's already set up on scanner. As I'm filming this time, it will pick up any anomalies. Not that I'm expecting any. Frank, can you unseal the door please."

The officer traced around the doorframe with a small pen spraying a fine jet. It dissolved the seal instantly. In the meantime David had begun filming. He ran one hand lightly over the door itself before opening, pulling on saniboots and entering. Rachel and the attendant officer did likewise. Like a tomb, the flat almost sighed as it released its trapped air, its suspended odours to the outside. Cold. Lifeless. Her stomach turned over in revolt.

Keep it together

She followed David, viewing the scanner screen as it read the environment, automatically cross-checking with its already stored data. As they came into the living area the large toothy smile that Josie had painted across the whole width of the wall greeted them. It said everything about her.

He was meticulous. Every corner of every cupboard was silently reinvestigated. No one spoke. In the bedroom she tried not to stare at the pillows. She tried hard not to wonder whose heads had rested there. David seemed to be pausing at the same moment. Bending, he filmed strangely across the top of the bed. Then he began to slide his free hand down the side and back of the bedside drawer. He found the button as she knew he would.

"Film me please, Fidelis Develin," he said grimly. She complied as he felt inside the hidden compartment and clearly found nothing.

The spare bedroom had been emptied apart from some bedding, Andrew's model collection of locomoters and turbines that he used to sculpt into the night, making him the butt of many jokes, and Josie's vast legendary scanimage collection. Anything sensitive had obviously been removed but there were still the familiar packed carousels. People would often give her unclaimed shots, the best of which she kept. It was generally thought that she had a good eye.

"Strange hobby for someone so unsentimental," David observed.

Rachel smiled. "Josie used to say it was... enlarging to have glimpses of so many different untroubled lives. I don't remember ever having made it through to the end."

"Well the collection's still intact, nothing missing." Rachel looked across at him quickly. He sounded relieved.

Suddenly she blurted out, "Would it be possible for me to have the collection, do you think? I mean I know it flouts convention. I am happy to sign for it, make copies for the records, not interfere with it in any way. I would just like to have something that meant so much to her..."

She stopped herself from continuing. She had made the request deliberately whilst he filmed, knowing it would be noted. She had nothing to hide.

"I don't see why not. If you can't be trusted, who can? I'll still have to put in a request with both our supervisors. I am almost finished here. Why don't I do that now for you before the flat has to be re-sanitised."

She waited outside, watching people glance upwards and then quickly avert their gaze. Such was the effect of the uniform.

He came out to join her ten minutes later.

"Senior Fidelis Butcher has no issues in principal with you inheriting the collection but would like it to be independently assessed before releasing it to you. To that end, I have arranged for it to be trollied over to Fidelis shortly."

"Thank you David."

"Now as far as my investigations today are concerned, I have three observations to make. Remembering that I conducted this same examination some days ago which included the sanitisation and resealing procedures, I am at a loss to explain the indentation of a body on the main bed, the faint but definite footprint 16 inches into the flat and the residue of sealant on the second panel of the outside door. I am always scrupulous in my attentions. There was nothing spilled."

"Could there have been some dripping from the top sill?"

"No." He shook his head firmly.

"There is also the fact that the ambient temperature inside is higher than I would have expected for an unoccupied dwelling."

"What are your conclusions?"

"That someone has been in the flat and resealed it... they did quite a good job but not perfect."

"Who would have the knowledge?"

"Well, in theory anyone within the force who has been trained but there are different areas of expertise required here. This was a... professional. I am sure however that nothing has been removed or added that was on the original schedule."

"Was the hidden compartment identified on the original?"

David appeared uncomfortable for the first time.

"Regrettably not."

"It was cleverly hidden. But it obviously contained something worth breaking in for. So if it is unlikely that Andrew himself was responsible then possibly he discovered someone else in the act and they reacted defensively?" she suggested.

And who was that struggle with? It was hard to forget all the animosity last night. So much rage locked in both their voices. Had that small row led to this wreckage?

Later, as she stared down at his bruised lifeless body, she was shocked at how wasted he seemed. She tried to concentrate on David's murmuring evaluation but as he cut she realised that she could not watch this one closely. It was too painful. She retired to the side and stared into the middle distance.

"Perhaps you would like to join me in the ante-room Fidelis?" David invited her afterwards.

"The thin line of bruising at either temple suggest two sharp scissor blows administered by hand. He died from a broken neck that could have been the result of the fall. His spine was shattered and both hips were broken It was an extremely efficient execution. Mind you, we all know how to kill each other these days! The other thing worthy of note is that he had stomach cancer that had already spread to the lungs. He may have had another six months."

"Oh," she bleated weakly.

"I'm sorry. Here are my reports."

An outsider would not notice the subtleties at play in Senior Fidelis Butcher's office. Her desk was arranged on the diagonal so that she had full view of the outer office. Her chair was set at its highest level so that she towered over any interviewee whose low chair was deliberately unpadded and therefore discouraged overstaying. The corner housed an alternative cushioned stool that forced one to sit forward in an even more supplicatory position. This, Rachel noted wryly, was today's choice. How could someone have graduated to such a senior level and still be so insecure. If she ever had the chance Josie used to swap them around. Nothing was ever said.

"So summarise David's conclusions for me," she listened to Rachel's account attentively.

"And your own impressions?"

Rachel reflected. "He is the expert. I could not appreciate the distinctions he was making because I could not see them. I would not have known where to look."

"Yes. Exactly. I don't know if you would agree but it strikes me he may have been looking to obscure some initially sloppy forensic work with a... new story... as it were."

Rachel felt uncomfortable. "Oh but his reputation is faultless. His attention to detail scrupulous."

"Yet he failed to notice the hidden compartment on his first examination. A fact that could be significant if this new break in were found to be... accurate."

"I think it would be a mistake to disregard his opinion."

"On the other hand, I have departmental resources to consider. We have had problems with that residential row over the last few days since Fidelis Kitchener's death. Various incidents. Lot of unrest. Tell me about Andrew Kitchener."

"Inconclusive. David described his death as an 'efficient execution'. There was obviously little struggle with his opponent. His neck was broken, possibly by the fall. He had stomach cancer."

"Oh," she seemed genuinely surprised, "then he wouldn't have lasted long anyway."

She must have seen affront rippling over Rachel's surface for she adjusted her tone to say, "The scanimage collection has been examined and I'm pleased to pass it into your stewardship."

"Thank you, Ma'am."

"Obviously I am sorry for the loss of a great officer and I know you will miss her. We live in changing times... Rachel. We must all learn to adapt. Fidelis Kitchener's untimely death may lead to further opportunities for you. I would like you to be able to take full advantage of them when they arise. I am to attend a conference at the Magnamater's offices in the next few days. There is concern about the growing disconnection with the Northern provinces. I expect that there will be moves to send an inspiring Senior Fidelis presence there."

"Thank you Ma'am."

My Dad used to have this nodding dog in the back of his car. He'd had it for years. Is that how you see me? Some gullible acolyte? D'you really think I buy all this warmth you're putting into your words? You think it pulls me into the fold? Too late. I'm not following anyone's footprints anymore.

Outside, she left the square busy with lunchtime traffic and fled to the far eastern corner of the Burgh where she contacted Andrew's sister. Watched her pale and disintegrate as she absorbed the news, watched her shudder with a new life where grief ruled and then watched her realise that she would have to break it to her parents. Heard her own offers of support as if from a different country.

Why didn't I ask Andrew when I had the chance? Now all this doubt will whine and flutter its wings in the darkness between Ben and me, just waiting to take another drink. How did I miss it? I feel like one of the old landfill sites. Full of old smells and things I'm supposed to forget about. Where does all that crap go? You can't burn it. I thought I'd forgiven him. Nobody teaches you how to do that. What did he say? "What about Rachel… Hasn't she got the right to know it's all a sham?" I have to see Ben's face when I talk about Andrew.

"Ben. It's me. I need to see you now."
"Riiiiight… could it wait 'til this evening?"
"No."
"Okay let's meet in the reception area in ten minutes. Won't have long."

She marched quickly back, zigzagging her way through the residential blocks and almost colliding with a figure emerging from row A. She wiped her tear stained cheeks abruptly.

Ben was already waiting with an assistant in tow.

"Rachel, you remember Dero? She's just been promoted."

"Yes. Well done." Rachel concentrated on Ben's face so that the girl would understand and leave.

"Oh… of course." The girl flushed and left.

"That was subtle," he said sarcastically.

She read his mien.

"I had to come as soon as I heard. Poor Andrew's dead. He was killed early this morning near their flat. No leads as yet. He didn't have long. Stomach cancer had spread. I have been assigned to the case. Thought you should know."

Instinctively she put out her arm as he sagged and rocked forward.

He was trained to know all the moves. But could anyone affect such total spinal collapse? This panting breath? Such immediate pallor?

"Had he talked to you about… anything?"

"Nnno," he replied weakly

"Are you sure?" she returned coolly.

"Yes. Yes. Of course I'm sure. What… what d' you mean?"

"I think we should go somewhere more private. And I think you'll be longer than ten minutes."

"I… can't…" He glanced at her face. "Okay. Wait here one moment."

He disappeared up the spiral staircase to the first floor.

This is so important. I have to get it right.

"Do you want to come up?" Dero called from the top of the stairs.

I don't need your permission.

She followed her to a small office off the main studio.

"If you'd like to wait in here, Ben won't be a minute," Dero said smoothly, carefully staring at the space just above her right ear.

Interesting. He couldn't keep me at any greater distance if he tried. And you're enjoying the moment, aren't you young lady?

Several chairs were stacked in the corner. She lifted one down and sat on the small table, facing the door. By the time he arrived her hands had stopped shaking and she had passed through irritation to control. Equally he had regained some composure. Lifting the chair, he re-positioned it near to the wall and leaned back into it, his hands interlocked round his head.

She remained silent. Finally he cocked his head and lifted an eyebrow.

"I asked you before if Andrew had said anything to you that might throw some light on his death."

"And I said no. D'you think that his death's connected with Josie's?"

"At this stage it's impossible to draw firm conclusions. When did you last see him?"

"About eleven. I left him at the flat when I had to come back in here."

"And was he in the flat when you returned at what time?"

"I didn't check. I crept in. It was about five am. What about you?"

"Me? I arrived earlier. I came in at an… unfortunate point in your argument."

His arms slid downwards and crossed defiantly on his chest.

"Is this an official interview Fidelis?" He jutted his chin upwards and sneered.

"Not yet. When it becomes so I will ask you to wear a veriband to authenticate your statement."

Funny that we both suddenly looked down at the same time. Maybe he can see the miles of deep valleys opening between us too

He bristled. "Do you have to be so, so brutal? We have just lost one of our oldest friends."

"There is a job to do. Andrew obviously believed that you and Josie were having a relationship. Were you?"

"Oh, so that's what this is all about. I thought we'd got over the paranoia, Rachel. Look, I don't like to speak ill of him. But it makes a lot of sense to know he was very poorly."

"Just because people believe something you don't like doesn't make them paranoid, ill or wrong for that matter Ben, as we both know. I repeat, were you?"

"This is ridiculous. Think about what you're asking. We're talking about Josie here. You know how Andrew digs his heels in and gets obsessive about things."

Yes sometimes he did. But Georgia and Luke do not

"I mean, it's hardly likely is it Rachel? Sadly, this is nothing more than a tired and, we now know, very sick man who never got as much of his wife as he wanted, in the clutches of grief and anger, needing to let off steam. I would have thought you would be able to see that. We've both worked hard to get through your insecurities. Don't let's go back there."

"I heard you say it was 'work' to him, Ben."

His arms opened and his hands slipped down to rest on each hip.

"Pardon!" He spat.

You forget that this is what I do best. I can't be rattled in quite the way I was.

"All the 'little notes' and 'snatched meetings'… you told him they were work related. So you didn't deny there had been legitimate cause for concern. Just that the interpretation was mistaken."

She watched his diaphragm rise and fall more quickly. It was the only sign of discomfort.

"You… have to be very careful… what you are jeopardising here, Rachel."

Suddenly she was overcome by the need to ask,

"Do you love me, Ben?"

Exasperation burst out of him "Of course I… just… hate… your… doubt."

"Then tell me, please. What work were you and Josie doing together. So secret that neither of you could share it with me?"

He blinked several times. Suddenly he stood, walked towards her and before she could stop him, curled his hand tightly around the back of her neck. Then he leaned forward and kissed her cheek slowly. His voice was low.

"I'm sorry. All I can say is that it involves a series of new initiatives concerning subliminal transmission manipulation. Only select individuals from a number of spheres are in the know. It is confidential and I can't discuss it further for the moment. You'll have to trust me. I said as much to Andrew. Okay."

As he moved back he patted her hand, as if placating an elderly confused relative.

I've got to get out of here. If I don't I might break his jaw

"And that's the truth is it?" She stood so that they faced each other.

"Absolutely. Hopefully soon I'll be able to…"

"And you are certain that you didn't speak to or see Andrew after that?"

"Yes." Momentarily he was taken aback, unsure if she was his once more.

She straightened her jacket crisply and stepped towards the door.

"I promised Andrew's sister that as one of his oldest... friends you would happily help out with any arrangements. I think you have her number."

"I... yes. Look Rachel. Let's talk tonight about..."

"The weather?" she interrupted, sensing her own storm rising inside her. "I think that we've lost too much here today already." She felt for the handle and looked at him so that he could see her distress. In turn she read something complicated playing across his face. It could have been pity. She turned abruptly and left him staring after her, open-mouthed and frustrated

From now on everything is camouflage

She spent the rest of the afternoon staring at pictures of Andrew's prostrate body lying on the concrete steps, his head lolling at an impossible angle. Had he reached the flat itself and then toppled backwards over the wall, had he fallen backwards down the stairs or had he been lifted and thrown over and clear of the wall? She contacted David and asked him.

"Given the length of the flight I would have expected more bruising over his body and possibly some smaller bone fractures and breaks. The angle of the body does not make it clear. The residual blood pool underneath the skull has been dragged slightly meaning that the position of the body was adjusted to confuse us. But clearly the injuries were sustained from impact at speed."

"If he were thrown it implies great strength, does it not? I know he was not the heaviest of men but a clean lift is difficult."

"His back was so damaged that it would be hard to distinguish specific abrasion marks consistent with being leant against the wall and levered over will. But I will look again."

Why would Andrew be killed? Had he uncovered

something in Josie's affairs that made him a threat? Or had he simply returned home knowing he wouldn't gain access and disturbed someone? Or was Butcher's assertion that he had been the victim of some local unrest plausible, since there was no Fidelis presence on that particular row?

All my working life I have been digging for buried bones. Stripping people clean. I can still smell Andrew's breath, hear Josie's voice. They're floating so close, substantial, demanding my attention. Don't let us go. If they were both still alive what would I say? Would I wreak havoc on their marriage the way she is doing on mine? Whichever way I look at it, she has just swept through, dragging us all in her nets, leaving me with the mess. And the moment Ben agreed to collude, he let me go.

Oh... I could run now. That stretch of wet sand... I could run...

No. I will not. I will be my own good dog. Focus on the chase, the scent under my nostrils. Nobody's hound.

The office had emptied by the time she left. There would be no time to rest. She hurried though the centre struggling with that rising light-headedness which seemed to plague her these days. It clouded her peripheral vision. As she turned into Residential she bumped hard into a wall. How could she not have seen it? The impact made her cry out and then quickly swing round to see if anyone had noticed. Quick enough to glimpse that same figure turn sharply into a side exit. Standard practise. She was not imagining it.

She did not go up to the apartment but slipped straight into the basement and unearthed her bag from its hiding place. Routinely she checked the hover's fuel cell, her torch and spare power chip. There was the rest of her kit. She arranged them in the order they would be needed. Capsules. Vicorder. Wrist strap. Glasses. Sedpen. Epipen. Whatever happened tonight would be memorised. Finally, she fitted an urethracat, took a fluid capsule, filled her flasks and dialled Ben's transor. It was switched off.

"Ben. It's Rachel. Listen, I have to work late tonight. Don't wait up. Bye."

She clicked the basement shut, reminding herself to stop and get food at the trolley, and re-climbed the hill.

The sound of his bleeping transor had woken Ben. Bleary-eyed, he fumbled on the surface, trying to focus on the clock.

"Lights On," he ordered and stretched, wincing as his pulled back muscle twinged. He stood by the window and listened to Rachel's message, his smooth brow furrowing as he watched her disappear from view.

CHAPTER ELEVEN

Marylebone

It was rare for there to be no seats on the locomoter, so with feet locked into the standing paddles she held on tightly to her carton of soup and tried to square her thoughts.

How did I get here?

"Putting one foot in front of the other," she answered herself out loud.

"Sorry?" asked the man to her right.

"Oh, nothing. Got to stop thinking out loud." He smiled sympathetically but looked away quickly. You didn't chat with a Fidelis.

If I'd just looked sideways more often and not always at the road ahead. Got a few less 'A' s at school and joined in instead of watching, maybe I'd understand people more. I've been so predictable which is a form of laziness in itself. Now I feel so light I could float away, as if I were losing gravity. What if I can't come back down again?

As soon as the first traveller left, she set out her food in front of her and forced herself to eat the soya roll slowly.

Sip – chew – sip – chew. Her appetite had disappeared.

This second journey mirrored the first and whilst it was busier at station 53, she exited with greater ease. However the sight of sheeting rain made her heart sink – this would make the hover trip even more challenging. Extending her visor she made her way to the viaduct and assembled the kit. Pure physical, mechanical function demanded little.

I trust my hands. It's my heart I don't recognise

Double-strapping her feet into the foot wells, she clipped her bag symmetrically across her back, conscious of balance. It felt heavier. Once more she started, rising up cautiously. Visibility was poor. At least it was a relatively straight line.

Be part of the machine. Use only eyes and fingers. Keep erect. Still. Stay kerbside.

It worked until an unexpected gust blew her off course so violently that she could not right herself and toppled onto the road.

How quickly we lose our childhood love for the tumble. The adult fall is a trauma.

Rachel's shoulder howled in protest as she clambered back up, cursing through tears. Somehow the dull ache and anger kept her more keenly focussed and, while the wind and rain continued, she reached the arterial and crossed, instinctively looking to the left and right.

What are you expecting, Rush-hour?

It was the same deserted landscape. She stared out towards the station and crept backwards up the small flight and into the portico.

There she dismantled and repacked her hover with her vicorder and transor and strapped the bag tightly up on the ledge. Then she fitted her wrist strap and glasses and adjusted her sound and visual levels. There would have to be some final tuning at the entrance. She swallowed the blood pressure capsule knowing the effects would be noticeable in half an hour.

I just hope that the light-headedness I know I'll experience won't incapacitate me. Anyway there's no choice – the sensors will pick me up otherwise.

The timing was critical. All she could do was rely on the surveillance information. The food trolley driven by two clones should arrive at seven fifty-five and would gain admittance at five past eight after security checks. This would allow her only ten minutes to sedate one of the clones and swap places. The sedpen would only take ten seconds to work. She knew what part of the neck to inject and at what angle she would brace his shoulders and lock his arms. These things at least her training had given her. But there was so much she could not anticipate and there was no reason to believe that tonight's routines might be flouted. It was the first time she had been without a transor in fifteen years. There were no orders to follow and as she zigzagged across towards the station, her tread already as spongy as a lunar walk, she felt the terrors of nakedness.

Following the railings that ran for some thirty feet from the entrance she reached a small gap and crouched down on the short flight of steps that led to a bin area. This is where she would leave the body. She would have to drag him about fifteen feet and undress him. The first will have gone to the door to start the security check. Then there was no more time. As the trolley turned the corner and trundled past, she examined her quarry.

So small, they seem like children in a slow game.

And so it unfolded.

He smiled sleepily up at her while she pushed his head sideways and held the pen to his pimpled skin. Although short, he was broad and flung a sturdy backward punch that surprised her. In reflex, she seized his left arm and tugged it sharply behind him. His right arm flailed momentarily before his legs buckled and gave way beneath him.

The first clone was already speaking into the vopass with his back towards them. Swiftly, she half-dragged, half carried the body to the railings and down the steps. Her hands slipped over the unfamiliar clammy flesh as she peeled off the white overalls and re-dressed herself in them. They were a little short. It was still raining and remorsefully, she looked back at his exposed slumped form as she pelted to the waiting trolley. She knew she had taken too long.

He sat, waiting patiently in the front seat. Without questions. Without initiative. She stilled her breathing and slowed down her movements. There would be no conversation or eye contact. Her dizziness indicated that her blood pressure had fallen. At least she would pass the initial metabolic security checks. However if it kept on plummeting she knew she would be at risk and that would draw unwelcome attention. She would try to avoid dismounting the trolley until serving was required. Briefly she activated her visible wrist strap then stroked it back under the cuff but allowed the antennae to remain slightly protruding. It's fineness belied it's extreme sensitivity. In the past she had used it to record events and conversations through highly dense surfaces.

"Proceed!" The disembodied order sliced the silence.

A dull siren. The clank of metal grinding on metal and a side door opened. There was only time to make the most minute of adjustments to her glasses before the trolley lurched forward into the darkness.

Marylebone's wide open concourse was gone, replaced by an enclosed, lightless space, like an old ghost train ride. She affected the rounded shoulders, the clone's lazy back and prepared to be startled, her whole being a porcupine state of alert.

"Outer doors shutting. Proceed!"

They moved on cautiously. A second siren sounded. Another louder clunk and like jaws opening on the mouth of an ancient beast, two massive panels gradually slid back, to flood the cabin with bright light.

A great sparkling hall recognisable but transformed. Their passage was obviously to be through the transparent covered tunnel that wormed into the centre. She stared ahead incuriously while every synapse shrieked as her peripheral vision caught the undeniable presence of three Fuchs Tanks.

The pride of the military Arsenal before the Age of Division.

Everywhere people walked and worked with purpose. Some in isolated cabins gazing at liquid screens and tubes networking to tanks, others in intense enclaves, nodding vigorously.

This was a hive.

They reached the top of the escalators. There was nowhere

else for them to go. Suddenly the trolley shuddered as the platform supporting them gradually descended to a new level where a well-lit lounge area interconnected with more workstations. Where the tube trains had once run there was now a moving walkway onto which they slowly drove. Through tunnels lit by more isolation cabins bored into the walls, they watched endless testing and sampling. There were even dimly lit living quarters with occupied sleeping capsules.

They emerged onto the next stop. Whilst the moving walkway continued into the tunnel, there was a natural break in the track and they followed a route round to the left. Here the layout was more informal with a series of open-plan lounges where people were relaxing and along one wall, Rachel noticed, with relief, a sign 'Trolley Bay'.

People noticed their arrival without comment but started to rise and move in drifts towards them. The driver swung his legs out as if they were weighted and worked his way to the back, apparently concentrating on arranging the cartons and trays for easy access. Rachel echoed his movements slowly always looking down to where the distant floor loomed. She held onto the frame to stop herself from falling as the first group approached. She listened uncertainly as they gave in their orders.

"I love these conferences. The food's always so good. Better then all that recycled soup and soy crap. Any meat? I had the chicken risotto, yesterday."

Rachel was able to lean her lower pelvis onto the dispenser and scan the various options. Most were unrecognisable to her. She could feel the rising impatience behind her. Heard the "Little slow today" aside. Desperately, she pulled a tray towards her and colourlessly read 'Pork loin with herb mash'.

"Fine." The woman was young and attractive. Her hair was longer than the norm and her clothes more casual. Her orbiting companions all exuded the same confidence.

"It's good to be back in the real world. O was stifling." They began to make it easier on her. They pointed. She handed them their selections.

The next group shuffled closely behind.

From the corner a woman approached and spoke directly to her.

"Please collect all the used cartons from lunch-time. They are over by room C. Don't go inside, there's a meeting in progress."

In response her clone colleague handed her a large tray. This might be a good opportunity. Silently she plodded the perimeter and began methodically arranging the used containers immediately beside the transparent sealed room where ten people were earnestly debating. She made sure that it took several laboured trips.

A new figure rose from the middle of the room and announced. "If I could just bring those specifically involved in the Viral consultation to the centre for a discreet meeting. By all means bring your food with you. The rest should continue in their allocated splinter groups for further briefings."

The screen to his right liquefied and the words 'VIRAL' re-formed.

Silence fell, as all eyes refocused and various individuals rose and moved towards him. When all were seated, screens emerged from the floor and joined to form a temporary but self-contained unit. Others regrouped in different areas leaving Rachel free to continue her clearance, now concentrating on the centre. She affected the vague clone gaze but lifted her head slightly so she could view him more fully. Although unfamiliar to her, he was obviously someone important. His long arms spidered across the screen and then returned to his side. His tonsure shone in the artificial light and his blue eyes beamed like lasers.

Slowly she scanned his audience. She wanted to record as many faces as she could. Clearly the discussion was not universally popular. She managed about fifteen minutes more before there was nothing left to clear and the same woman appeared.

"Thank you, I think everyone has finished."

Obediently, she returned to the trolley and shelved the trays with the clone before they climbed back into their seats and moved on.

They reached the lift port where an open lift descended, occupied by a group of engineers carrying apparatus. This, they boarded. The trolley rose and Rachel recognised the high vaulted roof space of Paddington Station. As they levelled, more tanks and unfamiliar light aircraft came into view. A hover capsule with a small fuel cell shot overhead, provoking cheers from a group of spectators. Another team gathered around a self-propelling suit.

"Forget what you've seen before, this recycles the waste in vessels which circulate the entire suit – in much the same way as the body pumps blood supply – fuelling the nanomotors and assisting thermo-regulation."

"Applications?"

She recognised these types. The glee of developing the new from the impossible.

At the trolley, they were also less careful, spilling and slopping the cartons' contents. Consuming without noticing what they ate. Sated like lions, they padded away.

"Is everyone done?" someone yelled. "Thanks you can go back now."

But the clone continued forward. Momentarily, Rachel panicked. They must not draw attention to themselves.

"I said we've finished," the voice rose slightly. The clone gestured forward to an Engineer who was waving two empty cartons from the end of the concourse.

"Sorry Sir, bit late finishing. Can they just collect these?"

"Yes. Carry on trolley."

Their drive back followed the same route, pausing in the conference area only to collect the refuse. It was the sight of the cushioned easy chairs that made Rachel's nostrils start to twitch uncontrollably and her palms sweat.

It's revolting. What are they planning form such a cosy, cosseted little camp?

Her deep sigh drew a glance from the clone next to her but he said nothing.

Throughout, they were ignored and left as they had come.

Once outside she had to move quickly. As the trolley drew level with the railings, she pulled out the sedpen from her right boot and injected his neck. He registered only mild surprise before his hands fell from the wheel and he slumped forward. She bent down, pulled his feet from the pedals and pressed the standby switch. Then, she dashed to the stairwell to the prone figure. He lay soaking, his scant hair floating in the pooled water underneath. His flesh was grey and icy to the touch. She had nothing with which to dry him.

How could I have left him like this? What kind of person have I become?

Filled with self-loathing she stripped off his overalls and redressed him. The rain began to drive harder as she dragged his body up the stairs, his foot catching on a corner railing. She yanked it free.

"Oh come on, damn you!"

Seated in the trolley they both looked less vulnerable. Waiting to be kissed awake. She used the epipen on the more needy one first. Shaking his arms, pinching his cheeks, finally he started to respond. Immediately she administered another dose to the second. His revival was quicker. As soon as their pupils were no longer dilated, she ran without a backward glance.

It was only as she stood dripping and shivering under the portico that she felt herself begin to unravel. Her vision drained to a blinding whiteness and she could hear nothing but the blood screaming in her ears. Her legs collapsed under her like a rag-doll and it was easier to curl. She pressed her head against the granite and wept.

Over! It's finished!

Time elongated and stretched and she had a sense of looking down from afar on her own prostrate form.

I could just stay here. Merge with the stone. But then someone's got to take the next step. Deal with all those clever people down there. So soon I'll have to get up and go back because no one has the right to define disposability. Where does it end? Who's next?

Up!

Grimacing, she forced herself onto buckling knees. Fighting this new terrifying frailty it took several attempts to pull down her bag and even longer to re-assemble the hover. She swallowed a fluid capsule and slowly worked the various muscle groups. Finally, with hands that seemed to have divorced her, she clumsily strapped herself back into the hover.

She kept as close to the ground as she dared, thankful that the machine had its own balancing sensor and looked only at the next few feet until she reached the station.

I can't do this again. Have I seen enough? What if the recordings showed nothing illuminating? What more do I need to know anyway?

She dissembled the hover and slid back through the portals into station 53.

She boarded the locomoter and sat inert in an empty carriage.

There is no trust.

It was her only incisive thought. She stared out at the miles skimming past and up into the inky sky, still spewing its load onto the land. Watching the years and causes fall in broken shards.

If anyone had seen her reeling return down the causeway, they would have reported a member of the Fidelis inebriate. She would have faced disciplinary proceedings.

She made the flat, struggled to open the door and once inside, sank to her knees in the darkness.

"It's getting later and later. Have you found his killer yet? Or is it something else you've got on, Rachel?" The disembodied questions floated to her. She breathed deeply, trying to contain the mounting nausea.

"Province C. Marchant case. I did tell you. Disgusting weather out there."

His lips curled.

"Don't… be… so… professional… Rachel. I don't feel we finished things well today. What's going on?"

There's ice in this air. Menace. The weight of his stillness. Ready to spring. Want to get away.

"Work... Ben... Work... I really don't need this right now." She forced herself up on one leg.

And he was upon her, snarling, gusting hot, alcoholic breath into her face. Vice grip on her shoulder.

"What exactly don't you need, Rachel? It's always work with you, isn't it? You Fidelis are all the same. Everything poor Andrew said about Josie... It's you... I'm only just seeing it. I didn't need you striding into Transmissions swinging your axeworth of accusations around the place. Don't ever do that to me again. Who d'you think you are? You know nothing!"

"Don't try and turn this around. I'm not the one with..."

"With what? What?" he shouted. "Secrets? Well who knows, eh? Why don't you just camp out at the office? Or maybe you've found somewhere else to bed down, Rachel?"

Spinning, the deafening whine. Was this how Andrew felt? The fear before the fall?

"Don't be ridiculous! Don't..." She raised her arm to ward him off and caught his cheek.

Ignition. She felt his weather. She felt him blow.

Grabbing, shaking and rattling. Her knee and fist rose reflexively and sunk into his torso, forcing him backwards

They both bent double. The ludicrous choreography of violence.

"Please... Ben..." As her gasp came, in mewling ululation, her bowels convulsed.

She wrenched away, driven by the primal need to hide her dirt and lurched into the bathroom, banging her temple on the marble as her vomit sprayed into the black.

She heard him shout, "Lights!"

There was nothing to do but retch and heave.

Finally, although spent, a clearing had been forced through her and huge wracking sobs blistered her surface.

She could only find one word. "Terrible!"

He stood over her, aghast. Using his own face cloth, he began to mop ineffectively around her.

She chattered uncontrollably and found a second word. "Lost."

"What?"

"Terrible!" Her head shook.

"Let's get you in the shower."

He switched on the water, carefully lifted her in, fully clothed and she leaned back, letting the water course her face and watched him clean up her mess.

After he had finished he disappeared and returned with a cup of water.

"I've put a couple of drops of mint in there – just sip it."

She could not move but tried to understand that this was a tender act.

Please let me be wrong.

He found himself stepping over, closing the gap and sliding one arm around her while the other lifted the cup to her lips. Whatever was soaking her and separating them, he wanted it too. Wanted it to drive away the ghost of his rage. He heard his mother's voice. "Ben, your problem is you don't know the difference between a slap or a stroke."

Stupid! Course he knew. He just liked them both. That's why acting had been so brilliant. You got everything in a single sentence.

She watched his lips trying to form words. Words that would never be enough. His mouth routed aimlessly.

"I…" she whispered.

He lifted his eyes to hers.

"I need to be alone now."

He winced and stepped backwards. He placed the cup carefully on the side and was gone. Bracing his shoulders to the cold he strode into the night.

"When am I going to learn?" He hissed, the cold stinging his tongue. "All that moral superiority, that detachment. I let her do it to me every time 'til the red cloud rises and the rest's a blur. It's her bit of control over me. Pathetic. Lecturing me on secrets when she's obviously doing who knows what!" His voice rattled round the square, bouncing off the lightless buildings. "Maybe... maybe... we've got to let go. She wants a transfer and I want something... different. I'm not running away after all these years of plodding on. This new thing's too important. I deserve it and if she'd been more supportive maybe I would have involved her. It's not my fault."

Finally he let himself into the Transmission offices where he curled up on the lounge area with the blanket Dero kept in the storeroom.

Across the Burgh Rachel lay herself carefully into bed.

It's not his fault. I'm digging my own trench here. Losing clarity. I expect him to trust me when I can deceive him so easily. It's like a wormery. We're layering misunderstanding on misunderstanding. Yet I've never been able to tell him much about work. He knows that. He's just using it to deflect responsibility for his own subterfuge.

She reached for a tissue and caught sight of her white bloodless face in the mirror. Its muscles frozen, its eyes staring fixedly back at her.

"What was he doing? Trying to attack me. ME! I could have broken his neck. We've been resenting each other for years. I'm sick of it all! Lights Off!"

And with the bedroom still swirling, she finally slipped away.

When she woke in the morning everything seemed normal but as she rose, her vision bled to white, the room faded and she stumbled forward.

It will pass. She urged herself on feeling for the walls, the edges of surfaces, the fittings and slowly her body adjusted. Relieved, she made herself eat a light breakfast. It stayed down for only five minutes.

Her transor sounded. David Poulter.

"Good morning Fidelis, Sorry that it's so early. I wanted you to know that I am being re-assigned from my current caseload as of today."

"That's very sudden, David. Were you given any reason?"

"Only a bland statement referring to forensic skill shortages in the North." He sniffed dryly. "Privately, I don't think they were happy with the Kitchener case."

"Oh, but it was a minor omission," she protested.

"Nevertheless, it was sloppy. But I stand by my conclusions."

"I'm sorry for that. They seemed eminently reasonable. There is no one I respect more in forensics."

"There was just one clarification though. The blows to the head caused a massive internal haemorrhage and were definitely the cause of death. I believe his assailant would have known this and the fall was merely camouflage. The exact time was twelve thirty am. I wish you well, Fidelis. Goodbye."

Wearily, she pulled herself to her feet. It was unfathomable. But her main priority this morning was to examine the recordings. It took a matter of minutes to download them onto diskette but she thought better of viewing them in the flat and went down to the basement. Last night seemed a remote madness. She felt her heart begin to race, her palms prickle.

What if the equipment hadn't worked?

But no, here it was sharp and undeniable on screen. The sound and images were a little shaky to start with but settled down to an acceptable quality as she had grown used to the slower pace. She relived every turn of the trundling trolley until the conference lounge when it was obvious that the discreet meetings were indistinct. The very heart of her hopes and she could not hear them. She thumped her opened palm in frustration. *Wait! After all this, there must be a way.*

She continued watching to make sure that the recording was complete.

I have to understand exactly what was going on, the purpose of it all. Oh for some discernment right now! I don't dare seek help from inside the Fidelis or any of the connected experts. But maybe there's an obvious alternative

She swallowed unwillingly and dialled his transor.

He answered immediately. A quiet "Hello" slipped through his barely open lips. She could see the studios in the background where he had probably stayed the night and thought regretfully that she had not considered his comfort at all.

"Hello. How are you?"

"Fine. Stiff. You?"

"Fine." She spoke lightly, disguising her own concern as she saw clearly how emotion had channelled his face. "Listen, Ben. I need your help." His chin lifted. "Can you get hold of an enhancer for clarifying muffled audio recordings for me? Something small. Portable?"

He stared back blinking for a few seconds. "Is that it?" he said finally.

"Yes. I need it as soon as possible though."

He looked to the side, as if he could not trust himself.

"I'll arrange for one to be left in reception." He inhaled sharply and collected himself.

"Rachel, we have to talk tonight about Bera's birthday. Can you… make sure you're around?"

"Of course." She smiled briefly and signed off. It had not been a request but a wooden order.

She made several copies and secreted them in all her concealed compartments in the flat and basement. They were infinitely better situated than Josie's had been. She enjoyed a moment of superiority while all the time battling with the same extreme light-headedness. It was the sense of disconnection that she disliked the most. As she sat trying to recover, her transor sounded.

Senior Fidelis Butcher.

"Good Morning, Fidelis Develin. Are you currently secure?"

"Yes, Ma'am."

"I have a new brief for you. A hard file is waiting collection at the office. As I indicated to you earlier this week, the opportunities in the northern provinces may already be presenting themselves. There have been reports of considerable unrest and the need for containment from N. Local Fidelis are requesting assistance. We would like an assessment as soon as possible."

"I will be in directly, Ma'am. But may I remind you that I have a day's leave booked for tomorrow. It is my daughter's birthday."

"Indeed. I had not forgotten. Perhaps you can continue up to 'N' from Abovo."

The pulse in Rachel's temple throbbed.

Oh, for one day's grace. Could I work through this?

She made a decision.

"Kate."

"Hello Rachel. Are you all right?"

"So-so. I'd be really grateful if you could give me a check up. Maybe I'm low in minerals or something. Don't you hate self-diagnosing patients! Can I come and see you this afternoon?"

"Of course. At three. Look forward to seeing you."

At the Fidelis offices, a bored cover clerk handed out files that each Fidelis took wearily before slumping into their cubicles.

"Is Ma'am not in then?"

"Just been called to A earlier. She sent her love…" the clerk offered facetiously

"What happened about your transfer request?" Rachel remembered to ask.

"Denied!" The girl replied shortly. "No openings. S.F Ma'am thought I would benefit from another six months in information – collation." She rolled the rhyme petulantly.

"It will happen."

"Not in her lifetime. She's like a reptile… wants everyone within easy reach of her tongue."

Rachel nodded sympathetically aware that at this point Josie would have come crackling in, rattling cages. She could see her now. Once after a particularly dispiriting week, Senior Fidelis had given them all one of her sermons and in her wake, Josie had cartwheeled round the office, gibbering like a witch doctor.

They had never liked each other and now Rachel suspected that her boss somehow felt vindicated. Even if rebellion was only implied, it should not be condoned and as Josie's friend, Rachel knew she was vulnerable.

I have to assume they're just waiting for me to betray myself.

She read the new assignment file. There was little further information apart from the reporting officer and Burgh. She snapped it shut more loudly than she had intended and looked ahead to the liqui-screen showing movements outside.

"Open!" she commanded the sealed cubicle doors. At the same time, Sandra Peters, an older colleague, was emerging from her station.

They nodded.

"Sorry to hear about Josie, Rachel."

"How are things?"

"Oh, looking forward to resorting – you know." She lowered her voice. "There is this island I went to before Division – surrounded by a reef made of coral... did you ever see any coral?"

"No."

"Pinky-orange – as you would expect. Living. The beaches were white and flecked with small nuggets and crumbs of this coral. And you walked out for miles in completely translucent water with these extraordinary coloured tropical fish and the odd eel swimming through your legs, stroking your skin as they passed. The blue was like nothing else..." she ended dreamily.

"What was it called?" Rachel asked, entranced.

"Bermuda... I think that I'll resort there instead. Had a bit of a reputation. Lot of traffic went missing around it. Maybe I can get lost there too, eh?"

"I will visit."

"It's a date. Bring men... or women." She laughed and together they left the building, despatched like drones.

The reception area of Transmissions was busy with preparations for an outside broadcast. Rachel grimaced but before she could make her way through the throng, she was tapped on the elbow by Dero.

"Good morning Fidelis. Ben left this for you." She handed over a small sealed package.

"Thank you Dero. Oh do you have access to the shift rotas this month? I have so many arrangements to make and I don't want to clash with any of Ben's shifts."

The girl nodded uncertainly.

"Of course. Excuse me. I'll be back directly." She was about to disappear upstairs, when Rachel stopped her.

"I think they have copies at the desk here, don't they?"

Dero flushed. "Oh yes," and walked reluctantly to the central consul where she paged the schedule and printed a hard copy.

She had wanted to check with Ben. But that was exactly what Rachel wanted to avoid.

"Was there anything else?"

"No thank you. Not for now."

The girl nodded once more, "Then goodbye," and turned away.

I wonder if she turned first deliberately? Does she realise Fidelis always dismiss a member of the public? Had there been a new insolence in her manner? I won't forget it. I never do. Oh get a life Rachel! You can't store everything! This enhancer could tell me everything

The basement was cold as the fuel cell was low. She sat in the semi-darkness, connected the equipment and loaded the recording. It was immediately apparent that the audio quality was improved. She realised that she was holding her breath as the conference scenes approached. The first of the discreet meetings.

"... And whilst Soya naturally produces phyto-oestrogens – protecting against the cancers, osteoporosis etcetera, the value of the omegas and the acids shouldn't be underestimated – a lot of the ground work was done before Division but our food engineering is much more advanced now. We can start to withdraw or boost, depending on the province. As we have shown, excess can trigger more problems than eliminate –

particularly with the already highly modified grains. So, we track all the way to Olim where, in certain sectors, we will start to introduce the protein group which will most likely effect neurotransmitter performance and then watch closely for the rise in dysfunction. This new greater mobility will make it so much easier to manage..."

The second meeting gave her... "Factor in reduced predictability allowing for some mutations. Province O is a good choice. Mostly Agricultural Sciences – active agents could be released into the water distribution plants – let's see if there's a natural increase in spontaneous pregnancy by releasing hormone levels. Track 'full-terms' and closely monitor mutation manifestations. It's a long- term proposal of course – I'd say three year cycle from ingestion to a year old child – if there are too many problems, we can deal with them in Abovo as we've done before..."

She stopped and listened again... "as we've done before..." Before.

I could stop listening now. Destroy the evidence. Bury the memory because if I carry on I will change.

Her finger made the decision and she watched her innocent foolish clone self by the central meeting.

"Finally, people to the emotive area of 'Viral Technology'. We have to accept that, despite the immensely decreased porosity of our borders, there is still risk of penetration from overseas. Our Intelligence is re-established but not consistent and because we know less about current research, we have to equip ourselves should that worst of all scenarios return. Now, we believe we have eradicated a great degree of unpredictability, but these new strains have to be tested in real scenarios. Laboratories will always be theoretical."

"How much work has been done on Clones?" A question came from the floor.

"We have had some success but the bottom line is that their immune systems are compromised anyway. The overall picture is unsatisfactory. We need a normal demographic."

He is so determined. Playing at consultation. He already

knows the future. What does such a mind look like? Housed within that spindly frame, etiolated like a sun-starved plant.

"Does that exist anymore? Genetic manipulation is one thing but George, if I understand you correctly, this is monstrous. How does one choose? It's barbaric."

"It is necessary, Carl. We scientists have always had to make the difficult decisions. It's part of our responsibility. We owe it to our people's future not to be coy. There are some obvious choices. It should be an isolated area, set apart. We could start with the one uncontributing sector – Cornwall."

"George, that's obscene!"

"Here is the simple truth, Carl. ASO cannot be sustained on its current scale. It will become necessary to concentrate our limited resources at the centre which means letting go of the outer regions who consume far more than they contribute. We have to look at different ways of achieving this and 'creative instability' is the preferred method."

"Is the Magnamater's office aware of your proposals?"

"Yes."

"And does she concur?"

"Initially she was… reluctant." He waved his hand dismissively, "But she accepts that to preserve, we must progress. Predictability is power. A fact that her predecessor was well aware of. But we must remember too, that our work continues regardless of the current Magnamatership. There is a world out there and we know that the dynamism of all our technologies is greatly admired. The opportunities for international cooperation may be boundless. Now if I could turn our attentions to some specifics…"

Her teeth chattered as if she had witnessed unspeakable atrocity.

Such clean easy words. Yet they're filthy with contempt. Every syllable hammering on my bones and snapping them in half like dry tinder-wood. As if he's parting my spine, reaching in and setting fire to my insides.

Once again she made several copies of the enhanced tape on different miniaturised formats. Onto each she programmed a security code to allow viewing before hiding them in secure compartments. She would keep two copies with her. It was her investment. Her protection. *What now?*

Later having endured the rigours of sanitisation, she found Kate hunched over a testing centre, scanning a pile of cardettes. She raised her head, frowning momentarily as her concentration broke.

"Rachel."

"I am sorry to bother you Kate. It is good of you to see me. I would normally apply for a consultation, but well, Ben is worried and…"

"Of course. It's unlike you to be unwell. Come through to my room," Kate interrupted, tapping her on the elbow. She shut the door behind her and waited.

"I'm feeling a bit… off… dizzy."

"Oh? How long for?"

"Well, at least a few days. I'm not sure… it's probably a virus or something. Lot of work on at the moment."

"Let me do some readings. Take a little blood. Could you provide me with a urine sample?"

Rachel grimaced. "I've just been."

"Maybe later then."

Swiftly, she moved over her body. Listening to her rhythms and pulses. Scanning her organs, her heat and colours. Taking hair, skin and blood samples.

"Stand for me please." She studied the measurements further.

"Right. Your blood pressure is low and pulse is raised but both normalise after a while. The tests that I have taken will give us a more detailed assessment of your general health, but I suspect that you are anaemic and potassium deficient which could explain the dizziness. It goes without saying that your cortisol levels are raised but I rarely see a Fidelis officer whose levels are not. Any sleep problems?"

"Just not enough."

"Any local pain?"

"No."

"Bowels and stomach okay?"

"I was very sick last night. I think it might have been something I ate."

"But you are feeling better this morning?"

"Just a little fragile... you know."

"Have you been anywhere, done anything out of the ordinary recently?"

She shook her head, unwilling to voice the lie.

Kate too remained silent, watching her carefully.

"All right," she said finally. "Look, I don't think there's too much to worry about. You may need to look at your diet. More salt and kelp for instance will help keep your blood pressure and potassium levels up. Most people have the opposite problem. Drop a urine sample off for me."

"I'll try. I have another imminent assignment taking me out of province. I may be gone a few days."

"When you return then. Going far?"

"Up north." Normally she would have been more evasive but Kate's discretion was unquestionable.

"So if you feel increasingly unwell contact me anytime. Can you rest a little more?"

"Thankfully it is a slow loco' ride."

"You take very good care, Rachel."

Kate gave her right elbow a fleeting tap. It was enough to comfort. Fidelis were rarely touched.

CHAPTER TWELVE

Abovo

As she climbed the steps to her flat she had a peculiar sense of disorientation.

Is this the right door? Or should I just keep walking? It's starting to feel less like home and more like a storehouse for disposables. Did Dad feel like this?

From the moment she opened the door she knew that Ben was there.

I'm not ready. What do I say?

"Ah. It's you. You're back then. I was just writing a note in case…"

"Yes… it's me."

She hung her jacket over the back of the brown seat, smoothing the creases from the shoulders. A snag in the fabric caught her eye and instead of looking towards him, she fetched a pair of scissors and carefully inspected every inch of the fabric, inside and out.

"I'm just making a snack before I go back. Can I get you anything?"

"No. I'm fine. You're working then?"

"Yes. Make sure it's all up and running before I leave them to it for the day tomorrow."

"What time are you planning to go then?"

"Well, I hoped 'we' might travel together. I think Mater said midday."

"You've spoken to her then?"

"Yes, to ask what time would be best. Was that wrong?"

"No of course not, but she had already told me."

"Well no problem. I just reconfirmed it. No big deal." He sighed.

"It makes us look so…"

"So what?"

"Separate."

The cold and lonely word hung out like obdurately wet washing.

Slowly he cut the crusts from his bread and grated pasty-looking cheese from a long oblong. Then tenderly, as if they breathed, he sprinkled the flakes from an exaggerated height.

"I'm just going to pack a bag. I'm straight on to N afterwards. New project." She whirled around, grateful for a diversion and conscious that as he ate, he was watching her. It took little time before her bag of essentials was packed.

"Efficient." He acknowledged. "You don't mess about. Take the minimum. I… like that. I always have to think a lot more about it."

"It's practise and… genetic."

"What d'you mean?"

"Dad was pretty similar. Years of brutally lightweight travelling made him unsentimental and the prospect of a change of scene thrilled him to the last. I can… I can remember running alongside him as he left on another trip. Trying to fall in with his jaunty, springing step. Trying to ignore the heat from Mum's eyes as she stared from the hall window."

He nodded, understanding and sensing that they were drifting upstream, out of the white water and into the blameless calmer shallow.

"Mum was the opposite. She depended so much on material attachments, filling her bag with 'what if' contingencies and burdening herself with foresight and fear. Nothing was left to chance and to move in unfamiliar territory was literally painful to her. That's why I prefer to forget those last few weeks. Physically she suffered terribly but it was the bewilderment in her eyes that I agonise over, even now."

"I know Rachel. You were a good daughter."

A white flag. At last.

"Thank you. Oh I've got Bera's card for you to sign."

Rachel placed the card she had laboured over in front of him.

"That's so pretty! Where did you buy it?"

"I made it. The shells came from the beach I take her to and the heather's from our trip. I weaved in the grasses to bind the whole thing together."

He stared at it. "It's lovely but I shouldn't sign it."

"Of course you should. It's from both of us."

"No I don't want to take any of the credit from you. I picked up something at Transmissions anyway. Someone had generated some three-dimensional images and mounted them onto cards just to raise a few extra Asos so I bought one of those. D'you want to see it? I can always re-seal the envelope."

"No that's fine. As long as you've signed something."

"I uhm, haven't wrapped her present yet so I can show you that if you'd like?"

"Oh but I'd already… yes I'd love to see it."

Why must he be so unilateral?

From their bedroom he carried a large box and lifted out a metal dog with a shelf area on its back.

"We're using them more and more on OB's to get mikes into shots without technicians. They're voice activated. Watch this. Roam!"

The dog moved forward. Rachel noted the small tip on the rear wagging.

"D'you see the tail?" he squealed delighted. "Stop! It's called Ben… though she could change the name obviously! Don't you think she'll love it?"

"Yes. How d' you think she'll use it?"

I hate it! I wonder if they'll allow it.

"Oh it runs on solar power. She just sticks it on the window sill in the dorm."

"I meant how… you know… when?"

"Well I dunno… sending messages to her mates in the

dorm... For fun. You remember?"

He ended peevishly. "It's a bit different anyway."

"Yes, I see. It really is. It makes the books I bought seem very ordinary."

"Well... you can never have too many books and you can share in this gift," he comforted

"But you know Ben. The best present of all will be having us both there."

"Course. It's going to be great."

Absently she prepared a snack.

"I thought you weren't hungry... or didn't you want to ask me for anything?" He finished sarcastically.

"I... sorry I'm not thinking straight. Maybe I'll take a bath."

Later she watched the steam glaze the mirrors, and sank gratefully into the water as she realised that her overwhelming need was not for rest, but solitude.

Yet after another dreamless night she woke feeling unexpectedly optimistic.

He was already dressed and talking when she came into the kitchen. The sight of their bags waiting by the front door made her heart flutter in her chest.

Like going on a holiday.

As she ate she watched him moving restlessly round nodding into his transor.

He's still the most beautiful creature I ever saw.

"So all you need to remember is to leave synchronisation up to Steve in A. C and D are a bit sleepy but we know that. Follow the new protocol closely and you should be fine. Any problems contact me straight away and I can talk you through. Worst case I can be back within a few hours. OK? Good luck."

"Right." He clapped his hands together briskly. "Shall we make a move soon?"

"Morning. It's a lovely clear day, isn't it?"

"Uh, yes." He glanced towards the window.

He locked the door behind them and in silence they fell into step as they crossed the square and climbed towards the station. Her heart skipped.

"It's a long time since we've done this, Ben."

"What's that?" He said absently.

"Left the burgh. On a trip. Together."

"I suppose so. It's all routine to you though, isn't it?"

"Yes. But I'm almost always alone. It's… nice to have some company."

He took the window seat and put the bags next to him so she sat opposite remembering that he preferred to face the travelling direction.

"So, what's happening at work today?"

"Well it's quite an important broadcast as it happens. It's the first time several different transmission centres will be linking up to do a multi-site, split screen simultaneous broadcast. Part of the new atmosphere of linkage and connection that Beatrice is promoting. Should be brilliant. As long as there are no glitches. Planning it for a long time. Shame to miss it really!"

Sorry I asked.

"You'll be having a special day in your own way though."

"Oh sure. So what's new out there then? Give me the guided tour."

"Well, Mr Develin, on the left we have the rather attractive land clearance awaiting the new hydroelectric plant. It won't be as impressive as the one we'll be seeing later on the Severn but nevertheless pretty exciting since they doubted it could be done for a long time."

"Mhm."

"In terms of transporting the water from various sites. Apparently the pipework has been engineered to self-pump… bit like our own peristaltic movement for digestion, you know."

"Uh-huh."

"And over there is the expanding eco-plantation. It's a biodiversity initiative to encourage specific wildlife which in turn promotes better quality cropping."

"I see."

"And is this new multi-split thing going to be a regular method then?"

"Well, possibly. Though it takes a lot of resources so I'm not sure how feasible that would be. Only time will tell. Look hope you don't mind but I do need to look at the schedules for the next quarter. Now's a good time without interruptions."

"No. You go ahead."

Because the alternative would be to waste some time talking idly to me and looking out at this stunning country we live in.

If he knew she was watching it did not affect his concentration and shortly before the most dramatic part of the journey where Rachel never failed to hold her breath she saw that he had fallen asleep, his sheets sliding down towards his hips.

His chest rose and fell.

Where does need disappear to? I used to imagine I was one of the air particles, slip inside him, coast through his vessels, see inside his heart, become a part of him. You can't burn on that level indefinitely... and there's been so many disappointments. We've both changed but as I look at him, vulnerable, sleep slackening his usually prepared face, I can't believe he's capable of killing anyone. He's too squeamish despite his temper. Though there have been times, glimpses of a potential. Like walking into a new room in a house you thought you knew really well. An unfamiliar smell that disappears so quickly it leaves you doubting it was ever there. I never thought I'd find his complexity dull.

She closed her eyes enjoying the sun's brightness filtering through.

Oh well. Another missed opportunity.

He woke sensing the locomoter slowing into the station and winced. "Ah!" His hand drifted to his right side.

"Is it that pain again?" she forced herself to ask.

"Oh yes," he sighed. "It's only a muscle spasm but it's agony.".

"Have you used the deep heat cream I got for you?"

"No! The whole studio complained when I tried it. It smelled dreadful."

She kept silent. Years of experience had taught her that he would rather have discomfort than compromise his vanity in any way.

Autumn had come sooner to Abovo. The trees lining the avenue were a dazzling future of reds and ambers. The low sun lit the Ark from behind and for a moment it almost looked beautiful.

"I don't remember it being so picturesque," Ben conceded.

"Senior Fidelis Rachel and Ben Develin for Bera." Rachel spoke lightly into the vopass.

It was as the gates slowly swung open that his transor sounded.

"Damn. I have to take it I'm afraid. You go on. I'll catch you up."

"Don't be too long. Bera will be standing at the fourth window of the first floor right now. She'll have hoist herself up so she will have been able to watch us approaching. Now she'll have seen you stop."

"Alright. It won't take long. Hi. How's it going? Right. On all three or just… ?"

Rachel kept walking until his voice faded. She remembered one summer visit when, because of the extreme heat, Abamater had let the children wait outside for their visitors. Once Bera had seen her she had launched herself from the top step so that Rachel had had to leap up several steps to catch her without allowing them both to topple backwards. Even now she could recall the relief.

It was a sign of the times that she now found herself knocking on the heavy doors and, glancing back briefly to see him still engrossed, she went inside.

"My husband will be in shortly," she told the young Mater.

"Let me take you to the visiting area, Senior Fidelis."

She followed her down a corridor that she had not been aware of and into a large reception room, filled with clusters of tables and chairs. Several were occupied with children and their parents. She chose a corner and waited.

Hope I look happy and pretty enough so I'll be able to lift her heart as much as she lifts mine.

After some considerable time her daughter came in.

Oh Bera. Try not to look so disappointed.

But the look was fleeting as from behind her, Ben appeared and said something inaudible causing Bera to wheel round and hurl herself at her father.

"Daddy!" It wasn't just delight. She watched her daughter's knees buckle as he swept her up into his arms. She was swooning.

She cares too much. What a strange cocktail. My insides are running with all sorts of feelings but there's something inky there too. Jealousy? I remember when I wanted him to do that to me... and now? I don't want to... catch anything I can't recover from. But listen to them squealing... It's joy. How can I begrudge either of them this?

He bounced her up and down until his pulled muscle gave up and he had to let her slide.

"Oh," she pouted.

"I can't – you've grown into such a big girl." They came towards her, hand in hand. A mixture of hormones and ozone.

"Hello Mum."

She drifted into Rachel's outstretched arms and was immediately enfolded.

"Happy Birthday darling."

Home to roost, my sweet treasure. When did I become Mum?

"This is so great. I've actually dreamed of this."

They sat and she reached out one hand onto each of their knees.

"Daddy you don't look any different at all."

"Well I am... a bit!" he offered, delighted.

"Mater says that youthful looks are genetic so I might..."

"Shame we can't be on our own, don't you think?" he whispered, nodding to the other huddles.

"I know! It's such a bore. New policy," Bera tutted, lifting her eyes to the ceiling. "They're just so paranoid!"

"Still. All birthday girls need presents." Rachel lifted the bags and laid the wrapped parcels on the table.

"Oh yes! Yes! YES! Can I open them in any order?"

"Absolutely"

Rachel shot a quick glance at Ben who was nodding vigorously as Bera fingered the biggest parcel.

"From you?"

Slowly she started to unpick the sticky tape.

"Oh don't bother with that! Tear it off!" He pulled impatiently at a loose flap.

"No. I like to… take my time. I want to enjoy every single tiny minute."

He slumped back in his chair in mock exasperation. "We'll be here for ever!"

No Ben. Only a few small hours. That's all we get.

Finally the box was opened and his interest re-kindled as she lifted out the metal dog.

"Wow!" She cooed. "What does it do?"

Ben lifted it down onto the floor.

"Watch. It's voice activated so you just tell it to do whatever you want. Move forward!"

The robot smoothly glided across the floor until it reached the next table where it turned and came back to them.

"It's got an in built sensor so it can avoid collisions. Now, I didn't show you this Rachel, introduce yourself to Bera."

"Hello Bera. My name is Ben." It's voice was small, staccato and slightly sickly.

"Oh sweet thing." Bera was enchanted. "Hello little Ben."

"You can call it anything you want. It just had to have a name for programming and you can alter the vocal tone too."

"I'm going to keep everything just the same, Daddy."

"So all we have to do is record your voice as the commander and then it will only respond to you."

"Oh thank you so much. He is the coolest thing I've ever had. Make him do something else."

"Ben. Are you pleased to see Bera?"

"Yes. I am pleased."

The small metal tail pulsed form side to side.

Bera roared, "I love him. Isn't he the best, Mum?"

"Brilliant!"

"Parents and children if I could just have your attention. It is time for your celebration lunch. Everyone has a named, allocated place. Please do make your way through now."

Mater stood to one side at the entrance and waved everyone along.

"Make Ben come and meet Mater, Daddy."

"Oh, alright. We'll just have to programme him up later then."

"I'll put everything back into the bags 'til after lunch. Shall I?" Rachel suggested, trying not to allow a sense of disappointment to cloud the day.

They followed behind the robot until they came abreast with Mater.

"What do you think of little Ben, Mater?"

She stared down gravely.

"He's very sweet."

"He talks too," Bera said already proud.

"Introduce yourself to Mater, Ben." Ben ordered

"Hello Mater. I am Ben."

"Indeed you are." She replied. "Will you be leaving Ben with us Mr Develin?"

"Of course. He belongs to Bera now."

"He's my birthday present." Bera chimed in.

"Mhm." Mater glanced quickly at Ben and Rachel. "We may just need to gain authorisation from Abamater. Certainly to see if she will permit it to be kept in the dormitory."

"Oh but surely," Ben protested, "you can't object to something like this. It's her…"

"Indeed. It's just that we normally prefer to have an opportunity to consider how new sorts of experiences will impact on the wider community and as such…"

"We understand that perhaps we should have sought

approval more formally but the gift was unexpectedly made available to my husband so there was no time to consult, but if you could on this one occasion ask for Abamater's consent as it is Bera's birthday we would be so grateful." Rachel could see the blackness gathering on both Ben and Bera's brows.

"I understand. I will speak with her as soon as I can."

"She'd better not say no," Ben hissed mutinously as they followed the queue to the Refresher.

"I'll... I'll keep him anyway. Under my bed. They can't stop me."

A section of the Refresher had been reserved for celebrating families. A dining plan showed that they were to share a table with two other families.

"This way," Bera trilled. Rachel followed, ignoring the low but clearly audible sigh that escaped from Ben's lips. They nestled again into another corner. As the second family joined the table the father greeted them broadly, "Well this is a bit of a day, isn't it? We're the Broadley's. It's Miel's thirteenth. Who'd have thought it, eh?" He scraped back his chair and beamed.

Ben returned a thin smile but said nothing. Rachel couldn't leave it there. Rudeness may come back on Bera at some point.

"We're the Develins. Bera is 12 today."

"Ah. Nice to meet you." But he was not dense and when Ben angled his chair away from them he echoed the gesture.

"So what are your best birthday memories Daddy?" She asked, pouring each of them a fruit punch from the tumbler.

"Mhm... that's a hard one. Probably when I was very small. I often stayed with my grandparents in summertime and grandma was a great one for picnics. They lived close to the river so we'd go out in the boat, grandpa and I would fish and she," He laughed suddenly remembering, "she played the ukelele. Always singing... now what was that song? Something about a dustman."

"Sounds nice. What's a dustman?"

"Well, when we grew up men would come round every week to collect the refuse from all the houses. They'd pile the rubbish bags outside on the streets and a big lorry would follow slowly on the road and the dustmen would throw the bags into the grinder in the back."

"It must have been smelly."

"It was."

"And what about your best present?"

"That's easy. My go-kart. Grandpa spent months making it. It was red and black and it went faster then anyone else's. He was a brilliant mechanic. He had really huge hairy eyebrows like caterpillars which curled down 'til they almost touched his eyes. He used to comb them. One day he had an accident with a lighter and it singed off one of them... think it was his right one. He looked so funny with one long eyebrow and one short," he giggled.

"I'm glad my grandparents are dead. I'd have hated not being allowed to see them." She cast a brief look at Rachel, "What about your Mum and Dad?"

His face fell.

"What about them?"

"Well what did they get you?"

"I can't remember. I had a lot of jelly and ice cream. Strawberry flavour." Bera watched him expectantly but it was clear that that whatever stretch of water he had drifted into, the gates were locked behind him.

"Do you look like your Mum or your Dad?" She persisted.

"Neither. More like my Grandma. She was an actress and singer too. Great voice. Lots of presence. She taught me loads of poems and songs and then she'd turn over a crate in the yard and get me to deliver them as loudly as I could."

"Sounds fun."

"She was. What about you Mummy?"

"Oh I know all about Mum!" Bera interrupted briskly. "Look here's the food."

Yes. I am known. Routine. Familiar. She wants to smell the exotic.

His transor sounded.

"Ah sorry ladies." Without hesitation he rose, "I'll go take it outside." He left without noticing the flash of resentment across Bera's face and the tightening of her jaw.

"So? Any hot gossip?" Rachel asked conspiratorially.

In response Bera merely lifted her eyebrows mockingly.

"In here? Hardly. Faith hasn't come back, if that's what you mean! Pajo's still not talking to me and I'm thinking about dropping animal biology next term."

"Oh. What does Mater say?"

"I haven't discussed it with her yet. It's just a thought at the moment. It's boring and I'm so bored of being bored."

Rachel was startled by the underlying sullenness in her manner.

"I'm sorry darling. Are there any extra-curricular activities you might like to start?"

"I hadn't thought."

"Well what sort of options are available to your year?"

"Like I said, I haven't thought."

I can't seem to say anything.

"Is there anything upsetting you Bera?" she asked tentatively. "Because if there is you can talk to me about it and it will go no further. I mean I won't discuss it with Mater or anyone else for that matter. I hope I haven't caused you any sadness. All I want is for you to be happy. Especially today."

"I'll put on my happy face then shall I?" Bera opened the curtains on her face and drew a large insincere smile.

Crestfallen, Rachel placed her cutlery on the plate.

"No. Don't. Don't ever pretend."

What an arsenal. I had no idea she had so many weapons.

Rachel flicked a pea across the table. It shot into the distance and landed close to Ben's re-approaching feet.

"Good shot," he nodded approvingly.

Several older teenagers served lunch on large white platters. A selection of soy-burgers, vegetable cakes and rissoles dressed with salads and unusual shaped breads. As one particularly beautiful blonde girl placed water jugs in front of them, Rachel noticed that she glanced quickly at Ban and flushed.

"Thank you so much." He angled his look, just for her.

He can't help himself. Everywhere he goes. It's always been the same.

Bera had also noticed.

"She's so wet that Doro. Always pulling her face about in front of a mirror."

"How do you know?" asked Ben, amused by this cattiness he hadn't seen before.

"Oh everyone knows. Her dormates are always saying so."

"Not very loyal of them!" He returned.

A brief but steady look of rebellion between them. Bera's mouth bulged, straightened and flattened.

"What does the Burgh look like?" she asked finally.

"Grey. Square. Functional. Lots of concrete." Ben answered.

"We could draw it for you. Give you more of an idea?" Rachel offered, sensing a sea change.

"No. Actually yes. That would be interesting."

"The Burghs are structured fairly uniformly but inside the buildings there's a lot more scope for variety."

"And colour? Are you allowed colour?"

"Oh of course. There's a limited selection but you can choose."

"And when I graduate will I have my own room?"

Ben and Rachel exchanged a look for the first time.

"What do you mean?" he asked.

"In the flat. Will I have my own room?"

Rachel collected herself

"Oh yes. It's a very nice one actually."

"If that's what you really wanted to do. It would be… fine." Ben added.

Bera seemed confused.

"But isn't that what happens?"

"There are no rules about…" Rachel began.

He interrupted. "Frankly Bera, no. Most people go and live where they get a job. It depends on what you want to do. Had you thought?"

"No. I don't know what I want to do," her voice had

shrunk small as she cut her food into ever more minute pieces.

"I just want to be... at home. I... I thought that's what happened."

"Well I would love that." Rachel spoke softly, aware of how important this moment was.

Bera lifted her head suddenly to see her mother smiling at her and her father's eyebrows twisting quizzically.

"Wait and see how you feel nearer the time, eh? So much can happen. You don't want to limit yourself. Opportunities can come up anywhere." Ben spoke briskly, expansively.

Does he not see how much she needs this? Can't he hear how scared she is?

"I can keep an eye on openings in our Burgh from now on. See where the areas of real need are and the necessary qualifications. If you'd like me to?" Rachel asked while taking out a blank piece of paper from her bag and beginning to draw a schematic of the Burgh.

"Yes. Yes if that's all right?" It was a tentative question for Ben.

In response he looked at his transor.

"I hope we can get out this afternoon. Give you a change of scene, darling."

"We should take Daddy to our beach. What d'you think?"

"Definitely. D'you like running Daddy? I bet I can beat you." She rallied to her own challenge.

"People. I think it would be nice to show how much we appreciate being together for this special day with a big clap and perhaps the birthday song," Mater beamed at the wall behind them myopically.

Bera scrutinised them for signs of dissent but for once Ben's feelings were not visible and the refresher soon clattered with the sounds of scraped chairs and rusty vocal chords.

"Let me show you my dorm."

As they followed her up the winding wooden stairs to the second floor, Rachel let her hand slide over the rail.

How many little fingers have run this way?

"Come in. This is mine." She sat territorially on the end of her bed.

From nowhere a flood of emotion almost overwhelmed her so she straightened the cover unnecessarily and pointed to the overhead shelves.

"You'll be running out of room soon, Bera. Isn't it cosy, Ben?"

"It's certainly smaller that I remember. There's four of you in here, are there?"

"Usually, yes. Sada, Jati and me at the moment."

He had walked over to the window.

"At least you've got a decent view. Will you get more space as you get older?"

She wrinkled her nose. "A bit. There's a communal leisure area in the older girls dorms. So I suppose they do feel bigger."

"And who has the fourth bed here?"

"Faith Orph was there. D'you remember me telling you Ben?" Rachel added softly.

"Oh yes. The Materini who wasn't." He chuckled until he realised his wife and daughter were silent. "Well it's very nice darling. *Very* nice."

"It's okay." Bera was non-committal.

"I can't wait for you to open your other presents, Bera." Rachel hugged herself gleefully.

"Well look, I tell you what, why don't we take advantage of the sun and light and get ourselves out now and when we get back we can take up where we left off with the presents." Ben clapped his hands together.

"Okay." They agreed. He strode out without a backward glance but Rachel lingered trying to imprint the room in her consciousness. Often when she thought of Bera she was just a rootless floating image. Now she would see her reading, propped up against this headboard, stepping over this floor.

The queue for the trolley was unusually long with people obviously having had the same idea. As they boarded his transor sounded once more.

"This is Ben. What d'you mean? Well have you spoken to Engineering? And what did they say? Well how long's that going to take? Right. Right."

"Your hair's grown, hasn't it? It suits you." Rachel stroked Bera's head wanting to distract her.

"Some of the Maters are so strict about collar and fringe length but Mater Ruth's a bit more relaxed. I'm lucky to have her. I could have ended up with Mildred. Wonder what they're saying to Daddy?"

"… What I'm saying is that you are going to have to be more assertive. Pull rank. There's not enough time to allow them to respond at their convenience. If necessary go to the section leader and make sure he knows how important the next few hours are. Magnamater is very excited by the potential. If we pull this off it will look great but conversely if its a disaster it will reflect very badly on the Burgh as a whole… because I'm here…"

Two red rings were growing on Ben's cheeks. Bera reached out and touched one of them.

Ben swatted her fingers away like summer flies.

She stomped onto the trolley steps.

"Sorry about that girls." He shook his head distractedly. "I don't know what's going to happen."

"We're going to the beach and you're going to race Bera and I'm going to take a few scanimages of this Olympic event for you to put in your Bera corner. You know we have a whole wall in our lounge dedicated to you darling," Rachel had had enough.

They sat three abreast with Bera in the middle. "What's the big problem, Daddy?"

"Well it's complicated to explain but basically we're broadcasting in a new way today. It's not been done before and everyone's very excited and very nervous about it. There are some fairly big technical problems my colleagues are facing right now and they don't know how to deal with them properly so they need to speak to me so I can advise them. D'you see?"

"Yes. I do see. I just wish it wasn't today."

"Well it can't be helped. At least I'm here for you."

Rachel breathed in deeply.

"Isn't the air clean, Ben? Coastal areas are just so different. I love the skies too."

"Mhm."

It was the sight and sound of the water that finally grabbed his attention and shook him out of his tree.

"Wow. I'd forgotten. Look at the size of those waves for goodness sake… and the turbines. They're so…"

"Big" they both yelled back.

Within minutes Bera had thrust her coat into Rachel's arms.

"Did you bring a…"

Silently Rachel handed her a plastic bag.

"Shells. Come on. We all have to contribute to the collection. I'm not even sure where most of them end up."

"Think I'll pass. Shelling's a girl thing. I'll just watch the tide."

"No you won't. You'll do as you're told. There's a prize for the best one."

"Oh yeh." He came up close to her until their eyes were level. "And what might that be?"

"I haven't decided yet. Anyway shelling's only part of this triathlon. There's running and…"

"And?"

"Well… a quick dip, maybe. Who lasts the longest."

"I haven't got anything to wear," he said huskily.

"Neither have I!"

"Mummee. Daddee. Look what I've found."

She hurtled towards them with palms outstretched.

"Oh look at that. It's a starfish. It's perfect."

"It's so beautiful. Can I keep it?"

"Don't see why not."

She ran her fingers over its five white arms. Then held it aloft towards Ben.

"No. I want you to have it Daddy. Something to remember the day by."

Rachel nodded, "That's a lovely idea, Bera."

Please be grateful, Ben.

"Are you sure? Thank you. I'll always keep it."

So here it is. This perfect moment of clarity. This piece of blue sky flecked with scudding clouds. This stretch of pebbled sand blushed orange by the sun's reflection and the thumping tide, whooshing in their ears as their feet crunched down into shelly fragments. White teeth bared within her upturned mouth. Six interlocking hands. Such a small calcite creature to play such an important part. Just for a moment.

"Race you!" he hissed and squealing, she tore away.

She pressed the shutter almost constantly.

I know so many will be blurred. Limbs will flurry and dissolve. Heads will be microdots. The distinction between land, air and water will be lost and their footprints will be re-filled. No calculated race with starter gun and finishing line but a gadarene. No trophy, just my voice screeching into the headwind, urging them on and on.

And now he slows, staring at his left wrist. Then stops. He shouts. At his wrist. Although I can't hear him I know he's shouting. Bera hasn't noticed. Oh she looks back while she runs to realise the race is over. She returns to him, waits for a few seconds and now starts to walk back towards me. I count forty-six disillusioned steps.

I can hear the seagulls are hovering overhead, massively entertained by the spectacle.

Bera's face was a collage of wrestling emotions. In between heavy pants she shouted.

"This isn't right. He shouldn't be…"

Unexpectedly she flung her arms around Rachel who watched as Ben's feet came slapping across the wet sand. Screeching to make himself understood over the gulls who thought they'd found a kindred spirit.

"It's hopeless. I can't hear what they're saying. Terrible reception here. All I can make out is that it's all going pear-shaped. I'm going to have to go back to the Ark. See if I can get it sorted out. I'll wait for you there. Sorry Bera."

She sprung out of her mothers grasp.

"This is so unfair. They have you all the time. Stay here just for a bit longer. Please."

"No I can't do that Bera. This is too important. I have to go where I can at least speak to them."

"No. They're hopeless. You shouldn't be talking to them on my birthday."

"Now listen to me young lady. You have to realise that there are some things that can't just be ignored. Work is very, very important. I must go and I'll see you back there and we'll open more presents and continue with the day. Or you could come back now with me."

He was already walking briskly back towards the road. Bera ran after him shouting miserably.

"You've got a useless, stupid job. I'm never going to work in Transmissions. Just doing stupid broadcasts of that stupid woman all day. I only have you just once in ages. And you can't even be bothered to just switch off your stupid transor for one day. Mummy always switches hers off when she's with me. I wanted this day to be so special and you're just ruining it."

He did not stop.

Wheeling round, she thumped the innocent air and stamped the sand, rage still foaming from her. "He…" she growled.

"I know." Rachel's murmur was lost in the wind

What can I do to rescue this?

As Bera drew near, Rachel kicked off her boots, peeled away her socks, her layers and her underwear until finally she stood upright. Steeling herself to the cold while her skin contracted.

Bera's mouth had fallen open in shock.

"Well come on then. What are you waiting for?"

She turned and walked towards the sea.

"Are we allowed?" Bera shouted, stumbling over her boots.

"Allowed? Bera it's your birthday. Get a move on!"

Bera stared at her mother's creamy nakedness. A mixture of curiosity and disbelief.

"Mummy. What if someone sees?"

"I don't care. Don't you like swimming?"

Mummy again. Why am I doing this? To camouflage his disappearance? Oh the cold.

Will she follow me? Exquisite biting painful cold spray fizzing around my thighs.

Will she follow me? Mystery dark water world swirling blindly underneath. I'm a charged electrified lightening rod. Her lighthouse. My granite feet will stay steady even as the sand shifts.

She submerged herself briefly and waited. Her daughter was laughing now. Rachel watched the pile of clothes grow on the shore. Bera's limbs seemed multiplied as she charged into the waves with her arms outstretched and mouth roaring.

Yes my darling, come to me. When did you grow pubic hair?

"It's freezing, so cold, brilliant!" she spluttered, falling against her. Despite her weight, Rachel swung her through the air and together they sunk underneath until only their heads remained above the water. Floating, they both suddenly realised how strongly the tide was pulling and, as Bera started to drift, Rachel grabbed her back and clamped her in the armpits. They fused. Legs encircled waist, arms curled round shoulders. Eyes shut.

Skin on skin. All those shared cells. One breath. Absolute. Undeniable. One. A few seconds?

Always?

Could we stay in this perfect moment? Slip under the waves.

Rachel stroked and crooned.

"I've never done this before Mummy."

"Me neither."

It was not really swimming – more a short walk, holding hands through shallow water. When they emerged the clouds were already gathering. They shivered uncontrollably and for the first time in many years, Rachel dressed her daughter.

"Shall we go back now?"

"Yes. Maybe Daddy will have stopped talking. And I've got more presents to open."

As beach gave way to track they both turned to give their customary wave.

"I love this place."

"Me too."

It was Mater Ruth who greeted them.

"Come inside. You both look very windswept and..." she glanced at their clothes, "... damp."

"Yes, Mater, it was very invigorating."

They exchanged a conspiratorial look.

Bera giggled.

"I'm glad to see you had a good time. If you want to have a drink in the refresher please go through, if not do relax in the lounge area."

"Where's my Daddy?"

For the first time Mater appeared a little discomfited.

"Ah yes. Mr Develin has had to return to the Burgh. Some sort of crisis at the Transmissions centre I believe. He was extremely sorry and upset to leave I know. He asked me to pass on this note."

Mater held out a piece of folded paper. Bera looked down at the floor, her arms locked at her sides. Mater clenched her lips and offered the note to Rachel. "I'm sorry, Bera. I know how you must feel."

"No you don't. How could you?" she yelled and pushing past them, ran up the stairs.

"Very unfortunate. She has pinned so much on this visit."

"I agree with you. I... I think I had too. Mater, I need to ask you, I have some concerns about her."

"In what way?"

"There's a certain volatility in her attitude particularly towards me. I know that she's reaching puberty and hormones can play their part but I worry that there may be more to it than that."

"Well, we have had an incident very recently that has made

me a little concerned." Mater said cautiously.

"What? Why has no one said anything?"

"We had to separate her and another girl who were physically assaulting each other. They were both put on report. When we investigated we found that the other girl had been calling you names and Bera had sought to defend you."

"What sort of names?"

"She said that you were a killer apparently. Bera didn't like this. Understandably. But I have to say that she became violent very quickly and would not desist until we literally dragged them apart. We suspected that this sort of taunting had been going on before, but you know what children are like. As soon as we started to divide them up they closed ranks and kept silence. Nothing if not capricious, they're now quite good friends."

"But that's awful. Poor Bera."

"Oh she's very robust. Strong-willed even. She has developed a tendency to shout rather then speak as you have probably seen. But I think the reason this visit was so important to her is that she craves a little normality. She wants an ordinary Dad not an absent one. If you'll forgive me, she perceives that your job separates you and therefore her."

"I can't do anything about what I do. Someone's got to keep the country secure."

She stared at Mater Ruth. Willing her to let her guard down. Show her true self.

Nothing. Instead she opened the note.

> My dear Bera. Please forgive me for having to leave without saying goodbye. My work colleagues really are in a desperate state and need me back there as soon as possible. I am as frustrated as you are. I didn't dare wait for you and Mummy to come back as I didn't know how long you'd be.
>
> It has been really wonderful to see you and share your special day. I hope the rest is great and I promise that I will be back very soon to visit you

again. I am so proud of you and love you with all my heart. Happy Birthday darling, your Daddy xxxx

"You must see these issues all the time, Mater. What can I do?"

Mater thought before answering.

"The children fall into different categories. Unlike some, Bera is curious about her future and seems to have a strong sense of her roots. She needs connections. Communication. Always be honest with her. Make sure that she's involved in your life as much as is possible given the obvious constraints. And, uhm, encourage the same from Mr Develin."

Rachel shook her head.

"I don't know if that's possible. You can't grow a seed without water."

"Some plants need very little."

"Please Mater I need you to keep me abreast of any developments here. I'll do anything as long as I know."

"Of course," she dipped her head before gliding away.

Upstairs Bera was faced down on her bed. The presents lay on the floor.

"Bera." She lay her hand on the small rigid upper back and with long steady sweeps, stroked her.

This seems so familiar. Eighth birthday and Dad had promised me he'd make it back from America I think. He didn't make it. I felt so let down but the only person I took it out on was Mum. Easy target.

As a friction heat began to grow on Rachel's palm she transferred her weight to the other hand and found herself giving Bera a much more deep massage.

Low moaning exhalations emitted.

Finally she stopped and waited. Her patience was rewarded when Bera sat up, red-faced and tousled but the furrow had disappeared from her brow.

"How d' you feel?"

She shrugged. "Not as cross I suppose. A bit hungry."

"Good sign. I'll go down and see if I can get something from the refresher."

"No Mummy, don't go." She pulled her mother's forearm around her.

"Mater Rebecca, you know the one with the funny lip, says that maths is the most pure subject because it has a natural order. That one thing has to follow another and that never changes."

"Yes," Rachel agreed cautiously.

"So when you have a child isn't that the next most important thing in your life. The next step? I mean more than anything else?"

How do I not condemn him here?

"This is a strange age we live in Bera. In some ways, an exciting new age. Things we used to count on don't apply anymore and we have to protect the society we have built."

"What does all that mean?" she waved her hand impatiently.

Yes. Quit the rhetoric woman.

She slid off the bed and kneeling, placed one hand on each of her daughter's legs.

Their eyes locked.

"The truth is Bera that from the moment you came into my life I was never the same. You made me new. It was the single most painful thing I ever had to do when I brought you here as a baby and then left you. I think about you every day and share things with you even though I know you can't hear. My most precious, most alive times are spent with you. When you hurt, so do I. You're my pride and joy and you will make a fine and brilliant young woman whom I hope to see every day when she graduates from here."

"I can't wait for that Mummy. It's so long away. I know Daddy doesn't feel the same."

Rachel started to reply but was interrupted.

"It's all right. I understand now."

She glanced over to the robot dog that stood near to her wardrobe.

"You're not saying much are you Ben? Oh that's right. You can't! Don't worry. I can use you as a doorstop."

She got up and picked up her unopened parcels.

Rachel's heart beat quickly as she opened the first. A bed cover she had sewn, painstakingly weaving in random words and messages culled from their time together. Scan-images of shells, wind-turbines, the sea, her own parents, trees, the Burgh where they lived, baby handprints and early family snaps all of which she had reproduced onto as many different sorts of fabric she could lay her hands on.

"I would have liked it to be a little more colourful, but there's a limited palate these days," she twittered, aware that Bera's still face said nothing.

"Did you do this all by yourself?" The child asked finally.

"Yes."

"When did you have the time?"

"Evenings. Whenever I could. I even took it on a few jobs. Got it out in the locomoter. Had a few looks I can tell you!"

"It's the most beautiful thing I've ever had. Nobody else will have anything like it. Thank you so much. So very much. I don't know what else to say."

"There's no need. I'm thrilled that you like it."

"Which shall I open next?"

"Your choice."

Relishing every layer she unwrapped the crystal heart pendant that Rachel had bought from a passing trader earlier that year.

They both noticed how her fingers trembled as she fastened it around Bera's slender neck. In the small mirror their eyes stared back at them. Merging from face to face.

"What I don't like about these days is that they end and everything goes flat again. I get scared that you won't come back. Sometimes I dream that you slip in and just whisk me away."

"Well. It would be an adventure that's for sure. You know that wherever I am, I'm always with you?"

"Yes. I think I do now. But will you call me more? Mater doesn't mind."

They switched off the lights and held each other. The distant bell sounded and sent a bolt through them.

Outside in the gloaming Rachel waved huge semaphoric flags, knowing that from her windowsill, Bera would just be able to make her out.

CHAPTER THIRTEEN

N

It would take several hours to get there. She contacted N and gave them an estimated time of arrival.

He'll be back now. In his element with a crisis to manage like a surgeon facing a long operation. All his acolytes fanning his furrowed but oh so capable brow. It's what defines him these days and I should just accept it. I haven't let myself look at those rotas yet.

She scanned her transor for the miniaturised rota files and found the morning of Andrew's death. Ben was listed as working from midnight to eight. She read the list several times knowing that David had been certain of the time of death.

Ben could have slipped out. Transmissions runs on a skeleton crew. But surely it would have been noticed. Did he command enough loyalty for someone to cover for him? What am I saying? I'm still thinking of reasons to condemn him.

Guilt prompted her to send him a text. *Ben. Hope all okay. Am travelling to N will contact you tomorrow. Rachel.*

She paused before sending and her fingers added... *love...*

Idly she looked at ASO's map and traced the journey with her finger-tip. Due east into H and then northwards through K, M and from O, west into N – on the borderland. For the first time, she might catch a glimpse of the legendary twenty feet high wall built by the Scottish, at Division. It could have been an ocean that separated them. There was little contact. They had been self-governing for years.

She had barely looked up from her wrist when another call came through. There was no visual.

"Fidelis Develin?"

"Yes"

"This is Celaeno, are you secure?"

She looked round the crowded carriage. "Not at present but I will switch to earpiece. One moment... Continue."

"Maia wanted me to communicate her thanks for your recent support. We understand that you have been assigned to the north. Which province?"

"You must realise that I can't tell you." She texted back.

"Indeed. However if you did find yourself in N we would be grateful for some water, crop and soil samples."

Their cheek was unbelievable.

"I have decided not to involve myself further."

"We understand and it is probably a wise decision. Nevertheless, having seen what you have seen, you will understand how urgent sample analysis is."

"Find someone else."

"You will be there. Imagine it were Josie asking."

Oh she was clever. Just one word, a call to arms.

"If I can help, which crops in particular?"

"Soya or Lupin. This is all we ask. We would not like you to endanger yourself or our cause in any other unilateral activity."

"I would not compromise my position. I only seek the truth."

"She is only concerned that you do not share Josie's need for an adventure. If you are successful please contact me and we will organise a meeting point on your return home. Will that be soon?"

"I do not know. I will be in touch."

"Then sail on Merope."

Letters grabbing each other's tails to fuse as words and harden into threats.

I know they saw me slipping into Marylebone. I'm glad of it. They'll realise I'm not theirs.

She slept.

At the interconnecting station between H and K, the compartments emptied. She found herself alone apart from one man who studied his portiscreen intently, only pausing to respond to his transor. He was handsome in a lupine way and sat on the seat edge as if he expected to leave imminently. She watched him for a while and then forced her gaze outside into the darkness.

At K, a clone boarded with the food trolley. She looked up into his widely set eyes, pale like a winter's day, the tell-tale pugnacious nose, the underdeveloped mouth and felt grateful. How would it feel to be so identifiable?

"Are the rolls fresh?"

"Always," he nodded sincerely.

"I will have two and soup and what's that?"

"Braised soy cutlets," he spoke slowly and with pride, remembering his training.

"Yes, thank you." She took the tray and ate purposefully, vaguely aware of her fellow traveller's eyes on her.

"Good soup?" The question threw her and she returned a more defensive "Yes!" than she had meant. Why did some people not know how to behave with Fidelis? He nodded slightly and went back to his screen.

N

Their arrival in N was earlier than she had thought but already it felt like the middle of the night. On the platform, she searched for Charlie Miller, her local Fidelis contact.

A lone figure waited. Fidelis certainly, it flouted convention and waited for her approach. She was unprepared for the squat balding man who saluted half-heartedly.

"Can't get the women up here," he said diffidently, reading her thoughts. She noticed his fraying uniform bore no rank and felt uncomfortable.

"I've brought a trolley."

Outside, refuse bounced through the cluttered streets. After the impeccably maintained southern Burghs where clones removed the first sign of dirt before it took a foothold, the deeply embedded grime spoke of neglect. He cast her a quick sidelong glance as he drove.

"So, do they always use you as their Reconnoitrer, then?"

"Quite often. Tell me whatever you want them to know or see."

She was deliberately handing him control so there would be no unnecessary preamble.

"We need new staff. There's no one coming in and most of us are in our fifties. There are problems now which even we experienced Fidelis don't know how to deal with."

"Such as?"

"Drugs. Mostly Hempole. Through street traders. We move them on, source the occasional dealer if we're lucky but it's getting beyond containment, especially as the new stuff seems to provoke a fairly psychotic reaction. The curfews are unenforceable. And what crawls out at night has to be seen to be believed. There's no provincial pride or morale, just a second class citizen mentality. The over-riding perception is that we're a disposable northern outpost for plant and fuel stations and agriculture, neither producing as much or as distinctively as other provinces. I've resisted asking for help but we need it." He glanced over at her.

"There is a new defiance we cannot afford to ignore."

He pulled the trolley up outside the Civic and they walked around the building to the Fidelis entrance. She took a few minutes to watch the centre. It was much smaller and this surprised her because all buildings and centres were built to a uniform specification. Then she realised her mistake. It was the congestion. No one was going anywhere despite the hour. They loitered, jostled, and overlapped; clutching bottles and cartons or in some cases each other. There was an urgency about this proximity, as if they would cease if they let go, became singular.

Overhead, the Asograph turned and the broadcast screen emitted faintly as Magnamater's face looked out and began her final evening address.

"Shut your trap!" bellowed a voice from the throng to her right, and a figure lurched out and hurled a soup carton at the screen – its contents splattered, eclipsing most of the Magnamater's features.

The act provoked a roar of approval.

"Shall we go in, Fidelis?"

His arm circled her shoulder and she followed stiffly, trying not to balk at the contact, the breaking of etiquette.

He showed her into a poorly-lit cubicle from where she could see three workers in the main office.

"Can I get you something?"

"Some soy milk please."

Silently he selected a small sealed container from the chiller which he inspected before handing it to her.

"Always check the seal."

They sat appraising each other.

"What do you think N needs, Fidelis Miller?"

He smacked his lips, his wide jaw opening like a bullfrog.

"Charlie, please. There's little enough time. A regeneration programme. We have been so consistently overlooked that this chaos was inevitable. It is not just Fidelis. There are less Restoration officers and Transmission experts per head than any other province. Fewer Fuel technologists who struggle to keep up with our compromised centres and have to maintain fused and cracked solar panels. The energy supplies are just generated and shipped out. In Magnamater's speech last week there was no mention of the special provisions for N that have long been promised. It is almost as if we are being deliberately ignored, sort of run down to prepare us for obsolescence. And the new mobility announcements have just prompted a flood of relocation applications. You should see my desk! And there's never a spare bed in Restoration. I've seen some things in the last five years…" He broke off.

"Such as?"

"I'll show you. Come on patrol with me tonight. Tomorrow I'll take you to Restoration and on to as many Burghs as you have the stamina for, just to prove that this situation is not isolated. Do you want to refresh yourself?"

"No. I am fine. However I would like to make lodging arrangements."

"My flat has a guest suite. You're welcome to stay there."

"Well, thank you. If that is convenient for you and your…"

"My wife's sick… in Restoration", he interrupted. "So we'll go across and you can leave your bags. Then we'll get started."

His flat was in the final row of Residential. From there she could see in the far distance an old, darkly sprawling metropolis.

"Newcastle," he read her thoughts. "You wouldn't believe how that place once burst with life." He spoke softly with a fondness reserved for old relatives, knowing he betrayed questionable nostalgia.

Rachel liked him for it.

"It had quite a reputation. You had to be tough but it was a real community… a lot of loyalty…"

He breathed deeply, as if reigning himself in.

"Are you ready?"

Outside, a bitter wind was rising.

"We'll trolley down to the fuel stations."

Once they had left the Burgh the track became increasingly uneven. She bumped along in her seat, her teeth rattling and her eyes narrowed, straining to catch a glimpse of their destination.

Eventually the fuel towers loomed, still shadows on the horizon. A strong sickly perfume drifted through the windowless trolley.

"What is that extraordinary smell?"

"Lupin crop. Field after field on either side. They say this new strain is an even better source of protein."

As the stations came into view, they slowed to a halt.

"We'll walk from here. I want you to see the state of the energy stations and the lack of maintenance to the network leading out to the Burgh. See the housing for these conduits – it's starting to crack. We shouldn't even be able to see the housing – it only needs re-aligning and refurbishing – it wouldn't happen if this were part of the main grid."

"I take it that this has been reported?"

"Of course! Engineering do their best but they are constantly being re-prioritised to the main grid."

She jotted a few notes into her transor.

Another rush of nausea overwhelmed her as the cloying odour rose to fill her sinuses. It was… unhealthy.

"Most of the recyclers are corroded and the fuel cell re-chargers are often faulty. Everything is sluggish. We have so many power cuts, the system never seems to work at full capacity, never gets flushed through."

"Power cuts are a fact of life."

"But not every night, Fidelis. Not every night. And lack of power has a huge knock on effect. Living in the half light is a half life – it distorts the perspective… makes madmen of us all."

As if timed for theatrical effect, the constant power thrum sighed and extinguished.

The Burgh fell into pitch blackness.

"Very impressive. Is that your party piece?"

"You overestimate me! I was just going to say that each night in Restoration, the staff struggle to compensate for absent technology. The relatives of those whose bodies need it's support grow more resentful and bitter."

He flicked on a torch. At the same time several fires were suddenly lit in the centre of the Burgh. It was a peculiar synchronicity – like an awakened pack wailing together.

"We'll go up into the centre slowly. When we get there keep close and hang onto your transor."

Quite touching really. What sort of protected life does he think that I've led? This is all very low key compared to what I'm used to. Then again that's exactly the sort of hierarchical thinking he's been complaining about.

"How long has it been like this?" she asked, following him along the uneven track.

"It's all been disintegrating slowly over a long time. Probably three years. I'd say the last six months have become more critical."

As they climbed up the final slope, they fell into step and she noted he drew closer to her. At home a curfew stilled the deserted burgh into silence and the people into an enforced hibernation. Yet ahead, an ungovernable noise grew.

"They've started early," he murmured. "There are six known tribes who congregate here. Mostly harmless posturing but occasionally it can get vicious."

In the corners, small groups of people gathered. Some beat upturned canisters while others chanted and clung to each other for balance. In the centre, large urns stood on battered trolleys manned by three figures. Notes were regularly exchanged for drink. Rachel looked at Charlie quizzically.

"It's a new currency system similar to the one we had before Division. They only use it for Hempole and Hempate. As I was telling you earlier, the new strain of Hemp has the psychoactive element, THC, reinvested but at an astonishingly potent level. Highly hallucinogenic. Scientists spent years isolating and then working it out of the genus and it took nothing to reintroduce it."

"How do you normally deal with this, Charlie?"

He shrugged. "What law enforcement officers have always done. We patrol, in a dignified yet vaguely menacing manner."

"Will we get a hostile response if we approach the traders?"

"Probably not."

The group gathered round the central stall parted slightly as they neared. But only just. She felt their body heat, smelled their sour breath. The tallest of the three traders saluted and bowed.

"Fidelis Miller. What a very pleasant change to see the whites of your eyes. And who do we have the honour of meeting here?" His clear eyes stared insolently.

A man used to control. A dealer is always a sober man.

"Senior Fidelis Develin," she responded coolly.

"And will you be joining our esteemed colleague permanently?"

"Possibly."

"Oh. Then what can I tempt you with, Senior Fidelis? A small tot to keep the night away? Or perhaps a little rush to make it shorter?"

His audience tittered.

"I have no currency."

"Have something on the stall. To remember me by."

"Very well. What do you recommend?"

He cast the briefest of glances towards Charlie before placing a small see-through wrap into her outstretched palm and decanting some hot liquid into a small sealed cup.

"Thank you. I'll save it until later."

"You've no shame, Rosh," a disembodied voice uttered from behind her.

"Do you make it all yourself or do your minions get their hands dirty, Rosh?" Rachel asked lightly.

"I have a trusted supplier. And that's as much as you'll get out of me. Isn't it Charlie?"

"We should move on," Charlie replied smoothly. He turned and pushed a path though them and she followed.

"You take good care now Fidelis and enjoy. You know where to find me now"

The table's not so deep. I could hit the jugular with one swift strike at the temple. Another time. I'm not up to dismantling the crowd tonight.

Smoke curled into the sky and clouded her vision. She remembered watching the fireworks pounding the night sky from her pushchair. Her parents had joined an organised march against something that ended in one of the big squares in central London. They had stopped so near to a fountain that drops of water spotted her face as she looked up. The sweet smell of congregation, of protest. Yet there was no danger because they were there together and she knew that she lived at the centre of their world. She wiped her wet cheeks briskly.

"The smoke is making my eyes stream," she whispered to Charlie.

Neither of them had noticed a youth tripping in their

direction. Too late, he grabbed both Rachel's shoulders.

"You have angels in your hair but your eyes are lidded boxes," he uttered.

She threw his arms back and jerked away. He scampered off, like a rodent, into the shadows. In the distance, elongated silhouettes danced to a rhythmic clapping and chanting. Paintings come to life on a cave wall.

They approached an enclave where several youths were whirling, shirtless, despite the cold. They became aware of their audience and one turned and lurched towards them, undoing his trousers.

"D'you want some of this pet?" he snarled tugging at himself.

It was not the shrivelled, almost non-existent genitalia that shocked her – but his pendulous breasts dangling redundantly in the half-light.

He was not alone. Others swarmed forward. This was an opportunity not to be wasted, to exhibit and luxuriate in their difference.

Charlie pulled her away, bellowing.

"All right lads. We've seen it all before. Pack it in!"

She stumbled back into a lone figure clapping gleefully and instinctively seized his hands to stop him from falling. It brought her close to his distorted face, his badly cleft palate and his milky, sightless eyes. He smiled, grateful for the contact unaware of her repulsion as she looked down onto his outsized, misshapen breasts.

"Shall we continue Fidelis Develin?" Charlie asked normally.

"Is it just the men?" she whispered huskily as they finally left the jeering behind them.

"There are reports of women with the beginnings of male parts but it's difficult to tell. People are starting to look very similar. As far as the drugs go – if it's out there, better that we can see it. We lose any modicum of control if it goes underground."

Later, they sat in Charlie's austere living room.

"Have you seen that sort of thing before on your travels?" he asked tentatively. She could hear how much he wanted his suspicions to be quashed, wanting to believe that N was not disintegrating alone. She had no comfort.

"No. I m glad to say I have not. What is your wife suffering from?"

"Duodenal cancer. Last stages."

"I am so sorry."

"Let me be frank, Fidelis."

"Rachel."

"I believe that if you could wipe us all out up here, you would. Instead, you are settling for guinea pigs – that's our lot. You don't need to deny it. Something is being stolen from us. My only hope is that we are able to retaliate whilst we are still able. I don't care either way – and if you've been sent to see how it's going or report back on dissent within the ranks, then report away and rot with the rest! I don't care. Just make something happen!"

"If I can, I will. Thank you for all your time. You… you have my deepest sympathy."

He sniffed, every pore enlarged with disillusion. Then he surprised her again by reaching out, taking her hand, upturning her palm and stroking it.

"Hmm. Do you feel drier than you used to? Do you remember your moist youth? Middle age slithers towards all of us in the long grass… you don't hear the rustle… but sometimes, when the breeze blows the right way, you get the faintest whiff, an intimation. And then suddenly you're my age and what you see ahead is so… disappointing."

He replaced her hand back on the arm of the chair and left.

Wearily she washed and climbed into the curiously high narrow bed.

I want to call Charlie back. Make him see that I'm not indifferent but he wouldn't believe me. Why do people feel that they can unburden themselves on me like this? It's always been so. The little go-between, unravelling all the family misunderstandings.

No room for any more drama, I had to keep detached, calm. And now the world thinks me cold. Perhaps everyone assumes the same about all professionals but that doesn't stop me from resenting it. So what if I've learned how to keep my face still. It doesn't mean I'm immune to rage or compassion. Only Ben and Josie had ever known what I was capable of and, ultimately, their own feelings were much more important to them. I know that now. Thank goodness for Bera.

I feel this aching loneliness pinning me to the mattress. Overwhelming. Why do I suddenly need to talk to Ben so badly? Because there's no one else? How do I judge what I've seen? Image after squalid sordid image. What have we people become to let this happen? The disgrace.

Offence pooled in her gut and shuddered through her. The bathroom was mercifully close but in the darkness she missed the toilet.

No matter. I'm getting used to my own bile. I will collect the samples and if it serves the Pleiades it also serves me. No more prevarication.

She began the following morning – the first water sample came from Charlie's bathroom. The second at the fountain in the Burgh centre, now strangely deserted after the chaos of the night before. The third from a communal laundry facility at the top of residential. She even persuaded a clerk to let her use his bathroom in a mid-row flat, close to the centre, claiming she was unwell. Later, in Restoration, Charlie escorted her through crowded corridors to one of the doctors.

"Doctor Jane Bannister. This is Fidelis Rachel Develin. She is here in response to our requests for additional support. She would like an evaluation of the health of the province."

"Aah. Of course. I am encouraged that some interest is finally being shown."

She had been expected. The selection and cadence of her words revealed it.

"Well as you have seen on your short walk to reach me, we cannot properly accommodate all the people who need care.

Ill-health is increasing dramatically. We used to have a low mortality rate here. Over the last five years it has risen by one hundred and fifty per cent. I talk regularly with other provinces, of course. The only one that comes close is O. Just next door. It cannot be a coincidence."

"Are the causes general or in particular areas?"

"Non-specific but extremely potent viruses – often leading to pulmonary failure and significantly compromised vital organ function. Infections set in and are unresponsive to broad-spectrum treatments. A range of untreatable cancers." She glanced awkwardly at Charlie.

"If you don't mind, I'll just pop over and see how she is this morning."

Jane watched him leave regretfully.

"It has been hard on him. They lost their son to the same thing two years ago. Knowing what the future holds makes it worse. Skin cancers are rife. In fact, let me show you a snap of our team here from four years ago."

She pointed to a group shot hanging on the clinic wall. Alongside hung another more recent shot.

"That was taken last week. Tell me what do you notice?"

Rachel examined the both carefully.

"Well, apart from the obvious march of time... I would say that... you all look very well... as if you had all been on a sunny holiday... tanned."

"Exactly." Jane nodded. "Without exception, the provincial complexion and skin tone is noticeably darker and ruddier... coarser. If I took you down to the mortuary, I could show you corpses whose cause of death was pulmonary failure but whose bodies are covered in black lesions and blisters. Then there are the significant eye problems which are not merely poor sight and normal presbyopic degeneration, but blindness. The area that is currently giving us the most concern is the profound hormonal imbalances. You will have seen the horrifying genital abnormality. Oestrogen levels are abnormally high. Male impotence is increasing yet conception levels are also up – usually followed by spontaneous miscarriage at the end of the first trimester. So we have the fallout from that to deal with. When they first started to occur, people were overjoyed – it was a sign of the tide turning here in N... now it's seen as some sort of punishment – a provincial scourge. Years of testing and all we know is that the water is likely to be the main problem – we just don't know how. I have sent constant reports and tissue samples down to the main research labs in A but they don't seem capable of anything more detailed than our own conclusions. The response is always a bland 'non-specific virus' statement. I have been hearing and repeating that for too many years. Whatever's going on, no one wants to discuss it. And..." She tailed off. "There are so many good people here, resigned to failure, to coping with the inevitable. You have heard of a collective consciousness? It is like war. Anarchy bubbles just below the surface in every walk of life. Can you not sense it? How are we to deal with the mutiny when it happens? Sooner or later it will not be safe to practise here anymore. I have to conduct a post-mortem. Would you like to accompany me?"

Rachel followed her silently down to the isolation annexe where she watched her swab the decaying flesh through the glass. Fleetingly, she saw her mother, flat on the slab, riddled with the voracious disease that had eaten her.

"Give me anything you can – I may know of an independent group who could test these. Unofficially, of course."

Jane paused momentarily and then continued her examination. "Thank you. I will have a collection ready for you by tonight. But don't leave it there. Make sure you take samples of everything. Air, water, crops."

"Yes. Tell me," Rachel lowered her voice unnecessarily, "do you know if the lupin fields are alarmed? I do not want to compromise Charlie by asking."

"Not as far as I'm aware, but they are patrolled – so you would have to be vigilant."

"Fine. Well thank you for your time. I..." she paused awkwardly, "I greatly admire your commitment."

The doctor straightened and stared over the corpse towards her.

"I would like to believe that you are sincere and that your concern will not abandon you on your return home to the sanitised south."

"I will speak to you personally with any results." They nodded briefly and Rachel processed slowly back to the foyer. Charlie stood in the corner, absently shifting his weight from foot to foot and staring at the floor. He did not notice her approach and started as she spoke.

"I think that I should see Burgh 2, Charlie."

"Of course. It's an exact copy but you are welcome. I'll take you wherever you want to go."

In the afternoon they shuttled on the locomoter. Occasionally she caught a glimpse of the grey sea, coated with mist that was being pulled inexorably towards the coastline.

"It gets to you after a while. No one could call it beautiful. It's too wild and mournful and the ground's little more than scrub at times. Aah. I used to love this stretch of sand. See how far it goes out. Bet you've never seen the remains of the old castle before. Perhaps in the end, it'll all just crumble into the sea and us with it. They say early Christianity started here. See, we've been doing martyrdom for centuries. Seems appropriate somehow."

She nodded, seeing clearly for the first time the archipelago of islands on the horizon. Out of the confusion of turbines she could distinguish the occasional red and white striped lighthouse and was surprised at her delight. History blinking.

He followed her gaze.

"It was a weekend treat. I used to take my lad out to see the puffins and the cormorants and the seals basking on the rocks. Once the wind farms became established, they all buggered off."

Burgh 2 was damp and the grey paint that coated every Asoan building peeled ragged. Inside, she found the Fidelis even more insular. They sat brooding over their desks, hunched and hollow-chested like ancient birds waiting for an easy rodent to pick off. The problems they had were similar but reported with a flatter acceptance.

"What would you like from the Administration?"

"Oh. Now why would I bother trawling through suggestions that you will diligently notate in your cutting edge transor package and submit to your superiors who will then tick the column marked 'checked' for another year?" drawled an officer from the corner.

"That's very cynical of you," she retorted, stung by the blatant indifference.

"I think that that Beatrice should stick to what she does best. Keeping us posted about crop yields and inter-Burghian sports leagues in those pretty broadcasts. We've been clamouring for extra resources for years. Frankly, sending a lone wolf out into the ghetto is worse than insulting. We're best left alone to manage as we see fit. Switch off the overhead lighting when you leave."

They all rose simultaneously and without saluting, emptied out of the office.

I've never experienced such contempt from fellow officers and if it's not just posturing then the decay's unstoppable.

"How extensive is the organised racketeering, Charlie?" she asked him over supper.

He sighed. "Is that the important issue? It's widespread. It has to be. These are times to survive in, nothing else. If you are asking for names, I won't supply them but I'm comfortable with my own position and that's all you'll get from me. I'm going to pop back to Restoration. Maybe I'll see you later."

She sat looking south out of his lounge, watching the racks of clouds scurrying a passage over the moor.

He is right of course. It's much more important to establish if there's anyone up here who could have actively been involved in environmental destabilisation. At Marylebone they made the research conference seem consultative but this manipulation's no recent thing. It's been going on for years. All a sham and if the scientists are lying to each other and successfully persuading the administration that their motives are altruistic, then how d' you stop them?

There I was a few short months ago. All wrapped up and swaddled in my own certainty. You bastards! What kind of fuel is disbelief? You've stolen my straight road.

CHAPTER FOURTEEN

Hunting

In theory, her status allowed her to conduct any investigations she saw fit, but anxious to avoid any unnecessary attention, she waited until dusk. She took several vials and a torch and made her way to the outlying fields where the bright blue and yellow bracts glowed vividly. There were no natural openings in the fencing, which stood much higher then she remembered. As she slid down into the dip, she checked the ground for sensors before climbing onto the metal rings. It was a higher climb than she had thought and, as she straddled the top wire and swung her legs over, she grazed the casing. Quickly, she catapulted forward onto the beds which were much more marshy than the impacted ground she had left. The erect spires matched her height and grew more and more dense as she made her way, sinking into the soil. Suddenly she saw flashing lights bouncing across the lurid flower heads and heard the sound of approaching voices. She must have triggered an alarm. She crouched, fingering earth into the waiting vial. Into another she tore fine shreds of leaves and into a third a section of root. For the final two samples she had to stand, snipping off sections of tightly packed buds from which she could later extract the pollen. Faintness and nausea overwhelmed her and, as a band of pain gripped her forehead, she was appalled to see two patrollers gazing straight at her.

Caught.

After weeks of waiting, it was almost a relief. But did it have to be here? So far from home?

A figure approached them, as slow as a lunar greeting. His distraction was enough. Fidelis. Charlie. She sank to her knees.

"Hello guys. You heard about this wild dog, have you? We've had several sightings now."

They snorted and ran their palms along their flanks, to release their tension, to bond in nonchalance.

"That'd be a real nimble piece, wouldn't it?"

The laughter was sceptical yet it lacked urgency.

"Creatures'll do anything to feed their faces. I'll let you know if we hear anything else. Rather deal with some feral than the stuff we get every night, up there. Just taking in a bit of fresh before the tribes start baying in the centre."

They nodded sympathetically. They did not want his life.

"See you again then, Fidelis."

Charlie waved heroically and walked on while they continued to scan the fields more casually. She stayed alert and cramped until she saw them return to the fuel station and then snaked a path northwards back to the Burgh.

All other sounds were drowned out by the regular brushing of shoulder on bract.

I could be gliding on snow, wading through water or jungle and I'd still feel this same disorientation.

When she finally reached the fence there were no detectable breaks or gates. She would have to risk setting off the alarms once more.

Suddenly he was in front of her.

"The sensors are on every other link from the third rung up. Place your first foot there when I say," he hissed through his bottom lip and looked around before nodding.

"Now!"

Once over she remained on her knees until he beckoned, and together they walked back.

"I don't need details. Just hoping that something good for N will come out of this."

It was only after she had raised her eyes and looked ahead for a few moments, that the whistling blood curdled to a screech in her ears and the ground tilted away from her. He grabbed her elbow reflexively.

"Are you all right?"

"I'm rather dizzy. Sorry. Unusual for me." She inhaled deeply trying to get on top of the breath.

"When d'you leave?"

"Not yet. There is something else you can do for me."

"Name it."

"Can you get me a list of mortalities for Burghs 1, 2 and 3 over the last nine months? Perhaps you could liase with Jane Bannister on this?"

"Of course. I'll have them for you tomorrow. For now, I would suggest that you stop."

He peered into her pale face as if she held all the answers and linking arms in a way that would have defied explanation to an onlooker, escorted her to his flat.

She lay, waiting for her heartbeat to stop thrumming in her chest. Every time she reached the edge and started to slip into sleep, the fall became a headlong topple and she had to haul herself back into her pulsing, overworked head where her eyelids remained resolutely open and determined to stare into the merciless darkness.

Bera. Conjure up the small bank of snapshots. Ben cried when she was born but I counted the digits and features. Ten. Two. Two. One. One. The wide toothless grin. Bowed, bent legs – I'd been convinced they would stay so – look at the gazelle now! The outsized hands – they had always been huge in comparison to the scrap of a torso, frighteningly frail. I remember wondering, was this shell really strong enough to grow? To make a real robust child? It was too small, too dependent. And if it didn't, then I would have failed. The sheen of her inky thick hair, falling in folds like a raven's wing before they hard pruned it into conformity. My own early fears of a squint dismissed as the wide bridge of Bera's nose became more defined. Her irises, brown like warm earth flecked with orange – like the sun was trying to get through. The drift of minutely tattooed freckles across her cheeks. The butterfly birthmark on her left shoulder... or was it her right? I should know. And now, changes fluttered down on her like rapidly falling leaves and I've missed most of her childhood whistling past like a high-speed locomoter.

Come back!

Her transor announced the rude morning.

Ben's face stared from the small screen.

"Morning. I... I just wanted to say hello. How is everything?"

She struggled to sit up.

"I... am not sure... only just awake." Her voice was small and hoarse. "How's the crisis?"

"Yes. Resolved thanks. How is the assignment?"

"Complicated. There are a lot of challenges for them here."

"Challenges everywhere though. Listen how were things with Bera when you left?"

Now we get down to it.

"Good. We had a lovely time."

"Ah," his face cleared. "That's a relief. It's just that I tried to contact her yesterday and didn't... didn't get to speak to her."

She stayed silent. *Do I tell him that there's been a shift? That she sees him more clearly now. Be honest with yourself. Isn't that what you think he deserves. More, what you want?*

"Will you be coming back soon?"

"I don't know Ben," she sighed. "I hope to. I am so tired but every day I realise how much there is to do."

He smiled briefly.

"You can't do it all yourself though, my darling. I know what's expected of you and that you want to be... the Fidelis star but you can't be all things to all people, can you?"

"Uhm, I think you're missing the point Ben. Don't project your own aspirations onto me. I don't need to shine but I have to do what's right, that's all."

"Very worthy, my love. No need to be so defensive though

– all I'm saying is… don't do anything you can avoid doing. Take care of yourself. I'll let you go."

Typical of him to rattle my cage so carelessly. But was it only his relationship with Bera he wanted to reaffirm? There was something else but I can't put my finger on it.

By mid-morning she was scrolling down a list of deaths without really knowing what she was looking for. She re-grouped the list into causes of death, ages and professions. There were twelve that stood alone and out of those she put aside seven who did not fit her profile.

Charlie returned at lunchtime and watched her silently as he prepared them some food.

"Any success?" he asked tentatively.

"Well," she replied slowly, "there are five whose post-mortem reports I would like to see."

Within an hour Jane Bannister had sent through the necessary discs over which she pored. *This could be a long and fruitless shot. Yet instinct's itching. I remember Mum painstakingly dividing strand after strand of hair, searching our scalps for the telltale white eggs while Georgia squirmed in horror.*

Deaths by strangulation, an explosion, a broken neck and two drownings. The strangulation was a domestic with a history of violence. The explosion happened at the local energy plant she had seen only yesterday. There had been a number of injuries but only one fatality. The broken neck belonged to Stephen Fellows, a forty-nine year old fuel engineer who had fallen down the cliffs at Hinge Point. These days everyone was an engineer. She watched the recorded interview with his wife Olive, who sat stiff-backed over the desk, slowly tearing the sodden tissue she clenched into tiny shreds as she talked. She kept her composure until she was asked about the suspicion of suicide.

"Well, that's just rubbish." She waved her hand angrily into the air. "He had everything to live for. Our son Stol was graduating this year from Abovo and had a position in Burgh 4. The family would be re-united. Stephen had just been promoted after re-training. He was a happy man. We were happy... I mean... We've lived here all our lives. He was a respected member of the Burgh. He knew Hinge Point like the back of his hand. It's nonsense..."

Rachel read the post-mortem. Multiple contusions over the whole body. Several fractures and broken vertebrae. Various head and skull injuries including cracked jaw, eye and ear damage and deep indentures in the temple close to the jugular vein. All consistent with the fall.

Charlie placed a salad on the table. "My wife knew Stephen Fellows. They worked at the same place. We went to the funeral. He was a popular man."

"Did you know any of the others?"

"Only their corpses. Although everyone had heard of the McKinleys. When a father and son are lost together at sea, it becomes a community thing. Sarah McKinley's gravely ill herself, I hear."

"Have they discovered what happened at the plant?"

"Faulty gas canister. Unsupervised trainee working in a confined roof void. Sent a fireball through one floor. Tragic. But you know, it won't be the last time. Stay in this job long enough and it's just a series of repeat patterns."

She nodded.

"I need to stretch my legs, Charlie. Have you time for a walk?"

The longer they walked the better she felt. Away from the claustrophobic breezeblocks and towards the pale blue which hung over the mauve hills and betrayed the hidden sea beneath.

"Over in that corner is Hinge Point." He pointed, breaking the silence, "Shall we continue?"

"Yes," her breath cut into the freezing air.

And as they followed the faint pathway that curved into the point, the breeze became a blast that buffeted against her back, almost forcing her onto her knees. Without his clutch at the folds of her uniform she would have fallen. Yet they both moved forward. So close to the ragged edge. She heard him hiss.

"It would be that easy!"

Cold twisted his features. He no longer looked like himself. "Pardon?"

"To slip over the top… If there was a gale up. They might never find you."

They could have been dancing. With huge effort she centred her body weight and tensed her legs, ready to spring out of his grasp.

"Lucky I've got you with me then Charlie," she grinned widely. "Lets get away from here!" She twisted suddenly and began to push against the wind, her head dipped but cocked slightly to the right so that she could see him on her heels.

Her exposed ears screamed with pain.

Could I sprint if I needed to?

The fast pace of their feet pounding the scrappy tufts, forced air from their lungs like a pair of moving bellows as they followed a steady slope downwards and out of the wind's direct path. The valley stretched before them like a reclining female and nestling into her belly sat the distinctive towers and tanks of the local de-salination plant.

"I'll bet you feel better now?" he said conversationally.

"Yes."

He jutted his chin forward. "That's where Brenda worked. She was so happy there. Except for the taste of salt everywhere. Even her hair. She'd give anything for that problem now. I've not been back since." His hands fell to his sides. "I should get on."

What was all that about? I'm getting too old for this. Losing it. Too neurotic.

"Thank you for indulging me Charlie," she said guiltily.

"Has it cleared the cobwebs a bit?"

She bit her lip, "I think I am on a wild chase going nowhere."

They parted in the centre.

She had intended to return to the flat but found herself sitting staring up at the idle Asograph and empty screen, noting that it's supports needed adjusting and watching the fine drizzle harden to heavier rain. All these structures and orders and systems. All they really needed was water. Water which was everywhere and yet still so precious and infinitely corruptible.

Repeat patterns…
Repeat patterns…
Repeat patterns…
Of course! I know who I've got to speak to!

The sanitisation process seemed to take longer than ever. She eventually found the chronic zone and asked for the duty doctor.

"She drifts in and out of consciousness. You will not have her attention for long."

The only adornment in her cubicle was a small scanimage of Charlie and her, at their uniting ceremony. They both had hair in those days.

"Brenda." She spoke softly.

She lay ravaged by illness and it's treatment but her eyes, when they opened, were remarkably clear.

"How are you?"

"Fed up. How are you? And who are you for that matter?"

"Rachel Develin."

"Don't you mean Senior-with-bells-on Fidelis Develin," she smiled wryly. Then fear crossed her face. "Is everything all right… with Charlie?"

"Oh yes. I am sorry. Everything is fine with Charlie. No, it is you wanted to see. I need your help."

"Really? I'm not fit for much these days you know."

"How's your memory?"

"Well you've got me on a good day. I'm awake. So?"

"Did you know Stephen Fellowes?"

"Aye."

"How?"

"I worked with him."

"Where?"

"At the Desalination Plant. I was a shift administrator. He was a senior engineer."

"What was he like?"

"He was a lovely man. Clever. Funny. Always had a smile. Kind too. Helped people out. Good to me when I was first diagnosed. He re-trained. Forget what in... Oh aye. Fuel."

"How long ago was that?"

She screwed her eyes up.

"I can't rightly remember. Maybe a year and a half ago. Just before I had to leave anyway."

"Did you know his successor?"

"Oh... I can see his face. Right sour specimen. No, it's gone."

"Stephen's death was a terrible accident."

"You're not kidding. We were all so shocked. He did like his hike though and he wouldn't be told. If you go up there you'll see how squally it can get."

"Was he popular with the rest of the staff?"

"Yes. You see he was one of us, never stuffy. A bit of a rebel." She winced. "I think that'll do for now love. Are you listening to my lad? He's been waiting a long time for someone to come."

"Yes. I really am. I hope I can help. You have been helpful. Thank you. And... all the very..."

"It's all right love. Difficult to know what to say, isn't it?" Rachel laid a hand on the thin arm lying across the sheet and on a whim, bent and kissed her.

She reached the door and Brenda murmured from the bed.

"Worthy... I think his name was Worthy."

Repeat Patterns.
Repeat Patterns.
Repeat Patterns

She still had David Poulter's transor number.

David. I need your help. Find attached a post-mortem report and a head scanimage. Have you seen injuries like this recently? This is highly confidential. I would be grateful for quick response. Rachel Develin

This time she approached the desalination plant by the official entrance. She knew that she would gain admittance but it was how to get an interview with him.

She took her first sample from the bathroom as she waited for him to come to the reception.

He had the yellowed etiolated look of a plant who had spent too long under false light searching for the sun. His irises were silvery pebbles buried underneath thick lenselets.

"Senior. Fidelis. Develin," he nasally over-punctuated each word. "What an honour. How can I be of assistance?"

This is a man un-used to women.

She set her tone to a breathless purr.

"Oh, Engineer Worthy. Thank you so very much for sparing the time to see me. Even without an appointment. You may know that there have been concerns about morale and instability in the workplace throughout the Northern provinces and so I have been sent to assess opinions at source, with the guidance of certain key personnel, before the Magnamater undertakes her proposed Northern Tour next year. It's more of a reconnoitre really. I do so feel that often desalination is overlooked as an area, in favour of the more glamorous Hydro-electric installations and Precipitation plants. Big is not always best. Do you not agree?"

"Indeed. An interesting. Area for someone of. Your rank to. Become involved. In." He blinked.

"It's a privilege. What is any structure without its people?"

"May I. Introduce you to. One of our. Senior Shift Administrators? Possibly. They would be. Better qualified to. Judge?"

"Yes. But I wanted to start with you. You have come so highly recommended. I am happy to join you on shift so I do not delay you."

There was a way of suggestion that ensured no argument. He was no match.

They had arrived at the main pre-processing tanks when she asked.

"With all the extra cuts and shut downs recently have you noticed much discontent? Or would your staff not feel comfortable expressing their views with you?"

"Oh I. Wouldn't say. That. I think we. Run a pretty. Happy Ship. Obviously there. Have had to. Be changes."

"I suppose everyone had to adjust after Stephen Fellowes death. It must have been hard to follow someone with such an established track record, with such style and... flair."

Don't overplay this.

"In. Deed. He was. And is. Sorely. Missed..."

"Is it really that salty?" Rachel interrupted conspiratorially. "I'm a bit seaphobic so I've never tried it." She pointed to the still tanks.

Amused, he leaned down and pulled a ladle of water up. She cupped her hands and slurped noisily.

"Ugh. That is more disgusting than I had thought."

"That's. Why we're. Here."

"I mean this is now one of the biggest plants in the north. You must have seen some developments over the years. What does the future hold?"

"Oh I. Think its. Potential is. Enormous. Although I. Transferred from. J just two. Years ago."

"Ah-hah. And tell me do you just extract the salt and then pipe the water on its way?"

"Yes we. Effectively do."

"And does it look exactly the same?" She asked archly.

"Well. You will see."

She managed a second desalinated tasting and, having left her in the administration suite, he returned to his own office, vaguely unhappy without really understanding why. As he combed the few strands of hair over to the far side of his balding pate, he reminded himself that he was not a man burdened with conscience or prone to stress. He could not know that she had detected his nervousness.

She conducted a less skittish second interview with a shift clerk who lamented Brenda Miller's absence but refused to comment on the morale or otherwise of the workplace.

"My supervisor will be in tomorrow. I'm sure she will be able to help you more thoroughly." She spoke clearly and deliberately as if they were not alone.

Finally Rachel left the plant, her shoulders tense with the suspicion that many eyes could see the three lots of samples sitting inside her jacket lining.

She took a chance that Olive Fellowes would be home by now as the administration shifts at Distribution conformed to daytime hours.

"Yes. Who is it?"

Rachel leaned into the vocom, "This is Senior Fidelis Develin. I would like a few words please."

The door slid back slowly revealing Olive's small figure hanging back in the shadows of a half-lit lobby.

"Yes?"

"May I come in?"

"No."

"I will not take up much of your time."

"I do not speak to Fidelis."

"I am sorry for that but I must insist. It is about your husband."

"I have nothing to say."

"Why?"

"There is nothing to say."

Rachel could not negotiate with this hidden voice suspended in the darkness, so she stepped forward. Immediately the woman lifted her left arm and grabbed a long-handled implement.

"Surely you would not attempt to use that?" Rachel soothed.

"Don't you believe it. I know what you people are capable of. I am not frightened."

"I only want to know why your husband re-trained?"

"Step back! Now!"

There aren't many who would show such steely defiance. It almost disguised her fear.

"I will. When you have answered my question. Why did your husband re-train?"

"When you have stepped back I will answer you."

"I do not conduct interviews like this."

"Then we will stand here in silence. I have nothing else to do."
Admirable.

"Neither have I! Mrs Fellowes, you are obviously very anxious. I wish I could understand why."

"I have learned to be careful."

"Brenda Miller has nothing but praise for Stephen. A people's man. Funny. Great to work with. Committed. She could not shed any light on your husband's career change."

"How is Brenda?" Olive asked more softly.

"When I saw her she was remarkably lucid and communicative but I gather the prognosis is poor."

Olive sighed, "Yes, I know."

"Olive? Are you all right?" A voice came from behind and involuntarily Rachel stepped backwards. The door slid shut immediately.

A neighbour scowled, "Can't you people keep away? She's been through enough!"

"I mean Mrs Fellowes no harm. I only had one thing to ask. An outstanding small detail. She seems so nervous." Rachel turned and spoke into the vocom, "Mrs Fellowes please tell me and I will leave immediately and not return."

She could hear the shallow breathing and then the hissed reply.

"He re-trained because I made him! Now go!"

She heard another door slide and knew the hall was empty. There seemed little point in staying.

Charlie's flat was dark and cold but she took advantage of his absence and organised her samples. By the time she had finished she had two sets that she insulated and stored separately. When she left tomorrow she would keep her set in her lining and carry the other to hand over to Celaeno. It was as she packed her small case that her transor sounded. There was no source caller listed but she recognised the reserved tone.

"Are you secure?"

"Yes. For now."

"How is N?"

"Fine. I am glad you contacted me. I have everything that you asked for and am planning to catch the nine o clock locomoter returning tomorrow. Will you collect them from me when I get back to B or earlier?"

"Earlier. Hand them to the same man who shared the carriage with you on your trip up to N. I believe he spoke to you. He is Asterope's brother and will join the locomoter at province I. He will find you and will remain on board for three stations. Obviously if there were any additional information you felt relevant from your time there, we would be very grateful to hear."

"I will give it some thought but you should know that it will be the last time. Too many conflicts for comfort."

I want them to believe me a war-torn dutiful officer, not a loose cannon firing into a lightless sky.

"I understand and I think that it is probably a wise decision. Do be assured that your efforts and contribution will probably have a great impact. Thank you."

Only moments elapsed before her transor bleeped once more and she was faced with Senior Fidelis Butcher's flat landscape. She clenched a fist knowing that it was perfectly possible for Fidelis to intercept and trace previous calls if they so wished.

"Good evening Fidelis Develin. I'm calling to find out how things are going up there?"

"Well, thank you Ma'am. I hope to return first thing tomorrow morning."

"Do you feel that you will have completed your appraisal by then?"

"Well yes!" Rachel was slightly surprised by the question.

Is she questioning my judgement?

"I think I have seen enough to draw some sound conclusions, yes Ma'am."

"Good. Well, I look forward to reading your report at the earliest opportunity then."

"Indeed."

"Excellent. Until tomorrow then." Like a thin soup, her

watery smile flitted briefly before her image faded.

I've got to be very careful how I report my experiences over the last few days. Make sure that l praise the professionalism of the local Fidelis and Restoration staff, outlining and legitimising all their areas of concern. Save the visuals I took in the square and the mortuary until the end. They'll blow everything else away. No one could ignore the extent of those mutations or dismiss the diseases, stealthily eating people away. A well kept secret until their bodies are laid bare on the cold slabs. I've seen death many times. But this is too much like the worst of times. Wasn't the carnage before Division enough? Hadn't most people lost someone? Maybe there'll be too much for the administration's sanitised palate and whatever I present will be watched and conveniently lost. The visuals showing the decay in the Burgh's infrastructure are pale in comparison but they do highlight the difference between North and South. My report to Maia will be more detailed and I'll give Charlie and Jane as future contacts. No one needs to know about my investigations into Stephen Fellowes. They're my business.

Once she'd finalised she made several secure copies then lay back in the chair and dozed.

No! I don't know enough.

Her eyelids forced themselves open like stubborn children who would not let her be. She accessed central records and read Stephen Fellowes' history. It gave no reason for his transfer from a job he had held for over twenty years. Carefully she scrolled through each entry. There was nothing inconsistent or irregular. His qualifications were extensive in the environmental sciences and he had attended all the appropriate conferences.

In some ways, I'm surprised that he had not advanced beyond a grade four. Remember that not everyone's ambitious. Oh just close the file. Forget it! But then why would the file have been updated again only two months ago? Perhaps an extra post forensic detail?

She typed in.

Request last entry.

No further information
Specify nature of last entry
No further information
No matter. There are ways round this. One of the advantages of my status.

She used her over-ride code.
Request details of last entry.
Information unavailable.
Request source of last entry.
Source unknown.
Request status of Stephen Fellowes. Of special interest?
Information unavailable
So something's being hidden and by an influential enough source to affect Fidelis coding. To push further might draw attention to my enquiry.

She heard the door slide and closed down the file. Charlie came in quietly.

"Evening."

The word slipped out of him in a long exhausted sigh.

"Can I get you a drink?" Rachel asked as he slumped into the chair and stared down at his interlocked hands.

"Just water."

She had taken to boiling and distilling her own since she had arrived and began to pour him a glass from her container.

"From the tap please!" he managed to shout.

So much of his crockery was chipped, grimy or without handles. The cupboards yawned and she ached for him knowing that he had already slipped into bachelor-hood without Brenda's loving eye to keep watch.

She placed the cup in front of him.

"I hear you've had a busy day."

"Yes."

"I wish you'd mentioned that you wanted to talk to Brenda. I mean I wouldn't, couldn't have stopped you, but… well it might have been… nice."

"Yes. You are quite right. I should have asked. It was a spontaneous thing."

"If you want my honest opinion I think that you're wasting your time on Fellowes."

"Yes," she agreed and laughed. "Maybe I have been doing this too long Charlie."

He should not be involved.

"Good sky tonight." He nodded outside, "Fancy a bit of fresh?"

They stood on the edge of the Burgh. A high wind forcing the occasional cloud to skate over the moon's surface.

"I am sorry about Brenda, Charlie."

"She had the most beautiful red mane of hair, you know. Wild. Of course, she wore it up for work but when she got home she'd take a couple of pins out and it would fall all over her shoulders and her tiny white ears like a big red wave and I'd cradle it. So heavy. Make me wonder how she could bear it scraped into a bun on top of her head. Always singing. Great pair of lungs."

"*… I remember the days, in sun, wind and rain, when a drover could roam the valleys,*

His herd was his own, to call with a song, and time enough to dally…"

His voice was sturdy until the last three words when she could hear his throat closing, swallowing the tune. She thought of the loves she had witnessed and slipping her arm through his, she laid her hand over his wet fingers and stroked.

In the morning he took her to the station early.

"Don't go through the official channels, it's a waste of time. If you have access to independent labs, use them… I know it would contravene… just about all the rules… but… I would like very much to know what's found. This is a secure transor number for which no one else has access. I understand you shouldn't but I'm asking anyway." He hesitated. "I wasn't always so hard bitten. The years coat you, layer after layer and remove you from your first skin. For the sake of the person I used to be and everything I held dear. I'll be waiting."

He glanced at her pale skin, noticed her clenched jaw

although he could not know how she struggled to remain standing and added, "You need to take care and get home."

They did not salute but shook hands in the old way. He waited and waved but she found herself looking down unable to respond.

CHAPTER FIFTEEN

Breaking

In the empty carriage she propped the bag discreetly against her seat. All she needed was patience. Outside, the landscape was often obscured by the rows of monstrous yew planted to obscure the fencing. Occasionally she glimpsed a ribbon of scarred landscape. Even after all this time, the surgery which had been performed at Division was only cosmetic and however they walled and contained their Burghs, the tangled jungle was only ever a spit away, somehow knowing its injuries and waiting for an opportunity to avenge and reclaim itself.

Damage. Everything was damaged. Is this all that was left to Bera?

She had been travelling for about an hour when her transor sounded.

"Rachel, it's David Poulter. Are you secure?"

"Yes, carry on."

"I've examined the post-mortem report you sent through and looked at the scans. At first there did not seem to be anything inconsistent with the fall and his injuries. But then I did as you asked and over-laid some comparisons with Andrew Kitchener. The two blows to the right temple are in exactly the same place, the same length and the same depth."

"Yes. I thought you might say that. Do you not think that it is too much of a coincidence?"

"Yes."

"Is it not more likely that these blows were inflicted by

hand? And more, do you think that it is possible that the same person may have been responsible for both?"

"It's possible," he offered cautiously. "And if true, it's likely that the assailant was left-handed. I'll do some calculations. See what I can surmise on height and weight and come back to you." He rang off.

At J it started to rain bad-tempered diagonals against the windows. It seemed that the loss of seasons grew worse each year.

Oh to have them back. The freezes, the thaws. Summer's dry heat, Winter's bright crispness, I miss them so much. Are we all going to wake up to the ultimate diluvian punishment one day? And who will I cling to then? The prospect of permanent separation from Bera and Ben actually hurts me so deeply, I feel like my lungs are punctured. I've spent so much time finding fault I forget that I still love him. She sent him a message.

Am on my way home. Hope to see you later. R xxx

Afterwards she asked herself why she had not heard the interconnecting door hiss.

At first she thought preposterously that the ceiling had collapsed. The blow was so hard and sudden that it shot her forwards onto all fours. The figure leaped through the air and was upon her before she had the time to turn. Her head was tightly clamped ready for the neck to be twisted. The floor swam in and out of focus. Her skull screamed with pain.

No. No. No. This was not how it would end.

Her left wrist was seized and her arm lifted upwards. But she resisted by forcing down and her assailant lost his grip. Immediately she heaved backwards and thrust her right fist at a trajectory she hoped would catch the side of his head. But the grip on her neck tightened. Her peripheral vision was starting to fade. The blood pounded at her temples and she knew it would have to be soon. She could not think of anything that she had been taught.

Tuck the elbows in! Jerk back hard!

She heard the grunt, felt the release and swung out of his grasp and round to face him.

Not so tall. My height. Combat uniform. Sealed black mesh hood

She swung out her right leg to kick the groin. He had the same idea. They matched and deflected each move until he ducked, turned and gained the space between them. Suddenly he was raining blows on either side of her jaw. She felt a bone crack in her face and reflexively returned the strikes.

As his fist worked her left side, his flattened hand started to side-jab her temples and she remembered and returned.

As she knew how.

As she had been trained.

The locomoter pulled into I.

Now it's over. Someone will board. The camera will be recording this. Just keep going.

A left kick to his centre sent him reeling. He recovered his balance and lunged forward.

This is to the death then.

Bolted against the window, she lifted her knees but felt one agonising blow at her temple.

That was the one.

She felt her legs buckle.

Such blessed weakness.

I can stop now.

Yet why is he falling?

He wants to gloat over me to the last.

What a circus! Two clowns down.

Oh. Maybe this other one knows what's going on.

When she came to, she found herself re-seated and Asterope's brother anxiously staring into her face.

"D'you mind if I sit here?" He grinned briefly, relief flooding his face. "Lucky I carry an epi-pen with me. I only came for a bag. Didn't think I was going to be entertained too!"

Too many teeth. Looks older close up. All those crows feet. My whole face feels frozen.

"Maia wants me to bring you to Olim. You're not in a fit state to travel alone and you need some work doing. I've cleaned you up as much as I dare."

He gestured gently to her face. She was not vain. She had never been vain but once again, the idea of damage made her cry.

"We're going to have to get rid of the body," he said reasonably. "I've taken a scanimage. Maia's doing an identity check. We should know anytime."

That seems sensible. But how did he die?

"We obviously can't leave her on the locomoter. There's a useful dumping point coming up at I and G's intersection before we'll have to re-route to Olim."

He knew what he was saying. Clearly. Who was he talking about though? She knew who she was and who he was and she recognised the word Maia. There was also obviously a body.

"Wan' shum help?" Talking was harder than she had expected.

"Can you just keep a look out?" he asked doubtfully.

She bleated a response and watched him straighten himself for action. In the corner of the carriage she saw a lone boot sitting erect and attached.

"I 'eed to shee... who?"

Painfully, with limbs splayed and unwilling, she clambered to her knees and crawled over to the prostrate body. He saw her approach and pulled off the hood with an executioner's flourish.

How features settle and slide into nothing as the personality departs. It had never been a face to feast on expression. Now it was a series of ideas. A drawing. And as shock and wild new speculation dawned on her, she realised what the definition of humanity really was. Who would mourn your passing? Who would miss the dull light in Senior Fidelis Butcher's eyes?

"I've checked the cameras... She must have already de-activated them. So nothing's recorded." His transor sounded.

"Yes. Really? You can't be serious." He glanced down at Rachel. "What should I do then?"

The words seem tunnels away. Must stay awake.
Some time elapsed and she found herself propped up alongside an opened emergency exit window.

"Just keep your hand on the button 'til I can get her through."

She stared at her wrist, uncomprehendingly and watched as he staggered forward with the body in his arms, hauled it over the ledge and shoved it out.

"Right," he gasped. "You can let go now."

The window slid obediently back up.

"Now put this cap on. We will get off in about five minutes and it's a little walk to the interchange. If I put my arm around you like this, can you manage?"

He seems like a decent man with a plan.
More than I have.
There is so much pain.

"Ben," she managed to say.

"It's Ray actually."

His grip around her middle hurt but the hurt kept her from swooning and somehow they reached the connecting loco. If anyone was around she did not notice.

In a corner seat she slipped into a timeless, muddy half-life.

Shadows and rustlings and murmurs and silence and red flints of pain darting across my inner eyelids and then more nothing.

It was a room she did not recognise. The walls were covered with clusters of small blue flowers. The air was cool, sweet and vaguely familiar.

My face feels so stiff.

From under the covers she lifted a heavy distant hand up to the light. The knuckles were enlarged and the two smallest fingers were strapped together.

She submitted to an urge to sneeze but unexpected searing pain forced a yowl to break the silence. Tentatively she touched her chin and moved up further, her heart lurching as she touched the bandages encasing the centre of her face.

What is this? Don't whimper.

A slight shift in the temperature gave Diana Fielding away. She stood still like a dark blue pillar.

"How do you feel, Rachel?"

"Hur. Wha' ha ha'?"

"Do you remember who attacked you?"

"es'. 'usher."

I didn't imagine it then. How can there be so much… occupation inside my skull? My tongue's far too swollen and stupid for it's space. Lolling about in there.

"You will have no explanation for your assailant. He will have come at you and beaten you senseless. You will never have seen Butcher. Officially she was supposed to have been working in province D. There was no reason for her presence on that particular route. Clearly it was her intention to dispose of you before you submitted your official report to her. But she will not be the only one. Others will follow."

"Ha' lon' haf' I bee' hi'?"

"Three days. Your nose has been re-set. There's a great deal of bruising. It's probably the most colourful you've looked in years. Other than that… you've been very lucky. I've spoken to Ben and promised that you would contact him as soon as you were able. In the meantime he has reported you as missing. I want you to stay and recoup. You will feel very battered for a while."

"'Sapples?" Rachel remembered.

"Yes. They're all intact and tests are currently being run." Diana replied.

There were things I didn't want her to know. But forgotten what they were. It doesn't matter here comes that wave again.

Sleep pulled her on an outgoing tide.

When she next surfaced, Diana was stroking her forehead in small slow drifts.

So long since anyone has been so tender.

"Rachel. I've brought you some chicken soup."

However manfully she tried to sit up, in the end, it was

easier to let Diana lift spoonfuls to her mouth. The first few gulps made her splutter but the taste made her persevere.

"My grandmother's recipe. I remember when I had scarlet fever as a child, she came by bus to our house and roasted lots of chickens and then boiled up the bones to make soup like this. But hers was better, much better. She'd slip in pulses, herbs and all manner of spontaneities which, when it came to the writing, she couldn't recall. She left her native Austria in the middle of the night with only the clothes she stood up in and my mother and uncle tucked in her skirts. And a head full of recipes that earned her a living here in a country that was not very interested in food. Wonder what they teach them in Abovo about cooking? It's probably all science now, eh?"

Rachel nodded.

"She had Sunday lunch with us almost every weekend of her life and afterwards we'd play cards or Monopoly or dominoes or dress up or play boules on the lawn in the summer. She had a wicked sense of humour. I found my teddy swinging from the light flex one time and if we stayed at her house she'd stand outside our door, rattle her false teeth and take them out if we begged long enough. She was the ultimate comfort zone. And I could draw her now if I had some paper to hand." Diana's large luminous eyes misted.

"Don't! Please don't!" Rachel pleaded, too late to stop two burning tears creep over the bulging edges of her bandages.

"I know what you are saying. And why. I have done my bit, Diana."

"I know. I know. Don't upset yourself. How does your face feel?"

"Less taut and more like my own."

"That's good. Perhaps you should contact Ben if you're feeling up to it. I've disconnected your transor. Use mine."

For the first time a transor felt unfamiliar in her hands. She started to wrap it around her wrist but stopped and held it freely while she contacted Ben.

His face appeared immediately, as if he had been waiting.

"Oh, Rachel... darling... oh. How are you feeling?"

She watched him struggling to conceal the shock.

"Better... I think. Stiff. I must look awful."

His bottom lip bulged, the lower part of his nose seemed to spread and his eyes disappeared back into his skull as all the recognisable contours of his miniaturised face collapsed, seeing worst fears made visible.

"It's good she's dead," he choked finally. "I would have had to kill her."

"What has Diana said?"

"I know everything."

What was everything, these days?

"I don't really know what state I am in, Ben. I suspect that it will be a few days before I can travel."

"Stay there. They will look after you. If you need me only contact me on this new secure line that I'm sending though now. There's a new round the clock broadcast they want me to start supervising as of today. Stay there. Out of the way. No independent travelling Rachel, promise me."

"Yes. Yes. Of course. Oh... What about Bera? Does she know?"

"No point in upsetting her unnecessarily. I'm sure she's fine. The less she knows the better."

"I'll contact her off visuals."

"I really would wait 'til you're feeling stronger but if it will make you feel better, I'll contact the Maters." His voice had slowed, his head tilted slightly in soothing appeasement. "Well, I must go. Rest now." He went awkwardly.

Yes. Rest. Drift. So easy. Time rippling like sand dunes, yawning, stretching and elongating. Awake and I can just make out the tree tips bending and yielding to the wind. I can't hold onto my thoughts, they just keep lifting from the bed covers like migrating birds. Stay. I wonder what's happened to all Bera's baby teeth. Surely someone's invented a way to recycle all that enamel. Or perhaps they could be threaded onto a string like worry beads and gifted to mothers. Diana always seems to be here, lifting me on and off bedpans, washing and changing me. I think I've said thank you. Someone came and removed the bandages.

A clear day and as she sat upright a stream of white blossom floated past the window. She called but Diana did not come and so she swung her legs over.

They're too pale and thin. Not like my legs at all.

As she stood, the bones in her feet cracked and realigned in protest, the soles strangely sensitive. She worked her way round the landing noticing the small painted beach scenes and collages of shells and netting lovingly crafted by small childish hands.

In the bathroom she had not thought to steel herself for the inevitable mirror. It took her breath away.

A swollen lunar landscape from which the features occasionally surfaced. A bloodshot, bruised mess. The twisted nose altered. Years of buried vanity broke loose and she crumpled over the sink thumping the enamel. "I want it back. Want it back!"

"It could have been worse, Rachel." Diana stood behind her.

"Just let me have my moment, can't you!" she sobbed.

"Look again and again and come to terms with it. It will take time but the bruising will fade. You have been lucky. I'm making lunch. Perhaps you'd like to join me downstairs."

Later as they sat at the kitchen table, Rachel was suddenly ravenous and although her jaw ached and her saliva glands shrieked from lack of use, she ate solidly.

I owe this woman a huge amount.

"I want to thank you for everything."

"It was the right thing to do. I felt responsible for you, after Josie." Diana smiled. "I can see your mother sitting there. You're very like her."

"Really?" *Keep it casual so she doesn't hear how hungry I still am to fill in the gaps, Grab back a few lost memories.*

"Did she come here much then?"

"No, in London. Marianne and your mother would often

be around especially as they were both married to men who travelled. I loved it. Made a change from my scientific crew and Gerald's politics. We always had a full house."

"Was… was she happy?" Rachel asked tentatively.

"She… had the capacity for happiness, I would say," Diana offered carefully.

"That's not what I asked."

"She was lonely," Diana replied finally. "Marriage to a man with wanderlust was very undermining. Every return would tilt the house off its normal axis and they would have to get used to each other again. Here she had stimulating company and it brought her out of herself. And she met a lot of influential people. Helped launch her career, really."

"Did she already have us?"

"Oh no, this was well before. Once she'd got the job in Whitehall and lost that self-doubt there was no stopping her. It was such an exciting time, so much stellar talent. She took it very hard when the Tories got back in. We all did. I don't think it was too long before your father changed his job and was around a lot more. I didn't see as much of her after that but I know that motherhood completed her. I remember that."

"Thank you."

She's no idea how much that means to me.

"I've been meaning to ask, have you had any results of the sample testing?"

"Still on-going but it has been established that the hormone levels are excessive and there are unknown modifying agents we've not seen anywhere else."

Now is the time I should tell her everything, finally reduce the distance between us. She's seen me at weakest and yet… I can't.

The silence grew.

"Edward Yorke was asking if he could visit."

"Oh. I'm not sure… oh why not."

In the garden she sat on a peeling wooden bench surrounded by glorious tall spires of pastel flowers and stared up at an azure blue sky. A beautiful blue winged insect drifted by so close it almost grazed her cheek and settled onto a stem nearby.

Enchantment.

She basked in the warm fresh air and did not hear his approach.

"Couldn't keep away from us then, Fidelis?"

She turned and saw him flinch.

"Hope you punched him back," he said gruffly.

"She came off lightly by comparison," Diana said as she joined them.

"By the way, one of your lot's arrived in the village. Been asking a lot of questions about your report, the line of enquiry you followed, your manner, who you talked to. She saw the Laceys this morning but just ignored me when I was in the garden."

"I didn't mention you in my report. But I did you Diana. I'm sorry."

"Then she will come and we will be ready," Diana replied robustly. "Would you like a drink Edward?"

"Got any beer?"

"Hardly. Tea or lemonade."

"Whatever you like." He grimaced at her departing back and sucked in his cheeks like a dotard. "Give the old boy a bit of soggy cake. Can't have too much excitement it might be bad for him!" He looked across at her.

"So, got any good jokes?"

She raised an eyebrow.

"Heard the one about the exhausted female mosquito who grew so sick of being taken unawares by her randy mate that one day she poked him in the tsetse, and said, "Gnats it. I'm fleaing. I've met a vegetarian called Birjit and we're off to join the circus."

She laughed. "Did you make that up?"

"Yep. Been doing a creative writing course. So when's your partner coming for you on his white charger then?"

She sighed.

"Not right now. He has other priorities. Why white charger?"

"Ah now that's the romantic in me. He should come." He stared down at the grass and lowered his voice, "If I were him I wouldn't let you out of my sight."

What on earth do I say?

"That's touching, Edward."

He shrugged and looked up defiantly.

"There. Said it now. Can't take it back. Ironic really. Lived with someone who needed to be told all the time and I couldn't. Thought it had to be rationed. Women want so much of you. Mother did. And of course William gave it to her with bells on. I, on the other hand, kept silent. She used to call me 'Clam'. Do you know he gave her a different coloured feather boa for her birthday for years. Right into her eighties. Completely ridiculous. Made her sneeze but I was sworn to secrecy. Suppose it was a sign of love. I didn't see it then."

"What is a boa?"

"A pointless feather frippery you wear round your neck. So what are these other priorities?"

"Work… but well… oh you don't want to know."

"You're right. I'm not that interested, just bored. So?"

She hesitated.

Josie was probably the last person I talked to about my relationship.

"A relatively sympathetic and incisive mind lurks underneath this finely honed but brutish exterior. If that helps, Fidelis."

"Rachel, please Edward." Her hands clapped together as if trying to prevent some truth from escaping and leaving her vulnerable.

He nodded encouragingly.

Finally she exhaled, "Ben and I haven't been communicating much recently."

"Well it's that horrible job of yours."

"No, perhaps in part. More importantly, I suspect that he's been having a relationship with someone… very close to me and…"

"Have you asked him?"

Diana reappeared.

"She's here. Both of you go upstairs to my room at the back. Left at the top of the stairs and stay there. If she decides to take matters into her own hands I'll have a coughing fit and you'll have to use your initiative."

"Lucky I'm here really," he hissed dryly as they quickly climbed the steps.

They sat and he noticed her curled hands clenching and unclenching.

I've spent years waiting in dark corners yet here I am twitching with tension while he seems so collected and still.

Each stared at the door for any slight movement.

I'm a storm-bringer. A Hyades.

They strained to hear the muffled voices creeping through the floorboards.

Suddenly, from the bedside table Diana's transor blared. Appalled they both shot forward. She reached it first and grabbing too swiftly, it shot out of her grasp like a recalcitrant amphibian and thumped onto the floor near his feet. Calmly, he lifted it and turned it off while she pressed her palms into her lips to stifle the heavy breathing.

Why didn't I turn it off?

They heard the voices grow and then the front door shut firmly.

She stood and centred her feet.

A firm tread on the top step.

"It's over," Diana said and came in.

Apart from the deep carmine bloom that crept up her neck, she appeared as composed as ever.

"That was challenging. If Senior Fidelis Gill Eales heard that noise she didn't show it. She said that she was investigating your disappearance following the murder of several Fidelis officers. She asked about the nature of your enquiries. Had you behaved professionally? Any surprising conduct given your position? Who had you spent time with? Where had you gone? I told her that I thought you were supremely professional. A real ice queen. A great credit to the service. I suggested she talk to the Laceys."

The three of them laughed, relieved.

"Look Rachel, I'm sorry," Diana began more soberly. "This changes things. It introduces a greater urgency to our plans. There are conversations I need to have that cannot be conducted in the usual way. I have to leave. I will arrange for protection for you but realistically he won't be here before tomorrow."

"Then I'll stay," Edward interrupted. Rachel lifted her hand up in protest. "Oh I know how magnificently invincible you are Fidelis but indulge me. I've got nothing better to do."

"With respect, Edward," Rachel began.

"Don't insult me woman! I'll slip out over the fencings and come back in an hour or so. Good luck." He nodded at them both and disappeared.

She watched Diana whirl round the house in a different time frame, collecting essentials that were eventually distilled to a small discreet hold-all at the foot of the stairs. A functional suit replaced her usual flowing robe.

"I'm sorry Rachel."

"No, I am the one who should be sorry."

"I have left you my transor. I have a spare. Remember the beach hut if you need it."

A fleeting hug before Diana walked resolutely down the avenue without a backward glance.

Seems like I've out-served my usefulness.

CHAPTER SIXTEEN

Olim

"I'm alone. She's left me. Fidelis Eales is down here sniffing," she told Ben who furiously rubbed his temple in response. "I don't know whether to stay or risk leaving."

"Shit! Well, I can't come. Not at the moment."

"I was not asking you to. Or perhaps I was. Anyway, I'm not in a fit state yet."

"Well there's your answer. Stay until you're stronger. Keep a low profile. Eales will be gone soon."

She tried not to notice his relief. "You may be right, carrying my head in a rucksack. It is lucky that I have Edward."

"Who?"

"I better go."

She signed off as he was frowning,

It's my own fault. I've been self-sufficient for too long. He's not capable of responding when I do really need him.

Systematically she checked every window and locked up rooms where she could, moving the furniture back to the walls and clearing the surfaces. She gathered together all the most lethal kitchen implements and kept only the smallest and sharpest knife on her. She packed all her own belongings, recharged her stunner and re-filled a sedpen. Exhaustion and breathlessness overcame her.

What am I thinking? I can barely eat, let alone fight.

As boredom set in, she began to rifle unashamedly through Diana's cupboards.

The contents were modest and unremarkable. Hand embroidered linen. Delicate china tea-sets. Candles, tablemats and an old pack of cards. A microscope with accompanying glass platelets and dishes. Various laboratory tools and an empty index card box. The wardrobes contained nothing but clothes and rows of tired shoes. In the hall she found four old scanimage albums and as she leafed through her heart leaped.

Epochs captured. The decades frozen. Old London's changing faces. The fashions, cuts, fabrics and hemlines identifying the different stages of Diana's life. Those high cheekbones lifting a younger yet still recognisable woman towering above her peers. Student plays and youthful gatherings on grassy quadrangles at dusk. Now, the working woman and her colleagues, outside important looking buildings at conferences, confident in their contributions.

She flipped over on to stills of the familiar coastline. Ball games on the beach. A young golden-haired tot clasping a painted tin bucket and offering the lens a large white shell.

Josie.

Her image swam. Lost in a cloud of tears.

And on to marches and rallies. Gerald outside Parliament making speeches, his arm outstretched. The victory podium at the 2005 election. More intimate shots of evening dinner parties. *I feel I should recognise these people.*

And then. A domestic scene. Three women at a table. Diana, older and more sophisticated. Josie's mother, Marianne roaring with laughter. At the centre, of course at the centre, her mother made real and glorious. Her hair falling in silky black ribbons about her shoulders. Her blue eyes glowing and her dazzling, impossibly wide smile leaping out of the frame making everything around her pale and uninteresting.

"Oh Mum. My beautiful Mum," she whispered into the silence. There was none of the dreaded unhappiness and introspection here. She flipped the leaf hardly wanting to lose the image.

Yet this time it was not at those perfect features that she gazed, but at the arm curled tightly around her mother's shoulders, at the hand covering hers so intimately on the table and the face nestling in close to her long white neck.

It was a face she recognised.

A face she had watched die.

A searing heat seemed to force her fingers from the page. Her head jerked backwards involuntarily.

Your mother would have been disappointed...

You have made monsters of us all and your actions will revisit you in the cold dispassionate gaze in your child's eyes as she hurries away from you, embarrassed by your outstretched hands. By the love that helplessly drips from us all, our life blood and we would spend our last drop for a moment of recognition...

She took out the scanimage and slammed the album shut.

I have to keep this. Marchant and Mum? It's dated just the year before I was born. Where was Dad? No, No, No! Don't let me have to carry any more guilt.

Painfully she made her way to the bathroom, stripped and washed herself from head to foot.

Then slowly she worked through the exercise programme she had relied on since her training. *Focus on the breath. The in and the out. The flex and release of each muscle. Reign in the renegade thought. The body is dormant and waiting for my higher self. And I will always drive the direction of energies flowing through me.*

She re-dressed in her old uniform. It did not matter that it was slightly torn in places. It temporarily reformed the clutter that she had become into one encased thing.

She heard her name from downstairs.

He was laying the table with meats, cheeses and inordinately large misshapen loaves of bread. A brown glass bottle sat in the middle. An old fashioned pistol and a curved ornamental machete sat incongruously in their midst.

"The liquor's for me Fidelis... I need it to keep me from getting anxious."

"And these?" She pointed.

"I always say you can never have too much weaponry."

"Edward. Thank you"

"Oh don't give it a second thought. I've cancelled all my important meetings. How are you doing?"

"I'm a bit desperate actually."

"Have you talked to Bob?"

"Ben."

"Oh yes. Well?"

"Yes," she said dismissively. "He was… consistent."

"Like I said to you earlier, Have you asked him about… well you know… the infidelity thing?"

"No."

"Sooner or later you'll have to deal with it. Maybe now's not the right time but… Is it a good marriage, sorry, what d'you call it these days? Unification?"

"It was… once… I still love him but is that enough?"

"You have to know. Honesty's more important than anything else."

"I'm not sure he's capable. But then, he could say the same thing.

He sighed. "I have an incredibly strong sense of déjà vu."

"Sorry?"

"I've heard this before. My brother. When the big 'O' finally got to where she wanted to be she just cut him off, denied him access, literally. So he got to witness her magnamatership and all of her short-lived sexual conquests at close quarters without actually being involved. She needed to keep him close you see. He knew too much. And when he finally resorted he was already desperately ill and riddled with guilt. But he could never say anything to her because it would hurt her feelings you see. And they had to be protected at all costs. He did things to himself that no one should ever witness."

"I'm amazed that you can bear to have someone like me near you. I mean I represent her heritage."

"Do you? Really? No. I hated her more than any other creature alive but it was her hypocrisy that I despised the most.

All that altruism. The greater good. Everything for the children. You've never met a more selfish, detached, unmaternal individual. She went on too long. A disease we just allowed to happen despite what history had shown us. This is all just the resulting carbuncles. I'll lock up. Then I need a drink."

"I need the toilet."

As she came downstairs she stopped by the landing window to hear the frantic screeching of nocturnal wildlife battling for garden supremacy under the vivid moon.

So Curious. All that panic's gone. I just feel fatalistic.

It stayed with her like anaesthetic until she walked into the darkened living room and the first blow against her left temple sent her reeling into the wall. She rebounded and found herself lying on her back, the creature's hand around her neck and other blows raining down onto her head.

And this is it. Finally. Get it finished and I can stop... being.

The blood sang in her ears

Do you have to grunt so? I can submit. Can you not assassinate quietly?

Every cell's shrieking. The crunch and crack of protest inside my skull won't let me pass out.

I am yours. Now let me go.

It was her legs that arched reflexively to position her knees and jerk into the back of the thing that mounted her. A shot blasted into the air and the form hung suspended before crumpling like a deflated puppet over her.

I refuse to be covered. If I have to die at least let me see the ceiling before I go.

But there was no pain and eventually she forced herself to sit up and roll the corpse onto the floor beside her. She hauled herself backwards and touched another.

He lay where he had crawled. The floor was wet and in the half-light she just heard the final stertorous gasps of someone who had sacrificed.

"Oh Edward. Please no."

She stumbled forward to switch on the light and under the electricity's harsh glare she saw the multiple stab wounds covering his torso, understood his last defiant moments. She couched beside him and stroked his lined, damp forehead, whispering into his ear.

"Edward. I'm so sorry. Thank you. I will always... truly, value, your friendship."

There were words that sounded like... "Big deal."

"Do you always have to have the last word?" she sobbed. "Who else is going to mourn for you... you annoying, irascible man? Why did you have to come back and add yourself to my conscience? Thank you."

Unsung Edward.

Through the years she had seen so much death and yet never spoken to a higher authority.

"Let him go to heaven." She cleaned his face and kissed his cheek.

She checked the other's pulse. Looked into its face. Cryo, robot, clone... like she used to be. Just another job.

The face in the bathroom mirror was no longer her own. She wiped the blood away but one eye was already closed. The nose looked re-broken. Peculiarly, she felt no pain.

In another time she would have fled and caught the next locomoter but she could not neglect Edward so and when she knelt beside him once more, she found herself screaming.

"I will not have this!!! There will be no more."

She took two wrong turns before she finally found the house. If Harry Lacey was shocked he recovered himself quickly and immediately became practical. A doctor would have to sign the death certificate. Edward would need to be buried.

"What to do with the Fidelis is a slightly more complex question."

Jennifer was insistent.

"We will have to report it. Otherwise there will be a never-ending stream of them crawling all over the village. But you will need to leave first... Fidelis..."

"Rachel, please. Whatever happens I will be incriminated and it is better to have it so. I would just like to have shielded Diana from further enquiries."

"Diana can look after herself!" Jennifer returned. "Let me look at that eye."

"Thank you. It's starting to tighten again."

As Jennifer tended her face she said gently, "You have been through a great deal since I last saw you, Rachel."

"I am not what I was. Did you know my mother?"

"Yes."

From inside her breast pocket she pulled the scanimage and watched for a reaction.

Jennifer merely smiled. "They were good times. Wasn't everyone beautiful back then?"

"I was there when he died, Jennifer. I… need to… know if they were…"

Jennifer interrupted, "I'm sure your mother would have been pleased. Now this cream really helps to reduce swelling and promote healing. I'll give you some to take with you. Have you decided where you will go?"

Rachel realised there would be no revelations from Jennifer and replied slowly, "Not ultimately but to start with, I need to go to the Learning Centre in Norwich. I want to record something. Do you know anyone there who might be able to help me?"

CHAPTER SEVENTEEN

The Learning Centre

So it was that early the following morning she found herself sitting in a sealed recording booth at the Learning Centre. Harry knew a recording technician who had shown her the equipment. Mercifully it was fairly old and straightforward.

She adjusted the frame and watched her misshapen self speak.

"My name is Rachel Develin. I have served as a Senior Fidelis officer for sixteen years. Until today. Last night I was attacked by Senior Fidelis Eales and last week by my immediate superior Senior Fidelis Butcher. Their intentions were to kill me. Both died in the attempt although third parties were responsible for their deaths.

I believe that Fidelis Butcher was also responsible for the deaths of my colleague and friend Senior Fidelis Josie Kitchener and her husband Andrew.

You will ask why the officers employed to protect and maintain security in ASO are trying to destroy me. It is because I have been investigating a series of cover-ups. Lies that have been told by the Magnamatership to you, the people, since Division. I have been into the supposedly contaminated Old London area. There I discovered a network of established research facilities in Marylebone to which people travel and work every day. Just like old times. I will show you the recorded evidence. You will hear scientists talking of their intentions to continue to control our environments by introducing more chemicals, pollutants and hormones into our water supply. These substances cause infertility, deformity, abnormality and disease. They openly state that it has been happening for years with the Magnamater's consent. I travelled to N province and saw there the appalling results of advanced contamination. I will show you the evidence. And water and soil samples confirm this.

Listen too for the extraordinary and terrible revelation that Magnamater Olivia herself coordinated the terrorist activity responsible for the devastation inflicted on Britain. This gave her the opportunity to supposedly rescue us and introduce her new social experiment. ASO.

I have believed in our system of Division all of my working life. But if our leadership is corrupt and if we the people are viewed as disposable social experiments, I can no longer support the system. I may not survive, but it is vital that you all know what I know and question your leaders and your lives in the same way."

She edited in the Marylebone footage and the visuals from N.

"Can I send this recording to a personal transor and could they then transfer it onto a Transmissions format for broadcasting?" She asked the balding man who had watched her curiously from outside the booth.

"Yes, technically."

"And is it possible for you to access Surisian Transmissions from here?"

"Technically." He added as an afterthought remembering her position. "Although obviously it's not allowed."

"What is your name?"

"Anthony Capwood."

"I need your help Anthony. Show me how to send it as a secure file to these transor numbers."

CHARLIE. You will receive a security file containing a recording I have just made. As you can see events have moved on and will continue to do so. If you have not heard from me in five days make sure that this is broadcast throughout N and further if you can get access. Do not trust any other Fidelis. Others will come looking for me.

BEN. You will receive a security file containing a recording I have just made. This is for your eyes only. I intend to broadcast it myself unless you can help. Rachel.

"I need some fresh air. Is there anywhere pleasant to walk on the campus, Anthony?"

"Sure. There's the lake. It's cool and quiet there."

She left the building by the rear entrance, seeing the oasis of water ahead, framed by stiff clumps of rushes and weeping willows. It had recently burst its banks so her feet sank into the marshy grass and, by the time she reached the bank, her lower legs were soaking. In the still, balmy air she found herself shaking uncontrollably and sunk to her knees. Her face stung as rivulets of sweat found their way into the open cuts. New pain from old wounds, subtle shifting of organ encased in bone.

The fever grew even as she sat, burning through her like a bushfire. Her body convulsed wildly.

Just stay here.

She lay on the ground, cooling her cheek in the wet grass and stared out onto the flat glassy expanse. Fragments of old lost legends came back to her.

Something should spirit me away now.

Nothing came.

Her transor sounded. She turned it to face her as the text came through from Ben.

Received. Implore you hold fire and position. I am being watched. Kate will come to you as soon as she can possibly as early as tomorrow... Ben.

Kate? Why Kate? But Kate was good and at least she will not leave me here dissolving back into the earth. Although there is no future. At best I'll just be a fugitive, an embarrassment to Ben and Bera, a void in conversation. What can any of this do?

"Please help me," she asked the indifferent water.

But the only visitor was a sweet melody from an old lullaby that she crooned until exhaustion overcame her.

Anthony Capwood did not enjoy dilemmas. As irritation grew it made his ulcer yowl with acid and he had left his tablets at home. What was he supposed to do? She was a Fidelis after all. Should he lock up as he was required to at the end of the day or wait for her return? He had the impression she would be back soon but she had been hours.

"Typical of that lot. Just typical! Well she'll have to come back tomorrow." He secured the facility and stomped through the complex. As he turned the final corner he had a flashback to her swollen face and stopped in his tracks. What if? He found his pace quickening, despite his bad knee, as he descended onto the grounds leading to the lake. He scanned the area but saw no one walking. If she were on the other side he wouldn't see her anyway. But he kept on until he reached the water's edge. Nothing. He gazed out and watched the swarms of mosquitoes hovering over the surface. A low sullen sun skulked on the horizon forcing him to glance a little further round the bank.

It was along time since his heart had lurched so.

"It's practically a bloody bog," he panted as his feet disappeared, slowing his progress.

She was so still.

"Don't you dare be dead," he told her as he felt for a pulse. He exhaled with relief after he had had felt the regular tap. "Now come along. Stop all this. You can't stay here. You... Fidelis," he added as an afterthought and shook her shoulder sharply.

"Yes," Rachel whispered faintly, stirring.

"Take it slowly." He crouched down and stared into her eyes. Glassy and unfocused. What now? He was no good at this sort of thing. Sarah was better.

"Can you help me up?" she asked doubtfully.

They made an incongruous pair as towering above she leaned heavily on him, while he encircled her waist and painfully they tottered back to the main annexe.

"I think she needs looking at," he told the Buildings Manager as if she were an animal.

"I'll call medical." The guard returned. They sat her down and shifted feet miserably, exchanging an occasional look.

A female doctor finally arrived pushing a wheel chair.

"All right. Let's get you down to the centre."

I'll do whatever you want. For now. Your voice is so far away. Here are my arms, legs, eyes, ears. This is my mouth. What d' you want me to swallow? Yes, you re-set my nose. I won't feel a thing. It's just a sickening sound that's all.

"You need to sleep now," were the final words she heard before sliding into oblivion.

She woke to the soft murmur of voices using words like 'responsibility', 'authority', 'condition' and 'linkage' and felt surprisingly clear headed.

The doctor came in. "How are you feeling?"

"Everything still hurts but I feel better in myself. Less foggy."

"Good. I'd like to run a few more tests today but you should eat first."

Her body was a map of bruising. Every twist an agony yet she worked her way through a large plateful of fresh bread and eggs. Afterwards she sat in a courtyard and watched plump orange fish drift around a small pool. The sun glinted through the tops of some ornamental trees in the corner.

Home. Years of accumulation. Room after familiar room. Open the wardrobes and run my hands over the uniforms with their high white collars, those plain dark pull-on boots. In Ben's area a colour change to brown to denote Transmissions. Rows of fawn smocking tops. Dreary. There was nothing advanced or superior about sludge. Ancient sophisticated cultures enjoyed colour. With all this technology there ought to be room for a wider palette. But that would be frivolous – twentieth century. Was that it? In twenty years time, the same? Perhaps a few more tones? There are other cupboards but I can't remember what's in them. Nothing important. Nothing I can't live without.

Well, there was Georgia. I feel terrible that I haven't spoken to her for so long. Ben won't have thought to. Maybe I'll send a message through Kate. Even if I were there I wouldn't let myself visit. What if I were carrying something? To my knowledge I've been exposed to at least two very differently polluted environments in the last few weeks. I don't want the responsibility for passing on an infection. All action has a legacy. A future ribbed with uncertainty and risk. I have to speak to Bera. Now!

She knew the connection code for Ark 60 by heart. Switched the transor to audio only.

"Good morning. This is Fidelis Develin speaking. Could I speak to Mater Ruth please."

"Good morning Fidelis."

There was hesitancy in the Mater's voice from the first syllable.

"Yes Mater. I'm sorry to call so early but I haven't spoken to Bera since her birthday. I would love to just have a quick chat. Make sure she's all right."

I'm pleading. Stop it.

"Well... uhm... Fidelis. I'm sure she would have loved to have spoken but she is, as you're probably aware, with her father on a day trip."

"Really? Where?"

"Oh just locally. He wanted to spend a little more time with her to make up for her birthday I think."

"Will they be back soon?"

"This afternoon. It was only a day pass. Perhaps you could contact us again later. Just after Joy-time?"

"Can I ask when did he make this request?"

"Oh, let me think. The day after her birthday, I'm fairly sure."

"Well... I'll contact you again later. I'm sure she'll have had a lovely time."

Now why are all my alarm bells ringing? It's perfectly reasonable that he might want to make things up with her. It's just not like him. And why would he have not mentioned it to me earlier? Oh stop. You're getting paranoid woman.

A transor sounded from inside and moments later a medical assistant stepped out.

"I think this must be yours."

"Oh, thank you."

A short message.

Have heard of recent events. Am concerned for your safety. Please contact me immediately. Diana.

She considered her response but before she had settled on an approach her transor sounded again.

"Yes," she answered

"Thank goodness Rachel. It's Diana. How are you?"

"All right. Considering. Better than poor Edward. I do not mind for myself any more but I am desperate about him."

"Yes. I'm so very sorry too. It must have been absolutely terrifying. Were you very hurt?"

"My nose was re-broken, more cuts and bruises to match the last lot but I'm not complaining. Yesterday was bad but actually I feel more myself today. More robust. I want to spend a little time deciding what I'm going to do next."

"Where are you at the moment?"

"At the Learning Centre."

"Good. You remember Ray, Asterope's brother? I will arrange for him to come there. He will stay with you for the foreseeable future. Then we can arrange for you to have a safe house for a while in province C or D. I've got contacts there. Or staying in Olim is another option. You just need to keep a low profile and hope that the heat dies down."

How breathtakingly arrogant! She is still trying to pull my strings!

"The heat will never die down, Diana. I think I have to face that and be more pro-active."

"Well you must remember that there are others involved in your life. I mean you would not want to jeopardise Ben's position or safety and of course Bera… and Georgia. They all will suffer if the Fidelis decide to make a scapegoat of you. And as you know, there are other factors to consider. You must not allow any personal crusade to… cloud your judgement. I blame myself entirely for involving you in the first place but I cannot tolerate the prospect of… interference."

"You sound a little like the Magnamater, Diana," Rachel spoke coolly but inside she was seething. "Are your plans so easily sabotaged by one impaired freewheeler like me?"

"This is a delicate time Rachel… a crucial time. The next few weeks will hopefully see significant changes. I will do my best to protect you but you have to be sensible."

"I've spent a lifetime doing that. I have to go Diana."

There was cold steel in Diana's voice, a determination to control at all costs. How far would she go? It won't end here.

So… the havens are growing fewer.

"I would really like to walk over to the information centre," she told the desk clerk. "I will not be gone long."

"I'm not sure, Fidelis. Doctor has to authorise and she's in a meeting."

"I will take responsibility for my decision. If I feel unwell, I will return immediately."

"If you are certain take a bleeper and contact me if there's a problem."

"Thank you. I will be back in half an hour."

She sat at the desk.

In another life I'd like to have studied longer. This place already feels… comfortable. There's a file I must re-read while I can. I want to go back further. I didn't notice how handsome Peter Marchant had been, how every frame revealed his huge open personality. A gleaming toothy smile, his arms and hands held out as if to pull life into his grasp and eat it.

Singing at a party conference. Dancing at a street party in his constituency in old Blackpool. I think it was partly submerged after a flood that altered the coastline. Much younger and marching on a rally. Holding a banner that said 'Give our mines a chance!'

Watching an open-air concert and sitting on steps with someone called Bowie who played a guitar.

Flashes of someone who put himself out there and stood resolutely in your field of vision.

There's no sign of Mum. This was a public life. I can understand her now. I'm sure if I'd been there back then, I'd have found him irresistible. And I've never said that about anybody. To think of him sitting in front of me, dying yet still defiant. To lose him so. What do you do with remorse? He was right. Mum would have been disappointed.

A message came through on her transor.

Rachel. I will be with you shortly. Kate.

Another message followed almost immediately.

Charlie Miller.

She returned the call.

His eyes were red, his voice soaked in misery.

"Brenda's gone. Last night. You look terrible."

"Oh Charlie. I am so very sorry. She was a fine person."

"Yes." He dipped his head and grimaced.

"Charlie, we do not have to do this now."

"Oh no. I want to. It's too important. I got the file. What an indictment. It's almost too painful to watch. I've set things up in Transmissions. Jane Bannister's brother works there. He knows how to get it into the main network and can loop it. Only problem will be if the main network's turned off in response. But he's looking into a back-up. Obviously he doesn't know the content yet. But I worry for you – this will make you an enemy of the state."

"Yes. But I already am. Keep the circle small and committed. Your ultimate response will be that the transmission was sent from the Magnamater's office with instructions to broadcast on Friday 16th at first light. If there are any changes then I, and only I, will be in touch. This is going to put you in a very vulnerable position, Charlie. Are you sure you want to be sticking your neck out so far?"

"Brenda would want me to. I haven't any other loyalties. But I've no idea how we'll handle the fallout. It's bad enough here already."

"Talk to Distribution. Make sure that stocks are as high as

possible, particularly foodstuffs and bottled water. As few Fidelis as possible should have access to the main weaponry stores just in case there are any sieges on the building. Maybe suggest a little local 'initiative' with the other Burghs, a pooling of resources. Tighter curfew restrictions just in the immediate future. Let it be known that you have heard about local insurgencies brewing trouble. That kind of thing."

She searched his implacable face anxiously.

He grinned suddenly.

"Stop worrying. We're all adults. Have you looked in the mirror recently? Eat something will you. You look all pinchy!"

"Nice way of putting it!"

"Goodbye, Rachel." He disappeared abruptly.

I can make this happen. Set spark to a dried out landscape. Get somewhere high enough to watch the bushfire spread. Someone should take me out now.

CHAPTER EIGHTEEN

Surfing

Anthony Capwood wished he had called in sick. But he could not ignore this woman with her multicoloured face and blazing eyes who seemed to make no sense yet was succinct and precise in her instructions.

"I need you to guarantee that in five days time you can commence a looped broadcast that will link into the main network but, should the main network go down, you can reboot from Olim independently."

"It can be done but you must understand Fidelis that if your lot come here and turn us off, I can't stop them unless…"

"Unless what?"

"Well." He stopped awkwardly. "Look I just want a quiet life, you know, Fidelis. I want the chance to see my grandchildren and with the talk of travel permits being re-introduced and…"

"My name is Rachel, Anthony. I am no longer Fidelis. *That's the first time I've actually said it.* Where do your children live?"

"In the north. L."

"Anthony. I need to take a chance on you. I want you to see this recording."

Obediently he sat and watched while she studied the clouds chasing and changing outside.

At the end she gave him a few moments before turning around.

He was still staring at the blank screen. Suddenly he gave a sharp intake as if he had been holding his breath, as if he had just surfaced.

"You've not escaped from somewhere have you? I mean… this is genuine?"

"I give you my word."

"I mean it's disgusti…" He choked and swiped at the tears rolling over his cheek.

He thumped the table to collect himself.

"We established satellite links with Europe and the United States a few year ago. The Magnamatership have their own but I can get onto my contacts and get them to circuit through if we're shut down here. So it'll give us a third option. There are people I need to get clearance from here."

"This has got to be handled very discreetly. There are still many supporters of the Asoan way here."

"You'd be amazed how few, but don't worry. I know who can be trusted and I don't need many. I still can't believe it. What's going to happen?"

I don't know, Anthony

"Yes good afternoon. This is Rachel Develin calling to speak with Mater Ruth please."

Come on. How much longer do I have to wait to speak to her?

"Hello Fidelis. Yes Bera has returned. Let me fetch her for you."

"Hello Mummy. It's me. Oh I can't see you."

"No sadly my visual link's not working. I can see you though."

"Oh is that because your work's taken you so far away? Daddy said it was."

"No… not at all. It's just a fault."

"We haven't spoken for SO long. And you promised we would speak more often."

"I'm so sorry. But this job's almost finished and I will be speaking to you every day from now on. How are you my darling?

"Fine. It's... it's been a funny day really. Saw Dad. Went to the beach. Doing lots of revision for my unit tests next week. Everyone's so jealous of my blanket. Dad tried to reprogramme the dog. Couldn't. So I gave it back to him. I keep banging my foot on it anyway! I... Oh... she's gone," she suddenly hissed. "Can you still hear me?"

"Yes." Rachel lowered her voice. "What's the matter?"

"They said I had to keep it a secret. Even from you. But I don't care. I didn't like them much anyway."

"Who are you talking about?"

"The women who came with Dad. At least they didn't come to the Ark. They were waiting for us on the beach. They set up a camera and everything."

"Who were they and how many women?"

"There were three of them. One was called Susan and she did the interview with me and Dad and then one was behind the camera and she fiddled with the equipment as well and I've forgotten her name and then the tall boss woman who was a bit older was called Diana."

"What do you mean 'interview'?"

"Well she asked us lots of questions about families and what is was like to not be together. And would we like to change anything? I said I would and being with you was like a little dream I had and Dad said how much of an agony it was and started to cry and then I said he didn't say that on my birthday and the Diana woman said 'AND CUT'. So we had to start again but I wasn't to say quite the same thing the next time. Anyway to be honest it got a bit boring after a while but they said I might be famous one day."

"Did they tell you why they were doing it?"

"Not really. Dad went on about a new 'initiative' and the Susan woman sort of introduced it. 'Here at Family Matters' she kept saying. I didn't think Dad could cry so much. Come to think of it, I didn't think he felt much about anything except work. I wish I didn't have to keep it such a big secret. Everyone would be so jealous."

"Well. Maybe. But best not say anything for now. I'll keep

it absolutely to myself. And... just to remind you... I have the same dream. I love you more than anything."

"Oh Mummy. I love you too. Here's Mater back so I'll say bye bye."

"Bye bye Bera. 'Til tomorrow."

Mater Ruth's voice spoke, "Thank you Bera, I'll see you in a few minutes."

Let me not have to speak to this woman or any of the witches again

"Fidelis Develin. Might I have a few more words?"

"Very well." She could hear herself snarling.

"I know what Bera has told you and I wanted to assure you most sincerely that I had absolutely no part in it's orchestration and indeed do not condone it. I hope that you will believe that my interests are first and foremost with the welfare of the children. I hope you will believe me."

"You will understand that I find it very hard to."

"If I have the opportunity to prove it to you personally, I will. Goodbye Fidelis."

A slow walk back to the centre.

I need some time to absorb this. They are all capable of so much perfidy. He's been with them all along. Was it easy for Josie to persuade you, Ben? You hypocrite! How could you use our child so? How many more strolls will I have without looking behind me?

Inevitably she was late and having reprimanded her for the absence, the clerk told her the doctor was ready.

"You are looking a little better, Fidelis. There's someone to see you."

"Oh, how nice. Who?" She asked casually.

"Sorry... she said... a friend, a member of the department. I assumed she was..."

"Ah..." Rachel thought quickly, looking for an exit.

"It's me, Rachel."

With relief she saw an almost unrecognisable Kate standing in the doorway. She wore a junior ranking Fidelis uniform, a wide cap covered her head but did not hide the heavy rimmed glasslets.

"Is that… all right?" The medic asked looking from one to the other uncertainly.

"Yes. Thank you so much," Rachel replied. "I have been expecting her but anyone else is…"

"Unwelcome. I understand. Hopefully we can alert you before it becomes a problem. Use the room at your leisure. I would like a chat with you myself on medical matters later."

"How are you?" Kate asked anxiously when they were alone.

"I have been in pieces… I think I… I think I have gone beyond reach now."

"I want to examine you. Head to foot. Inside and out. Can you give me a urine sample straight away?"

How much am I going to tell her? How many contaminants can be tested for? If I can just get through the next couple of weeks. If I am ill then at least… at least…

She lay undressed and vulnerable, willing herself to look into the middle distance and not try to read Kate's inscrutable features as her hands gently examined every inch.

"I want to scan you for breakages."

She slowly ran the small scanner over her skull, her cheeks, her neck, chest, abdomen, legs and feet. Then returned and spent much longer looking at her right cheek and temple, her chest and abdomen.

"Can you turn over for me?"

She hauled herself onto her front, wincing as her reluctant bones followed.

Kate scanned her spine and manipulated her shoulders.

"Fine. Thank you. Get dressed and I'd like to take some bloods now."

"How's Georgia?"

"Blooming. Trying not to think about Gelu going to Abovo. The Fidelis interviewed her and Luke you know. She was quite upset."

"What did they want?"

"When had she last seen you? How had you seemed? Any history of mental illness in the family? It was appalling really. She's called Ben a few times but heard nothing. I think he's been 'interviewed' a few times himself. Could you contact her? I know she would love to hear from you. She's been frantic."

"Yes, I will later."

"All right. There are a number of tests I need to run. I have what I need with me. I can stay until tomorrow night." She stopped and rested her hand lightly on Rachel's knee.

"You have not been feeling yourself for a while now, have you? Wherever you've been and whatever you've done, you have put yourself at great risk, Rachel. I hope it's worth it. For now though, you have to stop until I say you can go, remembering that I have your best interests at heart."

Rachel bit her lip and nodded. Restlessly, she padded round the room like the caged cats she remembered from her childhood.

Were there any hidden corners in what she just said? If I can only see over this hill, to this evening, to tomorrow, to stem the rising panic, to chase after the evening shadows of good health and good fortune. What have I already sacrificed to get to this place? The chance to see Bera grow? A normal life? Oh Josie, why could you not have let it lie? How could you have stolen into Ben's life without my knowing? If I am ill – it will be my punishment. Well... serves me right. Iconoclasts do not own a future.

She picked up her transor.

"Georgia. It's Rachel. I will switch to visual in a moment. How are you?"

"Out of my mind with worry. Where are you? What on earth have you done? How could you do this to me?"

"I can't say where at the moment but I am recovered, just."

"What do you mean?"

"I have been doing an undercover assignment and... incurred some injuries."

"But no-one knows where you are and that husband of yours refuses to answer my calls, he won't even talk to Luke. It's unforgivable. And I could do with the support you know... with Gelu going in a couple of months. It's too bad of you not to be here when I need you."

I can hear the familiar top-note of hysteria.

"I know, I know," she soothed. "The thing is my Georgie that life has been bad for me and I have not wanted to involve you in any way and I have to be honest and tell you that very soon you will need to distance yourself from me and deny even that we have had this conversation."

There was a vacuum.

Oh, do not always do this Georgia.

"I want to see you," she said finally.

"I do not look nice."

"I want to see you."

Rachel adjusted to visual and stared into her sister's flushed face. Waited and watched the child-like puckering and collapse. Georgia lifted her hand to the screen. At first Rachel thought it was to obscure what she had seen but then but realised that her sister was stroking the side of the screen while kissing into the air.

Such infinite compassion in so small a gesture.

It was too much and Rachel found herself weeping.

"Who did this to you?" Georgia whispered.

"Fidelis."

"Have you done something bad?"

"No. I found out things were not as they seemed and now... everything has changed. But... I want you to believe that I have not dishonoured anyone or any of the values I used to hold dear."

"You are frightening me. You know everything about me. You brought me up! We... belong. I could never deny you, Rachel."

"No. Listen I want you to be happy. Always. I wish that things were not so. I wish that Gelu could stay with you. But remember that I love you and that I will be in touch when I can."

"How can I help you?"
"I have to go now."
There's no point in prolonging the pain. I can't afford to weaken.

She stepped back inside the building and out into the corridor. As she passed one of the rooms she could hear Kate's voice... "because I am not prepared to and you should know better then to ask..." There was an unusual anger. Instinctively Rachel kept on walking, collecting her bag before she left the centre and walked in a new easterly direction towards an installation of bronzes set up on a hill.

The early evening sky was streaked with brilliant fire against its soothing blue. Light bounced off the rounded contours of the statues.

Closing her eyes, she breathed in and out rhythmically, stretching gently.

This is the moment. I am here in this moment. This is my moment. An old exercise. *Create a physical square to represent an aspect or issue of life and move it in space to another.* Technically challenging but in theory, one ended up with all areas assembled in a tower before you. The final task was to re-assemble them in order of priority. Requires huge concentration but the resulting stillness is worth it.

When she came to, the horizon had turned the soft amber before twilight catches and she did not notice the figure sitting in the shadows.

"Rachel." A soft voice broke the silence. "We need to talk, Rachel."

"Oh! Kate. Shall we go back?"

"No. Here is fine. Better in fact."

So ignorance ends here and I already know it is serious. So how will I work with it? How long have I left? Who will I tell? Steady the features into Fidelis mask.

Kate moved closer until their legs brushed against each other.

Was this the best proximity for sympathy?

"I have run a wide-ranging assay of tests on all aspects of your physiology. There are two hair-line fractures in your skull and your cheek bone is fractured. I would not suggest any treatment as long as you are not in pain. But if you notice any change you must let me know immediately. Things like headaches, vision or hearing disturbances might indicate encephalitic damage."

"Right."

Keep the monotone.

"You have two cracked ribs that will heal in time. As I suspected, you are quite anaemic – that is, your red cell count and ferric stores are low. As are your mineral levels – particularly potassium and magnesium. All this can be easily rectified with supplements. At the moment I do not see any evidence that your immune system has been fundamentally compromised although some of the tests I have run will need a longer lead time to give a fuller and more accurate picture. Given the extremes that your body has been through it is remarkable that you have sustained so few injuries and, of course, I will want to continue to monitor you rigorously over the next few months as…" Unexpectedly, she leaned forward and placed a small square freckled hand over Rachel's "…your pregnancy progresses."

This is what it must feel like to be electrocuted.

I'm surfing the sound-waves, riding syllables as they slip so easily over the skin and cartilage of my lobes, down into the canal, passing through the drum's membrane, tapping on the three tiny bones to reach the oval window where the vibrations are leaping through like flying fish and brushing along the cochlea's hairy surface. And look – the air has equalised and impulses are hurtling towards synapses in one glorious clear moment – and now I am only frequency.

And then there was ground and kneeling and in Kate's arms she was being rocked as only a woman can rock.

"Are… you… sure?"

"Yes."

"I did not think it was possible."

"Rare. But it happens."

She found herself laughing. "It is not authorised. I will lose my job."

"I think you have gone beyond permissions, haven't you?"

"Can you give me a few minutes alone, please Kate?"

"Of course. There are some more tests I would like to do but I had to tell you the news first. I am so incredibly happy for you. Come back down to the centre when you are ready."

She watched Kate's retreating back and swung round. A strong breeze had blown up, ruffling and bullying the field of ferns in the distance like waves roosting to the shore.

Her first instinct was a visicall so she could see his face. Her fingers hovered over his number.

If I were there, would I storm into Transmissions. Tear him out of his chair and yell

"Look what we have done!"

But no. I am here. And the air is surging so hard up into my chest and gusting out of my mouth. It is joy. And this is Joy. It is JOY.

"YES!!!!"

And I am cracked and splintered wide open. Volcano. A container full of stuff spilling out and irretrievably blown away into the smiling night. So everything is changed... again.

The cry stopped Kate in her tracks. She turned sharply to see Rachel swaying, her arms swinging wildly on the current. Then she sang and clapped and stamped until Kate felt she should look away.

Later they sat together.

"Kate, I have to tell you something. I know that I can ask for your absolute discretion."

"Of course."

"I can not go back to my old life. The nature of my most recent investigations means I would not survive. I am worried that the baby may have been exposed to unacceptable levels of contamination."

"How so?"

After she had finished her story Kate spent some time thinking.

"There are tests that we routinely run to check foetal abnormalities. We can check for placental cross-over of infections, diseases and some contaminants but we still can not predict the mutational capability of single cell elements present. So I can do these things for you but if you're saying that you are not returning to B, it will be hard for me to oversee this pregnancy in the way I would like. Talk to Ben and give yourselves a few days. You can't hole up here indefinitely."

"Ben has so much to deal with at the moment. I am not sure it would even register."

"But Rachel, he has to know. He has a right to know. He will be overjoyed – just like you."

Rachel beamed. "I still cannot believe it… after all this grim endurance. When could it have happened? It is a gift… Her face clouded. "What if there is a problem? I will not be able… be persuaded to let it go… whatever." She could only whisper.

"Let's get on with it shall we?"

I lie, suspended in deep, all encompassing fear. A petrifaction, while every measurement, prod and prick will define my future. Please make everything all right. If you are able. If you are out there. Please make everything all right.

"So, that's it. The neck width is good. There are certainly no apparent congenital abnormalities. The other results are going to take a little longer. Get some rest now. That is the single most important thing you can do for this baby. Rest and no stress."

She looked hard at Rachel then dimmed the lights of the sleeping cubicle and left.

What am I going to do? I can't have this baby on the run. And I can't go back. They wouldn't let me keep it anyway. Somebody tell me what to do. But not you Ben. Not you. You're just a flat surface. An idea I can walk around? I remember Josie and I lying on our backs after the sun had gone down and watching fireflies pricking the darkness? We used to say each one was like a quick flash of light on the future. So Josie, how do I decide which is the best mistake to make?

CHAPTER NINETEEN

Choosing

After breakfast she left Kate at work and walked around the campus. It was the start of a new week so she was able to blend in with the normal visitors. It felt good to be a part of an anonymous crowd again.

A poster at the entrance to a small building caught her eye.

"Come lay your problems at his door and he will make you lighter."

Without really thinking she went in and then understood that she was in a house of God. She turned on her heel quickly and narrowly avoided tripping over the chaplain who had followed her inside.

"Oh I am so sorry."

"Don't apologise please. Have we met before?"

"Oh no I just took a wrong turning I was looking for a... another place." She said limply.

"Don't let me chase you away. Can I help in any way?"

"No thank you I was just... just passing and..."

Don't look so interested... please.

"I am not a believer," she blurted out.

"No. But possibly you are searching for something?"

"With respect, surely everyone is?"

"Yes and many find their way here."

"I am sorry, I am just unconvinced that anyone is listening."

"Try me."

Why not, why not!
"I have this burden... this awful responsibility. If I do the right thing it will probably have dreadful short term consequences and if I do nothing I will continue to live and approve a massive social lie. Whatever I do I am in danger and yesterday I found out that I... this is confidential."

"Such conversations are only between the seeker and God."

"I am talking to you Chaplain."

"God is always listening."

"I am pregnant."

"How wonderful. Congratulations. Where is the difficulty?"

"Do I put myself and the safety of the unborn child before all else?"

"The Bible says if we put our trust in the Lord then he will protect us."

"That doesn't clarify anything."

"Why don't we both ask God for guidance right now?"

They sat and she mirrored his folded hands.

Oh the relief. To bow my head and listen to this genuine man who cares enough to pray for me. Am I mistaken? Where has this calmness come from?

"Thank you," she told him. "How will I know?"

"He doesn't use a transor but you just keep on talking to him. Thank him for listening. In my experience clarity comes when you least expect it."

"Yes. You've been very kind."

"Come again. I am always here."

Anthony Capwood was transformed. Animatedly he told her of his trans-national conversations held in the bowels of the night. He introduced her to two colleagues who would participate in the broadcasts.

"We will do our best to make this happen. It will be a challenge. Something to get our teeth into."

"Gentlemen. It is not without risk. The Fidelis will not

hesitate in doing whatever is necessary to stop you."

"Fidelis, I mean, Rachel, I have to be honest and say that when you first arrived I thought you were trouble but since I saw the footage and understood your commitment in the face of adversity, I think I realised that we are calcifying here in the comfort zone."

"What if I were obliged to leave early Anthony?"

He reflected.

"I always assumed you would. It's not as if you have the technical ability. Obviously you have many other things," he added quickly. "How early?"

"It could be as soon as tomorrow. A spare transor solely committed to this project would be vital. Could you help?"

"Yes. I'll set one up with a speed frequency linked to us here. Anywhere else?"

"Yes. This contact in N. I have given him your details. His name is Charlie Miller. He is Fidelis but of the disillusioned variety. His position is more vulnerable but he is absolutely committed. He also will be running the broadcast several hours before you start so that when they think the source is identified and attempt to shut it down, you will take over. Obviously timing is crucial so I was thinking if we set up a conference call now we can discuss the details. After that you will need to liase regularly so that if he is shut down you can cover his area from here."

Almost incongruous to be sitting here so calmly, planning the inconceivable and yet what else was there to do? And what on earth happens afterwards?

Her transor bleeped regularly to indicate missed calls. She knew who they were from.

Only when I'm ready.

It was as she sat in a courtyard of the residential quarter that she glimpsed two birds with wide wing-spans swooping down to skim the lake's surface and decided to take his third call.

Voice only to start with.

"Hello Ben."

"Thank Goodness. I've been frantic. Has Kate got to you?"

"Yes."

"And… And… How are you?"

"Exhausted, dizzy but better than I was."

"That's good. Listen, uhm, darling I don't want to add to your difficulties but I've had a call from Mater, apparently Bera's been ill overnight."

Her heart clutched and lurched into her mouth, as he knew it would.

"What's been the matter?"

"A virus. Very high temperature, sickness. Unfortunately her fever ran so high she had a convulsion but she seems to be recovering. She's on medication and is quite weak but eating again. I know how very busy you are but I thought you would want to be kept informed. She was asking for you but I told Mater that you had other… priorities at the moment."

"Oh don't bother trying to make me feel guilty, Ben," she spat. "I am desperate that she has been ill. Yes I do have other priorities, AS DO YOU."

"Mater did offer an unscheduled visit, if you had time," he returned casually, unruffled by her aggression.

I sense Diana at work here. A ruse to deflect my attention perhaps. But can I be sure it's genuine?

"I'm still not strong enough to travel Ben. Couldn't you take advantage of the offer and go. Bera would just love to see you."

"I only wish I could."

"Well then we will both just have to hope that it's nothing too serious, won't we?"

"When did you get so cold hearted? I've seen you be many things but never an indifferent mother. I thought she meant everything? Have you had all natural maternal instincts battered out of you on your stupid quests? No thought to how much you risk and the damage you might do."

"I am not the only reckless one in this shambles of a unification."

"Yes you are. I would never put myself in danger. My position has always been calculated. And if we're a shambles... it's your doing... shame on you. How dare you call us a shambles." His voice broke.

He is consummate.

A deep intake of breath and he started once more, "I won't be going to Abovo, I can't leave my desk at the moment. I assured Senior Fidelis Sharp in my interview earlier this week that I had not seen or heard from you for over a week and that I found your absence worrying but not entirely unusual. I know the flat's been under surveillance. Our flat, our home, you remember. It's a mess. I can't find anything. Even the doors won't shut properly and I've put a pillow on your side of the bed where you should be."

It's time he saw me

She stared at his hollow eyes, the fraught hair, the strain snaking his face. The brief flinch as he saw how battered she was.

"I..." He swallowed.

Must coat every word in ice. So I say what I must say. So hard when part of me wants to share the ecstasy. But look at him. Look at the shadow he's become!

"And how was Bera when you saw her yesterday, Ben?"

His mouth fell, he licked his lower lip and averted his gaze momentarily.

"Fine. On good form." The words were light as if they had no consequence.

She stayed silent.

Give him the chance to explain.

"A window of opportunity came and I just took it."

"Oh. Is that what you'd call it? You... are... such... a... disappointment to me, Ben."

"Oh don't start..."

"LISTEN. Little man. Of all of your betrayals this ranks highest. To exploit our daughter so!"

"Look if this is about Josie..."

"Josie... has become irrelevant. Everything behind us is

irrelevant. This is about your... other commitments. Be honest. Or are you incapable?"

He stared at her stonily. The look of a child whose crimes had been discovered. His mouth set defiantly.

"All right Rachel. All right. The opportunity came up to work for the Pleiades a long time ago. They needed someone in my position for covert communication and I'll be integral to the final... outcome."

"So it's not an ideological thing for you then? More career progression."

"Oh don't be so dismissive. Of course I believe in the objective."

"But you'll have a big part to play, won't you? And you've been missing those major roles for years haven't you?"

"I believe passionately in the family unit!"

"Oh save the performance for the programme, Ben. I thought you believed in the 'coherence of ASO', that it was the best way... just like I did. Or was that all just years of expedient posturing too?"

"People change. Believe me, I never dreamed that when we lost Josie they would approach you. I wouldn't have allowed it had I known."

"Allowed it! Who do you all think you are?"

"Rachel. You are an incredibly brave woman. You always have been. You've endured so much and yet you carried on. And I'm so angry with them for involving you but I have to urge you now to listen to me." He was panting now with anger and urgency to achieve the goal.

"There are only three important issues. Your safety, Bera's security and the success of our campaign. We can't let anything jeopardise what has been so long in the planning. I have to ask you to... disengage. Your account is spectacularly helpful... but in the right context. ASO is not quite ready. It would be reckless to broadcast right now. There will be total anarchy. Don't endanger yourself further. I can't lose you."

"I think you already have."

"Don't say that. Don't say that! I don't want you to become the scapegoat and be forever hounded."

"Understand, Ben. I'm being hunted down now. My life is over. I can't trust anyone. Least of all you!"

"Please, Rachel, don't make this about us. I committed to this a long time ago. I have to see it through conscientiously. And then…"

"Yes, Ben… and then?"

"We can start again and be a part of the new future."

I almost feel sorry for him.

Almost.

"Tell Diana that she has five days. After that ASO will hear what I have to say whether they are ready or not. We are no more worthy of the truth than anyone else."

His face fell divided, hopeless.

"Goodbye, Ben."

Over

How sure am I?

Do I just want wreckage for it's own sake?

Over

But her transor rang again. He would not be silenced.

"I hadn't finished. Rachel!"

"I think it is better if you do distance yourself from me for the time being Ben. Who knows what is ahead. We have causes, make choices and live with the consequences. We seem to have chosen different things."

"No, that's just it. We want the same thing, we just haven't talked about it," he pleaded.

"We have no more opportunity now. Such a pity… there is so much I would like to have shared with you."

"So… I can't change your mind about anything then? Despite the fact that I'm terrified for you, for us all?"

"No Ben. It's goodbye for now. Take care."

"I love you Rachel."

No… not love… I can't walk away on love. Yet I must. I know exactly what I have to do now.

Kate listened gravely until Rachel had finished.

"It is the only way, Kate."

"But Bera as well?"

"Yes. I know how much you have already done for Georgia and me. It is why I can ask for more now. Help me please."

"It's a huge undertaking. It will not go down well. Leave it with me."

She planned meticulously, studying the vast locomoter network and its timetables. Years of training enabled her to pack economically. Even the high- energy soybars would have been more suited to an astronaut. Under her dark blue suit she wore layers of expandable, waterproof hi-density clothing.

From the next room she could hear Kate talking. Sometimes a low murmur, then more strident and finally she heard shouting.

The only other call that she needed to make would be the most difficult, requiring all her powers of persuasion and diplomacy. It left her exhausted.

What if I am betrayed? I haven't the strength to think of an alternative.

When they finally met again Kate looked drawn.

"We are set. Tomorrow, we need to get away before first light. I don't know if anyone will be sent to stop us."

Rachel looked at her quizzically.

"Now I want to show you how to use everything. In this bag I've placed miniaturised blood and urine testing kits, vitamin supplements, portable pain relief patches, an ultra-sound scanner and early onset stabilisers. These are a list of acceptable result ranges and a I've downloaded a clip demonstrating self-delivery methods if necessary."

"I am not sure I am up to that."

"I know there are people there but if you need me I will come and if you have to be self sufficient… you will. You're capable of anything."

Later Rachel met with Anthony.

"I was sent a gift in meeting you. But you must know that life will change for you as soon as the first broadcast goes out. Things will not be safe or predictable. It is not too late to change your mind. I would not blame you."

"Thanks for saying that. Who would have thought at my time of life that I would signify again. There is nothing worse than the redundancy of old age. 'Time slipping uselessly through fingers' as my Sarah says. Until recently these fingers tinkered at the edge of perpetual boredom. And I was one of the lucky ones. At least I had a regular job. Now I've got a cause. Try taking it away from me. I made love to my wife yesterday for the first time in five years. All down to you! That's got to be worthwhile, hasn't it?"

"Yes," she blurted out. "Absolutely." They laughed before she held out her hand.

"Thank you Anthony. You have made everything possible."

He patted her upper arms awkwardly.

"Well done you and good luck. We will speak soon. I won't ask where you are going."

That night she recorded all relevant information onto yet more discs. She omitted nothing but the names of her most recent allies. She intended to leave discs like seeds so that if her plans were sabotaged in any way, someone else would be able to pick up the trail. As long as the knowledge was out there, it would be up to the people to use it. Her reputation may be lost but there were some truths that could not be dismissed as the ravings of a de-railed mind.

The Pleides... credited with clarity of sight while their half-sisters, the Hyades the storm-bringers, with blindness and trouble.

What if I'm wrong but too deluded to see and deaf to caution?

CHAPTER TWENTY

Abovo

Early morning was shrouded in mist and drizzle. They slipped from the campus and as they reached the station and parked their bycles, she remembered Edward once more. His gentle mockery as he taught her how to ride.

How could I say I have not been looked after on every step of this journey?

Inside, Rachel's eyes swept over the concourse as they walked across the platform and onto the waiting locomoter. Anyone could be watching.

For the first hour Kate's transor bleeped continuously.

"Someone badly wants you."

"Yes. I know who it is." Kate stared out of the window.

At every station they both tensed, scrutinising each boarding passenger as they settled.

As the flat landscape of F dissolved into G and they progressed further west Rachel spoke.

"You don't have to come all the way you know. Just come as far as the G-H border when I catch the northern line."

"And then I'll spend the return trip agonising over whether you got there."

The locomoter sped on eating up miles that she would not see again.

At the change, Kate linked arms as they hurried onto a

neighbouring platform and waited in the shadows until the link locomoter came. They were alone.

"Have you told him yet?"

"No."

"Will you?"

She shrugged.

"He's not a bad man, Rachel. Think carefully. And... I think you'll need him. You've never done any of this before."

"I know. And I am not dismissing what you say but he has made his choice."

"Don't all of us make mistakes and yet deserve a second chance?"

"Yes... but there comes a point when you run out of road. You can't wait any longer or be any more pragmatic. This is it."

"The scenery's stunning." Kate resigned herself. "Look at the crystal blue sky!"

"It is always so much bluer here on this side of the country. The air is fresher too."

At the end they disembarked and caught a trolley that rattled its passage up the familiar tree lined avenue. Rachel's heart leaped.

Kate looked up admiringly, "It's years since I've been here. You forget how unique the structure is. I'll wait outside."

"It could be some time. Just keep out of sight. There are deliveries all the time even if they are clone driven."

"Good luck. Be careful."

"This is Rachel Develin, here to see Bera," she spoke, rallying some of her old assertiveness.

The great gates slowly opened and breathing deeply, she marched up to the steps where the door remained resolutely shut. She knocked loudly several times and just as she was about to lose patience there was a creak from within and she found herself admitted.

"Please wait here." A startled young acolyte fled before Rachel could adjust her eyes to the darker interior.

She could hear the rustle of the Mater's cloak and glimpsed the headdress before the figure descended. It was not the face she had hoped for. If the Abamater was shocked by Rachel's changed appearance she did not show it

"Fidelis. This is somewhat unexpected."

"I heard that Bera had been unwell and since I was due to visit at the weekend I did not think there would be a problem."

The Abamater gazed at her steadily. "She is quite recovered now let me assure you."

"I would like to see her. Ideally take her for a small excursion."

The older woman smiled sweetly.

"Out of the question I'm afraid."

"Then perhaps a little time together since I am here."

"I…" Abamater lifted up her palms like butterfly wings. Conciliatory, understanding, regretful. "You place me in a very difficult position. You must know recent events, the circumstances…"

"I expect that you have heard confusing and disturbing reports," Rachel said smoothly. "Understandably and rightly you are concerned. My work has been very challenging recently and I don't mind admitting that I am looking forward to concluding this urgent and sensitive assignment when I submit my report to the Magnamater's office. It's unlikely that I will be able to return to Abovo for a few weeks. I would so much like Bera to feel that I had made time to come. The Magnamater herself always talks about this age as being the most emotional, does she not?"

She could see the Abamater wavering. Fidelis Develin was a senior ranking officer after all. What if the alert had been premature. If indeed she was involved in something undercover that in time proved to be defensible, her own conduct may be brought into question. She would tread the middle path, grant some recreational time and contact Fidelis Administration. They could act upon the information if they wished. It would do the child good anyway.

"Very well," she said finally. "A short visit then. Perhaps given your appearance it would be better to stay outside but strictly within our secure grounds. I think two hours should be long enough."

"Thank you," Rachel responded graciously. It was not what she had hoped for but it would give her a little time.

"Your injuries may be a little... overwhelming for Bera. Perhaps I should ask Mater Ruth to explain them to Bera before she sees you. If you would like to wait here for a while."

She could not argue and as the Abamater disappeared, she wondered how long she would have before other forces descended on the Ark.

It seemed long, too long but suddenly Mater Ruth was in front of her. Compassion flooding her face. "Oh Fidelis. I wanted to see you for myself so I could justly explain the situation to Bera."

"I would simply say that I fell and broke my nose. An injury that always incurs a great deal of bruising."

"Yes. Quite right. I'll speak to her and collect a lunch for you to take out into the grounds. Perhaps you'd like to go out there now and I will bring her to you. The east lawns are lovely at the moment. Such a good view of the valley and the beautiful banks of rhododendrons." Her tone, bright, and warm dropped to a low murmur. "All is in place... where Marchant arrived. You'll find everything you need and an exit."

Rachel knew where to head.

She's playing along so far... but there's still time for things to change.

Small figure, microdots of love, running towards her, growing bigger by the second. Powering into her centre, taking the wind out of her open sails. Bera buried her face for some time.

I can feel her whole body stiffening. She's preparing herself.

Finally, slowly, she looked up and recoiled. A small grunt escaped her compressed lips. She grabbed onto her Mother's arms.

"Oh Mum... Oh Mummy. How did this happen?"

Actually, I'm not going to lie any more. Our future depends on my honesty.

"It looks much worse than it is. I was attacked by a

criminal. It was bad at the time. I've spent a long time recovering but it doesn't hurt much any more."

"Daddy said you were working?" She wrinkled her nose quizzically.

"I was… before this happened. Look I'll tell you all about it later but it means we get some time together now."

Bera grinned and stretched up a tentative small hand. "Can I… touch your nose? I'll be gentle."

Lightly she stroked over her face.

"I… don't want you to do this anymore if people are going to do such horrible things to you."

"All right. I won't." Rachel said simply.

They both laughed

"This is so great. I'm missing double Fuel Technology. Tisa was mad because we were supposed to partner. She's had to share with Juin and Fran. And everyone knows what they're like." She rolled her eyes while Rachel suppressed an overwhelming desire to pull her close and cover her with kisses.

"So what are we doing?"

"We'll start with a quick picnic and then… well who knows? Overjoyed, Bera bounced uncontrollably. "Oh Bera, here is Mater."

"Bother. What can she want already?"

"The Refresher has prepared a picnic for you," Mater beamed and handed a large carrier. "And I thought that you might like to read some of Bera's work while you are here. You can return it to me tonight." Another carrier was handed over.

"I have insisted that Bera wear plenty of layers and take her coat. It is supposed to be very cold later."

"I know and I'm far too hot." Bera peeled off her jacket.

Momentarily, Mater allowed herself to glance over at Bera who was already running ahead into the sunlight.

A small imperceptible intake of breath. "Sail on," and she swept away.

Rachel forced herself to sit and enact the part. She ate sparingly knowing that the food might be needed later. Bera chattered on inconsequentially. Deliberately, she took them on a walk round the grounds to the opposite side where they could just see the old headland. They mimicked the turning turbines and flapped and screeched at the seagulls. Then they returned to the centre fields. Linking arms, Rachel gently increased their pace towards the perimeter.

"Now my darling, let's pretend that we are the greatest explorers in the whole of ASO and our quest is to discover the brightly coloured but rarely seen Trouper bird whose song is so loud and beautiful it can make the listener forget everything else."

Bera saluted crisply, "Yes Ma'am. Anything you say. Lead on."

"Firstly we must make a trail through the wild wood checking the treetops constantly but also in the undergrowth where it will often take shelter from the... heat of the sun."

She recognised the spot where the grass dipped away sharply.

A flap had already been cut in the perimeter fencing and Rachel noticed the sensors had been capped. It was just big enough.

Bera stopped, astonished. "Look at that!. Abamater will go dipstick! How did you know it would be here?"

"A hunch. It was where the Marchant thing happened... you know" she threw it in breezily.

"But they would have mended it. In fact I know they did."

Bera stood up straight, her hands on her hips, her legs slightly apart.

That's my girl. Question everything.

"They did mend it but I arranged for it to be cut open again so we could do this."

"Do what? Find this Trouper bird?"

The loose mesh rattled noisily.

I can't risk a lengthy conversation. Someone might see us from the tower.

"In part but mostly so we can escape. I'll make it good afterwards. But we really have to hurry. Now!"

The command jolted her and she immediately went down on all fours but Rachel knew she had to do more.

"What do you mean 'escape'?"

She prepared herself. *Steady, still voice.*

"I meant what I said to you on your birthday. You mean more to me than anything. We've got this one chance to be together... permanently Bera. It's not going to be easy. It means leaving the Ark, your friends and this life that you've known."

What am I doing? How can she understand the enormity of what I'm asking her?

"Can I fetch my best things?" she whispered finally.

"No. We have to go now."

It's best this way. She has to come for me.

A few long moments passed.

"Okay. Let's go."

"Good. Now dip your head and creep on through fellow hunter. Quick as you can."

With fumbling fingers she re-tagged the fence.

I hope Bera doesn't notice. She needs to believe me invincible right now.

It took longer to work their way than Rachel would have liked, emerging further on than she had promised Kate. She had begun to send a transor message when Kate came upon them.

"It's all right. I had to make myself scarce. There have been a lot of deliveries."

Bera had stepped back, startled.

"This is Kate. Our partner on the trail. Any sightings of the Trouper yet?"

"Not yet. But it's..." Kate searched for something to add, "...early days. We must hurry."

They marched in the dappled shade.

Finally at a junction they skipped onto the back of a trolley that took them to the station.

"We're going on a locomoter? This is... amazing. Tisa would flip. It's only my third time... ever. How do the doors shut? I mean how do they know when to shut? Are there sensors in the hinges or something or has the driver got a multi visual that sees into every compartment? Do clones drive or are they automatic?"

She chattered on, paddling in the novelty. Kate and Rachel maintained a discreet vigil, grateful for the girl's mood, but as the locomoter sped south through Abovo passing Ark after Ark, Bera peered out into the gathering dusk and lapsed into silence.

It was only at a busy station where Abovo intersected with G and E and the compartment filled that she spoke again.

"Where are we going, Mummy?"

Rachel glanced at Kate.

"D'you know. Originally I was going to tell you everything in small stages so you wouldn't be upset but as usual I forgot how grown up you are. Let me show you."

She unfolded the map and traced their route and destination.

"Do you know anyone there?"

"No. Not personally."

"Are you coming too, Kate?"

"No. Only for part of the journey."

"What about Daddy?"

I've been dreading this one.

"Daddy is incredibly busy with a big project and... doesn't know about our plans."

"But... but... will I see him again?" For the first time there was panic in her voice.

"Yes of course. But I don't know when."

"Suppose it's lucky I didn't see him much anyway."

As Bera grappled with what she was being told, Rachel watched her anxiously, aware of the figure nestled into a corner who had been paying them particular attention.

"How do you feel about it? A new life with just me and a few others."

"I think it's all right. I just might miss some things and I wish I'd known so I could have brought..."she tailed off.

"Mater packed for you." Rachel handed her the carrier. "We did talk about it."

"Mater knew?" Bera was surprised. "I hope she's not going to be in trouble. Abamater's quite strict about Maters not... doing that sort of thing. Who's going to teach me?"

"There will be people there. It will be an adventure."

"It's all right, I think I know most things anyway."

The women laughed.

At the terminus Rachel knew that they would have to leave the building and they would be met but not before they had parted from Kate.

There was no restraint in their final embrace. Tears soaked both their shoulders.

"There are not enough words to thank you for everything. I know I could not have done this without you."

"You underestimate yourself. Just follow my instructions as the months progress. Don't do too much or tire yourself out. Get Bera to help as much as possible. Keep your head down over the next few weeks at least. And I know you don't want me to keep on but tell Ben... please."

"Look after Georgia for me. She is... very young and the separation from Gelu is going to hit her so hard."

"Well, a lot may happen between now and then."

Kate smiled and turning at the door, leaned close towards her once more. She cupped Rachel's face. Such closeness, skin on skin – no longer strange. Her lips grazed Rachel's eyelids, light, as she remembered her mother's butterfly kisses.

"Sail on sister."

She ought to have had wings to disappear so quickly.

How could I not have realised?

Outside they huddled in the night air and as the wait lengthened and Bera grew restive, she felt doubt creeping over her.

We can't do this alone. I must be insane to think about the journey. The maps are so old. None of the new camps are listed. Too late for reservations now.

A squat woman in black wearing a cycling helmet strode past them at a brisk pace.

"This way ladies."

They followed, Bera tripping over the unfamiliar cobbled stones into a side-road. Then they turned a sharp first right into a covered bay.

Celaeno waited.

"Did you think I had forgotten? I'm the last of your guardian angels. The others could not be trusted. Maia's on the warpath with us."

She began to unpeel layers of hemp sacking from a large object in the middle of the floor.

"Fold these up for me," she instructed Bera. The final layer revealed a Har.

"Where did it come from?" Rachel was aghast.

"Its disappearance is currently causing a bit of bother in A. It will get us to Bude. No further. Kate's got connections there. Is that yours?"

Celaeno lifted the case that Kate had helped her pack the previous night. It looked too small to house everything that they might need.

They rode thought the night, passing through the occasional encampment. Unkempt folk, made plump with their many layers of ragged clothing, stoked fires and looked up suspiciously at the Har's noisy engine.

The old style houses boasted low lights from inside.

Even more locked in time than Olim. The wilful landscape lay untamed and tangled like matted tresses. *Open. Heart. Another country.*

She closed her eyes.

All the movement, the speed and nervous energy that has fuelled my life. Frightened to stop in case... what? In case I might notice my soul had rigor mortis? It's all been leading to this one final thrust.

Out of my hands

CHAPTER TWENTY-ONE

Suris

Senior Administrator Clare Willis had lost her customary cool mien. In its stead was a dyspeptic peevishness that Magnamater Beatrice would have found most unwelcome had she witnessed it. Beatrice had come to rely on her second-in-command's unflappable nature, as it contrasted with a certain excitability she so struggled to contain within herself.

As Chief Fidelis continued her reports of sporadic unrest currently rippling through the Provinces, she watched her superior's features twitch with affront.

"Games of Asonetta are regularly being disrupted, screens switched off, tables turned over. Non-specific but highly charged gatherings in the squares. Tribal music. Curfews flouted. The newly launched inter-Burghian leagues have been ending in brawls. Incidents of travelling without permits have rocketed. A general belligerence at Magnamater's transmission time. The incarceration centres are overflowing."

"Frankly, and with the greatest respect, I think that we have to be careful not to overreact to what could merely be the bleatings of local incompetence rather than a campaign as such. Are you asking for more resources and, if so, which Burghs do you feel have the greatest need? It has to come out of someone's budget."

"I am not saying that my forces are unable to cope. I am making a social observation. There has always been the bellicose element that will not be subjugated. It is the nature of people who no longer have wars to fight. No, this is a palpable change in attitude. Respect seems to be trickling out of our system. Quick and decisive initiatives are needed. I believe Magnamater should be made aware as a matter of urgency."

"Alright, thank you Chief Fidelis. You have made valid observation. I will speak to Magnamater this afternoon and we will meet again at the weekend conference."

Chief Fidelis nodded curtly, gathered her discs and left the office. Oh, she was mildly offended yes, but more she was deeply worried. She had been on the streets. She had seen the indifferent turned backs, the illegal trading, the nocturnal culture seeping out and claiming the Burghs as their own. There had been more fatalities than she cared to acknowledge committed by her own officers who were unused to such flagrant rebellion. It required effective leadership, new guidelines. And she was so very tired of guidelines.

The Senior Administrator stared down at her fingers gloomily. Alone she could not be so dismissive. On her desk lay the reports confirming the increasing levels of absenteeism throughout ASO. One Burgh actually ran out of food last week as there were not enough Distribution officers. At this rate they would be totally dependent on the clones by the next decade. Birth rates had fallen and pre-resortion mortalities were on the increase. How after all these years, with all their advanced microbiology and screening, could that be?

She called her dynamic young assistant Lida who had consistently scored top marks at every exam from the age of four.

"You have seen the figures? We need to get the team on this. We need new incentives. Initiatives. Games. Foods. Luxury goods... Holidays... We need to get them excited, wanting to contribute again."

Lida appeared alarmed. "Right."

"Well, you seem puzzled."

"It goes somewhat against our... well... Ethos. I mean... we don't have any... Luxuries."

"Well we need to get some. Make some. Find out what people want most of all. I want you to organise surveys. Get out there. Get Transmissions on something interactive. Where would people like to go if they could? Little… What do you call them… Breaks? 'Spend a couple of days in a different Burgh'. Ideas, Lida. This is your big opportunity."

"Right," Lida grumbled as she sat calling number after number. "Passing the responsibility to me more like. 'Come to sunny Burgh 14, exactly like 13 but… one more'!"

Ben almost laughed out loud.

"So let me make sure I understand you correctly. You want me to design an interactive transmission…"

"We were thinking of calling it a 'Show' to make it feel new and… different," Lida interrupted.

"Show then, inviting people to vote for their preferred luxury which the administration would guarantee to produce and make available for people to buy or win. And at the same time inviting ideas…"

"Calling it a 'Competition'."

"… Right, for a new sport or game that the administration would activate in the next six months. And also a short break allowance… calling it a… ?"

"Burgh Break."

A loose blonde curl escaped from Lida's grip, falling into her eyes, making her seem vulnerable and even younger then her twenty years. Ben's sardonic grin melted. Poor kid. They must be getting desperate.

"This is going to take a while. Would you want the interactive units just on public screens or installed in each domicile? You know most people have stopped watching transmissions at home."

"Oh, I think everywhere."

"That's a lot of units and hours. From a technical point of view it's not a problem but it would be pointless to go until you can maximise on the opportunity."

"Yes, but if I can get Installations working on it, you can design the format?"

"No problem!"

"It's such a relief to talk to a professional. Someone who can make things happen. I had convinced myself it would be a non-starter."

Too little, too late. But he admired her enthusiasm. Had he ever been that young? All that freshness. You just wanted to stay close to it and hope some rubbed off. Oh for a bit more time. He leaned forward and lifted the curl back into place. She blushed.

"Thank you."

"Welcome," he said softly.

His transor bleeped. Secure line… Maia.

"Are you secure, Ben?"

"No. I'll have to get back to you shortly." He switched off abruptly.

"So. It sounds feasible. Leave it with me and we'll talk soon." He offered his sunshine full-of-promise smile and showed her out of Transmissions.

There just weren't enough hours in the day at the moment. Won't turn it down though. Got to take advantage of everything offered… you never knew where it might lead. Sighing, he contacted Maia.

"Spoken to your wife recently?" she asked curtly.

"No. She's not taking my calls remember."

"We know she's left Olim. Despite my instructions. With Kate's help. Various 'others' refuse to commit to stopping her progress, wherever that might be. I'm just anxious she doesn't come blazing into Suris demanding to see the Magnamater and causing us endless problems."

"I'm more concerned that she may have left a time-bomb behind her. It puts me in a difficult position."

"Oh I think your position's secure Ben. I know you've publicly distanced yourself from her."

"Anyway, whatever she thinks, she's not a technologist and I doubt there are many there who could help her."

"Naïve assumption, Ben. Where d'you think the great minds end up?"

"Well yes of course. I just meant that I think it's unlikely they could pull it of in the time frame. I think she'll go see Bera. Make sure we haven't corrupted her with the promise of fame. But I don't know for certain, Maia. I don't recognise her any more."

"Well, we can't let anything distract us. Is everything progressing as it should?"

"Of course. I would have let you know if there were any problems."

Talk about suffocation. Everyone screaming for a part of you.

He should talk to Bera. Perhaps later.

Bera had already grown used to the wild ponies, sheep and goats wandering out in front of the Har. As they drove, the moors stretched out like drifts of purple bruising and the unpredictable road dipped and curved. She looked across at Rachel's still sleeping form. The tufts of grey sprouting from her head like coarse grass, the pale skin just below the collar line, below all those awful vivid colours, her bent swollen nose which used to be so straight and her full mouth slightly open with the jagged broken front teeth.

"I've never seen her asleep," she whispered. "I've never seen her cry and I can only remember seeing her and Daddy together once… except on a scanimage. She doesn't look like my Mum anymore. I wish… I wish… she'd given me some warning that this was going to happen. I'd like to have said 'goodbye' to a few people. Haven't even looked to see what Mater thought I would need or miss. It'll be like I never existed. I'll be another of those people like Faith Orph who no one talks about. I was doing quite well. I mean why do adults do this?"

Celaeno glanced at the small intense child.

"It's good that she's got you to look after her. Seems to me you're as brave as she is. It will all be very different for her too. She's used to Surisian life. This will be much more fun. She'll need lots of help setting up a home for you."

"You're right. I'm quite good at building things."

Abamater was not given to outward displays of emotion. She found them tiring and inconvenient so she encouraged her staff to keep emoting to a minimum. However on hearing of Bera's disappearance, the tears she shed were mostly of anger.

"I knew that woman couldn't be trusted. Outrageous. Makes us look so sloppy. I said two hours Ruth. Why was I not notified earlier?"

"I agree it was sloppy. And I must take full responsibility for not chasing up with the evening staff but if you remember I was visiting Ark 58 for the conference yesterday afternoon and didn't return until late. The absence should really have been picked up after Joy-time. I know the Fidelis visit was noted in the register."

The fact that she had deliberately omitted the details until this morning did not concern her. Mater Ruth had no compunction in lying. The cause was greater than the reputation of more junior staff.

"Does the father know?"

"I believe not. I can contact him if you would like."

"No, it ought to be me. It's Bert isn't it?"

"Ben, Ma'am."

His transor rang.

What was she saying? He found himself distracted by her facial wart.

"Well how does this happen? I mean surely you have a last register or something?"

"I will be investigating the exact circumstances in great detail Mr Develin, I can assure you. And of course we will review our procedures in the light of my findings which I understand will be of no comfort to you at the moment. In a small defence though it must be remembered that your wife's position does allow her a little more leeway, rightly or wrongly."

"Wrongly in this instance. You have allowed a woman who is clearly not of sound mind to kidnap my daughter. Where have they gone? Have your investigations so far afforded you any clues? I'd like to kept posted with anything you find out, please."

He thumped the table. Kate! Kate must have known.

He still had her secure line.

"Hello Ben."

"Back at work I see. You have been busy haven't you?"

"My patients need me," she replied coolly reading his heightened state.

"Where is she Kate?"

"In bed, cuddling her baby."

"Cut the crap, Kate. Rachel... where is she?"

"When I last saw her she was heading south."

"When is she going to stop being a pain in my side. It's all about one-upmanship with her. Stupid, misguided, half-baked conquests. She has no idea what she's doing. And she's dragging Bera into the mess too."

"Oh. I wondered when you'd mention Bera. She's fine by the way. Happy, healthy and safe."

"For now, Kate. I'll hold you responsible if that changes."

"Perhaps if you'd gone to her you'd have been able to dissuade her. I went because you could not. I am confident that I acted in the patient's best interests and that Bera will be well looked after."

"Rachel's no more idea than I about Bera's best interests. You elevate her into something she's not. And don't try to make me feel responsible!"

Kate fell silent.

"I want you to promise me that you'll let me know the minute you next hear from her."

"If there's anything to concern you I will definitely contact you."

"That's not what I asked."

"That's what I can offer, Ben." She ended the call. Worried that all their futures rode on such fragile egos.

Chief Fidelis had an aching right hand. It was possible that there was a fracture. The wall that she had fisted some forty-five minutes ago remained irritatingly smooth. Three Senior Fidelis killed in one night. This could not go on. It took five years to train a Fidelis. Let alone the extra three when a small circle of elite were selected for Senior status. But if that was not enough. To hear about that woman surfacing again. They had been so hopeful she had gone to ground permanently. Literally. Even though there had been no evidence. To have one of their own loose and lost. It was too dangerous. Especially now that she had defiantly appeared in Abovo and kidnapped her own daughter. It weakened everyone's credibility. She would have to be made an example of.

"I want all footage examined from every locomoter leaving Abovo in the last twenty-four hours. I want a committed team scouring E and down into Cornwall. I want her found but not killed. I want her brought to this office. And I want to see her husband today. Bring him here."

It was the usual assertion psychology. His cushion-less seat was placed at a right angle to the interviewer and of course, a suitable four inches lower. Ben noted wryly that she remained at the window without turning for a few minutes. He knew all the tricks. He had been united to Rachel for long enough.

She eventually joined him.

"Mr Develin. May I call you Ben?"

"Of course."

"I know that you will have heard of your wife's latest escapade. You must be very concerned about the safety of your daughter."

"Oh absolutely but only because she has been removed from the protection of the Ark. I know Rachel would not compromise her safety."

"You say that but how can you know? Obviously I do not want to alarm you unduly, but I wonder whether your wife can really be relied on any longer. Her behaviour has become increasingly erratic. And she has been 'involved' in the deaths of a least two Fidelis officers to our knowledge. It is probably hard for you to accept your wife's potential… but I wonder whether we can leave a helpless precious child in her charge?"

"I hear everything that you say and I agree that she is not what she was. But I still do not believe that Bera will come to any harm."

Chief Fidelis smiled sympathetically.

"I wish that I had your confidence. Tell me when did you last hear from her?"

"Three days ago. She finally contacted me to say that she was fine but she wouldn't tell me where she was or what her intentions were. Apart from to say that she would not be returning."

"Were you surprised?"

Ben sighed.

"I really cannot say I was. We have not seen much of each other over the last year or so. Rachel is Fidelis. You and I both know how exclusive the life is and frankly, if I can speak confidentially…"

"Of course, I will be absolutely discreet."

"We have grown so far apart. I am heavily involved and committed to my expanding role within Transmissions. The new initiatives are making it very exciting for us all there. I do not want you to think I am indifferent to Rachel's situation but…"

He lifted his hands helplessly, "If you want my honest opinion I think that she will return Bera to the Ark sooner rather than later. We are talking about someone who has never had to look after a child, who is used to being self-governing and needed to break out for while. It has been a tough year for her, I know that much. She took Fidelis Kitchener's death very badly. I would imagine that she is dabbling with a notion of being a more active mother. When she finds out how hard it is, Bera will be back with the Maters I am sure. I mean that is why we have the Maters. They have expertise the rest of us will never have."

"And what plans do you think she has for herself?"

Ben lowered his voice.

"The woman I saw was a broken… exhausted. I did not get

the impression she had any plans. I would like to think that she will come home. And if she did I would welcome her and help her to get some appropriate treatment. What do Fidelis do to support their damaged own?"

"We always respond... individually and with compassion. But I have to tell you that I cannot in good conscience leave Bera's disappearance like this. We have to actively try and find them. And trust that in so doing, Rachel will not prevent us from returning Bera to where she belongs."

"I understand and request that the Fidelis will not in turn endanger my daughter's safety. I hope you will forgive me but I am expected back at Transmissions shortly to coordinate the Magnamater's Peace Broadcast this afternoon."

He stood, aware that he should have waited for dismissal.

"Of course. The best of luck."

"And to you Chief Fidelis."

It was lucky that they didn't do a palm test. He waited until he left the building before wiping his hands. Hopefully he had headed her away from putting him in the spotlight further. This was one period of his life when he didn't need much attention. "Don't just suddenly materialise Rachel. I wouldn't trust myself. When did you get so selfish?" He muttered as he returned to Transmissions.

She played back the interview, watching his body language, listening for the key indicators for stress, camouflage or resistance. There was nothing to suggest that he was anything other than genuine. He was exactly the right sort of partner for a Senior Fidelis Officer. Independent. Pragmatic. Understanding. Ambitious in his own right. The relationship seemed to be floundering though. Perhaps Fidelis, like Maters, should not unite.

At what point had they lost Develin? And Kitchener for that matter?

CHAPTER TWENTY-TWO

Cornwall

It was a small cottage about two miles outside a place called Truro. The thick, grey, sweating walls were made of stone mined from the local quarries. The air felt damp and ancient. The property coordinator was a woman called Ruth. Bera tried not to stare at her violet-coloured hair that hung in long unconnected wisps nor at the silver stud that seemed to cling precariously to her tongue and darted mercurially in and out as she spoke.

"The cottage is number fourteen. We don't have names although you're welcome to give it your own stamp. There's an open fire as you see. You can burn logs or kindling but it tends to smoke a bit. I'll send the lad to help you clear the chimney and get the gas heater loaded. The septic tanks are emptied every six months so don't put anything unnecessary down there if you get my drift."

"What's a septic tank?" Bera asked appalled.

"We don't have a normal drainage system here love, for your business. So it goes in a tank. As you'll notice everywhere feels a bit damp. Can't be helped. Cornwall's a wet place. Takes the brunt of any weather from the west. And we have a lot of weather believe me. We don't get proper seasons anymore. It's wet and warm or wet and cold. I've seen some changes I can tell you. Every year we lose a bit more of that poor battered coastline which is why there's nothing built too close."

"How old are you?" Bera asked curiously.

"You should not really asked that, Bera."

"She's all right. Don't let my youthful beauty fool you – I'm older than I look… bit older than my teeth. You probably don't have bedding with you so I've supplied some to get you going. Generally though, you make your own or join the textile workshop. The way we work down here is on a barter or skill-swap system. You'll meet the team later and they'll explain everything. Food is available at the store. Newcomers get credits to start them off and then they get involved in the different production schemes. Have you ever milked a goat?" she turned to Rachel.

"No."

"Oh well, you'll have fun learning. Main milk source down here. I've put a welcome pack in your kitchen."

"Thank you."

"So hope you settle in alright. The team will be up later. Oh," she stopped in the doorway, "we don't tend to ask too many questions and we don't talk about newcomers. You've just chosen to be here. That's it."

From upstairs, Bera yelled, "Can I have this room? It's got a sink."

In the small back garden, Rachel looked out across the rolling valley. *A view at last.* She had never seen such a lush green before and beyond she could just glimpse the craggy pale froth of the shore. Even though the clouds hung heavy and low, the air was still warm and salty.

What on earth will grow here below that dry stone wall? My new border.

Suris

There had been days when Beatrice would have broadcast live. It was a sign of the times that she preferred to read her speech from auto-cues and needed several attempts to settle herself. In the end Ben, decided to inter-cut images of ASO with Beatrice talking over in profile and face to camera for only limited sections. In the wings, the Administration fluttered nervously.

"So to summarise these new initiatives. The interactive screens and units will be with you all soon. For the first time you will have the opportunity to tell us what you want. Don't waste the chance. Do get involved. This is your society. Help us to help you to improve it and make it an even more enjoyable life. Finally let us remember that ASO is a family. Sometimes we will not agree with each other but ultimately our strength is in our coherence. Coming together in commitment, co-operation and compassion, we will continue to build on our remarkable achievements."

Several forced smiles faced their leader as she stepped down from the podium.

"Marvellous, Magnamater. Marvellous"

"When do you think the interactive event will be ready?" Claire Willis asked Lida.

"Three days. Then the installation programme will take approximately two weeks with everyone working flat out. But I think we can plan for another major broadcast in three weeks. Today I've started another small programme of roving reportages in the Burghs themselves asking the same sorts of questions, which Ben has kindly said he can collate and broadcast when we are ready."

"Great work, Lida," the Magnamater beamed. "So good to hear something positive for once. Perhaps we could delay our status meeting until later Clare."

"Of course, Magnamater."

Senior Administrator Clare Willis returned to her office. She would have to work hard to keep this under control. At least she had the stamina for the difficult decision.

"Are you secure, Ben?"

He had slipped home for a quick shower and a change before Lida came up to Transmissions and view today's footage with him.

"I don't have long, Diana."

"How are things?"

"Everything's going according to plan. Susan and I have put the finishing touches to the Pleiades New Way campaign. It's ready for you. I've miniaturised it and I'll send it in a few minutes. How is your end?"

"We have undercover placements in every Province taking advantage of any opportunity so that when the time comes we can effectively target the weakest and strongest elements. I would have preferred a slower orchestration but maybe there are some advantages. I can't believe she'll have the commitment now she's got Bera."

"I suspect you're right. But we can't be sure."

"I will speak to you again tomorrow."

It was hard to believe that there was the space on such a tiny heart shaped face for such wide round blue eyes. In fact all of Lida's features were slightly over-sized. A small sliver of distinction between attractive and strange. Ben did not find her strange.

But the footage they were watching demanded his attention.

A square. Province F. Burgh six. Someone, probably from Distribution according to the uniform, was shouting, no ranting at the reporter.

"You patronising Robos! You want to know what we want... I can tell you what we don't want. We don't want your Fidelis state with that stupid figurehead blathering on... I mean is she real? Or do you just wheel her out? Maybe she's a clone. I mean she looks off her trolley. I bet she hasn't got her old mum dying without her being able to get to see her 'cos there's no more leave left. You tell her that's what us fodder want. You tell her." He swung out wildly and the camera fell to the floor where it rested still recording. There was a roar of approval and the soft thud of a body close by being regularly kicked.

"Oh no, Ben, no," Lida whispered appalled. "We have to make sure he's alright."

There were no more such violent incidents but the consistent level of hostility shocked them both. They talked until late. It seemed natural to offer comfort. She was so young. Brutality had not swaggered into her world yet.

Afterwards, it was like curling round a naked child.

In the morning she slipped away, an elfin wisp of the night and when he came to, there was barely an impression on the mattress. He changed the sheets trying not to think of Rachel.

"She shouldn't have left," he told the mirrored tiles in the bathroom.

Cornwall

They had both woken early, unused to the dawn chorus. Although small, the curtain-less windows let in a surprising amount of light. They had slept together for the first time. Even in Weaning, baby Bera was taken to the nursery at night. So they had never experienced that soft, tender, vanilla slumber, at once terrifying and moving, when a mother realises that all nights have been a dress rehearsal for these aching, sleepless love-soaked hours between dusk and dawn. At first their toes had touched unfamiliarly and shyly, their hands had searched each other out. Rachel opened her eyes and looked across the pillow to see the tousled blackness.

So this is how total contentment feels.
"Hello my darling," she cooed.
Rustling, nestling, limbs entwined.
I could stay like this forever.

Later, as they walked down the cobbled street to the centre where they would talk with the Team, everyone they met greeted them as friends.

There were three. Two men, Thomas and Manfred and a woman called Freya.

Manfred was small, broad and bald. His glasses did not contain the large brown dancing irises behind. Laughter lurked in every booming sentence he spoke. Thomas was more reticent and the physical opposite. Huge limbs emerged from shorts and a tee-shirt. His light brown hair grew mane-like from his brow, while most of his face was buried underneath a reddish beard apart from eyes the colour of summer sky. Freya was of average height, painfully thin and tanned. It was hard to tell her age as her dark hair was worn in long thick plaits. She had enormous hands for her size that she constantly wrapped and unwrapped as she spoke.

"We try not to make things too structured here but, for the sake of ease, I'm responsible for provisions, Manfred for training and Thomas for services. As far as possible we are a self-supporting community. We have a lot of expertise here and if we can't make something happen we have connections with the various other communities throughout the region. We are very aware that for all newcomers there is a great deal to adjust to. Most are highly skilled but unused to self-sufficiency. So we try to offer training in any area where you feel you are lacking whether it's cooking, gardening, manufacturing or fuel provision. There is an environments course that we all do. It covers most of the global issues like climate, pollution and agriculture that we all need to be aware of. But it's not all functional. There are music classes, games classes, history and world geography."

Manfred continued.

"We meet once a week on a Friday. Any community issues can be raised there. It's very relaxed and informal. We have our stunning cathedral where non-denominational services are held on a Sunday. There is a surgery where two general doctors practise and we also have three specialists who you can see for more specific health issues. We also have a small school," he said beaming at Bera. "We don't want our young people growing bored. Hours are nine until two, Monday to

Thursday. We also try and encourage all children to do the cooking and environment course."

"Can I learn how to fish?" interrupted Bera.

"Sure. I'm a big fishing fan," replied Thomas.

"I know a lot about fish except how to catch them," she added proudly.

"There are just a few dull adult things I wanted to ask. Bera would you like to wait in the square for me?" Rachel suggested.

"There's a pond at the back with a couple of beautiful swans and some new ducklings if you wanted to see." Freya suggested.

Bera leaped up and raced to the door. She turned suddenly. "Oh, thank you for… being here."

"Yes. She said it before I could," Rachel smiled. "With all my heart, thank you. I also felt that I owed you all an explanation. I know that Ruth said yesterday that there was an 'ask no questions' policy but in my case it is slightly different."

Thomas interrupted her, "We know the two most important things. That you are a retired Fidelis and that you are pregnant. Kate is an old friend."

"Yes." Rachel was slightly taken aback. "But I am not naïve enough to believe that they will leave me alone. I think it is likely that they will come after me. I have upset a lot of people and will continue to do so even while absent. I would hate to think that I might jeopardise the stability of your community. I wanted you to know that whatever happens I am prepared to move on if you or anyone else feels uncomfortable with my presence. I… also don't know anything about babies."

They all nodded sympathetically.

"We'll get you through I'm sure."

Is he smiling behind that beard? Hard to tell.

Suris

"How, when and where is the damage being done?" Beatrice asked Claire Willis fretfully.

They had just finished watching the reportages.

"It's impossible to say. There are Fidelis and my own networks working undercover in all the provinces but this unrest seems to have been carefully orchestrated. Sadly I think for the moment we should cancel your grand tour and any planned walkabouts."

"But I think that will send the wrong message. I have to be out there. They have to see that the Magnamater is in touch, caring and interested. No. I have to go exactly as planned."

Claire Willis recognised the tone. Once the Magnamater had decided there was no persuasion. It would be a major security nightmare. She called Chief Fidelis.

"She's going ahead."

"Even having seen the footage? It's madness."

"Put everyone you've got onto it. We cannot afford any mistakes."

"Ben, it's Lida. I just wanted to let you know that all future reportages have been cancelled. It's probably for the best. That poor man died you know. I feel so terrible. Thank you for all your help. I've been selected to go on the touring team with Magnamater starting tomorrow. Quite exciting. Anyway. Thanks again."

He listened to the message three times just in case he had missed something. He looked down at his palms and saw the deep grooves where his nails had almost broken the skin. Served him right. Then he shrugged. Got to focus on now, where the minutes were splitting and dividing and hurtling towards tomorrow.

Cornwall

It was the second time that a Har had passed through the straggling settlements. Inside, the two heavily armed Fidelis were receiving their final orders before the transor signal's range was exceeded.

"We have forty-eight hours before she wants us back in A to escort the tour. This is pointless."

Nevertheless, they stopped regularly always receiving cold blank looks or silence. It was a child who gave them what they needed.

"Another one." He pointed.

His mother pulled at his hand, too late.

"You've seen one before, have you?" the officer prettied her tone.

"No, he's mistaken," his mother interjected quickly.

"Was it as big as this one or a different colour?"

"Same." The child struggled with himself.

It was enough to keep them motivated. But by the time they had reached St Austell they were tired and had started to threaten openly with arrest at stunner-point.

"Yes all right. They went that way," one woman finally screamed desperately as they held her son. And as they re-boarded she spat, "You're not women, you're wolves. Hope you never get there."

"You are a long way from home Fidelis," Freya observed as she served the officers with food at the centre.

"We are looking for a criminal. A vagrant. She kidnapped a child. Have you seen her?" The officer held up a scanimage.

Freya made a study of it.

"Well, it's hard to say. We get a lot of people just travelling through. There were three people yesterday morning, I think. Would that be the right sort of time?"

"Possibly."

"Anyway, I think one of them said they were going on to Hayle. D'you know Hayle? Past Redruth and Camborne up on the west side. I can't be sure it was them though."

They left soon afterwards, their stomachs full, their senses a little dulled by the hard seats and the light-less roads. They could not have anticipated the force of the flash floods that engulfed them as they drove into the centre of Hayle, and as the Har capsized, battered along by an uprooted tree, the doors jammed and they could only briefly rail at the ignominy of such lonely deaths.

CHAPTER TWENTY-THREE

Suris

"I am for you and with you," Beatrice told dwindling gatherings in square after square. Her vigorous interest in every Transmission studio, Restoration ward, Distribution centre and Fuel plant was met with muted politeness at best. To her credit, her energy was unflagging and her ability to motivate her entourage admirable. Still, she could not blind them. In J the Har was attacked and cartons of black paint were dropped from a walkway, leaving them all in occluded darkness. As the jeers rose outside, she conceded that the tour should end.

And so it was on a beautiful, clear September morning, after a prevailing wet front had moved over the island that Magnamater and her team met at A's headquarters for what everyone knew would be crisis talks. A new strategy would have to be developed. A courageous, possibly even drastic reconfiguration. Temples were damp, cheeks flushed within the sealed airless conference suite where ideas ricocheted and swarmed noisily like a plague.

Yet outside Asoans were stopping and watching and listening with more commitment than they had in years.
  There was a new face on their screens. A crushed, devastated face. A face that once they might have mistrusted. But how could one not believe her words and the horrors she showed.

Recordings of an underground life at Marylebone where scientists planned Asoan's genetic futures; intermittent footage of Beatrice talking of Transparency while images of N's mutants danced in the background.

They gazed, revolted, as the looped transmissions repeated throughout the day and Fidelis frantically scoured the system for the source. When power was finally shut down, plummeting Suris into chilly darkness, Anthony Capwood was able to reboot the supply in Olim and continue the transmission from that old station at Norwich's learning centre, where he had also successfully established a new satellite link with some parts of Europe and the United States.

People stayed out on the streets and lit fires. Stunned paralysis was overtaken by blistering outrage, yet no one harmed the screens because they did not want to stop watching. Old hovers were unearthed from basements and while Chief Fidelis had instructed all officers to maintain a high and heavily armed visibility, most had begun to dart through the crowds like bats.

In N and O people spilled into the Burghs like boiling liquid. Years of neglect gave them purpose and not content merely to rampage, they hunted down the Fidelis. Charlie could not bring himself to resist. He understood. He had done what was necessary and as he was carried out into the night he thought only of Brenda, their son and Rachel. Would he have been comforted to know that in a chaplaincy he had never visited, a candle was kept lit and prayers offered in his name?

The following morning Magnamater Beatrice and her administration could only watch transfixed as footage from 2026 showed Magnamater Olivia in secret meetings with various discredited heads of biotechnology companies and with the later to be convicted electronics warfare terrorists from Korea. The disks had recently been unearthed from a vault in the house of a leading Democrat. His grandfather had held office in 2030 and had left instructions for them to be released into the hands of his old friend Peter Marchant on his death. They had been Peter's parting gift to Diana who now sat in F's transmission centre, overseeing the link-up to Ben and waiting for the first Pleides broadcast. In effect, it was Susan Pelucci's inaugural address as she challenged Beatrice to defend her office.

The Magnamater's abdication was immediate. The ensuing re-grouping, re-affiliation and courtship would have been a fascinating spectacle had Claire Willis not needed a signature and discovered her body. She had been dead for six hours.

"I knew that you never had the long fight in you," she hissed at the corpse. "You should have gone long ago. There was supposed to be a succession plan. You promised me."

There were two choices. Either she fled or stayed to ride out the backlash. And ultimately she needed little persuasion. There were plenty disenfranchised from the Administration who had nothing to do but wait in the wings and groom a new candidate and a new party. The detail would come later.

It was the Fidelis who felt things most keenly and it was with the Chief that Susan held her first meeting. There had been many immediate resignations but it was agreed that, with some adjustments, a re-branding might succeed.

Thus the new Police force flanked the crowd who flocked over the bridges towards the derelict centres of Old London, Birmingham and Manchester. With Diana at her side, Susan called for the tunnels to be opened and rode a Fuchs tank out onto the middle of London Bridge. Many of the research community had already fled but many more were walked out into the sunlight, silent and defiant. They would be the first detainees under the Social Protection Programme. In the de-briefings, many cursed and named their leadership but, despite every effort, George Lonsdale, Senior Science officer proved impossible to find until months later a short transmission from Chinese state television showed his appointment to Viralto, the state sponsored viral technology unit. Six months later, his premature death would only warrant a fifteen second announcement.

Ben and his teams stood and filmed Susan's announcements

with hand held cameras and there was even mirth as they drove through the streets seeing shop windows where mannequins stood frozen in fashion time. Did people ever wear that? The Thames glittered, its tide continuing to ebb and flow, indifferent to the spectacle.

Anti-contamination units would be set up straight away. Water purification and anti-viral treatment programmes were a priority. They had access to so much expertise from overseas that the Pleides managed to inspire confidence and optimism from the start.

Most of the Maters had elected to re-join the community and continue in their teaching role, leaving the Abamaters to run the Arks as Specialist Academies. There would always be those who would struggle to embrace a less distinctive future. The creation of a vast and complex programme of re-integration occupied most of the administration's waking hours. Temporary housing within sprawling conurbations extended beyond the Burghs in preparation for the Day of Sharing and Reconciliation that finally launched the future.

The locomoters creaked with the weight of Maters escorting children out of Abovo.

Extra services were arranged to bring Olim's entire population to their requested destinations.

In any one of London's great old parks and in similar events throughout the country, after hours of patient shuffling, generations were re-united in a deafening thrum of hearts and feet as they walked, ran, then stampeded towards each other. There was a distinctive look as people first glimpsed a loved one. It became known as the 'Sighting' and part of many future Pleiades broadcasts.

CHAPTER TWENTY-FOUR

Home

Rachel pulled the door to, fondly stroking the iron ring that countless hands had lifted before her. A distant bleep came from a small shelf at the back her oak wardrobe. Pausing, her hand wavered before she shrugged and walked down the hill. Above, screeching seagulls hovered, hidden by the sea-mists that would not clear before lunchtime.

"Yes, I know how loud they are," she told her swollen stomach which rippled and contorted with the baby's wild acrobatics. "And now we will pick up your sister and go on that walk."

Bera was waiting on the Cathedral steps. Her hair hung below her shoulders and she had suddenly grown taller and broader.

"Mum, did you know that 'Truro' comes from the Cornish 'Tri-Veru' and it means 'three rivers' and it developed as a port between Truro, Kenwyn and Allen rivers? Thomas said that he'd take me surfing in Newquay at the weekend. We're decorating our boards in Art and Design. Hello baby, me little 'andsome."

She bent and kissed Rachel's navel. "There's a trip to Newlyn's pilchard factory and on to the Tidal observatory on Thursday, if you give permission."

"Yes of course."

It's getting harder to keep up with her as she tears up the narrow paths and onto the cliff-tops. I'd never say though. I'll follow her anywhere and she knows it. It's worth the effort once you get here. Filling my lungs and clearing my head with the most pure, clean air I've ever breathed. And then the ocean. It's like a magnet. I try to hold back but my gaze just gets pulled out towards the horizon. How have I lived my life away from all this blue?

He had taken them everywhere. Shown them the endless rocky coastline, only interrupted by the odd promontory or small inlet where cottages nestled too close to the water's edge. They had climbed the moors to find disused tin mines. Visited the gardens at Lostwithiel and Glendurgan and marvelled at the exotic shrubs and trees thrashed by the sea-breeze into a twisted grotesque ballet. They had followed ancient tracks to reach Iron-age fortresses and Neolithic stone circles. Stood among the Merry Maidens and imagined the Sabbath dance that ended in such punishing entombment. She had struggled with a new claustrophobia in the underground passageways that lead to the supposedly holy burial chambers of Chun Quoit. Five minutes of shivering nausea in the flickering light were enough. "I've had enough of such dark tales and places," she murmured into the biting wind. They played games with the unpredictable tide in Perrinporth and cut off, had sought refuge at the back of caves, on the old ledges hewn by smugglers. In Penzance they had clung together as the huge grey waves crashed mercilessly onto the barren coast. Bera had dragged her to Madron's sacred well where she tied a ribbon round the tree and they both made a silent wish. It was there that she told her about the baby.

It could have gone either way. She could have hated the idea but every day she gets more excited. I'm forgetting things. Little slopes of time from which I ski and dip into the white horizon, free falling 'til I came back to ground, to the present where I'm left wondering what's happened and how I might have revealed myself.

    Sometimes I think about what I've left behind... I never feel like I've sacrificed anything important. We're all attached to something but it's only when you have to use a knife and cut loose that you understand what has any weight. Maybe I'm the lucky one. I had the choice. And I look at that child. Watch the bud bloom and know I was right. In this new land I've seen a thousand pictures and almost every one has made my heart sing

New settlers arrived daily. Bera called them 'Emmetts' in her newly acquired Cornish accent. They sought Rachel out thinking that she would want to be updated. Once, a man shook her hand but she pulled away, not wanting his thanks. Charlie Miller's face was always with her.

Ben found it hard to imagine their first conversation. Almost seven months. A roller-coaster of key assignments. A prestigious new role. He was a someone. Two letters addressed to Rachel and Bera had been passed to him from Peter Marchant's estate. It had given him a good excuse to visit. But as he embarked on the long journey, his confidence faltered.

Crantock was her favourite place. Thomas stretched out his hand to pull her up over the high dunes and together they walked onto the creamy sand. Freedom. Miles of freedom.
　"You still haven't told Ben?" he asked gently
　"No. He comes because he can." She flung her hands out and let the breeze carry them. "Is there any mead? Kate said a little will not hurt."

I called my son David after the rebel who wrote my Dad's favourite song. Who would have thought that so many years later I'd be listening to Faith Orph teach Bera the words written in nineteen seventy six while I sit on a wide golden beach looking out to sea.

About this CD

ASO – a productive society born from the remains of an old Britain. Founder Magnamater Olivia deemed any reference to the recent past irrelevant and provided three new formal songs.

'Joytime' serves as ASO's anthem, aiming to encourage coherence and loyalty. 'United' accompanies the marriage ceremony, and at funerals, 'Heartheld' celebrates a life spent.

In Rachel Develin, we see all the inherent contradictions and conflicts of ASO itself. Powerful and ruthlessly dedicated to her prestigious office, 'Running' follows her pursuit of the truth, as her causes gradually betray her. Fiercely loyal in her relationships, aching for her daughter and the remnants of her marriage, her heart breaks in 'Tender Assassin':

"Stop your Tender Assassin,
 hunting down all the lost things,
 like a missing limb,
 I feel you still."

All songs written and recorded in 2007
by Lindsey and David Mackie.

For more music, stories and Mackieism explore

www.lindseymackie.com